THE
DRAFTER

Center Point
Large Print

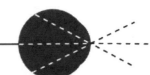

**This Large Print Book carries the
Seal of Approval of N.A.V.H.**

THE DRAFTER

LP
FIC
Harriso
2016

KIM HARRISON

CENTER POINT LARGE PRINT
THORNDIKE, MAINE

This Center Point Large Print edition
is published in the year 2016 by arrangement with
Pocket Books, a division of Simon & Schuster, Inc.

The text of this Large Print edition is unabridged.
In other aspects, this book may vary
from the original edition.
Printed in the United States of America
on permanent paper.
Set in 16-point Times New Roman type.

ISBN: 978-1-68324-223-9

Library of Congress Cataloging-in-Publication Data

Names: Harrison, Kim, 1966– author.
Title: The drafter / Kim Harrison.
Description: Center Point Large Print edition. | Thorndike, Maine :
Center Point Large Print, 2016.
Identifiers: LCCN 2016034834 | ISBN 9781683242239
    (hardcover : alk. paper)
Subjects: LCSH: Large type books. | GSAFD: Fantasy fiction. |
Suspense fiction.
Classification: LCC PS3608.A78355 D73 2016 | DDC 813/.6—dc23
LC record available at https://lccn.loc.gov/2016034834

For Tim, who still reads my rough drafts—
and some of the rewrites

ACKNOWLEDGMENTS

I'd like to thank my editor, Lauren McKenna, for her insights into making Peri's story everything it is, and my agent, Richard Curtis, for believing in Peri's story when it was raw and new.

THE DRAFTER

PROLOGUE

2025

The room was a featureless eight-by-eight, the monotony relieved by a single chair and the door pad softly glowing in the recessed overhead lights. Pulling up from a stretch, Peri stifled a shudder as a feeling of electricity crawled over her skin, pooling where the training suit pinched.

Concerned, she passed a hand over the spiderweb of white stress lines in the otherwise black leather, frown deepening when her hand turned to pinpricks as the electric field in the fabric phased. *Seriously?* The slick-suit ran from her neck to the tops of her boots, elevating her slight form to dangerous and sexy, but a wardrobe malfunction would slow her down.

"Hey! Excuse me?" she called toward the ceiling, her high voice laced with demand. "I'm getting excessive feedback from my slick-suit."

A soft chime fell flat in the tiny room as the audio connection opened. "I'm sorry," a man's voice said, the hint of sarcasm telling her they knew it. "Possible suit malfunctions are acceptable under the parameters of the exercise. Begin."

Again the chime rang. Adrenaline surged with her quick intake of breath. She didn't see the cameras, but people were watching, comparing every move to an unattainable perfection. Squandering a cocky three seconds, she stretched to show her confidence along with her lithe shape. *Challenge one: technological fence,* she thought, glancing at the locked door pad.

In a swift motion, she grasped the back of the wooden chair, flinging it into the wall. It hit with a startling crack of wood, and she knelt before the pieces. Nimble fingers bare of the slick-suit's gloves sifted through until she found a metal pin. Rising, she padded to the locked door and used it to wedge open the door pad.

This task is mine, she thought, then walled it off, concentrating on the maze of wires until she found the one she wanted. Hand fisted, she tensed to yank one of the wires free, then hesitated. With her "malfunctioning" suit, she might end up on her ass, blowing out smoke as she tried to remember how to focus. *Not worth the risk,* she thought, following the wire back to the circuit board and shorting the door with the pin instead. The ceiling chimed her success. Peri saluted the unseen cameras, smug as the door slid open. *Eleven seconds.*

Pin set between her fingers to gouge, she dove into the cooler air and into a spacious, spongy-floored room. The ceilings were higher, the light brighter, and at the far end, a closed door beckoned, the light on the lock already a steady green. Beyond it was everything she'd been working for, everything she'd been promised. She just had to get there.

A faint whisper of air gave her warning. Peri ducked, lashing out with a back kick to send a man pinwheeling into the wall. *Shit, he's huge!* she thought as his slick-suit flashed white. But it was fading to black even as she watched. He wasn't out of it—yet.

"Nothing personal, right?" she said, her eyes jerking from his holstered weapon to the two men sprinting toward her. Three against one wasn't fair, but when was life ever?

They attacked together. Peri dropped, rolling to take out the closest. He fell and she swarmed him, jabbing his throat with her elbow. There was the telltale thump of a pad, but she'd struck hard enough to make him gag. His slick-suit flashed white as she rolled to her feet. *One down.*

The second grabbed her, a glass knife shadowed with electronics at her throat. Screaming in defiance, she stabbed his ear with the chair pin. He howled in real pain, and she threw him over her shoulder and into the first man, now recovered.

Following them both down, she scrambled for his blade, running the glass training knife across both their throats. The glow of the technological blade against their skin flashed, indicating a kill, and their slick-suits turned white. Gasping, they went still, paralyzed. Real blood, looking alien on the training floor, dripped from the one man's ear.

Peri straightened, keeping the pin as she turned her back on the men and walked confidently to the distant door. *No more lame excuses,* she thought, the adrenaline high still spilling through her, though shifting to a more enduring burn of anticipation. She'd been working toward this for months. How many times did she need to prove she was ready?

With a heavy thunk, the lights went up. At the door, the pad shifted to a locked red.

Peri jerked to a halt. "Excuse me?" she directed at the ceiling, and the audio connection pinged open.

"You failed to demonstrate proficiency with projection weapons," the man said, but she could hear an argument in the background.

Peri cocked her hip, knowing the time was still running, ruining her perfect score. "You mean a *gun?*" she asked with disdain. "Handguns are noisy and can be taken away, and then I have to do more damage to fix it."

"Your time is still running," the man said, smug.

"How can I prove my value if you keep changing the rules?" she muttered, stomping back to the three men, still paralyzed in their white slick-suits. Jaw clenched, she snatched the nearest man's handgun. "I already killed you," she said when

14

the man's eyes widened, and she spun, shooting out the cameras in the corners instead: one, two, three.

"Reed!" the man shouted as his screens undoubtedly went black.

Peri dropped the weapon and waited, shaking the pinpricks from her fingertips. The audio channel was still open, and a smile quirked her lips as she caught some argued phrases, "best we have" and "it's that shitty attitude of hers that makes her perfect."

Glancing at her watch, Peri shifted her weight. "So am I going, or do you want me to try it again with feeling? I have stuff to do today."

There was silence, and then a younger voice took the mic. "You will report to medical tomorrow at nine. Congratulations, Agent Reed. It's yours."

Her breath caught, the quick intake lighting a fire all the way to her groin, and then she steadied herself. "Friday," she countered, ignoring the men behind her, groaning as their slick-suits returned to a black neutrality. "I want to say good-bye to my mother."

Again the silence, and Peri's good mood tarnished as she caught a whispered "might not remember her when she gets back."

"Friday," the young voice finally said, and Peri's jaw clenched at the pity in it. Her mother didn't deserve anyone's pity, but that didn't mean she wasn't going to say good-bye.

The lock shifted green, a solid thump echoing as the door opened onto an empty, white hallway. Her thoughts already on a shower and what was in her closet that her mother might actually approve of, Peri paced forward into the light.

CHAPTER
ONE

FIVE YEARS LATER

Peri Reed reclined in the plush leather chair across from the CEO's desk, her feet up on the coffee table, enjoying the adrenaline pooling as she waited in the dark for Jack to find what they had come for. His mood was bad, but that wasn't her fault. Bored, she helped herself to a foil-wrapped, imported chocolate from a nearby dish.

"Really, Peri?" Jack said at her *mmm* of appreciation.

"So hurry up." Licking her lips, she deftly folded the foil into a tiny hat, which she set jauntily on the statue of the naked woman holding the dish. "This guy knows his chocolate."

"I prepped for glass. Wave technology isn't even on the shelves yet," Jack complained, his tan face pale and distorted through the holographic monitor. The touch-screen projection hazed Jack's athletic shape and black Gucci suit, and Peri wondered whose ass the CEO of Global Genetics was kissing to get the new holographic touch-screen technology.

"My good heels are in the car. Waiting. Like me," she prompted, and he hunched, his jabbing fingers opening and closing files faster than a texting fourteen-year-old.

Impatient, Peri stood and ran a quick hand through her short black hair. Her mother would hate its length, insisting that a woman of quality kept long hair until she was forty, and only then allowed it to be cut shorter. Moving to the window, Peri smiled at her manicure in perverse satisfaction. Her mother would hate the color as well—which might be why Peri loved the vibrant maroon.

Shaking her hem down to cover her low-heeled boots, she exhaled her tension and focused on the hazy night. The black Diane von Furstenberg silk jumpsuit wasn't her favorite, even if it had been tailored to fit her precisely and was lined with silk to feel like ice against her skin when she moved. But add the pearls currently in the car with her heels, and it would get second and third glances at the upscale pool hall she'd picked out as a spot where she and Jack could decompress.

If we ever get out of here, she thought, sighing dramatically to make Jack's ears redden.

The projected monitor was the only spot of light in the office suite with its heavy furniture and pictures of past CEOs. Surrounding buildings were lit by security lights dimmed to save power. Low clouds threw back the midnight haze of Charlotte, North Carolina. This high up, the stink of money had washed away the stink of the streets. *The corruption,* Peri thought, stretching to run a finger over the lintel to intentionally leave a fingerprint, *is harder to hide.*

"One of these days, that's going to bite you on the ass," Jack said as she dropped back to her heels. Her print would come up as classified, but it would also tell Opti that they'd been successful—or at least that they'd come and gone. Success was beginning to look questionable. Five minutes in, and Jack was *still* searching for the encrypted master file of Global Genetics' latest engineered virus, the hidden one that made it race-specific.

The faint clunk and hum of the elevator iced through her. Her head tilted to the cracked door, and she shocked herself with the sweet candy still on her lips. She never would've heard it had the floor been busy, but in the silence of a quasi-legal, government-sanctioned break-in . . .

"Don't leave my sight," Jack demanded as he hooked the rolling chair with his foot and pulled the leather throne toward him to sit. His fingers hesitated, jabbed the holomonitor, then waved the entire field to the trash. His brow was furrowed, and the glow of the projection made his face appear gaunt and his blue eyes almost black. Feeling sassy, Peri sashayed to the door, liking being paid to do what anyone else would be jailed for. Jack looked too sexy to be good at the computer stuff, but in all fairness, he was as proficient as she in evasion and offense. *Which is why we've survived this long,* she thought as she slipped the flexible, palm-size wafer of glass out of her pocket and powered it up. Her Opti-augmented phone was glass technology, and up until seeing the CEO's wave, she'd thought it was the best out there. Hitting the app that tied into the building's security, she brought up the motion sensors.

The screen lit with a harsh glow. Dimming it, she crouched to peer into the secretary's office. One wall of the outer office was open to allow for a view of the common office area beyond. Intel said the night guard was cursory, but intel had been wrong a lot lately.

The app finished its scan and vibrated for her attention. *No movement,* she thought as she looked at the blank screen, not trusting it. "I can't do my job from here," she whispered, tensing when the elevator hummed to a halt and a beam of light lit the ceiling. Keys jingled. The translucent screen in her palm lit up with a bright dot. *Shit.*

"I can't do mine if you leave my sight," Jack said. "Stay put, Peri. I mean it."

Arcs of harsh light played over the ceiling—

closer, coming closer. Adrenaline coursed through Peri once more, and the soles of her feet began to ache. "Catch," she said, rolling the phone into a tube and tossing it at him. He scrambled for it, his silhouette tight with anger against the city lights.

"Let me know if we get more than one," she said as she yanked on her pendant, jerking the tiny felt marker from its cap. "Otherwise, keep working."

"Don't go out there without me," he said, his sudden alarm at the click of the pen uncapping jerking through her.

"Just find the files. I'll be right back." J IN OFFICE she wrote on her palm, avoiding him as she blew it dry, recapped the pen, and tucked it behind her top.

"Peri . . ."

"I wrote a note," she said, nervous at his angst, and she slipped out, easing the door nearly closed behind her. Dropping to the flat carpet, she wiggled across the receptionist's office and peered around the end of the desk, propping herself up on the flats of her arms to wait for a visual on the guard. Jack was right to be concerned. He had to witness a draft to anchor her. But to fail meant the deadly virus might reach an already decimated Asia.

That's why they were here, to find and remove the files concerning the virus before a second wave of death washed through what had once been nearly two-thirds of the world's population.

Opti had commissioned the first wave three years ago, when Asia's political hierarchy thumbed their noses at the new CO_2 levels set by the United Nations and therefore threatened the entire world with continued rising global temperatures. But this second wave of tactical bioengineered population reduction was illegal, funded by the Billion by Thirty club with the sole intent of broadening their financial interests in Europe. Peri thought it amusing that she and Jack had helped almost half of its members gain their admission.

The light on the ceiling became focused. Warning prickled her skin as the jingling keys grew louder and a uniformed man came around the desks. Peri's brow furrowed.

It wasn't the guard that Bill, their handler, had told them would be here. This man was younger and thinner, and wasn't singing along with his phone. As Peri watched, he tucked his flashlight under his arm and used a card reader to go into one of the private offices ringing the floor. Lips pressed, she waited until the guard came out with a square bottle of something sloshy.

Damn. He was a lifter: familiar with every office and comfortable with treating the building as his personal, no-card-required shopping mall. The best case would have him on the alert for anything out of the ordinary as he strove not to get caught. The worst case would have him in the CEO's office sampling the chocolate.

Breath held, Peri crept back to Jack. He looked up from her phone as she eased the door shut, frowning when the lock clicked on and a red light from the door pad glowed in the dark. "Don't leave my sight!" he whispered, yelling at her in a soft hush.

"We got a lifter," she said, and Jack's fingers hesitated.

"He coming in here?"

"Give me a second, I'll go ask him."

Mood sour, he returned his attention to the crystalline projection. Peri padded over for her phone, breathing in the light scent of his sweat as she tucked it away. Her mind drifted to the sensation of his touch on her skin as his quick fingers searched folders and files. "Maybe the files have a biometric lock?" she suggested.

"No. I simply think it's not here. We might need to hit the labs downstairs," Jack grumbled, doing a double take when he realized her lips were inches from his ear. "Peri, back up. I can't work when you're that close."

"The labs? Good God. I hope not." Peri leaned to put her arms across his shoulders. Her bag— filled with all sorts of interesting things that needed an artist's touch to get past TSA—rested on the desk, and she wondered if she should get something out of it, but everything was noisy. "Why don't you shut it down. He's just shopping, and we've got all night."

"It's not here," he muttered, and she pushed off his shoulders and went to listen at the door. Hearing a sliding clatter, she roughly gestured for Jack to cut the light. Grim, Jack stood, fingers still flicking files about the screen. "I thought wave technology had a sleep corner," he whispered.

Peri tensed. Footsteps. Coming closer. "Shut it off. Now!"

Jack's face was creased in the dim glow. "I'm trying."

The guard was in the secretary's outer office, and she settled into a balanced readiness beside the door. He was coming through it—she knew by the prickling of her thumb and the itch in her feet. "Damn it, Jack. I haven't drafted in six months. Don't make me do it now."

"Got it!" he whispered, fingers waving across the monitor as he found the off switch.

"Got it" wasn't good enough, and with a tiny beep from the locking pad, the door clicked open and the security guard came in, flashlight searching.

He was a cool customer, she'd give him that. Silent, he took in Jack, standing behind the desk like a guilty teen found looking at his dad's porn. Expression twisting, the man dropped the bottle and reached for the pistol on his belt.

Peri moved as the bottle clunked on the carpet. The man yelped, shocked when her crescent kick slammed out of the dark and into his wrist, knocking his handgun into the secretary's office. Hand to his middle, the security guard dropped back. His shock turned to anger when he saw Peri's slim figure cloaked in chic black. True, it looked suspicious, her in the dark and in an upper office where she had no right to be, but add some jewelry and Louboutins, and she was ready for a five-star restaurant. "You're nothing but a little bitty girl," he said, reaching for her.

"I prefer the term *fun-size*."

Grinning, Peri let him grab her, spinning around and levering him up and over her shoulder. He'd either go where she sent him or he'd dislocate his arm. He went, hitting the carpet with a muffled thump.

"Ahhhhoow!" the guard groaned as he pulled the unbroken whiskey bottle out from under him. The flashlight rolled, sending shiny glints across the black panes of glass.

Jack frantically worked at the computer, his head low and blond hair hiding his eyes.

Enjoying the chance to take the big man down, Peri gathered herself to fall on him. Eyes wide, the guard jerked away, and she changed her motion into a heel jab that never landed, then fell into a ready stance between him and the handgun. *We have to get out of here, like now.*

The guard spun upright, fumbling for the radio on his belt. "Put a wiggle in it, Jack!" she exclaimed, lashing out with a crescent kick, a front kick, then a low strike to his knee as she drove the guard back—anything to keep him from his radio. She loved the adrenaline, the excitement, the knowledge that she had what it took to beat the odds and walk away without reprisal.

The man shook it off, and she lashed at his ear, lurching when she hit his jaw instead. A solid thump on her right shoulder sent her reeling. Peri stumbled, feeling the coming bruise. Anger fueled her smile. He was good and liked to cause pain. If he landed a clean strike, she'd be out—but beating those odds would only make her win more satisfying.

"Quit playing with him!" Jack shouted.

"I need to burn off some calories if I want cake tonight," she said as the guard felt his lip, thoughts shifting behind his eyes when his fingers came away shiny with blood. Suddenly he ran for the door and his handgun.

"We're having pie, not cake, and stay where I can see you," Jack called.

She jumped the guard, snagging a foot before he reached the door. He went down, dragging her across the carpet. Chin burning and eyes shut, she let go when he kicked. Peri jerked away, gasping when the guard turned, looming over her with his fist pulled back.

"No!" Jack shouted as the guard struck her full in the face and her head snapped backward. Dazed, Peri wavered where she sat.

"Don't move! Or I fucking shoot her!" the guard shouted.

She couldn't see straight. The gun pointed at her held no meaning as she tried to figure out what had happened. Dizzy, she felt her face, jerking when the pain exploded under her fingers. But it focused her, and she looked at Jack behind the desk. Eyes meeting, they silently weighed their options. Jack had a handgun and she had a blade in her boot. They'd *never* needed extraction from local authorities in their entire three years together. She wasn't planning on starting now, and certainly not getting fingered by a dirty rent-a-cop.

"You at the desk!" the guard barked, and Peri's gaze on his handgun narrowed as she estimated the distance. "Come here where I can see you," he said, one hand fumbling behind his back for his cuffs. "Hands up. You make a move to lower them, and I shoot her."

Hands in the air, Jack edged out from behind the desk. He coughed, and the barrel of the guard's gun shifted to track him.

"Bravo!" a clear, masculine voice exclaimed from the doorway.

The guard turned, shocked. Peri lashed out in a spinning kick. Impact against the guard's hand vibrated through her even as she followed through and rose into a crouch and from there to a stand, the flat of her still-swinging foot slamming into the guard's head.

Spittle and blood sprayed and the guard crashed into the coffee table. His handgun fell, and she kicked it to the far windows. Jack went for the man in the doorway. Knowing he had her back, Peri followed the guard down, fist clenched to hit him somewhere painful.

But the guard was out, his face bloody and his eyes closed. Resisting the urge to hit him anyway, she looked up as Jack shoved an older man in a suit into the office at gunpoint.

"Impressive," the man said, nodding to the guard. "Is he dead?"

"No." Peri stood. *What the hell?* she thought, unable to read Jack's tight expression. This couldn't be a test. They'd already had their yearly "surprise" evaluation job.

"Good. Keep it that way," the man said as if he was in control, regardless of having no weapon, if Jack's hasty but thorough pat-down was any indication. "I've been meaning to take him off the payroll, but I'd prefer unemployment over a death benefit to his wife."

This isn't how we do things, Peri thought as Jack shoved the man into one of the cushy chairs, where he fixed his tie, affronted. Peri looked from the slightly overweight man to his photograph on the desk, posing with a stiff-looking woman in too much makeup. This was his office. *Bloody toothpicks, Bill will have a cow if I off a CEO.*

"I have what you came for," the manicured,

graying man said, his soft fingers reaching behind his coat to an inner pocket.

Peri lunged. Her knee landed between his legs and he gasped at the near miss. One hand forced his head back; the other pinned his reaching hand to the arm of the chair. "Don't move," she whispered, and irritation replaced his shocked pain.

He wiggled, wincing when she shifted her knee a little tighter. "If I wanted you dead, I wouldn't be here myself," the man said, his voice strained but angry. "Get off me."

"Nah-uh," she said, fingers digging into his neck in warning, then louder, "Jack?"

Jack eased close, the scent of his aftershave familiar as he reached behind the man's coat to slip free an envelope. It had Jack's name on it, and Peri went cold. *He knew we'd be here?*

"Get off," the older man said again, and this time, Peri eased back in uncertainty.

Jack passed his handgun to her, and she retreated to where she could see both the CEO and the downed guard. The crackle of the envelope was loud, and the older man readjusted himself, giving Peri a dark look. "What is it?" she asked, and Jack unfolded the paper inside and shook a pinky-nail-size memory chip into his hand. "Is it the files?"

Her attention shifted to the CEO when he palpated his privates as if estimating the damage.

"No. I printed out the highlights to justify my request. You tell Bill that what I found warrants more than a paltry three percent," he said, shaking his arms to fix the fall of his coat. "Three percent. I just saved his ass and he thinks I'm going to take three percent?"

"Jack?" Peri whispered, disliking her uncertainty. *He knows Bill? What's going on?*

Face white, Jack angled the printed page to the faint light coming in the window. Fingers fumbling, he tipped the chip onto his glass phone. It lit up as the data downloaded, and Jack compared the two, going even more pale as he verified it.

The man leaned toward the side table, his gaze lingering on the foil hat before he took a chocolate from the dish. "You're very good, missy. Watching you . . . I'd believe you myself." He smiled, white teeth gleaming in the ambient light.

Jack looked more angry than confused. Peri's gut knotted. The CEO knew Bill. Was he proposing a *deal?*

"You made a mistake." Jack folded the paper around the chip and tucked it away with his phone.

The man snorted and put an ankle on a raised knee. "The only mistake is Bill thinking he can get something for nothing. He can do better. I only want a fair price for what I have."

Shit, Peri thought, her alarm mutating to anger. He was trying to buy them. They were Opti agents. Drafters and anchors had to be trustworthy to a fault or the government that trained them would literally kill them. Drafting time was too powerful a skill to hire out to the highest bidder, especially now.

Fear settled in her like old winter ice, cracked and pitted, as Jack cocked his head at the angle he always had when he was thinking hard, and a weird light was in his eye.

"Jack?" she said with sudden mistrust. "What's that list?"

His expression cleared. "Lies," he said blandly. "All lies."

The CEO bit into a chocolate. "The truth is far more damning than anything I could invent. It's a list, lovely woman, of corrupt Opti agents," he said as he chewed. "Your name is on it."

CHAPTER TWO

Peri's finger tightened on the handgun, and she forced her finger away from the trigger. Shock filled her, doubt and anger close behind. "Liar!" she cried, jumping at him.

"Don't!" Jack shouted, and she landed on the man, pinning him to the chair and wedging the muzzle of the gun under his chin.

"You made that list up!" she exclaimed, and the

man's head jerked as she shoved the gun harder against him. "Tell him! *Tell him!*"

"Peri, get off!" Jack demanded, and Peri gasped at the echoing blast of a gun fired in close quarters. Pain was a stake of iron pounded into her chest, and she looked at the man under her, his eyes fixed on hers and his face unblemished. She hadn't shot him.

Peri took a breath, agony stabbing her again. *Oh shit,* she thought, and then she fell back as Jack pulled her to the carpet. The guard she'd downed had shot her. Damn it, she was dying, the bullet still in her as she choked, bloody froth gathering at her lips as pain made it hard to breathe.

"What the hell are you doing!" Jack shouted at the CEO, Peri's head cradled in his lap.

The CEO stood, and she could do nothing, pinned by a thousand-pound weight. *Oh God, it hurts.* But Jack was here. She'd be okay if she could hold it together long enough . . . to draft.

"She's on that list," the man said, pointing down at her like God's avenging angel. "She can't walk out of here knowing she's been marked. I'm doing you a favor. Bill owes me. He owes me big."

"You cretin," Jack snarled up at him. "She won't remember any of this in about thirty seconds. You think we don't know her past? Who she is? That doesn't mean she's not useful! She's a goddamned drafter! You know how much she's worth? How rare she is?"

What . . . what is he saying? He thought she was . . . corrupt? Selling her skills to the highest bidder? Oh God. Her name was on the list?

And then the pain grew too much. Adrenaline pooled, tripping her over the edge and jumping her brain into synaptic hyperactivity. She was going to draft. She couldn't stop it—and it would save her life. Again.

Eyes widening, she felt the tingle of sparkles gather at the edges of her sight, flooding her as she breathed them in, swirling through her mind until she breathed them out—and with a soft hush of gathered energy, she jumped into the blue haze of hindsight.

Peri's vision flashed blue and settled as her mind fell into knowing. Her breath came in without pain, and she knew it for the blessing it was. She was drafting, and she stood before the CEO, watching as he reached for a chocolate. Fear made her aim shake. Her name was on Jack's list? But how? She knew who she was, and she wasn't a dirty agent.

Peri looked at Jack, his expression tight. He was frustrated and angry, but at the CEO, not her. As an anchor, he knew they were rewriting the last thirty seconds, unlike everyone else, who would never even notice the small blip apart from perhaps a faint sense of déjà vu. Until time meshed, she'd remember everything.

Afterward, she'd remember nothing until Jack returned the final timeline to her—and now, she had a doubt.

"Jack?" she whispered, terrified of what her gut was telling her. He was angry, not shocked—as if he'd already known. But how could she be something she knew she wasn't?

Jack turned away, and her fear redoubled.

"The truth is far more damning than anything I could invent," the older man said as he bit into a chocolate, oblivious to the new timeline forming. "It's a list, lovely woman, of corrupt Opti agents. Your name is on it."

She was not corrupt. A fire lit in her. Screaming in anger, she pivoted to the guard crawling slowly toward the windows and his forgotten handgun.

"Peri, wait!" Jack lunged to knock the gun spinning from her.

Panicking, the guard scrambled for his weapon. Peri shoved Jack out of her way. The guard scooped up the Glock, and she kicked him into the window. Snarling, he brought his gun down on her and she snapped a front kick to his wrists. The gun went flying.

Face ugly, the guard grabbed her around the neck and slammed her to the floor. Peri's eyes bulged as she tried to breathe. One hand clawed at his grip, the other reached for the knife in her boot. Stars spotted her vision as she jammed it into him, angling it up under the ribs. If she died in a rewrite, she'd be dead. It was him or her.

Gagging on his own blood, the guard rolled away, hands clenched to his chest.

Free, Peri sat up, hands on her neck as she rasped for air. The strong scent of whiskey wafted from the guard. She coughed, bile-tainted chocolate blooming bitter at the back of her throat.

"How am I supposed to explain this!" the CEO shouted, standing over the guard, who spilled bubbly blood from his mouth as he panicked and began to choke.

Jack stomped back to the desk and scooped up Peri's short-job bag. "Haven't you ever heard of the chain of command? We know who she is. We always have. You really fucked this up."

"Me?" the man exclaimed, voice rising. "I'm not the one who killed him."

"I don't kill anyone who doesn't kill me first," Peri wheezed. Beside her, the guard gurgled, not quite suffocated in his own blood yet—but close.

The CEO spun to stare at her. "What?"

"Get out," Jack said, and Peri jerked away when he reached to help her stand. "Go hide under your secretary's desk. I don't want to have to explain you when she snaps out of it."

"Snaps out of what?" The CEO's eyes widened.

"Then it's true? She can change the past? Are we in a draft? Right now? But it feels real."

"That's because it is." Pissed, Jack picked up the gun—the one that had killed her. "It's the first draft that's false—or will be, rather, after she finishes writing this one."

"You know who she is and you still trust her?" The man hunched over with his hands on his knees as he peered at her. She hated his wonder, his amazement—but if he knew about drafters, he was dead.

"With my life." Jack checked the pistol and snapped the cylinder closed. "In about ten seconds, she's not going to remember anything but what I tell her. Now, will you go hide? I don't want to have to explain you."

Peri sat on the floor, her fingers clenched in the flat carpet as she shook. She'd thought she was capable. She'd thought she was strong. But she was vulnerable. People were the sum of their memories, and apparently hers were whatever Jack told her. They hadn't come here to find the virus files. They were here to secure a list of corrupt Opti agents—and Jack didn't have a problem that her name was on it. Maybe she *was* corrupt. How long? How long had this been going on?

"Who else has the list?" Jack said, glancing at his watch.

"No one. I assumed Bill would be . . .

reasonable," the CEO said, voice faltering, and Peri's eyes flicked up with knowledge of what was going to happen. He knew about drafters, and that was unacceptable. Jack would contain the information—whatever the cost.

The CEO's eyes widened as Jack aimed the guard's pistol at him. Peri watched, numb, as the older man lurched for the door, almost making it. The sound of the gun firing jerked through her. She gasped, the burst of air clearing her thoughts and sending her hand to her middle. Legs askew, she leaned against the desk as her lungs ached. She'd been shot in the original timeline, but that's not why her chest hurt. They thought she was corrupt? She'd given Opti everything!

Jack vanished into the outer office. She could hear him dragging the suited man away, and still she sat. "Stupid deserves to die," Jack said in anger, and then he was back, avoiding her eyes in the dim light as he wiped her print from the top of the lintel. The gun was next, set carefully in the guard's outstretched hand after he wiped it clean.

She looked up as Jack extended a hand for her to rise. Scared, she recoiled. She'd know if she was a dirty agent—wouldn't she? "Jack," she whispered, wanting to believe there was another explanation. "I'm not corrupt. He's lying."

Jack dropped to kneel beside her, his arms enfolding her like a warm promise. "Of course you aren't, babe. That's why I killed him. You're safe. No one will know. I can fix this."

Shocked, she stared into his eyes as she felt time overlap and begin to mesh. For an instant she saw herself on the floor as she choked to death in the original timeline. The guard was standing, and the man in the suit watched it all as Jack held her head in his lap.

"This is very bad for my asthma," both she and her shadow-self whispered, one dying of confusion, the other just dying confused.

And then time mended and everything flashed the most beautiful red, scrubbing it away.

Peri pushed back, her heart pounding as her shoulder thudded against the leg of a desk. Jack was kneeling before her, and she looked at a door and the green light blinking on the locking panel. She was on the floor of a midnight-dark corner office. Her chin hurt, but the rest of her face was in agony. A bloody knife lay beside her, and a man in a security uniform twitched not three feet away, his life's blood soaking the carpet.

"It's okay, Peri," Jack soothed, and she scrambled to her feet before the blood could reach her, slowing when she realized everything hurt. "It's done."

I drafted, she thought, looking at her palm to see

J IN OFFICE. She'd *left* him? Heart beating fast, she picked up her sticky knife, conscious of Jack's sudden wariness. She'd left him but she'd made it back, obviously, and he would return her memory of the night's events.

A security guard was dead. Her knife thrust had killed him—she recognized the entry wound as one she knew. A handheld radio hissed, and a Glock lay in the guard's grip. She smelled gunpowder. They were in a high-rise, the thirtieth floor at least. It was night. They were on task. She'd drafted to rub out a mistake, and in doing so, had forgotten everything. *Charlotte?* she wondered, spotting the crown building out the window.

"Did I die again?" she whispered.

"Pretty close. We gotta go," he said, and she winced when he touched her elbow. Her short-job bag was under his arm and she took it, feeling unreal.

"Did we get what we came for? How long did I draft?" Peri asked, numb as she looked at the dead man. She only killed someone when they killed her first. Damn it all to hell, she hated it when she drafted.

"Not long, and it's in my phone." Eyes pinched, Jack stuck his head out the door and looked around. The office beyond was quiet. "What do you remember?"

Less than I like. "Wait." Peri knelt beside the

dead guard, cutting a button from his uniform with the knife still bloody from his own death. It wasn't a trophy, but re-creating a memory would be easier with a talisman to focus it on: blood, the feel of the sticky blade, the scent of gunpowder, and the taste of . . . chocolate?

"You made a reservation, right?" Jack asked, looking awkward in his concern. "Did you write it down? I don't know why you insist on keeping our post-task date a secret."

"Because it's fun to watch you squirm," she said softly, still trying to find herself. He was overly anxious, wanting to move and keep moving, but as she glanced at the dead man, she didn't wonder why. Pulse slow, she felt the new aches settle in, clueless as she looked out the huge windows at the dark city. "What day is it?" she said, and heartache marred Jack's handsome face as he realized how deep the damage was.

"We'll check your phone. I bet you wrote it down," Jack said, avoiding her question as he took her elbow and carefully helped her through the secretary's office and into a maze of low-partitioned cubicles. "Do you remember where the elevators are? I have a lousy sense of direction."

"I don't remember the friggin' task, Jack. What day is it!" she snapped, and he stopped.

Facing her, he gently turned her right hand up to show her a watch. She didn't wear a watch. Ever.

"February the seventh. I'm sorry, Peri. It was a bad one."

Peri stared at the watch. It looked like something Jack might have given her—all black and chrome, having more functions than a PTA mom with twins, but she didn't remember it. "February?" The last she knew, it was late December. "I lost six weeks! How long did I draft?"

Emotion flashed over Jack, relief and then distress. "Thirty seconds?" he said, putting a hand on the small of her back and getting her moving again. "But you created a massive potential displacement. You were going to die. The guard? He was the one who did it."

And now she was alive instead of him. That was a lot of change to absorb. She was lucky she'd lost only six weeks in those thirty seconds. She'd once drafted forty-five seconds, but the changes made had been so small that she'd lost only the time her draft had created. There were rules, but so much impacted them that estimating time lost from time rewritten was chancy at best.

"The car is outside," Jack said as he led her through the dark to the elevators. Jack walked just a shade faster than she, falling into a well-practiced role of filling in the gaps in a way that wouldn't make her feel stupid. If she didn't move too fast, she could at least look as if she knew where they were going. There was an art to it, and they'd both had time to refine it. "We fixed the camera on the south elevator, right?" he asked as he hit the down button.

His nervous chatter was starting to get to her, but it was because he was worried, so she bit back her sharp retort, not wanting to make Jack feel any worse. Her body ached from a beating she didn't remember getting, and her face felt as if it was on fire. Dancing was out, but they could still play some pool, relax before they turned to the task of rebuilding her memory. It was a tradition that stretched back almost to their first meeting.

They stepped into the elevator together, and she jerked when Jack was suddenly there, his arms around her and his lips beside her ear. "I'm sorry. Sometimes I wish I wasn't your anchor. Seeing you get beaten up is hard enough, but being the only one to remember it is misery."

He pulled back, and they shared a weak smile. Peri steeled herself against the wave of emotion that washed over her. She could cry later. But she wouldn't. Holding the world together while a new timeline formed was her job. Witnessing and rebuilding her memory was his job—and had been for the last three years.

She took a slow breath as the elevator halted with a cheerful *ding*. She would have written down their reservation. The night was not entirely ruined, and she would appreciate a good wine and the release that flirting with Jack would bring. "What were we getting, anyway?"

Immediately Jack relaxed. "Remember that virus that Opti used to reinforce the United Nations' pollution limits three years ago? It had an ugly stepsister," he said. "I'm sorry, Peri. At least you didn't lose the summer."

A faint smile eased her worry, and she twined her fingers in his as they got out of the elevator. No, she hadn't lost the summer, but if she had, she knew that she could've fallen in love with him all over again.

CHAPTER THREE

The stairway was cramped, lit with tiny flashing lights and glittery with the hearts-and-roses banner someone had put up for next week's Valentine's Day party. Peri had to go up almost sideways in her heels, the music thumping through the walls seeming to push her up to the loft where the pool tables were. Jack was still downstairs talking on his phone to their handler, Bill, under the guise of arranging payment, and Peri stifled a surge of jealousy. Couldn't they have even one moment of relaxation without Bill interfering?

But her frown shifted to a blank nothing as the memory of the guard surfaced, a hole in him the size of her knife. Quashing it, she continued upstairs, eager to push out the faint—and admittedly ridiculous—feeling that something was wrong.

This will help, she thought, pleased as she emerged onto the second floor and took in the six tables of masculinity replete with beer, wings, and camaraderie, liking the wide range of attire from jeans and plaid to suits and ties. It was the love of the game that brought them here and wiped out their differences like blue chalk in the wind, and she breathed in the faint scent of smoke that lingered in the green felt and relaxed.

But someone noticed her and jostled an elbow. Another cleared his throat, and soon everyone looked up, their gazes traveling over her in appreciation and lingering in question on her black eye and TSA-approved cue case instead of her curves. Three tables were open, but it was the one in the back corner that caught her eye. Sashaying to the supply rack, she took a finger towel and an old chalk.

Jack was just coming up when she turned, his smile wide as he noticed every eye on her. "I can't leave you alone for even a second," he said, tugging her to him for a welcome kiss.

His lips met hers, and she leaned into him as the spark dove deep, kindling a desire that the coming evening would only fan higher. The music thumped with a suggestive rhythm, and the post-adrenaline crash made her feel flirty. Their lips parted, and she sighed, happy to have him in her life.

"It's the clothes, believe me," she said, and he shook his head.

"It's what they're wrapped around," he said, one arm lingering around her as his gaze lifted to the room. "Which one looks good? Corner table?"

Nodding, she headed that way, shivering when his hand slipped from her. Eyes were still on them as she crossed to the shadowed corner, wincing at the electronic whine coming from an out-of-phase holo table and glad the place had only the one. No one was playing it, probably because it was out of synch and the graphix were jumping.

Music thumped up from the floor through Peri's feet as she set her handbag on the small drinks table and slid up onto the high stool. A heartbeat of electronic dance music seemed to carry the colored lights to the corners of the two-story, upscale club, but the spinning flashes were mere hints under the strong glow of the nearby low-hanging pool table lights. The atmosphere, even on a Thursday night, was alive and electrifying, a heady mix of angles and vectors surrounded by chaotic movement and life.

Just what I need right now, she thought as Jack ran the play card to free the balls. Smiling, she idly spun through the club's at-table menu system, ordering a basket of wings and two red wines as usual. Tradition dictated that dessert would be determined by the winner—which would be her if she had her way.

"My break?" she asked when Jack lifted the rack up and away, not liking that she didn't remember how they'd left their last game.

"As I recall," he said as he handed Peri her cue stick.

Slipping from the stool, she leaned to rest the flat of her arm on the smooth finish of the pool table. Her swollen eye throbbed as she held her breath and lined up the shot. The cue slid between her fingers like silk, once, twice, and then away . . . and she straightened at the familiar thump and crack.

Smiling, she watched the balls scatter as the nine dropped in. With the noise below, it was more a feeling than a sound, but satisfying nevertheless. Around them, the men's interest waned, her excellent break telling them she belonged.

Jack sighed. "This might be a while," he said with mock glumness.

"I might miss," she promised as she exhaled and lined up another shot.

"Doubt it," he grumbled, the slim wafer of glass glowing in his palm as he checked his messages.

"Ten in the corner, off the bank," she whispered, feeling better already. The thump of the cue against the ball pulled her upright, and she stood as the ball dropped in. She missed her next shot, but their wine had shown up, and she decided to order dessert when Jack wasn't looking. He wasn't going to win, even if it required cheating.

"Your go," she said as she came back to the table and touched his face just to feel the faint stubble. *I love seeing him this relaxed,* she thought, wishing she could remember more nights like this. "I sank two."

"You're off your game," he said as he took his cue. "Looks like it's apple pie tonight."

"Doubt it," she said, sighing as he moved forward to study the table. From below, the music shifted to something slower, the lights lowering to spin at the floor in lazy circles. Jack settled on his shot, and she scrolled through the menu, ordering chocolate cake as she waited for the exact . . . moment . . . to distract him.

"How's Bill?" she asked suddenly, and Jack jumped, miscuing. The cue ball spun in an awkward spiral to hit nothing, and he frowned, knowing she'd done it on purpose. "I've seen you check your messages twice now," she added as he straightened.

"As antsy as always," he said. "I know this is our time, but I was tired of avoiding his texts. They found the body already, and he wanted to make sure we're okay."

Peri grimaced. Sloppy. Leaving bodies was sloppy. "You told him I drafted?" she asked, not yet ready to think about the additional debriefing that a draft engendered.

Jack wouldn't look at her, and she disliked the unusual avoidance. "He wants us to check in when we hit Detroit," he said. "No rush, but no . . . what did he say . . . lollygagging?"

Peri rolled her eyes, imagining the heavy, somewhat prissy man saying just that. Blowing the dust from the tip, she smiled, forgiving him for bringing up work. The lights had risen again, playing on the ceiling of the open floor below the loft. "You didn't leave me much," she said as she sashayed forward. "I think you missed on purpose."

"I like watching you shoot," he said as he stood behind her to look over the layout.

"You just like seeing my ass in the air," she quipped back.

He grinned, tucking her short hair behind an ear. "It's a very nice ass, Peri."

Laughing, she shied away from him. "Maybe if I bank it off there . . . ," she said, losing herself in the math. Stretching over the table, she tested the angle. It would be tight.

"You're a little off," Jack said, and she felt him lean in, hanging over her to see her shot setup. "I think you need to angle it more. This might be a little *hard* for you," he said, pressing into her.

"It's not how hard it is that worries me." She liked his nearness, the way she could feel his warmth against her. "It's how long it is."

"Mmmm." He grinned, inches away.

"Is this better?" she said, not looking away from him.

He licked his lips. "Better. Nice and smooth now, and I think it will go right . . . in."

He was far too close for an easy play, but he was trying to make her miss, among other things, and she focused on the shot, exhaling when she tapped it and knowing before it moved a foot that it hadn't been enough.

"Well, darn," she complained as she pushed herself up. "Your go," she said, returning to their table and levering herself up on the stool. Her cake had arrived. She couldn't help but wonder how she'd found this place. Maybe Bill suggested it. He knew their after-task tradition of pool and dessert.

Her smile faded at the reminder of what lay ahead. *Six weeks.* Jack could never bring that all back. But then, what does anyone really remember, anyway?

There was a thump of a ball. "That's two," Jack said. "You're not eating that if I win."

Feeling good, Peri ran a finger across the top of the cake. "Just keep dreaming," she said, making sure he was watching as she licked off the whiskey-infused frosting. The shock of it burned in a pleasant surprise, and as Jack focused on his game, she breathed deep, feeling it add to her slight buzz.

The balls cracked, and she cheered when the

eight went in too early, making it her win. Clearly not caring, Jack set his cue on the table and came to stand behind her. "You win," he said, his arms going around her and rocking her slowly. "You always win."

She sighed, feeling the love as the music shifted, becoming even slower as the evening lengthened. Together they looked out over the dance floor below them. She could dance to this, black eye or not. Hell, they were almost dancing now, Jack slowly swaying with her as she sat on the stool, him standing behind her where he always was.

"Peri, have you ever given any thought to retiring?"

She stopped his motion, looking up and behind at him in surprise. "Quit Opti?"

"Why not?" he said, rushing to talk before she said anything else. "I can't think of a better way to live out my life than with you, doing nothing more than this. Maybe on a beach."

They had talked about this before, but never when she was feeling this relaxed, this . . . vulnerable to his idea. She couldn't quit. This was who she was. "Sand in your shorts would get a little tiring after a while, don't you think?"

He turned her in his arms and kissed her forehead. "Not if you were with me. I'd get you chocolate cake every day."

Quit? She couldn't do it. "Jack," she protested, biting back her argument when the pattern of lights shifted from rosy colors to a stark white, bathing Jack's face, and she stared at his pasty complexion, her gut twisting. *Don't leave my sight* drifted up from nowhere, an image of his anger superimposed on his content face. It was his voice in her mind.

I left him, she thought, breath held as she looked at her open hand and the faint J IN OFFICE that hadn't washed off completely.

"Jack," she whispered, the taste of the chocolate and whiskey strong on her lips.

Blinking fast, she leaned into him as a sensation of vertigo swept her. Her breath caught, and it felt as if she'd stepped out of time and was just watching.

It's a list, lovely woman echoed in her thoughts, and an image of a suited man eating chocolate, smug and confident, surfaced. She licked her lips, tasting it. The bitterness kindled more, and anger flashed through her, its source unknown. "Jack," she whispered, unheard over the music, but the anger vanished, smothered by a feeling of desperation and loss. No, betrayal. Eyes wide, she looked up at Jack, squeezing his hand until he looked down at her.

"What?" Jack's content expression vanished in concern.

She blinked, gaping at him through a flood of questions. She tried to speak, shocked to silence when he leaned close and the scent of chocolate and whiskey suffocated her. Panic unfolded. Her hand hurt, and she looked at it, cramped and tight as if holding a knife.

"Peri!" Jack gripped her arms. "What is it?"

Her head dropped. The light on his face made it worse. Unable to look at him, she was alone in her terror as she relived shoving the guard off her. He'd smelled of whiskey, and the taste of chocolate was with her still. He'd choked her, and she'd killed him to save her own life. But she shouldn't be able to remember anything! Not until Jack brought it back and made it real.

"Peri, look at me." Jack yanked a chair closer, sitting so he was inches away, his blue eyes worried as he gripped her arms tightly, keeping her upright. "I'm here. Look at me."

"I'm . . . okay," she rasped, but she wasn't. "Memory knot," she whispered, and Jack's eyes widened in fear. One hand still supporting her, he turned to the stairway. Swallowing hard, she silently agreed. When things go wrong, you minimize, and things had gone wrong.

Memory knots were nasty little snags of unremembered thought triggered by scent and images. On its own, a memory knot was frightening enough, but if it was attached to a rewrite and left unattended, it could lead to a MEP, memory-eclipsed paranoia, as the twin timelines lurking in her subconscious fought to be remembered. Anchors didn't have a problem remembering twin timelines, but drafters . . . Drafters would quickly lose their mind. It was an anchor's job—apart from doing half of everything else—to bring back one clean memory for a drafter to find closure with.

That a memory knot had snarled up before Jack had even had a chance to defrag her memory didn't bode well. Something had happened, something so bad that her mind was fighting to remember it. Killing a guard to save her life wasn't enough. It was something else.

It's a list, lovely woman, she recalled, and the taste of chocolate and whiskey rose anew. "We need to go," she said, light-headed as she slid from the stool. "Jack, I want to go home."

Home was eight hundred miles to the north, but anywhere would be better than this.

"Right. Okay." Jack's arm slid around her, holding her upright without looking obvious about it. His eyes went to their cue sticks, and she made a small sound.

"Don't you dare leave them. Hand me my purse," she said, and he nodded, steadying her as she found her chancy balance and pushed through the dizzying sensation of memory trying to beat its way to the surface.

She hardly recognized the stairway, Jack almost carrying her down.

"Going out for a smoke!" Jack said loudly to the doorman, and he opened the door for them. "Don't give our table away."

But Peri knew they weren't coming back.

The door to the club shut behind them, and Peri looked up in the muffled thump of music and the damp February night. She flushed, embarrassed. She hadn't passed out, but it was like being afraid of ghosts. "I'm okay," she said softly, and Jack shook his head, his expression in the streetlight hard as they made their way to the car.

"Memory knots are dangerous," he said, pace slow. "We head back now. I'm driving."

"I said I'm okay," she protested, not liking the fuss.

"I never said you weren't," Jack said. "But we're still going back."

"Fine," she grumbled as she found her balance and pulled away. The fresh air had revived her, but she still felt foolish, and Jack refused to leave her side, even when they found her Mantis right where they'd left it.

"In you go," he said as he opened the passenger-side door for her, the biometric lock recognizing him and releasing. The car chimed a happy greeting as she sighed, fingers shaking as she slid into the leather cushions. The door thumped shut with the sound of money well spent, and with her purse on her lap, she reached to start the car with a push of a button. The warming engine rumbled to life with a satisfying growl and, ignoring the onboard computer's cheerful greeting and question whether it should prepare to register a new driver since she was in the passenger seat, she hit the button for the heated seats and turned off the music as Jack broke their cues down and dropped them in the trunk.

She didn't like leaving her car on the street. Not that anyone could steal it, but the Mantis was illegal outside Detroit because of the solar-gathering, color-changing paint that charged the batteries. Though, to be honest, most cops would only ogle the sleek lines instead of impounding the two-seater. It sort of looked like a Porsche Boxter, only sexier.

Jack jogged around the front, giving her an encouraging smile as he got in and waited for the car to recognize him and release the controls. "Home by dawn, Peri. You'll be fine."

"I'm fine now," she protested, but she'd be glad to get home.

Damn memory knot had ruined everything. She had saved Jack's life more times than she could count, and he had saved hers more than she could remember, but as he flicked the warming engine off and found his way to the interstate, a little niggling of warning bit deep and burrowed deeper.

She was only going to remember one past, and Jack . . . he'd remember both.

CHAPTER
FOUR

His head hurt, but it was the smell of electronics and polymers from the slick-suit that pulled him awake. Silas snorted, jerking upright only to groan and hold his head. He was sitting at a small table. Squinting, he recognized the small, featureless, eight-by-eight room immediately, and anger pulled his shoulders stiff and made his pounding head worse.

"God-blessed idiot," he muttered, pushing the sleeve of the slick-suit up his arm to find the tiny puncture wound where they'd darted him—darted him like an animal and dragged him back into something he'd worked hard to leave behind. He'd been in his car the last he remembered, on the way to the restoration site. He rolled the sleeve back down, struggling because it was a size too small.

"I'm not doing this," he said, directing the statement at the watching eyes. "You hear me?" he said louder. "I'm done, Fran. Done!"

He frowned as the chime rang out, hating that they knew his pulse had quickened. God-blessed slick-suit. God-blessed idiot for helping them design it.

"Good morning, Dr. Denier," a woman said

pleasantly over the unseen intercom. "I'd say I'm sorry, but you and I both know you wouldn't have come if I'd just asked."

Silas sat back from the table, thick arms across his chest, making the slick-suit run with stress lines. "I fulfilled my contract. Open the door."

"Open it yourself," Fran said, her confident smugness irritating.

Silas's face twisted in frustration. He was not an agent. He was a designer, a tinkerer, an innovator whose playground was where the surety of electronics met the vagaries of the human mind. And they wanted him to run a maze like one of his rats? "You can't make me do this."

"Yes we can."

A wave of sensation rippled over him, cramping his muscles and making him grunt in surprise. It was the slick-suit. Silas reached for the sensitive brain of it, then choked as someone tightened the wavelengths. Gagging, he fell prostrate, shaking with convulsions.

They stopped as quickly as they had begun, and he lay on the asbestos tile floor, his anger turning cold. *Son of a bitch . . .*

"Begin," Fran said, and then the chime.

It rankled him no end that he'd chosen the sound himself.

Seething, Silas pulled himself up. Grasping the back of the chair, he flung it at the door lock, shattering the chair and damaging the panel. With a primal shout of anger, he punched it, satisfied when the light went out and a wisp of smoke trailed to the floor.

"Don't be stupid, Denier," Fran said, and Silas sucked on his bleeding knuckles. "You want to talk to me? Tell me how wrong I am? Get out of the room."

"I'm no one's lab rat," he muttered. Levering himself up onto the table, he stood and hammered his way into the ceiling. The audio link was still open, and he couldn't help his satisfaction at the sudden uproar.

Years of bench-pressing paid off, and he pulled himself up into the low crawl space above the training floor. It was cooler up here, and the outlines of the various rooms were easy to see. Besides, they hadn't changed them. Keeping atop the sturdier walls, he walked to the hallway in a low hunch, clear of the training room's potential immobilizing field.

"Silas, get back on the training floor!" Fran demanded, faint through the ceiling.

"Maybe you shouldn't have forgotten that I designed it," he grumbled, gauging that he'd cleared the active areas, and jumped clear through a ceiling panel and down into the outer hallway.

He'd landed badly, his ankle twinging as his arms pinwheeled to keep him from falling outright. Dust and ceiling rained down, and he slowly rose through it, grimacing at the five men in combat gear pointing close-range weapons at him. He felt vulnerable in that outrageous slick-suit, clinging like a second, uncomfortable skin.

Her heels clicking, an older woman with short, dyed blond hair styled back off her face pushed through to confront him, an aide tight behind. "You designed it. Isn't that the point, Denier? You owe us."

"I don't owe you anything. I quit Opti. And I quit you."

"If you're not Opti, you're alliance. And you are alliance," she said, and he held his breath against the sneeze her perfume tickled forth. Most women would have looked odd in a flamboyant red business suit with an orchid-and-silk corsage, surrounded by squat men in bulky combat gear, but not Fran. Her sure confidence made it all work.

But she had a right to be confident. The alliance was made up of renegade Opti personnel who believed the government shouldn't control the ability to manipulate time. They'd make their fight public except that their ranks consisted of anchors and drafters themselves, and if word got out, the populace would panic and kill them all. So they worked in the shadows funded by benefactors, benefactors like Fran. It was exchanging one power-hungry boss for another as far as Silas was concerned.

His file was in her hand, the photo of him with

his close-cropped hair and lab coat three years out of date but still accurate. He'd put on some muscle since then, but his frame had always been bulky, earning him the nickname Hulk from those who didn't like him, and that had been more than a few.

Fran ran her attention up and down his body, smiling in appreciation. Weight shifting, he clasped his hands into a fig leaf, trying not to look obvious about it. "I was done three years ago. Nothing has changed. You going to shoot me?"

"But it has changed." Fran gestured for the men ringing them to fall back. "We got word this morning that she might be ready for extraction."

Twin feelings of elation and betrayal flooded him. "Might be?" he said softly. "You have *nothing!*" He gestured wildly, catching his anger when the men tightened their grips in threat on their weapons. "This idea was flawed from the beginning. It will not work. Not in a year. Not in ten! Every time she has something, they scrub her and she loses more. It was a bad idea, Fran. All you're doing is making it worse, and I'll have nothing to do with it."

Fran smacked his file against his chest. "Update your info. You leave tomorrow. The way in is already prepared. Even have a friend waiting for you."

His lip curled, and he refused to take the file. *Toy soldiers playing war.* "You're not listening to me."

"No." Fran leaned into him, and he backed up, knocking into one of the guards. "You're not listening to me," the woman said, her head tilted to look up at him and the light showing where she'd had some work done. "She's got what we need. She doesn't know it yet, which is why it is going to work this time. Go in. Get it. Now, before they figure it out and scrub her. You want to end it? Then end it."

But even ended, it would never be as it had been. Angry, Silas turned to the man he'd bumped into, glaring until he shifted aside to show an empty hallway. Truly, they had no call to detain him, and they knew it.

"I need you, Silas," Fran said, not pleading, but close to it. "What are you going to do? Go back to your hobby? Clean your historical relics and pretend you're something you're not? You are a master, Silas. You are the best. And you are pissing your genius away."

He turned, seeing her surrounded by her guns and men, playing at a war that no one knew existed. He wasn't a genius, just lucky in how he saw the world. "You used me."

"But it all worked out, didn't it?" she said with a false brightness. "If we have any chance of ending this, it's going to be through you. You're the only one smart enough to see the extent of the damage and fluid enough to adapt a program to fix it. Don't walk away from her. Not now."

Jaw clenched, Silas turned. Arms swinging, he strode down the corridor, the slick-suit pinching. His clothes were around here somewhere, and, he hoped, his car.

"Tonight," Fran called after him, her smug voice irritating. "Five sharp."

"I don't think he's going to do it," Fran's aide said, and Silas's neck warmed when Fran laughed.

"He will. Make sure you have something that fits him. That's one big man."

Ticked, he strode faster, knowing the way to the garage. He hated that she knew him so well. He'd sulk and stew, and probably break something expensive. Then he'd show up at ten minutes to five because she was right. He wasn't the best they had, but if anyone could do it, it would be him.

CHAPTER
FIVE

Peri lingered under the motel's shower, the tiny world of warmth and fog working over every muscle to ease her aching body. Post-task injuries weren't unusual. What was unusual, what had Jack so unnerved that he'd driven all night, was that damned memory knot.

Brow furrowed, Peri reached for the shampoo. She felt fragile, as if something in her past might loom out of nothing and bring her down. It was obvious what had triggered the knot: the taste of chocolate, the scent of whiskey, Jack's face, stark in the club's lights. But she daren't even think about it. Not until Jack got back with breakfast, anyway.

It had been hard to bring Jack to a halt this morning, so intent was he on getting back to Detroit. He'd driven all night, watching over her while she slept. The man was dead tired, and she was going to insist on finishing the last leg behind the wheel herself. It was her car, damn it. She was fine. She'd be even better after a defrag. Besides, it wasn't often she had the chance to open her Mantis up and let it joyously run until the voltage-sensitive paint paled from its usual black and silver to an energy-saving, low-state white.

She'd needed to play the "I'm hungry" card to get him to pull off at a sad-looking truck-stop restaurant. That had led to the idea of taking a shower at the even sadder-looking adjoining motel while breakfast was being prepared. If she got her way—and she usually did—their break would extend into a memory defrag. Then Jack would sleep. He wouldn't be able to help it. After three years of saving each other's asses, her trust in Jack was absolute, but her gut said to stay off her employer's radar until Jack returned her memory, especially if a knot was involved.

Jack was right to be concerned, but defragging

her thoughts was the quickest way to unsnarl and prevent another knot. *Before I start to hallucinate,* she thought as she squirted cream rinse onto her palm. Though, to be honest, it would take weeks of unattended memory issues before that happened.

Her arms ached as she worked the cream rinse through her straight black strands. Her hair was longer than she remembered, but that wasn't unusual. Unfortunately, neither were unexplained rug burns and bruises. She hated the disconnection that drafting left her. If not for Jack, she'd be adrift. Alone. Lost.

Jack will tell me, she thought, lingering under the water as she wondered if her mother might have died in the last six weeks. Not knowing how she felt about that, her thoughts turned to her first draft—or at least, the first one she remembered. She'd been ten, swinging too high at the playground. A fall had broken her arm, but it had probably been getting the wind knocked out of her and the accompanying surge of adrenaline that had caused the jump. She'd since learned to control it and could draft at will, but the fear of dying would always trigger an unstoppable draft. She actually thought she had died that afternoon, when she suddenly found herself again swinging, watching a ghost image of herself gasp for air on the ground, her mother frantic.

At least, that was the memory she'd eventually defragmented with the help of Dr. Cavana, a child psychologist she'd been referred to after the episode at the park, teased from her over the span of several months. Stress-induced amnesia, they called it. But when she kept waking from nightmares of suffocation and a broken arm when she clearly didn't have one, her mother had gotten scared, overreacted—and unknowingly changed Peri's life.

Dr. Cavana had been a nice old man, part of the covert government-funded group that found and evaluated potential drafters and anchors, the same branch of government she now worked for. Far more than a mere anchor, he could delve into a drafter's mind and painstakingly rebuild memories he hadn't witnessed. The skill had made him unique and therefore sheltered, but she'd always harbored the idea that he could kill a man in five seconds if he needed to.

Cavana had been the one to tell her about anchors and drafters, and that if she worked hard and took the right classes, she could join the clandestine, elite government force developed in the '60s to counter the Cold War intel, the drug war, the war on terrorist activity, and any war they felt like in between. Opti agents tweaked the present to set the future, and they had their fingers in everything from the development of soft fusion, to the legalization of replacement organs, to making sure U.S.-financed Finland made a manned landing on Mars before Putin.

Anyone who'd ever experienced déjà vu could be trained to remember altered timelines, but the anchor's ability to mesh his or her mind with a drafter's to *rebuild* those timelines was a rare skill. Drafters were even harder to find, seeing as they forgot both the history they changed and the history they wrote. There was a reason Cavana had been posing as a child psychologist, and even today, recruits were pulled from youth mental health wards.

Cavana made sure she got into the best schools, and she eagerly took the classes he suggested, wanting to be just like him, not minding having to lie to her overbearing, controlling mother, who thought her master's degree in military tactical innovation meant she was in a lab designing weapons, not that she was one.

The two years spent in a special branch of the military were like heaven on earth, both the hardest thing she'd ever done and the best. It was there that she learned how to use her body as a weapon that couldn't be turned against her, how to shoot when she had to, and how to avoid it by using her wiles. The science geeks helped her develop the framework of rituals to keep her balanced after a draft and ease the confusion. Some drafters, the men especially, could draft longer than she, but it was her opinion that the best draft was the one you didn't have to make.

Hearing Jack's footsteps outside the door, Peri

turned off the water and got out, trying not to drip on her overnight bag. Wiping the mist from the mirror, she palpated the skin around her swollen eye. It was turning purple already. She jumped at the soft knock, even though she'd expected it.

"I've got your usual on the table," Jack said, peeking in to hang a robe on the back of the door and set a steaming cup of take-out coffee on the glass shelf.

Still dripping, she leaned to give him a kiss. "You're too good to me." His lips tasted of coffee, and her eyes dropped. "My mother didn't die in the last six weeks, did she?"

Jack gaped at her. "Good God, no! What brought that up?"

Feeling silly now, she shrugged. "I don't know."

"Oh, Peri . . ." He awkwardly edged his way in, taking her in a damp hug and pinning her behind her towel. "You talked to her last week. Everything is fine."

"So am I," she insisted, not liking the lump in her throat. "But I want to get last night's task back before I get in the car." His arms eased, and she looked at the guard's button sitting on the shelf. "Can we build the defrag around that?"

He nodded solemnly and took it. "Um, yes. I talked to Bill. He's freaking out. Are you sure you don't want to wait and defrag at Opti?"

"Opti?" she blurted, thinking the request was unusual. But there was a memory knot, and he was tired. "I'd rather do it now if you're okay. You are okay, aren't you?" she said, and he nodded, head down as he backed out and shut the door to leave Peri with a lingering unease.

The six weeks she'd lost wouldn't come back on their own, and there was only so much Jack could reasonably return to her. Sandy, her Opti-assigned psychologist, who'd been with her from the start, said that the larger the difference between the two timelines, the deeper the damage went. Six weeks for saving her life wasn't a bad exchange. Six weeks was manageable. But she had to know what had happened up in that room.

The scent of sausage and egg began to permeate the bathroom, mixing with the lure of coffee on the shelf. Her stomach rumbled as she reached for the robe Jack had brought in, and it pulled free from the hook to send her pen necklace behind it swinging like a pendulum. Peri brought the cotton to her nose, breathing in the scent of her detergent under the cold, stale smell of luggage, then slipped it on, silently thanking Jack for putting the robe in his bag. If she wasn't relaxed, nothing would come back. That Jack knew her so well made her feel needy and dumb, but patterns kept her sane when the world was jerked out from under her.

Reluctantly Peri tucked the sterling silver pendant pen away in her bag. Most drafters had a way to leave quick, impromptu notes to themselves in case they drafted without an anchor, but wearing it during a defrag would be a show of mistrust.

The quick gulp of coffee hit her like a bitter, welcome slap, and she sat on the edge of the tub and pulled her overnight bag closer. Most of the clothes in it were unfamiliar, but she almost always wore the same thing so she'd never feel lost—solid, bold colors and tailored cuts—and she hung a fresh pair of slacks and new top on the back of the door to unwrinkle in the shower's residual fog. *White panties?* she wondered, the thin cloth sticking as she put them on under her robe. When had she started wearing white? They were so . . . pedestrian.

The boots were her familiar kick-ass style, and she gave them a quick wipe to get rid of a scuff, flushing when the cloth came away red with blood. *That explains my swollen foot.*

Her tight brow eased at the knitting project shoved in the front pocket for the drive there and back. *I've gotten brave enough to try gloves?* she thought as she set the double-pointed needles aside and kept digging. The domestic art was more than an Opti-sanctioned stress relief, and she liked being able to carry spikes of wood through TSA. In truth, it was a big part of why she'd agreed to it when Sandy had suggested she learn the homebody hobby. In a pinch, the needles could fit beside her knife in its boot sheath.

Her phone was next, and she checked to see

whom she'd been talking to lately, glad she hadn't forgotten how to work the glass technology. There weren't many names, and she recognized all of them. An odd exchange gave her pause until she realized it was out of Charlotte, probably the club, a restaurant, or the hotel they'd stayed at.

She found her knife wadded in Jack's handkerchief, and she meticulously washed the blood off with a DNA-destroying wipe, using a drop of oil stored in an unused contact lens case to lubricate the blade before tucking it in her boot sheath where it belonged. The bloodstained handkerchief she threw away, knowing that the maid would dispose of it more surely than she could. She didn't like that she couldn't remember ending a life. She never killed anyone unless they killed her first. Jack, though, wasn't that picky.

Tired, she looked at herself in the mirror as it fogged back up, not liking the shadow of her mother in the slant to her narrow jaw and the upturned curve of her nose. She'd pieced her life back together as much as she could on her own. It was time for Jack's help, and she headed out, coffee in hand.

A sagging queen bed with a faded print bedspread took up one interior wall. There was a large window overlooking the parking lot and interstate beyond, and one small window opposite that looked out at scrub and rock behind the hotel. The maroon carpet was matted, and the furniture was decades out of date. A TV was bolted into a corner at the ceiling. There was an actual rotary phone on the nightstand, but beside it was a universal etherball plug-in/charger that connected any device to the Net—a necessity when catering to truckers. The one spot of high tech made the rest of the room more dreary. It was a far cry from the tech-rich, five-star service she was used to, but it was safe, and that was all that truly mattered.

"Better?" Jack asked as he scooted a second chair to the tiny round table he'd arranged.

"Getting there." There was an omelet with toast and sausage across from a plastic bowl of yogurt and walnuts. The early sun streamed in, glinting on the button sitting at dead center of the table. Slowly her smile faded as she tried to both remember and forget the face of the man she'd taken everything from, his eyes open as he stared up at her with his last breath foaming the blood at his lips. Sometimes forgetting was a blessing.

"You, ah, going to shower before we hit the road?" she asked, hearing the whoosh of the interstate traffic leaking in along with the golden sun.

Jack glanced at the bathroom. "Probably. After I eat. I'm starving."

"Me too." The sausage smelled wonderful, and though the plastic spork was annoying, it didn't seem to matter when the fatty bliss hit her tongue.

Sighing, Jack flopped into the chair across from

her. Peri took another gulp of coffee, freezing when she set it next to Jack's cup—sitting right in front of her. *Great.* Eggs and sausage were apparently not her usual anymore. Six weeks ago they had been.

She looked up to find Jack glumly poking at the yogurt. "Ah, this is your breakfast, isn't it," she said, and he sheepishly reached across the table to take his coffee.

"Ye-e-e-eah. You've been on a health kick lately, but go ahead. You look hungry."

"Oh, Jack," she breathed in chagrin, and pushed the plate to him, getting up and moving to sit in his lap when he protested. His arms felt right as they went about her, his grunt of surprise making her smile. The smell of gunpowder lingered on him, way down under the dry scent of blue chalk and old beer. The bitter odor penetrated deep into her psyche and kindled a tingling desire born of memories of adrenaline and joined danger.

"We'll share," she whispered, and he shifted her weight. "Here. Take a bite."

His eyes lit up, and he held her securely on his lap as she angled the spork and sausage between his teeth. "I could get used to this," he said around the mouthful, and relief dropped her shoulders. She hated it when she made a mistake this obvious.

It was all about routine. Routine wouldn't bring her memory back, but she had to have stability to notice what was out of place—and she was making mistakes.

"Mmmm, good," he said as he shifted her so he could help himself. "You know, Bill is really not happy about the knot. Wants us back ASAP."

"Of course he does." But her gaze went to the interstate. If something deeper than a memory knot cropped up, Opti could handle it. Fix her. Returning immediately was a good option. "What do you think? Back by noon?" she asked reluctantly, still wanting a defrag before she faced the couch warriors with their psych tests and evaluations. But if he was too tired . . .

Jack nodded, picking the walnuts out of the yogurt to eat them one by one. "If you drive. I gotta get some sleep." He hesitated at her suddenly wide eyes. "I'm good to do a defrag, though," he added, and Peri exhaled in relief.

It wasn't as if she could force him, and if he had begged off because he was too tired, she would've had to wait. Most people at Opti thought the drafter was the ruling force in a drafter-anchor pairing, but the honest truth was, the anchor held the sanity of his or her partner—and every drafter knew it. "Now?" she asked, feeling as if they were running out of time.

Jack nodded. Pushing the half-eaten omelet away, he levered her up, his hands familiarly on her hips. A last bite of egg, and Peri took up the button. It was cold—as if it held nightmares. Jack closed the curtains, and she sat in his chair, the fabric still warm from his body.

A yellowish, amber light seeped through the thin fabric. It was like muffled sunlight, golden and warm. She sighed when he came up behind her, his strong fingers pushing into her forehead. Like a top-dollar massage therapist, he began to work the tension from her, starting at her brow, avoiding her bruise as he found and held pressure points until she exhaled the energy from her. The hot shower had eased her sore muscles, and Jack worked from her eyes to her forehead, to her jaw, to her cheekbones, and back again until Peri's slight headache was gone. She stifled a moan when he turned to her neck and shoulders. There were lots of ways to calm the mind and body, but this was her favorite.

Peri was still holding the button lightly, her fingers flexing around it as Jack eased her tension. All drafters tied memories to objects to help make them real, but it was only the final timeline that was allowed to remain. In essence, anchors were creating a memory knot, but it was tamed and safe because there'd only be one timeline associated with it. That anchors could remember both was a wonder to Peri. How could there be two pasts? It didn't make sense.

"We ate in the city at sunset," Jack said, his voice low, almost unheard over the distant traffic. "Champagne, strong cheese, and crackers amid gold and pink light. You flirted with the waiter until he brought you a plate of almond cookies off the menu," he said, and Peri smiled, thinking that sounded like her. "You drove the long way to the building so you could sing with the Beatles. We were the happy, tipsy couple when we entered, and no one gave us a second look. You timed me decrypting the floor's main door. I was three seconds slow."

But two minutes better than my best time, she thought at the memory of burning circuits. Her closed eyes twitched, and Jack's words made her blood hum as the night became real.

"You sat, admiring the view as I worked," he said, and she breathed easy, remembering the deep purples and shining golds of lights between the street and night sky, her confidence that they'd be back at their hotel by sunrise eating breakfast on their balcony and Jack complaining that she was poisoning him with health food.

"You pointed out the planes stacked for landing," he said, and she drowsed, recalling her good mood. "You sampled the chocolate, everything going well. Then you heard the elevator, and you were feeling daring, so you left me."

I left him. His worry twined about hers, magnifying it. An anchor had to be within a drafter's reach to recognize a jump, and drafting out of his sight might have left Jack unable to bring back her memory at all. *It must have been worth the risk,* she thought, her grip tightening on the button, the holes sharp on her skin.

"It was the security guard," Jack said, his touch returning to her jawline to work the new frown from her brow. Memories were coming back stronger now. She could feel Jack with her, their mental connection tightening until his emotion in her mind was as real and recognizable as hers. There'd been lights on the ceiling, doors opening that should have remained shut, a dangerous, aware lifter instead of a cream-puff guard.

Jack's fingers fell away as their connection solidified and her closed eyes began to dart in earnest. Together they saw the man she had killed. She recognized his expression, gave Jack the knowledge that the guard had smelled like whiskey and sweat when they had collided. Jack felt her confidence when the guard opened the door, felt her pain when his fist found her eye. Peri's heart pounded as she recalled the taste of her blood when he shot her, the smell of gunpowder, the shock of adrenaline. She was falling away from a man with gray hair. . . .

And then Jack wrapped his mind around the blood, the pain, the scent of gunpowder, and the image of a confident man in a suit—fragmenting them. Peri's breath came easier as the broken weave vanished, replaced by the memory of fear and the sudden give as her knife scraped on the guard's ribs and found his lungs.

The memories came in no order, with no reason to them, a mixing of the first timeline and the second as Jack, deep into her psyche, burned the first one away—long before the chaos of two realities could linger and drive her insane. Peri's darting eyes slowed in the first hint of release, and at his urging, they ran through the night again, both of them looking in the shadow places of her mind for remnants of the original timeline that could trigger a mental crash.

Peri tensed when they found it, feeling Jack's grip on her mind tightening. There'd been someone else—a man in a suit. Remembered panic pooled from her to Jack, and she gasped when Jack followed her fear deep into her mind and plucked from it the memory of a man eating a chocolate, reinforcing that she'd eaten a chocolate as she sat in a chair.

But she *knew* they hadn't been alone, and an oily voice crying *Bravo!* echoed against the black edges of burned memory. Jack blotted it away, soothing her.

Her hand throbbed as she recalled pinning a man to a chair, the disdain in his eyes, her fear at his confidence.

In her mind, Jack folded the edges of the first-weave memory in on itself, erasing it. It wasn't there. It hadn't really happened.

And then it was gone.

She was left with the memory of Jack standing

before the wave screen, cursing the files' lack of organization, his face lit and pale in the glow. It was comforting—knowing this was real—and she basked in it, feeling the night's memories in her unfolding like a crumpled paper, the sequence choppy but structured as Jack insisted that they go over it once more, defining a clean memory from both his and her thoughts.

It was only when she eased into the satiated state of a successful memory defragment that fear bubbled up again, rising through the carefully stacked memories, welling up around the jagged edges and swamping her. An unreasonable fear that she was wrong, that she'd made a mistake she couldn't come back from, took her.

It was from the first weave, the one she no longer had memories of. She had been lied to! She was in danger, foul, loathsome, untrustworthy. . . .

Peri's breath caught as Jack's presence strengthened. *Not you,* Jack said, his unspoken words ringing in her mind as he sponged up her fear, dissolving it with his confidence. *Not you, Peri. You're clean. You are uncorrupt, my dove.*

Her chest clenched as his love soaked into her, hiding the fear behind it, and the trembling of her arms eased. Jack burned the fear to ash, telling her he loved her, trusted her, that anything else was a lie. Slowly . . . she believed. She had to.

"I'm here," Jack said aloud, and she felt his fingers find hers, both of them touching the button she'd taken from the dead guard. His calm seeped into her as she worked the rough, round edges of the small chunk of blue plastic. Jack had been there, had seen both times, and had burned away the mistake they'd made until there was only one memory, the last.

Peri's bruises ached anew as she remembered last night and they were given meaning. Her almost-death had never happened, and she only knew of it because Jack had told her about it last night. Secondhand knowledge was safe—a real memory deadly. New Year's and their anniversary were still gone, but there were ways around that, too: her diary waited at home.

Her eyes opened. Jack was kneeling before her, and he smiled as their eyes met. Her thumb was catching on the button's holes, and she stopped rubbing it like the touchstone it was. "Thank you," she said.

Jack leaned forward and brushed the hair from her eyes. "You're welcome."

His voice was husky, and sweat had beaded on his forehead. It had been a hard one. Peri set the button on the scratched table, accidentally dragging it off, and it hit the carpet and rolled under the bed.

Jack's arms went around her, and she leaned into him, breathing the scent of his hair, her arms tightening when she realized he was shaking. Her eyes warmed with unshed tears. "I almost lost you," he said raggedly. "I *did* lose you. I don't know if I can do this anymore, babe."

She parted her knees and pulled him closer, close enough to feel the warmth of him rising between them. He grounded her, kept her sane when the drafts grew too long and the weaves too elaborate. Most people would say he had the easy part, out of the line of fire as she protected him while he got whatever they were after, but the truth of it was that his job was harder. He saw everything, lived everything, relived it again and again until she remembered it, too.

He was still shaking, and Peri tilted his head up. "It's so hard," he said. "Peri, I love you."

"I love you, too." She kissed him, tasting walnuts. "I'm okay," she said, holding him close and breathing him in. "Let it go."

"But what if I hadn't been there?" A tight anger eclipsed his grief, his fierce expression hurting her, almost. "What if you hadn't come back and I had nothing to anchor you? You would have lost everything." He reached up and touched her jawline. "And I'd lose you."

Peri took his hands, feeling his strength. There was no answer, no sure thing. To agonize over it would leave them both questioning. "Don't do this, Jack. It's part of the job."

"I don't know what I'd do if you forgot me."

"I can't forget three years," she said, pulling him close so he couldn't see her face. It was a wish, not a promise, and they both knew it. A traumatic enough draft could make her do just that.

Heads bowed together, they held each other, and her shoulders eased when he reached behind her robe and ran his thumb down a line of her muscle. Exhaling, she looked at the ceiling as heartache was suddenly pushed out by desire. His hands rose to find her breasts, his motions trapped under her robe, somehow more throat-catching than if she'd been naked under him.

Peri curved her hands around him to feel the strength in his shoulders. Relations between anchors and drafters were expected, as it took commitment and trust to merely do their jobs, but love, real love, was frowned upon for just this reason. How could anyone prepare for the pain of loving someone who might forget them tomorrow?

She knew his frustration was because she was forever losing parts of herself, a renewable distraction with a reset button. He gave, and gave, and gave, but he needed her as much as she needed him. Today she remembered. That was all they ever dared to try to keep.

Peri traced the line of his shoulders, liking the sheen of hazy morning outlining his biceps. With a sigh, he dropped his head to find her breast with his mouth. Peri's breath caught. Wanting more, she wrapped her legs around him and ran her fingers through his hair, following the curve of his head down to his neck and then his smooth chest. One by one, she outlined the defined edges of his abs, teasing as she reached down as far as she could. It wasn't far enough.

Jack pushed her robe open. She shivered as the golden light bathed them. Her eyes met his, her own desire kindled deeper at the need rising in his gaze. With a happy sigh, she pulled him back to her, mildly frustrated that she couldn't take his shirt off without making him stop what his lips were doing.

Her fingers stretched, reached, and finally, unable to resist, she slipped from the chair, sending it toppling over behind her as they knelt together. They kissed, the hint of his tongue sparking through her. His lips tasted of coffee and walnuts, the scent of hotel soap a whisper rising between them as their breaths quickened.

His hands moving, always moving, Jack's kisses spun from her lips to her neck, becoming more aggressive. His grip became firmer, more demanding. She found his mouth again, and wouldn't let him leave until she reached to pull his shirt over his head, her shoulder aching from her bruise.

But she got it off him. Relief was a flash, followed by wicked desire as she groped for his zipper. His teeth on her neck shocked through her. One hand traced his tight backside as the other unzipped his pants. He sighed as it went down, but she needed two hands for the button, and she teased until she got it undone and reached to find him.

She squirmed as he pushed her panties down, careful when he skimmed over her bruised hip, and she shivered as she met his mouth with hers, stiffening in delight when his hand traced a firm, demanding path up the inside of her thighs, defining her with his touch. He was a beautiful man, sculpted and toned by the needs of fast action and evading death, and her pulse quickened. He was hers. All of him. And she loved him.

Breathless, she sent her hands everywhere, gentle here, demanding there, until he found her breast again, and she gasped, back arched. They needed to reaffirm that they were both alive and that she was here with him and not dead on the floor of an upstairs corner office.

"Oh God. You're going to be the death of me if you don't do something more," she whispered, almost humming with desire.

His lips lifted from her, and he smiled, reaching behind her to pull the cover off the bed. Her robe had come undone, and he lowered her to the faded bedspread, their passions hesitating as she sent her eyes over him, loving the way he looked, the way he made her feel.

He knelt above her, his pants kicked off and his shirt in a corner. In the rich light filtering through the curtains, he looked like an amber-skinned god. Peri traced the lines of his abs again, drifting lower to make him growl and lean down over her.

"Jack . . . ," she whispered, pushing suggestively into him, and then her hands on his shoulders tightened as he entered her, first warm, then cool as he withdrew and slipped within her anew. Breath fast, her motions became demanding, the pains from last night forgotten as he moved with her, his hands in her hair, his mouth on hers. She bit his lip, and he tilted his head, lunging into her neck with a motion that was both loving and aggressive. Her passions began to peak, and her grip on him grew tighter yet, pace quickening with a desperate need.

She wanted this, she wanted it now. The barest slowing, a widening of motion and catching of breath warned her, and she slowed, knowing it was close and wanting to prolong it. She strained, legs wrapped around him.

And then she found it, gasping with release as waves of ecstasy pulsed through her, shaking them both.

Jack groaned. His hands sprang from her hair as he clenched his fingers into the bedspread, shuddering. She could feel him inside her, and her body responded again as their motions with each other slowed and stopped, warmth eddying between them until all was still.

Panting, she slowly unkinked her hands from his backside, not remembering having put them there. Smiling, she looked up at him, liking what she saw in this moment of unguarded contentment. Sweat sheened his tanned skin, making him glow, almost. His eyes were still closed, his breathing heavy but slow.

She turned to see his hand dug into the bedspread beside her ear, still white-knuckled. There was a sock under the bed that she didn't want to forget, her talisman button beside it. Not wanting time to move, she pulled him down to her to breathe him in. The floor was hard and the smell of dirt in the carpet unnoticed until now. A line of sun glowed in from under the door, and the scent of cheap soap and coffee added to her contentment.

At peace, she looked at Jack, seeing that same happiness in the faint lines just now starting in about his eyes, seeing the reaffirmation that they belonged together. *He wants to retire?* She wished this would never end, but she'd be content if she could hold on to it forever and never forget.

CHAPTER
SIX

"**D**id you remember to plug in the car?" Peri asked as she trundled her overnight bag past the row of Sity bikes waiting for warmer weather. Her building loomed over her, and she couldn't wait to be back in her apartment, finding herself.

Looking tired, Jack pocketed their access card and held the door for her. "As always."

The stairs were unheated, and it was cold despite the low February afternoon sun shining into the glass and cement stairway of the residential tower. Peri's bag thumped up the steps behind her, conspiring to make her shoulder ache and her black eye pound. They could take the elevator, but it was slow and their apartment was only one flight up.

She'd picked the place out five years ago, liking the balcony overlooking the engineered pond and surrounding shops and restaurants collectively known as Lloyd Park. Even then her job had paid enough that she could have afforded one of the larger units on the top floor. But she couldn't jump out of a top-floor window and survive the landing. The second floor, on the other hand, was perfect. Jack had moved in six months after becoming her anchor, but it still felt like hers.

Jack jogged past her on the stairs at the last moment, his dress shoes scuffing as he got to the fire door. "I said I'd bring that up for you," he said, and she puffed her bangs out of her eyes.

"And I said I had it," she muttered, her mood bad. She hurt, and that brought out the worst in her.

"As you wish," he said, his dry humor making her smile as he pushed open the fire door. He'd been distant and preoccupied since defragmenting the draft, and a return to his normal, cheerful self was a relief. Perhaps he was worried about Bill. Their handler was a stickler about her mental state, demanding tests and sessions when their earned downtime would accomplish the same thing.

Peri followed Jack into the warmer hallway, giving the solar panel–covered, snow-edged parking lot shared by the twin residential towers a last look as it glowed in the setting sun. Detroit was a pretty backdrop, Opti a short ride in by magnetic rail or car. *Much better,* Peri thought, remembering streets so choked with cars that you couldn't drive, and then the frightening emptiness when everyone who could left.

She'd watched Detroit falter, was there when the city fathers tore it down to use the old infra-structure to create defined pockets of clean industry, commerce, and housing, then connected them with green relief and quiet transport all layered over the original foundry steel. Though still known for her cars and music, Detroit had become home to the developing human and technology interface industries. Her Mantis was a part of that, a pretty, monstrous bauble that showcased Detroit's new technologies. Hiding the Opti military installation amid the new medical park hadn't been difficult.

Unlike many of the restructured areas, there hadn't been a landmark used as a stylistic cornerstone at Lloyd Park, but Peri loved the Frank Lloyd Wright theme gone neon that the architects had played with. The stark patterns of angles and lines were everywhere from the street-lights to manhole covers to the roof over the taxi charging stations, even the fencing around the park. But it was at the nearby commons where the neon took over. Surrounded by high-end shops and eateries, the red, gold, green, and white blazed loudly between the ever-changing e-billboards and big-screen communications monitors to keep the courtyard alive with people even in the dead of winter. The façade of her building continued the neon theme, and though the style was heavy in the lower common areas, it was a mere hint in her apartment.

Just enough to make a statement, she thought when the fire door clicked shut behind them. She was glad to be back—impatient to do some-thing normal. Having lost six weeks, she felt as if she was coming home from an extended vacation, not three days. The shadow of cat feet moved back and forth at the crack under the door, and she smiled. Jack had named the stray, thinking it hilarious to call the cat after a late-night TV skit character who could divine the arcane. "Hi, Carnac," Peri said, and his meows grew louder.

"I think he's in love with you," Jack said as he opened the door and Carnac came out, tail high as he wove between her feet, the bell on his collar ringing.

"Sorry, sweetie, I'm a speciesist," she said fondly to the marmalade cat, and they followed Jack in.

"Change setting. Weekend," Jack said loudly to shake the apartment out of extended-leave mode, and the environment computer dinged, recognizing him and turning up the heat.

Peri's shoulders slumped in exhaustion as Jack called for more light, and she trundled her overnight bag into the large, open-plan, high-ceilinged apartment. Leaning against the wall, she unzipped her boots and kicked them out of the way. Her feet stretched, pressing against the hardwood floor in relief. It was cold. She should've called ahead and gotten the house warmed up when they crossed the Michigan border.

The spartan apartment felt spacious, decorated with solid blocks of color, mostly whites and grays with some teal and brown for contrast. There was a big screen with a gaming console for Jack, and a formal dining table for her that they never used. A ball of yarn and a project she didn't remember starting sat in the crook of the couch, hidden like the compulsive behavior therapy it was. *Scarf?* she wondered, eyeing the scrumptious red yarn in passing and thinking it was a good match with the gloves in her bag.

The den was to the left, and the doors to the bedroom and bathroom on the right. The kitchen took up an entire interior wall, and she enjoyed looking out over the living room and to the view when she cooked—which was often. Again, something that had begun as Opti-therapy, but Jack seemed to enjoy her efforts and she'd learned to find satisfaction in it. She loved the lazy summer afternoons when she and Jack would retract the balcony windows into the walls and the entire apartment felt like it was outside. Shelves lined an interior wall, holding her talismans from previous drafts. Remembering the button in her pocket, her smile faded.

Jack dropped his bag. Remote pointed at the huge plate-glass windows, he shifted the glass to an opaque one-way. It was a measure of privacy she appreciated, seeing as they sort of lived in a bulletproof fishbowl. Detroit glowed in the near distance, the buildings red in the sunset. Random reflected flashes showed where the droneway paths hung. High-Q traffic and security drones were allowed above the city streets 24/7, but low-Q delivery and recreational drones were not, and the mid-skies were busy with last-minute payload drops.

Tossing the remote aside, Jack went into the kitchen to stand appraisingly before their small wine cooler. The answering machine on the counter beeped, and Peri picked Carnac up, collar bell ringing. Jack was trying to hide it, but he was on edge and growing more so. He'd slept most of the second leg home, but he'd been closed and distant ever since waking up.

"You miss me, sweetie?" she whispered to Carnac, breathing the words between his ears. Grabbing a few kitty treats from the canister, Peri ambled to the huge windows, Carnac still in her arms. Her winter-dead plants waited in sad-looking clay pots on the cold balcony, the chopsticks she'd stolen from Sandy and used to tie up weak stems still jammed in them.

"Are you going to change for tonight?" Jack asked, his back to her as he took down two glasses and opened a red. "Bill wants to meet at Overdraft to debrief."

"Overdraft?" she questioned as Carnac spilled out of her arms. The bar was one of the few places that drafters could call home, intentionally kept unchanged to help ease rough transitions and therefore somewhat stuck in the '90s, when it had been bought by Opti's psychologists and staffed by the same. It was generally too busy for a proper chat, with Peri's psychologists manning the bar, but it would be more comfortable than a sterile office. Maybe that's what Bill was going for.

"I thought you texted Bill that I was fine," she complained, button in hand as she went to her talismans. "Can't he wait until morning to start poking at me?"

"Apparently not," Jack muttered. "He wants us there at one."

"In the morning?" Peri sighed. At least at that hour, it would be close to empty. "Sure. I don't have anything else to do." *Other than read my diary and catch up on the last six weeks of TV eye candy, that is.* "I might cover the black eye. Change my blouse." Sandy would still see the shiner, but that woman saw everything.

Out of sorts, she set the button beside a picture of Jack and herself. It was night, and there was a huge fire gone to coals behind them. And stars, thousands of stars in patterns she didn't recognize. She was dirty, her hair even longer than it was now. Jack was relaxed with his arms around her. *New Year's?* she wondered as she picked up the heavy frame.

"Jack? It's Bill," came from the answering machine, Bill's voice sounding tinny through the speaker. "You home yet?" The heavyset man was as American as she was, but living abroad had given him a faint accent. Peri knew he used it to give himself the polish his Bronx beginnings lacked.

Peri's eyes closed as the machine beeped. Something told her that she'd used the picture as her own private talisman. She could feel it as clearly as the silver dagazes tooled around the frame. Carnac's collar and the half-knitted scarf both sported the hourglass-like glyph as well. That it looked like Opti's logo on its side didn't hurt. She only put it on things she'd want to recognize as her own if she ever forgot them. She knew with a guilty certainty that Opti's psychologists wouldn't approve, and she hadn't even told Jack about her experimentation, but she was hoping that with some preparation, the images in the photo and her imagination might—just might— bring this moment back.

Cavana had given her the idea, after a cryptic conversation about how memory knots might not be as lethal as Opti made out. That had been right before Opti had moved him out west. She still missed their occasional chats over dessert coffee.

Anticipation simmered as she brought the frame to her nose and breathed in the scent of the weighty metal. She tried to remember the feel of the thick red dust between her toes and the heat against her face, all of which she could see in the photo.

With an om-like sigh, she exhaled, and like magic, the entire night came back with a tingle of adrenaline: it had been New Year's after all. The Aborigines who had found them, the meal they'd shared, the stories she and Jack had gifted them with, the reading of their souls that they'd given back, the blessing the old man had pronounced over each of them. It had been heaven, and Peri stood there, elated as the memory held and returned a small part of herself to her. She had remembered. She had remembered on her own!

"Jack, you there?" Bill's agitated voice came again, pulling Peri from her private celebration. "I know I gave you the day off, but that was before Peri's memory knot. Call me."

"How come you didn't erase the machine from your phone?" she asked, her joy hesitating as she saw Jack hunched at the kitchen counter, one hand propping him up, the other wrapped around his wineglass.

"I haven't figured out how yet." He took a drink, his lips curling at the bitter taste. He hadn't waited for it to breathe.

"Impatient bastard," she said, scared when he didn't laugh. "Jack, what's wrong?"

"Nothing. If you pull your clothes out, I'll get them to the cleaners tomorrow."

He was brushing her off, and, peeved, she stood for a moment, arms crossed, staring at him. "What?" he finally said, and not liking his belligerence, she took her apartment card from her purse beside the door. Something was wrong, and she wanted him to know she knew it. "Where are you going?" he said, sounding almost afraid.

"Executive gym."

"Peri . . ." It was contrite now, but he'd snapped at her twice, and she wasn't in that good a mood either. She didn't want to argue. And if she didn't leave, they would.

"I want a sensory sauna before I see Sandy," she

said tightly. "I'll be in either Brazil or Arizona." Lips set, she yanked the door open, not caring she was barefoot but for her nylons.

"Peri," he cajoled, and she shut the door hard. Feet silent on the carpet, she strode down the corridor to the elevator, hitting the up button several times in fast succession. She raised her head as the doors opened, and she got in, tapping her apartment card before pressing the button for the top of the tower. The doors closed, and she fell back against the wall of the car, feeling every bruise, every sore muscle. Slowly her anger dulled in the new silence as she saw her reflection. Her eye was ugly, and she leaned toward the mirror to cautiously poke at it. Peri pulled away, a feeling that she'd been inexcusably remiss slithering up over her.

"Where's my bag of magic rocks," she whispered, watching her lips move. There was no bag of magic rocks. There was an old fable of a lazy man regaining his dwindling wealth by throwing magic pebbles into the farthest corners of his holdings every morning, in essence, catching the thieves who were nibbling away at his wealth. Lazy, she'd become lazy and complacent, and she didn't like it. Something was going on and Jack wasn't talking.

The lift dinged, but she stayed unmoving when the doors slid open and the translucent light of the gym, warm with the western view of the sunset, cascaded over her. "Good evening, Ms. Reed, the attendant said cheerfully as he looked up from his screen, already knowing it was her by way of the card tap. His smile hesitated at her black eye, then steadied. "Will it be the Caldas Novas hot springs or the Jordan Hot Springs in the Sequoia National Forest tonight?"

His question hung unrecognized in Peri's mind as a hundred inconsistencies swirled and condensed into one clear realization.

Something was very wrong.

"Um," she hedged, the feeling she'd made a mistake growing heavier. "I forgot my flip-flops." Peri forcefully hit the button for her floor and the doors slid shut, sealing her in a Frank Lloyd Wright box. She didn't want her flip-flops. She wanted Jack to talk to her. Now.

Finally the elevator doors opened. Pace fast, she strode to her apartment, the need to get back to Jack a sharp goad. Her card was soundless, but she gasped when a scared Carnac ran out over her feet, then was gone in three seconds.

"She's upstairs!" Jack was saying, spinning her head back around, the anger in his voice stopping her cold. "Everything was fragmented. It's under control. Get off my case, Bill!"

Peri shoved the door all the way open. "Bill!" she exclaimed, seeing him inches from Jack, almost shoving him up against the wall beside the big windows. "What are you doing?"

CHAPTER
SEVEN

Bill spun, and Jack slid out from between him and the wall, lurching into the kitchen. Fear rose through her as the bigger man's anger vanished behind a pleasant mask—and her skin crawled when he moved to where he could see them both. "Peri!" he exclaimed, arms spread wide as if she might come right over there and give him a hug. "Thank God you're okay. Jack said you lost six weeks."

Jack wouldn't look at her, hunched and angry, fixing his hair. She glanced toward her knife, still in her boot and halfway across the room. For a fleeting instant, confusion reigned. She shouldn't need her knife. Bill was their handler. This was their home.

"I did," she said as she came in. "I'm fine. I went upstairs for a sauna and forgot my flip-flops. What's going on?"

Jack straightened, but his ears were still red. "We had a misunderstanding is all."

Peri stiffly shut the door and dropped her apartment card on the table. She could almost taste the tension in the air. Bill wasn't in uniform, but he might as well have been, with his white hair in a bristly flattop cut and the stiff formality with which he carried himself. He was half military, half CEO, and more clever than a cornered snake. Though older than Peri by several decades, Bill worked hard to keep his shape, but you could see his age in his lumpy nose and veined hands.

Bill's welcoming smile faltered. "I'm sorry, Peri. I was worried about you."

"I went to take a sauna," she repeated warily. "Twelve hours in a car. Now, is someone going to tell me what's going on, or do you boys want to play charades?"

Again, neither man said anything, and the tension coiled tighter. Peri pulled her face into a mask of balanced poise as her intuition sparked.

"Bill thinks you need a full workup in the hole," Jack said, voice flat. "I disagreed."

"The hole" was one of the nicer terms for the underground medical floor where drafters went when they had . . . issues. The walls were a horrid purple and bounced back a specific light wavelength, which caused the release of a hormone that hampered the ability to draft. Opti went further to pump a steady 741 MHz from the speakers. Both prevented drafting, both were as annoying as hell, but they were required safety precautions when someone might freak out and MEP.

She could hear the lie in Jack's voice, but long association told her to go with it. "Full workup," she said, pretending to relax. "I lost six weeks, not six months, Bill. Jack already brought back the rewrite. I'm fine."

Jack took a too-casual sip of his wine. "See," he said, but his face was pale and she could smell his sweat. "I told you she was okay."

"Good!" The enthusiasm was one hundred percent Bill, but the recent sight of him pinning Jack to the wall was too real. "I'm glad to hear that. What about the memory knot?"

"It untangled with the defrag," she said simply. Bill seemed genuinely relieved to see her, and when he strode forward with his usual sparse motion, she forced herself to smile as if she hadn't walked in and found him threatening Jack.

"Whoa, who gave you the shiner, kiddo?" Bill said, reaching to touch it.

"The man I left bleeding his life out on the thirtieth floor of Global Genetics," she said, leaning out of his reach. *Why do they always try to touch it? It hurts, damn it!*

"No-o-o . . . let me see," Bill cajoled, and she grimaced, not moving as his rough hand encompassed most of her face, concern thick and honest on him as he looked it over. "When my best drafter takes a deathblow, I want to make sure she's okay."

"I'm going to have a lousy night trying to find Carnac, but I'm fine," she said for the third time. "Jack took care of me." She looked at Jack, his hand steady as he topped off his glass. His other hand was in a fist on the counter, and he opened it as he saw her notice. "Are you here for the data? I thought we were meeting at Overdraft tonight," Peri said, casting about until she saw Jack's phone on the counter. *Is that what this is about? Bill thought I'd left with it?*

Pace fast, she went to get it, ignoring Jack's uncomfortable *umm* when she snatched it up and went to stand toe-to-toe with Bill. Everything she knew said Bill was her confidant. Everything she'd spent the last five years doing had strengthened that trust. He gave her the chance to prove herself, and she rewarded him by giving him all she had. But if there was one thing Opti psychologists drummed into their drafters, it was to listen to their intuition. Emotion was never forgotten, and it lingered to guide them until enough new memory was laid down.

"Here you go," she said, not liking her new mistrust as she extended it, and he took it, Jack's phone small in his thick hands, misshapen from being broken too many times in his martial arts practice. "Task accomplished."

Bill took it, his smile a shade too wide. "Thank you. Well done."

She fought the urge to back up. "Jack was the one who found the file," she said, to keep the silence from becoming awkward.

"Then thank you, Jack," Bill said jovially, and it

felt even more wrong. "I'll get your phone back to you tonight."

"Great. Thanks." Jack poured another swallow into his glass and downed it.

Still standing in the middle of their apartment, Bill tapped the phone against his palm and tucked it away. The Opti logo on it meant it probably did more than her phone did. The memory of Jack's face, pale from the city's lights, flashed before her. "You don't want to do the entire debrief now, do you?" she prompted.

"No. It can wait until tonight," Bill said. Peri stiffened when he reached into an inner coat pocket. But he was only after his driving glasses, and she mentally kicked herself. She was on high alert, and she couldn't say why.

Jack was pouring a new glass of wine. "That's for me, right?" she said to try to ease the tension and pretend everything was okay. "Bill, can you have a glass, or are you working?"

"I'm always working," he said, halfway to the door. "I know you just drafted, but if Sandy and Frank green-light you tonight, we have an emergency. Everyone else is out on task."

Jack handed her the glass, avoiding her eyes. Peri set it on the granite counter with an attention-getting click. "What happened to my two weeks' downtime?" she complained as the man's heavy fingers worked the buttons on his overcoat to bring himself back to a full military mien.

"Delayed." He opened the door. "If Sandy okays you, will you work or not?"

If she didn't, she'd be in the hole having a full psych review. "This sucks, Bill," she said since she had a right to be pissed if they made her work this soon after a draft.

Bill hesitated at the open door. "Yes, it does. I'll see you tonight for your full debrief."

"Tonight," she echoed sourly.

Nodding, Bill stepped into the hall and closed the door. She didn't move until she heard the fire exit door bang. Peeved, she went to stand at the balcony. The small visitor lot was right under her window, and if Bill looked up, she was going to flip him off whether he could see her or not. The sun was setting, and the towers' shadows seemed to stretch all the way to the city's rebuilt, redesigned, and renewed core, miles away. The glow of the raised magnetic train wove like a ribbon through the neon-rich common, making it into a glorious pendant. Behind her, Jack heaved a frustrated sigh.

She was done wasting time. "Jack. What was Bill here for?"

"Global Genetics' latest biological nightmare."

Her hand went to her hip, and she stifled a flash of anger. Something had happened up in that corner office and Jack had destroyed it, wiped it clean from her mind, erased it from her memory—something he shouldn't have done. He had said as much right before she'd walked in. "Bullshit. Why was he here?" she demanded.

Distress crossed him, real but not moving her. "It doesn't matter, Peri. Forget about it."

He came out from behind the counter, and she put up a hand for him to keep his distance. "Screw that. You fragmented something you shouldn't have. What was it?"

Jack took a breath as if to protest. He looked torn, desperate. Her eyes narrowed, daring him to stay silent. And then he exhaled, his eyes pleading. "I only wanted to stay with you. Bill said if I kept quiet about the list, did a few jobs on the side, nothing would change."

Jobs on the side? "What list?"

"Um." Jack looked away, then back. "A list of corrupt Opti agents."

Her eyes widened, and she looked out the window in time to see Bill get into a black Opti car and be driven away. "How . . . ," she started, then sat down as a flush of cold washed through her. *I just gave Bill a list of corrupt Opti agents?*

"Peri," Jack pleaded. "It's worse than you think. The list is Bill's personal stable of drafters and anchors. He's giving it to his superiors after he takes his best agents off it. He's cleaning house. I got us on the right side of things, but we're on borrowed time and the interest is stacking up."

My God. He knew? How long? Her outstretched hand faltered and she turned, the blood falling from her face. Bill was dirty? Their handler was corrupt?

Seeing her understanding, Jack nodded, head lowered as he took up her wineglass and came forward. Shocked, she sat there, trying to figure it out. "You kept a copy, right?" she whispered.

Jack hesitated, but when her gaze sharpened on him, he set their glasses down beside her and reached for his wallet. "It's in your wallet?" she exclaimed.

"I haven't had time to squirrel it yet." He sat down, metal-woven wallet in his hand. It was impervious to scanners. Her favorite handbag was lined with a similar material. Breathless, she sat beside him, light-headed as she took the hotel stationery he extended. "I, ah, decoded the chip while you were in the shower," he said as she scanned the list of eight names. Every one of them was familiar, every one of them in high-profile tasks.

"I don't get this," she said, looking it over. "Nathan and Chris? I've known them my entire Opti career. And you're telling me they're corrupt?"

"Remember when they ended that three-week grounding of international flights by exposing a terrorist cell? There were no terrorists, only scapegoats." Jack took the list from her, and she scooted closer so they could look at it together. "It was a planned shutdown to keep the U.S. clean while that smallpox outbreak in Iran ran its course. A non-Opti task."

Peri's eyes widened as she recalled thinking it was a bit of luck that the shutdown had happened right before the first smallpox case surfaced. "Please don't tell me Opti caused the outbreak, too?" she said, and Jack pointed to Brandon and his anchor, Julia.

"Also a non-Opti-sanctioned task. We thought it was an accident until recently," he said. "And the brain-Web interface trials? The innovation that was going to give us a direct link to Internet everything through the new glass technology?"

It was supposed to have been the biggest breakthrough since the vacuum tube, having everyone from those in Washington to religious leaders around the world in an uproar at the possible culture upheaval. "They failed. Everyone died of brain hemorrhages from the implants," she said, and Jack tapped Gina Trecher's name, his finger lingering on her anchor, Harry.

"Oh, they died all right, but not because the technology was bad. The company behind wave technology wanted it buried, knowing if people could see the Internet in their heads, it would make their product look like it was from the Stone Age. Not Opti-sanctioned.

"Nina and Trey didn't end the Africa uprising in 2026," he continued, and Peri held her breath, remembering how pissed she was when the older couple got the high-profile task instead of her and Jennifer. "Opti sent them to help the transition from the existing government to one the U.S. approved of, but what they were being paid the big bucks for was to install an extremist faction instead. That the extremists went on to slaughter everyone with white skin was . . . not a surprise."

Peri sank back into the cushions, remembering the horrific newscasts coming out of the tip of Africa. They had called it the White Plague, and it had been little more than organized murder. No wonder Nina wouldn't talk about it.

My God. This is real. "What were we really doing at Global Genetics?" she whispered, and he folded up the list.

"Getting this, but I didn't want you to know. Bill threatened to take you away from me if I—we—didn't do a few jobs for him. It's gotten out of control. We have to run."

Her head came up as she started to think again. They couldn't run. The same patterns that kept her sane would make her easy to find. Besides, Opti had the backing of the U.S. government, and they had no proof tying the corruption to Bill. It was his word against theirs. "We have to do something with this."

"You mean give it to someone?" He flung a hand into the air. "Who? You think Bill could do this on his own? He's a cog. Someone else is pulling his strings, and if we take it to the wrong person, we're dead." His head drooped. "We might be dead anyway. Or I might be. They'll always need you."

A new fear slid through her. She was reasonably safe. Rare. One in a hundred thousand. Jack, though . . . She stifled a shudder as she remembered Bill threatening him. But it all made sense now, and her lingering distrust of Jack vanished: his pensive mood, the conversation with Bill he hadn't discussed with her, her gut telling her that something was wrong. She stood, frustration replacing her panic. Their only option was to find the root of the corruption themselves. But if they blew the whistle too soon, she'd lose everything. Everyone in Opti knew how to smother the guilt of a cold-blooded killing. That it might be one of their own wouldn't slow them down at all. *Did Nina really facilitate genocide? For money?*

"I can't lose you," Jack whispered, and she blanched at his heartache. "I'm so sorry. This is all my fault. I should have told you right from the start."

"Yes, you should have." Her brow furrowed. "Running is out," she said, knowing it would be futile. "Bill thinks I'm in the dark, right? Let's do a few of his jobs."

"You'd do an illegal task?" Jack said, and she searched his face.

"It will be our cover as we figure out how far this Opti corruption really goes," she said, heart pounding. Running would be a fast death; staying and ferreting out the depth of Opti's sickness would be a long game of cat-and-mouse. Same ending most times, but occasionally the mouse got away. "Once we know who's running it, we can go to the alliance."

"The alliance!" Jack's expression held a moment of shocked fear, and then it was gone. It hit Peri like a slap and she fumbled, trying to figure it out.

"They can give us protection if nothing else," she said, and Jack violently shook his head and pulled from her grip.

"Peri, the alliance is nothing but a vigilante group trying to wipe Opti out of existence. Good and bad. Everything. We can't trust them."

Fear. He was afraid, and Jack was afraid of nothing. "They're made up of drafters and anchors themselves," she said, suddenly unsure. "They won't turn us in, and they won't tell the world about us or they'll end up as science projects as well. Jack, they'll help us root out the corruption if we give them the proof. It's all we have."

Brow furrowed, Jack looked at the kitchen. It was where he stashed most of his firearms, but they couldn't fight their way free, and he knew it. "Opti knows everything. They'll find out."

Frustrated, she bit her lip. "Then we minimize. You said there was a chip. You didn't give it to Bill, did you?"

"No, of course not," he said as he teased a tiny, pinky-nail-size chip from his wallet.

Her hiding things was a bad idea, but his keeping it in his wallet was even worse. Peri crossed the room to her knitting bag, feeling like this whole unfolding mess was somehow surreal. It was as good a place as any, better than most, because if she forgot, she'd eventually find it. As for the list itself? She could knit herself a message tonight in the tail end of the scarf like a modern-day Madame Defarge.

Needles clicking, she found the blue size 8. It was fairly large, and it was unlikely she'd lose it since a half-knitted scarf resided on the second needle of the pair. Fingers shaking, she wedged the cap off the blunt end and dropped the chip in. Unhappy, she gave it a shake until it wedged itself and was unmoving.

"There." She recapped the needle and dropped it back into the bag. "Hard copy?"

Jack said nothing as she reached for the lighter beside her candles, the quick whoosh of fluid igniting the only sound as she lit the scrap of paper and let it burn in his empty wineglass. The ribbon of smoke was sharp, the scent reminding her of the single memory she had of the last six weeks: her in Jack's arms as they connected with the universe beside a fire gone to coals.

Miserable, Peri sat on the edge of the couch, her elbows on her knees and her head hanging as she realized how deep in the crapper they were. Jack drew her close, holding her sideways as he took a sip from her wineglass and passed it to her.

Fingers shaking, she drank the last swallow and set the glass down with a clink. It was as if she could feel her world realign as the enormity of what they were up against became real. They'd have to play a very dangerous game, and there was no one they could trust but each other.

"I'm so sorry. This isn't what I wanted to happen," Jack said, and she saw the heartache in his eyes, his guilt that he hadn't told her sooner.

Her hand rose to touch his face, needing to reassure him. "We'll get through it together," she said, tilting her chin to find his lips with her own. They met with a soft passion that flashed hot, and need arced through her, more potent because of the danger they'd have to survive. His hands tightened on her, but he pulled away first, even as she reached for more.

A heady emotion flickered over his face, reassuring her that they could do anything together. "We find the key players?" he said, and she nodded. They'd plumb the depths and find out how far the corruption went—or die trying.

And if all else failed—she was a damned special ops agent. She knew how to lie.

CHAPTER EIGHT

"The mic is at the thick end, see?" Matt said, his fraternity ring glinting on his chubby finger as he held the pliable wire out. Silas took it, slumping in the folding chair at the stupidity of it all. The SWAT-size van smelled like his first college apartment, and the snap of ozone, electronics, and locker-room BO curled his lips. He felt cramped even sitting in the oversize aisle, and the faint but insistent electronic whine of the floor-to-ceiling surveillance equipment went right through his head.

It didn't help that he was mentally exhausted after an afternoon of putting his life on a shelf for who knew how long. Despite everyone's belief that it was a three-hour job, Silas knew better. Acquiring her might take one night, but to bring her back successfully would take longer.

"On its own, it has a reach of about four feet," Matt was saying, and Silas tuned out the slightly overweight tech geek, almost embarrassed at his enthusiasm. "That's why you need the phone, see? Just coil it up in a pocket out of sight, and the phone will boost it to me."

Just kill me now. Silas's gaze slid to the white slab of plastic beside the duffel they'd prepped for him, the oversize phone looking out-of-date and clunky. "All the way out here to your van?" Silas said, but Matt didn't recognize his sarcasm. The tech's tie was loose about his neck, and the black pants and white shirt screamed off-the-rack. His index fingernail was notched to snap nicotine caps.

"It's mostly one-way, but if we have something need-to-know, we'll text. No wires behind your ears to give you away. Nice, huh?"

Silas sighed. His fingers were too big to hit the phone's tiny buttons. Texting would be a pain in the ass. "Can I use my phone?" he asked, and the curly-haired tech started, aghast.

"No!" he blurted, as if Silas was being stupid. "It's not just a phone. It's full of stuff you need! God! Why do they keep sending me newbies?"

Silas rubbed his aching head as he imagined what Matt had wedged into the tiny bit of outdated electronics. Tracker, certainly, addresses for safe houses, contact numbers, and apps to find the nearest coffee shop. But it was too small for him to use, and if he tried, she'd realize he was some-thing he wasn't. Besides, his phone was glass, the technology light-years ahead of what the alliance had.

"Keep it," he said, and Matt fell back into his rolling chair, vexed. "I'm not wearing a wire."

Matt filled the silence with downing his Dew, making it into a show of frustration and disdain. "It would be better if you wore it. Sir."

"Why don't you just hang a sign around my neck saying ABDUCTOR?" Silas said, his voice growing louder. "You don't think she's going to see the buttons are too small for me to work? She is a finely tuned piece of paranoid intuition."

"Only because we made her that way," Matt said, and Silas leaned in, shoving the wire into Matt's front shirt pocket.

"Then maybe I don't want you hearing what I have to say. Everything you've given me is old tech and no-name brands. No one buys this stuff because it's military crap. I'll stick out."

Expression dark, Matt pulled the wire out and dropped it into Silas's open duffel. "That imported coat of yours will stick out worse. And the wire doesn't need to be showing," he added angrily. "It's designed to coil up in a pocket. That's why you need the booster."

Impatient, Silas glanced at his watch. It was almost six. He'd been here an hour, and his first impression that they were going to get her killed hadn't changed. "I didn't say she'd see it," he said, scanning the van for anything useful. "I said it would give me away. If I need you, I'll call. On my phone. You have the number, right?"

"Yeah, I got your number," Matt said sullenly, then sucked down another gulp of caffeine and sugar as he eyed Silas's coat, carefully folded over the back of his chair.

Silas pulled the duffel closer and threw the

coiled wire up into the driver's seat. Pushing past the military gray sweats, he took out the tasteless, no-name running shoes. *Like I'm going to run anywhere?* The clink of medical vials drew his attention, and anger simmered as he recognized the heavy drugs. My God, they were butchers.

"You can keep these, too," he said, dropping the vials on the counter in disgust.

Matt shifted his rolling chair back and forth in agitation. "How will you know she's got the information if you don't do a defrag?"

He didn't want to get into her brain, afraid he might find himself there. "Maybe I can just ask her?" he said, ready to walk away. If they didn't give him the freedom to do this right, it wasn't going to work. "I can use this, though," he said, leaning to take the slick touchpad hidden under a coffee-stained cup. It wasn't glass, but he was betting it had this year's operating system.

"Hey! That's mine!" Matt protested, and Silas flipped it open, his eyebrows rising in pleasure. *All the right apps in all the right places.*

"So it's not going to be bugged, then, is it?" Silas tucked it behind his coat. It was scratched enough to be real, and if it belonged to Matt, it would have everything he'd need.

"Give it back," Matt demanded, afraid to force the issue.

"Soon as I'm done with it." From outside, a car door slammed, then another. The flickering vid screen at the front showed a long black car and a tall woman in formal cocktail dress striding forward, flanked by her driver. Beyond the car was the river and one of Detroit's casinos, looking dead in the low sun. "Someone's at the door," he said, and Matt spun at the sudden hammering.

"Dragon lady," the tech whispered. Face reddening, Matt shoved off the counter to send his rolling chair to the front of the van.

The driver hammered again, and Matt punched in the code to unlock the door. *31415. Pi,* Silas thought, moving Matt's pad to the duffel bag and hiding it under the sweats. *How original.*

The door swung open, and Silas breathed in the cold fresh air coming off the river in relief. Diamond- and ruby-strewn, Fran stepped up and in, her six-inch heels making her more formidable than usual. A white fur shawl was draped over her shoulders and she reeked of perfume. "Stay," she said, pushing her driver back onto the pavement with a white-gloved hand before shutting the door behind her. "I have five minutes. Impress me."

"Mrs. Jacquard, come in!" Matt said, already standing and shoving his rolling chair out of the way. "Welcome to Reed recovery central. Completely mobile, and ready to go."

And as conspicuous as a dog in a cat show, Silas mused. Wrapping the surveillance van in a furniture logo only worked during business hours.

Even here at the docks, the homeless had been avoiding them.

Fran's nose wrinkled. "Why are we still using these? Couldn't we have gotten you a real trailer?"

"Yes, ma'am." Matt lurched backward as she came deeper into the van. Silas got to his feet, impelled by ingrained manners, not respect. "But I know where everything is," Matt added. "All the information feeds into here, and from here, I can direct everyone's movement."

Eyebrows high, Fran looked at Silas, chuckling at his obvious annoyance. "Right."

"A small ship turns fast," Matt tried again, starting to sweat.

And it sinks faster, too, Silas thought, sitting down before Fran could take the chair.

"It has an air conditioner, doesn't it?" she said, looking around. "Turn it on. And straighten your tie. We pay you enough to look better than a university reprobate."

"Yes, ma'am."

Matt fumbled his way to the front and Silas pushed his cuticles back, ignoring Fran. He didn't like her. He didn't like Detroit. There was too much steel, in the people as well as the streets. The new layer of green wasn't fooling him. Detroit was a hard, unforgiving mistress.

"So how is our man?" Fran asked, her voice dry as she realized that the only other place to sit was

Matt's rolling chair, sticky with electrical tape.

"Ahh . . ." Flustered, Matt finished tightening his tie and reached for a printout. "He's fair with a gun, okay with hand-to-hand simply due to his size." He chuckled in dismay and shook his head. "Good with electronics, though. Mrs. Jacquard, I've got better—"

Matt jumped when Fran snatched the printout, then gasped when she dropped it into the shredder.

"I meant," she said as it roared into silence, "does he have his equipment? Is he ready to go? Reed is meeting Bill at that drafter bar in less than six hours."

Silas loosened his tie and slouched in his chair—daring her to say anything.

"Ah, no," Matt said, eyes flicking between them. "He keeps taking my equipment out of his duffel."

"I'm so surprised," Fran mused, clearly not, and Silas grinned insincerely at her.

"My way, or no way," Silas said. "You said it yourself."

"I most certainly did not."

Silas closed his eyes. "I distinctly remember you saying I was the only one smart enough to see the extent of the damage and fluid enough to adapt a program to fix it." Eyes opening, he sat up. "I'm adapting and fixing. Get them out of my way."

"Mrs. Jacquard," Matt said, clearly upset. "I've got six other agents more than able."

"Oh yes. Put them on notice," Fran said, her perfume finally overpowering the BO as she got angry. "But Dr. Denier goes in first. His charms are not ones that you can put on paper."

Matt hesitated. "Wait," he said, looking at Silas in a new way. "*Doctor* Denier?" Silas slumped again. "Denier, who invented slick-suits? Who pioneered memory cushions and talismans? How anchors rebuild memories?"

Silas exhaled, wanting to get out of the van. "It's not that hard when you are one."

"Shit, man!" Matt lurched close, flushed. "What are you doing here?"

"Trying to make up for it," he muttered. "Fran." He sat up, uncomfortable as Matt began to all but giggle, lurching about and . . . tidying? "This isn't going to work."

"Why not?" She shifted out of Matt's way as he threw out a bag of chips. "Matt is extremely proficient on paper."

"This wouldn't work even if I were a real agent," Silas protested.

"And you aren't!" Matt chimed in enthusiastically. "Damn. Dr. Denier in my van."

Silas scrubbed a hand over his face. "I can't walk in there, take out Jack, subdue her, and expect to get any information. She is a soldier, Fran. She kills people."

Fran looked at her diamond-encrusted watch and frowned. "She only kills those who kill her first. And you'll have help. An old friend of yours."

Friend? Silas stood, hands clenched as he made an educated guess as to who that was. "I can't do this your way."

Lips pressed, Fran clicked her way to him, being careful not to touch anything. "You will," she said, eye to eye with him in her high heels. "All you have to do is find out if she has the info or not. Matt's people will bring Jack and her down. You don't even have to be there for the actual . . . reacquirement."

"In which case she will be so adrenaline-soaked that retrieving anything will be impossible," he said, desperation creeping into his voice. "You don't understand. This isn't something you can go into with both barrels blazing. It has to be subtle."

Again she looked at her watch. "So we hit her with 741 MHz. Or Amneoset. Or any other of the wonderful drugs you helped pioneer to stop her from drafting."

Frustrated, he forced his hands to unclench. "It's not the drafting I'm worried about. If there's too much going on in her head, if she's not relaxed and comfortable, there's no way to retrieve hidden memories. None. I can't do it your way and expect any results."

Fran stared at him, the hunched figure of Matt behind her. "Make it work," she said. Turning, she looked Matt up and down, gaze lingering on the burrito stain on his middle. "Get him suited up. Now."

"Yes, ma'am."

"Bloody fantastic," she muttered, looking at her watch once more. "Now I'm late for the symphony. Matt, keep me posted."

"Yes, ma'am!" Matt called as the van shifted with her leaving and the door snapped shut.

Silas fell back into his chair, hand scrubbing at the faint bristle on his cheeks. This was going to kill her. Drive her mad. There were too many variables to plan this. It had to be done subtly, by feel, by one person, not a team that tripped her into fight or flight. She was going to fight him all the way regardless, but he'd rather have the battle in her mind than a physical one. He'd lose the latter, but in the former he had a chance. A good chance.

"You want her or not? This is all we have," Matt said, and he looked up, startled at the man's empty expression.

"No. It isn't," Silas said, coming to a decision. "I'm sorry about this."

"Sorry about wha—hey!" Matt exclaimed, back-pedaling.

But it was too late, and Silas's chair fell over, clattering into the back of the van as he sprang at Matt, fisted hand swinging forward with the force of a train.

He hit him with everything he had, all his anger,

frustration, and fear focused into six inches of bone. Matt's head snapped back, and he fell, out cold even as Silas shook his hand out, not even bruised.

"For that," he said, pulse fast. Silas snatched up the duffel, stuffing it with equipment he wanted from the shelves and cubbies. Finished, he threw it out of the van, tossing his coat to land on top of it. The sun was setting, and he took a moment at the door to breathe in the cold, snow-tinged air. Low-Q drones, barely visible in the dusk, skimmed up and down the river, their only legal pathway now that the sun was down. There was a chance that Fran would simply proceed without him. But the longer he gazed at the river, the wider his smile became. Maybe he could learn to like Detroit.

Breath held against the smell, he ducked back inside for a last check before he sank the van.

He needed to get her alone was all, away from Jack Twill in such a way that she didn't freak out. It would be nigh impossible due to the heavy conditioning against being alone that Opti had instilled in her. It would have to be her idea; she'd have to be the one in control. But if he could get her alone and comfortable, five minutes with the right drugs ought to do it.

"But not these," he said, looking again at what he'd taken out of his duffel. Angry, he yanked open the med drawers, riffling through until he found what he wanted. Something softer, something she was used to.

Vials clattering in his grip, he slammed the drawers shut, the memory of how sensitive she was lifting through him. His shoulders slumped, and then he hardened. Shifting the van into neutral, he shoved the vials in his pocket, then grabbed Matt's arms and dragged him thumping down the back step to land against the duffel. It was a job. That was all.

Matt moaned and sat up, holding his head. "What are you doing?" he asked when he realized he was sitting on pavement.

Feeling a new sense of purpose in the chill evening, Silas went to the back of the van. He put his shoulder to it, and pushed.

"Hey! Stop!" Matt staggered to his feet and looked at the nearby river. "Dr. Denier, what are you doing?"

With a groan of success, Silas got the van moving, creeping slowly and pebbles popping from under its wheels. "No!" Matt shouted, running after it and trying to pull it to a halt. Silas's smile widened as the van hit the water, slowing but not stopping as it crept deeper.

"Are you crazy!" Matt shouted as he stood at the edge of the water and shook. "Everything we need is in there!"

Silas put on his coat and went to stand beside him, satisfied as the van stopped in four feet of water. Clapping him across the shoulder, he said, "I'm not."

Matt turned to him, aghast.

"Tell Fran that I'll get the information." Silas swung his duffel up over his shoulder like a backpack. "I need at least three days to learn her state of mind and come up with an idea. If I see Fran or one of her stooges, I'll spook Peri myself and she'll never get anything."

"B-but my van . . . ," Matt stammered, lost.

Silas smiled. "I need three days," he said, then turned and walked away. Matt was already on his phone, but by the time they got the van out and dried up, Silas would have something to placate Fran with.

He'd get Peri back, and he'd do it his way, so she might survive it. But even as he strode forward, Matt's curses and threats growing faint, a worry wedged itself between his thought and his reason.

He knew she loved the control, the money, the sense of superiority and independence that Opti had lavished on her and used to lure her into self-blindness. It was why she'd volunteered for it in the first place.

The harsh reality was that there was a chance she might not want to come back.

CHAPTER
NINE

Peri tugged at the thick oak door of Overdraft to find it locked. Frank was a blurry image through the stained-glass window, standing on a ladder with his head in the sound system. Below him, the silver disk of a floor sweep moved in its methodical path, a purple haze of UV light glowing. It was just shy of one in the morning, but clearly they'd closed early.

Frank looked up as Peri tapped on the window with her car fob. She drew back, disconcerted as she realized the cut glass formed Opti's hourglass-like logo, glowing in the dark like a beacon. Frank's voice was muffled as he shouted to someone before returning to his task.

"I'll talk to Frank, you take Sandy," Jack said, fidgeting as he scanned the barren parking lot dusted with new snow; Peri's Mantis was a sleek shadow under the security lights, recharged and back to its usual black and silver.

Cold, she hunched into her long cashmere coat and scarf. The thin wool wasn't enough to block the wind, but she'd bought it for the way it looked, not its thermal ranking. "You think our psychologists might be involved with Bill?"

"That's why I brought my Glock." Jack patted

his coat, worrying her. His coat was thick enough that the bulge of the weapon didn't even show. She didn't particularly like guns, though she agreed they were handy in the right setting. The six-inch knife in her boot sheath was more her style: quiet, unexpected if done correctly, lethal only if she wanted—but always attention-getting.

Sandy's slight form darkened the window, wiping her hands on her jeans as she reached for the lock. Sandy had evolved from psychologist to friend a long time ago, and Peri smiled wanly as the long-haired woman pushed open the door. If Frank looked like a Viking in plaid and jeans, then Sandy was an Asian princess, slim, demure, and capable of dramatic outbursts when the situation called for it. Peri had seen her drive drunk twenty-one-year-olds out the door with her voice alone. And she was the only person Peri knew who was smaller than she was.

"Peri! Jack," the late-thirties woman said with the faint Seattle-Asian accent that always made her sound slightly exotic to Peri's midwestern-bred ears. "Bill said you were coming for a debrief. I locked up to keep it more private. Come on in. It's cold tonight." She glanced at the light snow before ushering them in and giving Peri a hug. "Everything okay? You're still in your work clothes."

Cursing herself, Peri looked at her black slacks and matching blouse. She even still had on her pen necklace. Her subconscious had her ready to run—and Sandy had noticed. "Could be better," she said as she scanned the bar with its low stage plastered with '90s band posters, scuffed dance floor, never-lit flagstone fireplace, and lotto kiosk in the corner, its flashing lights even brighter than the Juke'sBox online music panel that Frank had put in after someone blew out the '70s antique it was named after. Even Peri admitted it was easier to load a night's music from the tabletop ordering pads, but she missed the clunky singles stacked neatly in rows waiting to be chosen, knowing everyone was watching her as she stood before it.

The lights were down in the adjoining gaming lounge with its low tables, couches, and the testosterone magnet of a six-by-ten gaming panel, but she could still smell electronics over the varnished wood that held sway in the main part of the bar. Somehow the shadowy cushy booths and black ceilings with their bare support beams and hidden state-of-the-art sound system felt ominous tonight, even with the band novelties that Frank collected and stuck on the walls amid the illegal drone shots of celebs, public figures, and the occasional sunbather seeking her no-tan-line perfection.

Chairs were atop the tables as the cleaner ran, and the floor was scuffed to a bland haze the color of spilled beer everywhere but a thin line along the walls. The dance floor's yellow parquet was so scratched, she could hardly see the original lines.

Bill wasn't here yet, which was both a relief and a concern. Jack gave Peri a reassuring touch before making a slow beeline for Frank, still on the ladder.

Sandy smelled of polish, a rag stuffed into a back pocket, and Peri felt a sudden wash of affection for her longtime friend and confidante—and more than a little guilty at suspecting Sandy's motives. "Hard day?" Sandy asked, and Peri nodded. "I worry about you two," Sandy said, arm muscles showing a wiry strength as she returned to the bar and scrubbed at the brass. "Bill said you drafted. You lose a lot?"

Bad news travels fast. Peri slid atop one of the stools. "Six weeks." Taking off her coat, she set it on the gleaming black counter beside the glass jammed full of chopsticks. Frank liked his burgers, but Sandy had more cosmopolitan tastes, and every restaurant in a four-block area could be accessed for delivery from the tabletop pads. "It could have been worse," Peri added as she decided to leave the scarf on. She didn't recall knitting it, but her fingers remembered the pattern, and it felt familiar.

Dropping the polishing rag, Sandy went behind the bar, the light from the UV hand sanitizer flashing as she stuck her hands under it for a few seconds. Frank had come down from the ladder, and he and Jack were talking in hushed but strident tones. Peri jumped when Sandy handed her a chipped mug of lukewarm coffee. "How about you start with the black eye?" she said, leaning against the bar to make her long black hair fall in a curtain to one side of her face.

"Someone hit me." Peri looked into the oily, rank depths of the coffee. Sandy's coffee invariably sucked. "I hit him back. What's to tell? Especially when you don't remember."

"You always remember, you just don't recall," Sandy said, and Peri blinked fast at the pity in her voice. Sandy put a hand to her mouth. "You killed someone, didn't you. I can tell."

Peri's thoughts touched upon the man twitching on the floor as stuff that should be inside leaked out through a hole the size of her knife. Both hands around the mug, she took a sip of coffee. It was old, bitter, and burnt. "Jack tells me he killed me first," Peri said softly. Guilt pulled her shoulders down, but it wasn't from killing the guard. No, her unease was that she would have to work Sandy over. She had to know if she was in on it. She had to get her reacting.

And the best way to do that is to start a rumor, one that accounts for Bill's erratic behavior in a nonthreatening way. "Sandy, is there talk about splitting Jack and me up?"

The woman's eyes widened. "Oh, honey, I'm not supposed to say even if I know—and I don't. Why would you even think such a thing?"

Peri looked down as she worked over her friend. "Bill showed up five minutes after we got home. They're watching us." She took another sip, gauging Sandy's expression over the rim of her mug. "It's so unfair. Bill has us going out again on task already. It's got to be one of those stupid evaluation ones, and if they don't like what they see . . ." Peri made a small sound.

Sandy held her thick-walled mug of untasted coffee before her. "Already? You're supposed to get two weeks after a draft—especially if you're being evaluated. I'm glad you came here for your debrief and orders, otherwise I'd assume you were on leave. You want some Baileys for your coffee? You're tense enough to crack eggs on."

Sandy touched her shoulder, but Peri had gone still, looking at the wall where pictures of retired drafters and their anchors hung in the shadows. "No, I'm driving," she whispered, but something Sandy had said had pinged in her intuition.

Two weeks. Frank and Sandy would be the only people to know she and Jack were out on a new task. Everyone else would assume they'd taken their break and gone to a sunny beach to recover—no one would suspect they were doing anything outside Opti's legal parameters—and Sandy didn't seem upset about it.

She should have been.

Shit. Peri looked at Frank and Jack still talking. Their own psychologists . . . *We have to get out of here*. "Would you excuse me for a moment?" Peri said as she put her coffee down.

"Sure. Go ahead, honey."

Peri crossed the room, her boots leaving puddles of melted snow on Frank's dance floor. Her back was to Sandy, and for the first time, she didn't like it. The men turned to include her, and she forced a smile. The big bear of a man was both the bartender and the bouncer, but he had a past, like everyone else connected with Opti. "Hi, Frank," she said, heart pounding as he gave her a one-armed hug that made her feel like a little girl.

"Hey, sweet pea." His voice rumbled through her slow and easy, and whereas it usually calmed her, it was all she could do not to jerk away. "How you doing?"

"Fine." She smiled convincingly. "I need to ask Jack something. Can we have a sec?"

"Sure, hon." Giving her a grin, Frank ambled to the bar.

Peri's breath came in slow, shaking on the exhale. Taking Jack's arm, she turned him so they couldn't read her lips. "We gotta go. Now."

Jack's focus sharpened on her. "Huh? Why?"

"Because they're in on it. Both of them." Peri pulled him back around when he tried to look over her shoulder at them. "If we go on a non-Opti-sanctioned job, right after I drafted and lost time—no one will think twice about our absence. We're supposed to be gone. Sandy doesn't care that we lost our downtime. Neither does Frank. They're our psychologists, for God's sake."

His eyes widened in understanding. "We have a problem."

"You think?" She had a bug-out bag in the trunk. So did Jack. Getting to them was step one.

From the bar, Frank's gruff voice called out, "Either of you want a beer?"

Peri turned to see him holding a cell phone to his ear. Looking tiny beside him, Sandy pulled a chopstick from the water glass on the top of the bar. Hips swaying, she wound her hair up as she paced a slow path to the back door. With a last acknowledgment, Frank said something and ended his call.

A sliver of fear wedged into Peri, driven by Frank's knowing look. Sweet adrenaline poured in behind it. By the front door, the floor cleaner finished with a cheerful *ding* and shut down. "We're fine," she said, but she knew Frank heard the lie.

Jack's expression when he turned back to her was thick with concern. "Any ideas?" he muttered, lips hardly moving.

"Working on it." Peri gave his cold hand a squeeze. Bill wasn't here yet. They had a chance.

Jack's eyes flicked over her shoulder. "I'm sorry, Peri."

"It's not your fault," she said when Jack reached inside his coat to touch his handgun.

But the sure and steady *snick-snack* of a rifle cocking cracked through her and he froze.

Peri cursed her slow understanding when Frank came out from behind the bar with that squirrel rifle he kept hidden, now pointed at them.

"This isn't how I wanted to do this, babe," Jack said as he shifted to stand between her and Frank.

"Not my first choice either," she said, then started when the sound of keys drew her attention to Sandy returning from the back door. It was padlocked, the excess chain still swinging. Frank pulled a handgun from the small of his back and tossed it to her.

"You know the old saying, too smart for her own good?" Sandy said as she checked the clip, and Peri grimaced. She'd thought Sandy was her friend. *Lies, it was all lies.*

The front door opened, and Peri looked at the thirtyish man coming in and stomping the light snow off his shoes. His long face was red from the cold and his coat too thin for the weather. A gray scarf was around his neck, and Peri stiffened when his brown eyes found hers and his thick fingers unwound the gray wool. Though his black slacks and shirt were casual, she could tell he was Opti. It was his grace, the way his eyes traveled the room, lingering on her in what might be guilt as he flicked his curly black hair from his thick black glasses.

"I told you she was verging on one of her epiphanies," Sandy said as the new man caught the keys that Frank tossed him and locked the front door before pulling a chair from a table to sit in it, his feet spread wide and his confidence absolute. "That intuition of yours is both your saving grace and your Achilles' heel, Peri," Sandy continued. "I blame Bill. He'd rather believe Jack's fairy tales than split you two up. You're his best operatives. Three years. I don't know if I should congratulate you or decide that you're especially stupid."

Peri tried to get in front of Jack so he could draw his gun, but he wouldn't let her.

Still holding that infuriating, sweet smile, Sandy eyed Jack with appreciation. "But if I had a man like Jack waiting on me hand and foot, I might be keen on a little self-blinding, too."

Heart pounding, Peri thought of her knife, peeved at bringing it to a gunfight. She suddenly realized how fit Sandy and Frank were. Overdraft was a trap.

"We're going to have to get that furry orange mouse-eating bug back into your apartment," Sandy was saying coyly, as she sashayed closer. "We could have lost you on your 'evaluation mission.'"

They bugged my cat? Peri flicked a glance at the man by the door. "Jack?" Peri muttered. "I'm open to suggestions here."

"Play it out," he said grimly.

"Frank, let's get this going," Sandy said, a new, ugly look on her face. "Shoot her."

"Not me," Frank said indignantly. "I want her to like me tomorrow. You do it."

Sandy sighed. "Maybe you're right. Can you shoot Jack?"

"Oh, hell yes," the big man said, bringing up his rifle.

"No!" Peri screamed, lunging forward. The rifle fired, stunning her ears. Jack fell into her arms, his hands across his stomach. Together they hit the yellow parquet floor, both staring at his middle as blood seeped past his fingers. It was a gut wound. It would kill him, not right away, but it *would* kill him. Even getting him to the hospital might not save him.

"You shot me!" Jack said, voice high. "Frank, I can't believe you shot me!"

"Why are you doing this!" Peri raged, Jack's head in her lap as she held him tight.

"Because you're valuable, honey, and he's just firmware," Sandy said sweetly, and Peri hated her all the more. "Now. Either draft to save his life and become who we need you to be, or let Jack die. Your choice. Tick-tock."

Somehow they'd found out, but how? Frantic, Peri wadded up her scarf, using it to stanch the blood. Jack was okay. He had to be! They'd survive this.

I will. He won't.

Peri's teeth clenched. Jack's blood stained her fingers as it soaked through her scarf and he made a heartrending gasp. "Fuck, that hurt," he moaned, face white.

"Suck it up, Jack!" Sandy barked. "You knew the risk." Turning back to Peri, she smiled. "Go ahead and draft, honey. We'll scrub you back to where you don't have any disturbing thoughts about Bill, or me, or Frank here. Everyone wins," she said brightly.

Peri's arms began to shake, the stress of holding her and Jack together beginning to tell. "It doesn't work like that," she said, terrified. "You can't predict a draft's mental damage."

"Sure you can," Sandy said, and Peri's fear coalesced when the man by the door came forward. "This is Allen Swift," Sandy continued. "He can scrub your memories until you forget everything I say. I'm thinking . . . four months? The six weeks Jack managed weren't enough."

They can't do that! she thought, and then her mind seemed to jump. *Jack took me back? As in intentionally?* Had all those lost days and weeks been engineered? On purpose?

Peri looked at Jack as her hands pressed into him. A wash of nausea flooded her, and the world seemed to turn inside out. Frightened, she stood, and Jack's head hit the parquet floor with a thunk.

He's in on it, she realized as Jack yelped. *He always has been.* He'd told her exactly what he needed to in order to get her to come here tonight.

She wasn't corrupt—but Jack was.

CHAPTER TEN

"**O**w!" Jack sat up, annoyance joining his pain as he rubbed his head with a bloody hand—clearly not dying. "Way to go, Sandy."

"What? Like she's going to remember any of this?"

Peri started when Frank was suddenly behind her, the rifle now in Allen's hand and out of her reach. His meaty fingers pinched her arm as he pulled her away, but she was too shocked to react. Her heart pounded as Allen set the rifle on the bar with a sliding click, brown eyes evaluating. Sandy's aim never wavered, her expression mean, as if she wanted an excuse.

Not Jack! But it felt like a wish, and she tensed as the truth cycled down to one ugly certainty. If she jumped, she'd lose everything—be exactly who they wanted. She'd be whatever they told her she was. *How many times have they done this?*

"And now she gets it all," Sandy said sarcastically. "Welcome to the party, Peri."

"Jack?" Peri said, and he winced, not in pain, but in guilt.

Anger flared. "You bastard!" she shouted, lurching for him, only to be brought back by Frank's iron grip. "You stinking son of a bastard! You knew? How many times have you done this?" she shouted, thinking over the tasks she could remember, seeing the gaps, the anomalies. A fragment here, a missing hour there. That time she lost eight months? Peri's fury grew, and Frank's grip tightened. *I trusted him. I let him do it.*

Flinching, Jack scooted himself backward until he was propped against the low stage. "I'm sorry, babe. I did it because I love you. It's the only way to stay together."

"Stay together?" Peri exclaimed. *"You lied to me!"*

She fought to get to Jack, but Frank had her, arms pinned to her sides, helpless. "How long? How long have you been doing this? Lying about our tasks, making me into . . . a corrupt agent? Was my name on that list? It was, wasn't it. And it wasn't me, it was you!"

Jack lifted the scarf from his middle and let the blood-soaked yarn hit the floor with a sodden plop. "You can't tell me you don't love the adrenaline," he said, shifting his torn shirt to show the body armor dented and smeared with synthetic blood. "The excitement. The money."

He looked up at the last, giving her a shit-eating grin.

"I'm not a mercenary. I don't kill for money." Peri wiggled as Jack levered himself up gingerly to sit on the low stage. He must have known he might be shot tonight, even down to where to put the sack of fake blood. *Damn it all to hell.*

"If you're not doing it for money, then you're doing it for kicks." Jack reached awkwardly to the straps, and the sound of Velcro ripped the air. His innocent blue eyes were full of knowing. "Admit you like it. The thrill, knowing that you might have to kill someone to survive. The sense of superiority you get from it. Otherwise it wouldn't have taken you this long to figure things out."

"Let me go," Peri muttered, twisting in Frank's grip as Sandy watched in amusement. "Let me go!" she demanded, throat raw. She was a soldier. She did not do this for kicks!

But she was caught. The doors were barred. Jack was unhurt, and they were going to shoot her to make her draft. And that man now over by the bar—Allen—was waiting to spin her back four months to where her ignorance lay. Not this time. Not again.

"I won't forget this," she vowed as Jack set his body armor on the stage and cautiously palpated his middle. "I don't care if you take away a year. I'll remember."

Sandy looked at Allen as if for his opinion, and

the man pinched the bridge of his narrow nose in thought. "She's right," he said, and Jack's head snapped up, his fingers fumbling as he rebuttoned his bloody shirt. "There's too much to fragment and not enough to form a memory from. Not after Jack's been in there already, making holes."

"Hey, I gave her a clean memory," Jack said, and Peri's heart thumped at the glimpse of his holster under his coat. "Do you know how hard it is to fragment an entire person? Make a realistic timeline from two?"

He can do that? she thought, her lips tasting a memory of chocolate, nothing more.

"Four months isn't enough," Allen said. "There are too many residuals, and the gaps will fester until she digs the truth out or MEPs trying. I have to take her all the way back."

Peri went still in Frank's grip, scared. "All the way? What is all the way?"

"Hey. Wait a moment." Jack awkwardly got to his feet, hand to his bruised ribs. "I've got this. I know her mind. A year maybe, but no more. She trusts me."

"Not anymore," Peri snapped.

"I agree," Sandy said. "Take her all the way back. It's the only way to be sure she stays useful." She beamed at Jack. "Just think. You get to fall in love with her again."

"Aww, fuck," he muttered, infuriating Peri.

"Let me go!" Peri demanded. She'd had enough,

and when Sandy looked away, she acted. Heart pounding, she breathed fast, enriching her blood. Frank's grip tightened as he guessed she was going to do something. It was exactly what Peri wanted.

Peri went loose in his grip. Frank leaned forward to keep their balance. His chin dropped, and Peri slammed her head back, teeth clenched; his nose crunched and he howled in pain.

Peri dropped again, breath held and core tight. Frank instinctively tightened his grip until she could lever him over her. Her breath came in fast as his weight arched over her then slammed into the floor to knock him breathless. She was already moving, barreling into Jack on the stage and grabbing his Glock from behind his coat.

"Get her!" Sandy screeched, but Frank was trying to breathe around the blood and broken cartilage. Jack didn't move, his own weapon now pointed at his head, shaking in Peri's hand.

Peri held Jack before her like a shield, his body armor useless on the stage. "How long have you been lying to me?" she demanded as Frank sat up and Sandy ran to him. "Tell me or I'm blowing a hole in your head right now!"

"Three years," Jack said dully.

Three years? Their entire relationship? She could hardly think, she was so angry.

"Sure, go ahead, but leave the gun here," Peri

heard Frank say to Sandy, napkins pressed to his face. The tiny woman smiled and handed him her pistol. Peri stiffened.

Howling, Sandy threw a side kick over Jack's head. Her foot hit Peri square on, shoving her backward and dazing her. Sandy screamed again, poised to do some major damage. Instinct moved Peri and she dropped Jack's Glock to catch Sandy's foot, but Sandy jerked it free before Peri could break her ankle.

Sandy crouched to attack, fingers crooked to gouge and teeth clenched. The lump of Jack's discarded body armor pinched under Peri as she got to a kneel. Her fingers twined in Sandy's luscious black hair and she slammed her head into the stage. Sandy shrieked, elbowing Peri in the gut as Peri pounded her head again. She'd always wondered if she could take the little dragon down. Looked like Sandy had entertained the same question.

But when Sandy got a good hit in, Peri had to let go. Both women staggered upright. Peri struggled to breathe, hunched as she wiped the blood from her cheek. Frank had gotten up. So had Jack—creeping to the locked front door, the little pissant. Panting, Sandy touched her lip to find it bleeding. Seeing the hair-twined chopstick in Peri's grip, Sandy's eyes narrowed.

"Allen, will you just shoot her!" Frank shouted, and Sandy rushed Peri with a high-pitched howl.

Peri swung, that stupid chopstick set to gouge. Sandy blocked her, dropping back to the bar and scrambling atop it.

"Not me," Allen said as he tossed the rifle to Frank, the stock smacking his meaty hand with a solid sound. "She might remember, and I want out when this is done."

"I don't want her remembering me shooting her either," Frank said.

Peri smiled grimly. Everything could be fragmented, but emotion lingered to fuel the intuition and there'd be mistrust, even if she couldn't place why.

"You spoiled, entitled little girl!" Sandy shouted from atop the bar. "I'm sick of you drafters complaining. You have someone waiting on you hand and foot, treating you like a god, and all you do is bitch about it when you lose a little memory. Life isn't fair. Love is not real. I'm doing you a fucking favor! Love?" Sandy shrieked. "There is no such thing as love!"

Teeth clenched, Peri slipped her six-inch blade from her boot with her other hand and threw it at Sandy. It wouldn't hurt her much, but all Peri wanted was for her to shut up.

"No!" Frank cried as Sandy gasped, twisting to avoid the knife. She fell behind the bar and into the mirror, shattering it. Bottles rained down when the shelves collapsed.

"Jack, no!" Allen shouted, and Peri staggered

when a gun popped. Something slammed into her, and recognizing the sound of Jack's Glock, Peri looked at the blood seeping from her chest, then to him standing beside the door. The muzzle was smoking.

Peri staggered. The chopstick in her hand clattered to the floor, and she clutched the table. Shock took her down. She hit the floor hip first, then collapsed. Twin pains, one in her skull, the other in her chest, throbbed in agony as she stared at the black ceiling. Her fingers were warm and wet, and she coughed, scared when it came out bloody. *Not again.*

"Jump," Jack said wearily as he stood over her and holstered his weapon. "Go on and draft. I like you better when you're stupid."

"What are you doing? You're her anchor!" Allen exclaimed, and suddenly he was there, shoving a wad of those stupid napkins onto her chest. Jack must have nicked her lung. She had time, but only until it filled with blood. The longest she'd ever drafted was forty-three seconds. If she staved it off longer than that, it wouldn't matter.

"I can't fragment the trauma of you shooting her," Allen protested. "It was going to be hard enough with Sandy or Frank doing it!"

Oh God. She was going to jump. She'd give anything to be able to draft a day, an hour. "I won't," Peri said, teeth clenched against the pain. "I'll die first." She coughed again, the ragged sound filling her with fear that she was tearing her lungs to shreds.

"If she dies, Bill is going to be pissed." Hunched and wiping the blood from him, Frank went to Sandy, her loud swearing behind the bar saying she was okay. Peri hated them. She hated them all.

Allen, though, was holding her, his eyes soft, and even that small compassion from a stranger almost brought her to tears. *His eyes are so pretty,* she thought, deciding that his long nose suited him where it would look wrong on anyone else, and his thin hands were blessedly warm. She wouldn't draft, not even to save her life. Bill would just have to deal with it.

"Peri, draft," Allen said, and she blinked, wondering why his beautiful brown eyes were scrunched up as if he were the one in pain. "You can't do anything when you're dead."

"What, and have all this go away?" she rasped. "Eat shit and die."

Frustration pinched his brow. "If you draft, I'll let you shoot Jack."

Peri's eyes flicked past Allen to Jack as the man popped up from behind the bar where he'd been helping Sandy. "Hey!" he exclaimed. "She can't rewrite a draft. I'd be dead!"

"You'll give me the rifle?" she wheezed, clenched in pain.

Frank came out from behind the bar. "Ah, Allen?"

Nervous and looking small, Jack backed to the door. "I'm not dying for her."

"Then maybe you shouldn't have shot her," Allen griped, and he turned Peri's face to look at him, his thin finger callused and rough. "How about it?"

"You'll wipe me down to nothing," she groaned. "Use me."

He nodded. "Someone will. You'll never remember Jack, but I'll give you the chance to shoot him before you forget."

Revenge wasn't a good weight in the balance of actions, but right now . . . she didn't give a shit.

"You guys figure this out. I'm leaving," Jack said, and Frank cocked his rifle. It wouldn't matter, though. If Peri drafted, he'd be right back in here and he knew it.

The pressure to jump was building, and Peri looked at Jack, white-faced with anger. Her fingers felt that awful slick stickiness of blood on the varnished floor. The feel of blood was in her mouth. Pain crushed her as Allen knelt beside her, a wad of napkins pressed to her chest. She squinted at the ceiling, wondering if she could see the ghost of herself up there. Everything was important, and she sealed it all away, trying to make a knot of memory as she panted in agony. She would remember this . . . but she'd need a trigger. Blood, varnish, slick fingers, the hardness of the floor, the pain of loss radiating through her, betrayal, Sandy's hair twisted in her fingers. Allen was going to take the last three years from her, but killing Jack would be worth it.

"Deal," she said, and then . . . she jumped, and the world flashed silver sparkles that dissolved into blue.

Hunched and hurting, Peri stood on the stage and wiped the blood from her cheek. Sandy rose up between her and the bar, panting as she touched her lip to find she'd bitten it. The woman's hands clenched into tiny fists.

Peri reoriented herself, knowing that in thirty seconds she was going to be dumber than a stone. She was drafting. Jack had betrayed her. Bill was lining his pockets with Opti's agents' efforts. Her own psychologists were working for him. So was Allen, but he'd promised to give her a rifle so she could shoot Jack's head clean off.

She turned to Allen, watching her from behind his thick glasses and from under black curls. Frank's rifle was in his hand. It had one shell in it. It had to be enough.

"You spoiled, entitled little girl!" Sandy shouted, still before the bar but her words unchanged from the first draft, telling Peri she wasn't a drafter or anchor. "I'm sick of you drafters complaining. You have someone waiting on you hand and foot, treating you like a god, and all you do is bitch about it when you lose a little memory. Life isn't fair. Love is not real. I'm doing you a fucking favor!"

"You got that right." Peri held out a hand to Allen, her fingers and toes tingling. What if he'd lied to her, too? Why was she so trusting?

But Allen threw it. The rifle hit her palm with a solid thud. Confidence flowed, and Peri turned, cocking it with a sure motion.

"We're in a draft!" Frank shouted, and Sandy went ashen-faced. "Twenty seconds and she's done! Sandy, get down!"

Plenty of time to take care of business, Peri mused, filing Frank's anchor status away. He had to be an anchor, otherwise he would've been as oblivious to what was going on as Sandy was.

Jack was backing to the door, his bloody hands outstretched. "Babe, let me explain."

"There are no words," Peri said, and with an unhealthy satisfaction, pulled the rifle up.

He ran for the door.

She didn't have a problem shooting him in the back, seeing as he'd been working behind hers for three years.

Peri sighed through the recoil as she pulled the trigger. Jack hit the door, arms splayed as he fell flat against it. He slipped down in a tangle of legs and arms, knocking the floor sweeper upside down, where it beeped for assistance. Sandy's hands muffled her scream.

The shells were spent, and Peri watched Jack twitch and go still.

Jack is dead, she thought, and the sudden shock of that hit her.

She did nothing when Frank wrestled the rifle from her, numb as Sandy ran from behind the bar to kneel over Jack. "Call an ambulance!" she cried, but no one moved.

"You let her kill her anchor," Frank said as he spun the rifle to the floor. There was blood on his hand gripping her, and Peri wondered whose it was. Hers? Jack's?

Allen looked at his watch, his expression grim. "I just saved Bill's best drafter. She needed closure or she'd never forget."

"In about five seconds, she's going to need an anchor," the large man said. "She knows I'm not hers."

"Not my problem," Allen said, and Peri blearily looked up, still in shock. "I don't know how to rebuild memories, only destroy them."

Peri's heart thudded as Sandy rose from Jack's broken body, her face pale.

"It's not mine, either," Frank said as he shoved Peri at Allen. "You think you can hold her while I get Jack out of sight?"

She fell into Allen, the sudden motion reviving her. She took a heaving breath, but it exploded from her in pain when Allen twisted her arm behind her, threatening to dislocate it.

"Sandy, some help here?" Frank said brusquely as Allen tightened his grip, and she gasped, seeing stars. "I don't want to have to explain him when Peri finishes the weave."

"Don't do this," Peri demanded, hating her inability, and then adrenaline flashed through her as time began to mesh. Suddenly, forgetting was too high a price to pay, and she panicked, fighting Allen and sending them both down.

"Get your ass over here and help me!" Frank shouted, and Sandy screamed something in a singsong language, bitter and angry.

"Let me go!" Peri exclaimed, but it was too late, and she seized as time snapped and her head exploded in a red wash.

"Her scarf! Get her bloody scarf," Frank exclaimed.

"No!" Peri raged as Allen slipped into her mind, the way opened by the meshing of the timelines. Images sped past her, curling up in flame, destroyed: the button from the security guard, New Year's under the stars, throwing flowers from the bridge in Paris in the rain, a total eclipse of the sun seen from a cruiser in the Bahamas, their toes rising out of a tub of bubbles, their first kiss, a shy smile and introduction as she was given a new anchor. She was going to miss Jennifer, but Jack seemed nice.

* * *

Pulse hammering, Peri looked up, confused when the man kneeling beside her staggered to a stand, a hand to his chest as he panted. *Heart attack,* she thought, and she felt her own chest, not knowing why.

Suspecting that she'd drafted, she lurched to her feet, reaching for the table when suddenly everything hurt. *New hurt layered over old.* She was at Overdraft, but not the one she remembered. It was closed, with chairs on the tables. Sandy was behind the bar, pale and unmoving as she stared at her with wide eyes, her beautiful hair mussed. Frank was with her, dropping a red towel into the sink and turning the water on full. The smell of spent gunpowder was obvious.

Sandy—always-in-control Sandy—was quietly panicking, muttering in a singsong until Frank told her to shut up. His back was to Peri, and he watched her through the mirror. But it was the mirror with its shelves of bottles that Peri stared at. They looked wrong in their orderly smoothness, and she couldn't say why.

"Where's Jennifer?" Peri whispered, glancing at the unfamiliar man. Her hand went to her throat. It was sore, and she was sweating. Confused, she looked at her wrist, red where someone had twisted the skin. Her shoulder felt as if it had been wrenched.

"Call 911," Frank muttered, and the man beside

her jerked his head up. Peri's eyes widened. Frank was covered in blood!

"We're *all* okay," the man beside Peri said firmly, a ribbon of sweat inching down his neck, and Sandy looked at her feet, her lips parting.

"B-but . . . ," Peri stammered.

"I said we're all *okay*," the man said again. "Frank doesn't need an ambulance. It's just a bloody nose, for God's sake."

Frank turned off the water, motions small as he edged out from behind the bar. Shaky, Peri sat against the edge of the table and tried to figure out what had happened. At least she knew where she was and who she was with. Her eyes slid to the Opti stiff now sitting on the raised fireplace hearth, his elbows on his knees and his head in his hands, his curly black hair hiding his eyes. *Mostly, anyway.*

Feeling ill, she staggered to the bar. Sandy made a tiny noise, looking scared as Peri moved to stand right before her. Frank, too, became oddly alert. "Shit, I've got a black eye," she said as she caught sight of it in the mirror. She carefully prodded it, deciding it was a day old. They'd just come back from task, then. That would explain the aches.

Just that small knowledge made her feel better. "Where's Jennifer?" Peri asked, her flash of good mood dying when Sandy's eyes darted to the man at the fireplace.

Peri turned, her growing hunch that she'd over-drafted growing when the man on the hearth looked up, his eyes haunted. "Ah, what day is it?" Peri asked him weakly. Crap, the jukebox was gone, replaced with some new system she'd have to relearn.

"Er, it's Saturday now. I think." The man glanced at Frank when the big man cleared his throat in warning. "I'm sorry. I should have asked you before. Are you okay?"

Peri's throat tightened. Something had gone very wrong. "No," she said as she turned back to the bar, laying her arms flat on the smooth wood and dropping her head to hide her face against them. It was bad, really bad—so bad she felt sick to her stomach.

"I'll give it all to you later, but the guy you were watching tried to rob the place. He shot you. You drafted. He ran out in the second weave."

Why is it I can handle both when told, but remembering them will cause a psychotic episode? "I don't remember you," Peri said, her breath coming back from the bar warm and stale. She tensed at his footsteps, then jumped when his hand landed on her shoulder and fell away. A tear brimmed but never fell. Knowing he was still there, she looked up at the stranger with whom she'd been sharing her life for who knew how long. His glasses drew her, as if she should recognize them. "What year is it?"

His smile faded. "Year?" The lump in Peri's throat grew, and when she did nothing but silently stare at him, he whispered, "It's February 2030. Valentine's is next week. . . ."

Peri's stomach caved in and became a knot. Oh God. She'd lost three entire years. Someone had tried to kill her and apparently succeeded. That'd be the only reason she'd lost so much. Turning away, she held her breath. "I'm sorry, I don't remember you." *Three years? How could I lose three years?*

"Oh . . . ," the man said, and she jerked, heart pounding when he touched her again. She was angry, as if she'd done something unconscionably stupid. "I'm Allen. Ah, Allen Swift," he said, his hand falling away with a guilty slowness.

Taking a deep breath, Peri met Allen's eyes. She didn't know this man, but Frank and Sandy did, and she was tired of looking stupid. Besides, she'd lost time before. This man would help her find her way. "Can we go home?" she said, and Allen looked so relieved that she couldn't help but try to smile back.

Her hand in his felt okay as he helped her off the stool. She might not remember him, but he clearly knew her. "You have this?" he asked Frank.

"Yes. You?" the big man answered. Sandy was still pale as she stood behind him, glancing at her feet again to make Peri wonder if she was avoiding broken glass. Her continued frightened silence behind the bar was odd.

Allen took Peri's coat from the bar. "We'll

figure it out. Peri, you've got the keys, right?" he asked as he helped her into it.

Peri touched her coat pocket to find a fob. "Looks like it," she said, doubting it belonged to the little Beemer she remembered. Her taste in clothes had improved in the last three years, and the coat was everything she liked. Allen pulled a gray scarf from a table and got her moving, and she paused, more curious than shocked at the blood on the door. With a small grunt, Frank hustled over and unlocked it, accidentally kicking the floor sweeper into the wall, where it gave a pained whine and died.

"After you," Allen said as he wound his scarf about his neck. The cool night air shocked through her as the door opened, and Peri took one last look at Sandy standing stiffly behind the bar. There was a strand of black hair caught in Peri's fingers, and she pulled it free to let it drift to the cold pavement. Frank was watching from the open door, and Peri's unease grew.

"Ah, Allen?" Frank said. "I suggest you get Peri checked out before you go home. I'll let Bill know where you are."

"I'm fine," Peri protested, but Allen seemed to start, visibly collecting his thoughts.

"Mmmm. He's right," he said, thin fingers touching the side of his long nose as he scanned the nearly empty lot. "You hit your head. It won't take long."

"It will take all night," she complained. "I don't need to go in." But he was ushering her forward, his hand familiarly on the small of her back. It didn't feel wrong there, but she didn't like being pushed. "I haven't changed my apartment in the last three years, have I?"

"No."

"Is my mom still alive?" she asked, the cold night making her bruised eye throb.

"Yes. You called her yesterday. Now, will you please get in the car?"

She had talked to her mom? Clearly things had improved. Either that, or gotten much worse. "Sure. Which one is it?"

Allen took the fob right out of her hand and clicked it. Across the way, a sleek black car flashed its lights. "Maybe I should drive," he said in sudden avarice, and her eyes widened. *Holy shit, it's a Mantis. I own a Mantis?*

"This is ridiculous, I'm fine," Peri complained. "Allen, give me my keys back," she protested when he held them out of her reach like a playground bully.

"No, I'm driving," he insisted, and she gave up, hands in her pockets as she stomped beside him.

"This is really bad for my asthma," she muttered, angry and becoming depressed.

Allen started, turning to her in surprise. "Asthma? I didn't know you had asthma."

Peri blinked at him, confused. *Why did I say that?* "I don't," she said as she pulled her coat closer. "Sorry. Bad joke."

Kind of like her life.

CHAPTER ELEVEN

She'd had to reinstate Allen into the car's system before he could drive it. That hadn't bothered her as much as Allen not knowing what she'd had her Mantis in for or why the technicians had accidentally blown him out. *A Mantis,* she thought in satisfaction, wondering what color palette she'd programmed into it. You couldn't even get on the purchase list unless you'd lived in Detroit for ten years.

'Cause only those who never gave up on her should be allowed to play with her toys, Peri thought, as the bright neon of one of Detroit's casinos came and went between the e-boards, green spaces, and community gardens lit like a fairyland for the night.

Uneasy, she glanced at Allen as they slipped into an industrial park. She felt as if she'd left something behind, like her wallet or a sweater. *Or maybe a gun,* she thought, stealthily feeling the edge of her boot to find her knife. Her angst was growing, but she dismissed it, knowing it was likely the shock of losing so much time. She was fine, damn it!

But the unease only grew worse as they took an easy curve and Opti spread before them, two empty lanes of dim lights and stiff regulations at two in the morning. "I don't want to be here," she protested, even as she dug in her purse for her ID. An odd pane of glass caught her eye, and with a shock, she realized it was her phone. *Glass? I've got glass? Cool.*

Allen slipped his ID from a shirt pocket. "I can tell," he said as the woman on duty stepped forward. "You hit your head. I'm not letting you go to sleep until you get checked out."

"I'm fine," she complained as the snow-crisp air slipped in his lowered window, but she dutifully showed the security woman her ID across the expanse for her to scan it. "A good night's sleep would do me more good than being here."

"Let me do my *job,*" Allen said, the bitterness catching the security woman's attention. "We're going to the med offices," he said to her, though he didn't have to. "She overdrafted, and I want her checked out."

Overdrafted, as in losing too much memory to function properly, Peri thought. Bullshit. She'd probably lost large chunks of time before. *And therein lies the problem. . . .*

The woman waved them through, and Allen's grip on the wheel tightened as he drove toward the small Opti infirmary across campus from the larger office building. His frustration was obvious in the occasional glimmer of a streetlight. "I know you're tired, but you drafted twice in twenty-four hours. I want you checked out before I go mucking about in your head."

I drafted twice? Uneasy, she dropped her glass phone into her purse to figure out how to use later. "You think I might MEP?"

He didn't answer, worrying her even more. MEPs were usually preceded by multiple drafts with no time between to sort things out, but occasionally old damage or a memory knot could trigger it. Peri suddenly felt fragile.

"I don't want to muddle it up," he said softly, the car slowing as he pulled up right before the door of an unassuming three-story building. "I'd feel better if we checked your synaptic activity levels."

His uncertainty bothered her more than anything else, and she looked straight ahead as he turned the car off. Her gaze went to her broken nail, and her pulse throbbed at her eye and at the back of her head. Her hip was bruised, and her shoulder had been wrenched. The faint scent of gunpowder lingered in the seat cushions. Her Mantis could be cleaned and the sundry hurts in her body would mend. The damage to her mind . . . that's where the darkness lay.

Seeing her unmoving, Allen set a tentative hand

on her knee. "It's going to be okay," he said, but his smile held doubt, and she was glad when he took his hand away.

They got out at the same time, the doors shutting loud in the crisp, snowy night. Opti's infirmary building looked like all the rest. There weren't many Opti operatives, and their unique ailments didn't take up much room.

Allen held the heavy glass door, and she murmured her thanks as she went in, too tired to smile at the receptionist. Allen could be personable for both of them. "Special needs," he said by way of explanation, but Peri was already following the teal line on the floor. Allen jogged to catch up, the cadence telling her he ran regularly. She felt only a minor flash of irritation when he looped his arm in hers to slow her down. He was only a few inches taller, and that seemed odd somehow. Muscle memory never vanished, and her suspicions tightened.

"Why are you in such a hurry?" Allen said, and she forced her pace to ease.

"Sorry," she said, and the large man in a lab coat riffling through his paperwork glanced up at them and away. The guy was tall without an ounce of fat on him, his tie loosened as if at the end of a hard day, but his face was clean-shaven—only hours ago. He'd be good at subduing unruly patients. Maybe that was why he worked nights.

Stop it, Peri. She was seeing assassins in the

shadows, but all she had to go on at the moment was intuition, and it was in overdrive. "I can't believe anyone is here," she said when they turned the corner and the man was out of earshot. "It's two in the morning."

"You don't think Frank called ahead?" he asked. The teal line made a sharp left to a glass door and window wall. Beyond it was a tiny waiting room with an efficient-looking woman in purple scrubs behind the reception counter. She'd be in a suit during normal work hours, but things relaxed on the night shift as she'd have to do everything from file the paperwork to draw blood. It was Ruth, and Peri didn't have to fake a smile as she and Allen went in.

"Peri," Ruth said as she stood, her relief obvious. She vanished behind a wall, and in half a second she was coming through the heavy wooden door that separated her from the waiting room. "I just heard," she said, giving Peri a hug that was so honest Peri's eyes shut as she basked in the other woman's warmth. "I'm so sorry. You okay?"

Peri nodded when Ruth held her at arm's length and searched her expression. "I'm okay. Really," she added when the nurse looked doubtfully at Allen.

"Hi, Allen," she said as she let go of Peri, and paranoia pinged at Ruth's guarded tone.

"She hit her head, but it's the proximity drafts

I'm worried about," Allen said, his tone just as telling. He didn't like Ruth, either. "I'd like to get moving on this. Is Bill here?"

Ruth frowned, her pique obvious at his implication that she was slowing things up. "No," she said, pushing open the heavy door and leading them back. "We'll have you out of here in an hour, though. Get your synaptic baseline and send you home. No need to check you in."

"Thank God," Peri said softly, feeling the late hour all the way to her bones.

"Bill is only a few minutes out," Ruth was saying as she led them down the hall past dark offices and diagnostic rooms. "He must have been putting in a late night."

Peri's gut tightened, but if it was because of Bill or the diagnostic room Ruth was ushering them into, she couldn't tell. Allen filed in behind her to stand just inside the door.

"Jewelry off," Ruth said brightly, moving about with quick efficiency, her short black hair swinging as she turned a soft, indulgent chair for Peri. "And your jacket. Here's a bin for you. I'll be right back to get your drip started. Bill wants to watch the diagnostics, so as soon as he gets here, we can get going."

Peri took off her coat and gingerly sat in the big chair, her shoulders easing as she sank into the soft cushions. The low-ceilinged room had a flat brown carpet and drapes on the walls as if there were windows. There was no examination table, but there was a little desk with an outdated computer plug-in beside the etherball, and a trash can for hazardous waste. A second door probably led to an adjacent room. There was a mirror on the same wall—clearly a one-way for observation. It was desperately trying to be a comfortable room, but the diagnostic tools were ruining it.

"I don't want to leave," Allen said, looking helpless beside the door, and Ruth seemed to soften as she pulled the shade on the one-way mirror.

"You can stay." She smiled at Peri, halfway out the door. "I'll be back with your IV."

Needles, Peri thought glumly as the door shut, and Allen sat in the chair beside the door. It was placed carefully—set on the outskirts and not very comfortable—to imply that he was allowed to be here but would have no power. He was here on sufferance.

Neither of them said anything as she took off her pen necklace, setting it beside her purse in the plastic bin with a picture of a mountain pasted to the bottom. A watch was next, and then her magnetic-backed earrings that wouldn't rip out in a fight. Reluctantly she set her knife beside them. Peri eased into the chair, the watch especially catching her eye. She wondered how long she'd had it. She never wore watches, especially one with so many gadgets. This one looked brand-new. Significant.

"I'm sorry this happened," Allen said, his voice low as if someone might be listening.

Peri handed him her coat and he draped it on the back of his chair. "Shit happens."

He shifted his feet, hunched over his knees. "I'm sure we can bring something back."

Three years? The silence of the building soaked into her along with his obvious doubt. Her head was scrambled like Sunday morning eggs. You couldn't bring back three years, and she didn't know if she even wanted to try. *What could have happened that I'd lose three years?*

Allen straightened at a rattle in the hall. Peri tried to smile but only managed not to frown as the door opened and that same man from the hallway came in with a bag of saline drip on a stand. A tablet was tucked under his arm, in startling contrast to his buff physique. His tie had been straightened, and the familiar packaging of a sterile IV kit showed from his lab coat's pocket. Peri's pulse hammered, and she took a steadying breath, quelling her paranoia.

"Hello, Ms. Reed," the man said, his voice professionally bland as he ignored Allen apart from a cursory, somewhat peeved look. "I'm Silas. Ruth asked me to get your IV started while she prints up some paperwork she forgot."

"Sure." Peri nervously tucked her hair behind an ear before she began to roll up her sleeve. Her scraped knuckles caught her eye, and a flash of scratched parquet flitted through her thoughts. *I will not MEP. I will not MEP.*

"And you are?" Silas said to Allen as he set his tablet on the desk.

Allen shifted in his seat. "I'm, ah, Allen. Her anchor."

"If you're staying, you need to be quiet. I don't want you screwing up the results."

Allen leaned back in his chair, his arms crossed resolutely over his chest. "I know how to be quiet."

Satisfied, Silas sat in the rolling chair as if it were a throne, cracking his knuckles as his tablet connected. She wondered if his nose had been broken once or twice, which wouldn't surprise her, with his brooding manner and the iron-pumping arms stuffed into his lab coat. Even so, it only added to his rugged good looks. He *had* just shaved, and the spicy pine of his aftershave was . . . different but good.

Exhaling, he typed into his tablet with surprising facility. She leaned to peek, and he turned it so she couldn't. Her memory loss–induced paranoia fluttered. *He's wearing dress shoes.*

Eyebrows high, he ripped the IV package open and swabbed her inner elbow. "Rough night?" he said sarcastically.

"That's what they tell me," she said, then added a dry "Ow?" as the needle went in.

"Sorry." Smile insincere, he taped the needle

into place. "You have nice veins. They're popping right up there."

"That's because I don't poke them all the time," she said, and at the door, Allen shifted his feet. Peri glanced up, having almost forgotten he was there.

Silas used too much tape, and she watched him set up 2cc of something from his pocket into the drip port. Immediately her aches retreated. Shit, it was good stuff.

Peri watched the drip, enjoying the lassitude plinking into her in time with the drops.

"Does it wear off fast?" Allen asked, his wary tone sparking dully through her. She'd tell him to shut up so she could enjoy her high, but it seemed like too much trouble.

Silas put a pulse clip on her finger. "Yes." Her arm was slack as he stuck another electrode to her, made her knee jump, and shined a light into her eyes. "No concussion. Good."

He's wearing jeans under his lab coat? "How long have you been in Opti?" Peri asked, lips slow from the drug.

Silas didn't look up as he plugged both the pulse meter and the electrode into the tablet. "A while. I work nights most of the time because the light hurts my eyes."

But you have dark eyes. And a surfer tan, Peri thought, wanting to run her fingers over its delicious smoothness. Then she smiled at the loss of inhibition that came with the muscle relaxant. *The things I could do with you, lovely muscleman. . . .*

The loudspeaker crackled in the hallway, and they all listened as "Allen Swift to the reception desk, please. You have a phone call" came over it.

Allen wrangled his phone out, frowning at it. Grunting, Silas turned back to his tablet. "There's no service this deep in the building," he said as Allen stood. "It's a bitch, isn't it?"

"It might be Bill," Allen said as he looked toward the front of the building. "Will you be okay for a minute?"

Peri's pulse increased as her body metabolized the drug and the haze she was in eased. "I'm not a baby," she said, sitting up when she realized she'd been slouching.

"No, you're not." Allen touched her shoulder and leaned close. His curls brushed her cheek, and she breathed in the scent of his shampoo, thinking it smelled all wrong but not sure why. "I'll be right back."

Peri touched his fingers as they slid from her shoulder. "I'm not going anywhere," she said, feeling centered for the first time in a long while. She didn't care if it was the drugs finding her baseline. She was calm and relaxed, hearing everything, seeing everything, and right now she was glad to be rid of Allen. He was distracting her from something important. If he left, she could probably figure it out.

Allen eased into the hall, leaving the door open a crack. Chuckling, the tech rolled over and closed it with his foot. He stood as it clicked shut, taking a card from his breast pocket and running it through the door panel to make the green light shift red. "I thought he'd never leave," he said softly.

"You're kind of snarky, you know that?" Peri said. He'd locked the door. She should be upset, but she just . . . couldn't find it in herself . . . to care.

Still standing, Silas ran his finger across his screen to follow a line of text. "What else am I, Ms. Reed?"

She watched him increase the drip. "Too old to be doing intern work," she said. "Your shoes aren't right and jeans are a no-no, even after normal hours. Who are you?"

Turning from the IV, the man evaluated her. "And they wanted to send in a team," he whispered, leaning over her with his palms on the arms of her chair, his face uncomfortably close as he stared at her. "I didn't know about the no-jeans rule. Thanks."

Peri blinked, her lethargy reasserting itself. "You're not Opti. If you've hurt Ruth, I'm going to kick you in the balls."

Surprised, he straightened, shifting out of her easy reach. "She's fine," he muttered.

"Who do you work for?" she asked. Everything was hitting her with a peaceful crystal clarity that felt too good to risk breaking with movement.

Silas sat back down. Something on his screen pleased him, and he smiled. "The alliance for clean timelines. Mind if I ask a question?"

She wanted to pull the electrode off, but what would be the point? "Seeing as I'm drugged out of my mind, I do. What did you give me?"

He looked at his watch, inadvertently relaying to Peri that he was in a hurry. "Nothing you haven't had before. Relaxant, mostly. Peri, are you aware of any illegal Opti activity, recent or otherwise?"

At that, she blinked. "You mean like dirty operatives? Just rumors. You look too smart to be alliance. Who are you really?"

Frowning, he looked at the screen. Peri leaned in, catching sight of a graph before he turned it away. "Are you aware of who is giving the orders?" he asked.

"Orders for what? The illegal activity?" Peri glanced at the drip running into her arm. "I told you. I've only heard rumors." It was the usual stuff, but he'd given her too much.

"Who is giving the orders?" he demanded more forcefully. "How far up does it go?"

She wanted to stop talking, but "I don't know" came out of her mouth. *Shut up, Peri.*

Silas glanced at the drip, then the readout on his

screen. "What do you remember from Charlotte? Did you kill Jack tonight because he found out you were taking jobs on the side? Or was it the other way around?"

Peri's eyebrows rose. She'd been in Charlotte? Then she blinked. *Taking jobs on the side?* "Who's Jack?"

That set the tech-who-wasn't-a-tech back, and he pushed away from his tablet. "Just how much did you lose tonight?"

"Three years," she said, distracted as she tried to process what he had said. She knew she'd been on a task yesterday, thanks to that day-old black eye. But was he implying she was corrupt, or just fishing for answers? Even with her memory missing, she'd know if she was a dirty agent. *Wouldn't I?*

"Three years!" he echoed, looking disgusted. "What am I supposed to do with that?"

"You can . . . put it in a pipe and smoke it," Peri said, staring at the ceiling as the wonderful lassitude took over.

Silas stood, his motions fast and angry as he unplugged his tablet from both the wall and Peri. The electrodes were still stuck on her, and she suddenly felt violated. "I could almost be sorry for you," he said. "So worried about not looking stupid that you walk out of a bar with a man you don't even know simply because people assume you will. Intuition can only take you down a path you already know, and right now you know nothing."

"It's all I've got, ass-hat," she said. The IV drip hung between them, and she stared at it, thinking it would be easy to rip it out of her arm. Painful, but easy. With a small nudge, she got the fingertip pulse monitor off. Silas looked at it as it thumped on the carpet tiles, clearly surprised she'd managed even that. He took a breath to say something, freezing when a voice in the hallway shouted, "He's in there with her right now!"

"Security!" bellowed a familiar voice, and Peri smiled smugly.

"That's Bill," she said. "He's almost as big as you. You'd better run, rabbit man."

"What a waste." Silas was shoving things in his pockets, his motions full of grace. "You didn't see me tonight," he said as he tucked the tablet under his arm.

"The hell I didn't." Peri's pulse quickened as she shook the drug off. It had been a psychoactive sedative, not a hypnotic suggestion drug.

Frowning, he leaned over her. She drew back, thinking his skin looked . . . irresistibly smooth. Her focus blurred as she imagined it shining with sweat, muscles moving evenly as he pumped iron. "You didn't see me," he repeated, his brown eyes scrunched up.

"You're the one who filled me up with drugs that make me want to talk, doofus."

He pushed back, clearly frustrated. A rattle came at the doorknob, followed by a shout for the key. Jumping, Silas went for the second door, flinging it open to show a dark, tiled room beyond. "If you're smart, you'll keep your mouth shut."

"Screw you!" she exclaimed, then fell back, lethargy taking its toll. *Who the hell is Jack?*

Allen shouted and hammered on the door. Silas ran out, his lab coat furling, shoes silent. Slowly the door arced shut.

Peri rolled her head to look when something crashed into the hall door. The frame began to split, and with another blow gave way. Allen and Bill rushed in, two security guards behind them. She wasn't corrupt. The creep had been fishing for information.

"Where did he go!" Bill exclaimed as Allen knelt beside her.

To stay silent would take too much effort. "Through there," she said, looking at the door.

Bill bolted, security tight behind. A buzzing alarm began in the hallway. Peri didn't care, and she watched dispassionately as Allen took the IV out of her arm with more finesse than Silas had used putting it in. His hand was red where he'd hit the door, making it easy to see where his fingers had been broken in the past. *Martial arts?* she wondered, having seen the same damage on Bill's thick hands before. Not on Silas, though. For all his size, his hands were baby soft.

"I shouldn't have left. Are you okay?" Allen said as he bent her arm up to keep it from bleeding. "Did he touch you?"

"He drugged me," she said, the blood seeming to rush to her head to clear it. "All he did was ask me questions."

Suddenly still, Allen looked at her over his glasses. "What did he say?"

Peri's focus sharpened. He was more concerned with what Silas had said than with what he might have done to her? Suspicion flared. "Who is Jack, and why did I kill him?"

Allen's mouth closed, and he looked at the door Bill had gone through. "Ah . . ."

Angry, she sat up as the drug filled her with the sensation of pinpricks. *So worried about not looking stupid that you walk out of a bar with a man you don't even know simply because people assume you will.* "Who is Jack?" she insisted, and Allen stood. Men ran down the hall, and the alarm cut out and started again. "Allen?"

"What did he tell you about Jack?"

"He was more asking than telling," Peri said, then started at a distant but loud bang. The hall alarm cut out again, this time for good. "He wanted to know if I was taking side jobs and who the orders came from. Jack's name came up. Who is Jack? Was he dirty?" *Oh God, what if I'm a corrupt agent? How would I even know?*

Allen pulled the rolling chair close and sat in it, elbows on his knees. "I'm sorry, Peri—"

"Stop it!" she exploded, and his head snapped up, eyes wide. "Just stop it! Everyone keeps saying they're sorry, and I don't know why. Who is Jack?"

Allen's eyes searched hers, the pity in them scaring her. "Your previous anchor," he said, and her breath caught. Silas had said she'd killed him. . . .

"A few days ago, while on task, you found out some of your past missions weren't Opti-sanctioned," Allen said, and her heart pounded as she grasped another truth. She wasn't corrupt—Jack was.

"Jack tried to kill you when you found out," Allen continued, and Peri's vision sharpened as she looked for the lie but saw only his regret that he hadn't told her sooner. "We thought you were safe, but he followed us to Overdraft." Allen's hand was warm as he took hers. "He shot you. You jumped. Peri, I'm sorry. I wasn't there for all of it. I can't bring it back."

Memory tried to rise, shredding even as she focused on it. "I shot my own anchor?"

"You lost everything." Allen made a helpless gesture. "It seemed cruel to bring him up. Maybe . . . you forgot on purpose."

Never, she thought as two men ran down the hallway. Peri sat, stunned as her world shifted and resettled. Jack had been her anchor, and now he was dead. What it meant was that apart from the memories tied to her talismans, the last three years of her life were beyond recall. She was probably suspected of being a turncoat as well. "He's dead?"

His hands still cradling hers, he nodded. "I'm so sorry."

The subtle clues that had been telling her Allen was wrong now added up. Ruth's words in the reception office, her pity. Hell, Ruth knew more of her past than she did. "Did I love him?" she asked softly. Emotions never die, even when the memories tied to them are erased, and judging by the amount of bitterness in her, she must have loved him deeply.

"Yeah," Allen said tightly, as if it bothered him. "Yeah, you did."

Something in Peri snapped. Maybe it was the drugs wearing off, but she was suddenly ticked. "I want my memory of tonight back," she said. "You were there. I want everything you saw. Now. Right now."

She tried to stand, falling back into the chair when the pinpricks rose in a new wave. Silas had accused her of being a dirty operative, and the only one who knew if she was—Jack—was dead.

"It's going to get better, Peri," Allen said. "I promise. Give it some time."

Time? Peri started when Bill came in through the open door. "Peri." The head of Opti's agents looked both irate and comforting, his hands extended. "Are you okay? Did he hurt you?"

Peri blanched, feeling the strength in his hands as he took hers. "Tell me you got him."

But his creased brow said otherwise. She watched Allen closely as he stood, deciding that he was truly upset, not acting, and something in her eased—just a little. No wonder Allen had been pinging her paranoia meter. She'd probably known him less than a day.

"Not yet, but we will." Bill gripped her shoulder reassuringly. "We know who he is."

"Silas, right?" she said to shake a reaction from him. "From the alliance."

Bill hesitated, his hand falling away. "How . . . He told you his name?"

Two lab techs went by, talking excitedly. Peri looked up at both men, feeling out of control. "He also mentioned Jack. My previous anchor?"

Bill's eyes darted to Allen. Allen raised his hand as if to say "What could I do?" adding, "Bill, I know you wanted a clean break for Peri, but Denier told her she killed her last anchor because he had her doing non-Opti-sanctioned tasks. She doesn't *know* any more than that." His hand found hers, giving it a squeeze.

"Am I a dirty operative?" she whispered. *Damn it all to hell, how could I love someone who could try to kill me?*

"Good God, no. But Jack was," Bill said,

surprised. "I never would have guessed it. Maybe it's good you lost the last three years. Start fresh with Allen. This might be a blessing."

Allen's fidgeting became obvious. "I'm not taking her home until I know that alliance nutcase is apprehended."

"I agree," Bill said sharply. "I was going to check you in for observation—"

"I'll regain more at home than in the hole," Peri protested, but Bill had a hand in the air, asking for patience.

"But if the alliance has gained access here, the entire campus is suspect. You need some time off. Both of you," he said, voice demanding obedience. "Go to Allen's tonight, try to get some sleep, and we'll get you an early a.m. flight out to somewhere warm."

She didn't want to go to Allen's, but a hotel would have been worse. Someone was lying to her, and all she could do was trust her gut.

Too bad her gut was telling her to run.

CHAPTER TWELVE

Peri hated the airport chairs in the Detroit terminals. They were not made for the comfort of passengers, despite what they claimed: the worst of them had a severe slope that was supposed to be relaxing but wasn't. She had to believe the open back was there so security wouldn't have to worry about what people were leaving behind.

Knees crossed, she sat out of the late-morning sun glinting through the windows, fingers swift as she knitted, purled, knitted, purled the edge pattern of a scarf she didn't remember buying the yarn for. It was easier than she remembered, and she didn't even have to watch what she was doing. Clearly she'd been knitting a lot the last three years—which wasn't very cheering since it was an Opti-encouraged activity to relieve obsessive-compulsive stress.

Across from her, two Opti security agents bitched about the Big Ten being renamed to include an expanded twenty teams. A projected, muted TV hung over them, the code to listen in on an intuitive phone flashing for attention. Peri sourly glanced at her glass phone, wondering if it was intuitive or just smart, and how long it would take to find the right app to change the station. *Good Lord, when did Twitter get its own TV channel?*

A third female guard had accompanied Allen in search of coffee. It was the second trio of security they'd had since leaving the hospital. That the detail had camped out in Allen's hallway was probably why she hadn't slept well, but at least she knew *why* she and Allen weren't cohabiting. He'd been her anchor only a day, and she wished Bill had let her return to her apartment to at least pack a bag. What Allen had come back with looked great but lacked functionality.

The sleek white cashmere sweater she had on fitted tightly in all the right places and the wide collar fell off her shoulder to show her neck, but it would be problematic in a fight. She remembered buying the fitted jacket, lined with silk to be light and free-moving as well as warm. A matching black cap sat atop her carry-on, the red embellishment accenting her earrings, necklace, and nails. Black traveling pants finished it off, the traveling designation meaning they had pockets deep enough for her to stuff her ID, ticket, and phone for easy access. The boots from last night were still on her feet, but no knife in the sheath. She looked *good*—good enough to *feel* good—but the only thing on her mind was worry.

Fingers fumbling, she looked down at the soft red as she worked. *I killed my own anchor? No wonder I lost three years.*

"What was I trying to do?" she muttered, unwinding the red yarn from her fingers and spreading the scarf flat on her leg. It was nearly done, which was why she'd brought it with her. The completed end had a dagaz made of raised purls against a flat background of knits, but the end she was working on had a weird band of odd stitches she couldn't figure out. There was no pattern apart from three flat rows between nine individual rows of knit-and-purl nonsense.

Head tilted, she angled the nine odd lines to see if she'd been hiding an image in the knits and purls, but that would've needed a pattern, and there hadn't been one in the knitting bag Bill had brought from her apartment in his attempt to give her psyche something familiar to build on.

"This doesn't make any sense," she mumbled, sliding the stitches off the needle to unravel it. She'd just repeat the dagaz pattern and bind it off.

Her focus went distant as she pulled the stitches out, her faint grimace deepening as she looked at the black, cheap fabric bags on tiny plastic rollers that she'd bought this morning, Allen patiently walking her through how to do it with her phone. Apparently no one used cards anymore since the system-wide hack in '28. She was sure she had better luggage at her apartment, something with thick leather and big wheels that turned when she did. She'd tripped on her new stuff twice going from the car to security. Their escorts weren't happy about having to check their weapons, but her knitting needles went through with no problem—the smug satisfaction of which helped rub out her embarrassment at not knowing how to pay for things.

They were on their way somewhere warm that required a passport, and she kept shoving her vague unease down. Bill had blamed the alliance as the reason to avoid her apartment, but Peri suspected that Bill knew that she, like most drafters, kept a private diary. They wouldn't let her in until they found it and ascertained if she was dirty, or if it was just Jack. Sighing, she wrote off finding her past that way. She wasn't on vacation, she was on paid leave while they investigated her.

The only thing that had come from her apartment besides her knitting had been a cat named Carnac whom she didn't remember. He remembered her, though. Bill was watching him while they were gone, though it was likely his secretary who was checking the cat's food and cleaning the litter pan.

Her head hurt, and she felt the bumps and hesitations of the knits and purls of one of those odd rows pulling out all the way to the backs of her eyes. *Who names their cat Carnac?*

Bump . . . bump, bump, bump, and a smooth patch of knits pulled from the scarf, and then bump . . . bump, bump, bump again, the knots thumping like dots and dashes.

Shit. Peri froze, recognizing the Morse code end symbol knitted into her scarf. Panicking, she looked at the yarn spilled on her lap like the wasted message it was. She'd knitted herself a message in Morse code in case she drafted, like writing a message on her palm. And like an idiot, she hadn't recognized it. She'd never done that before. At least, not that she remembered.

This is wrong. Pulse fast, she looked up.

179

Impatient businessmen and parents wrangling toddlers fought for the chance to preboard. The two security stooges across from her were oblivious, one stretching as he looked for Allen, clearly anxious now that the area was getting busy. Suddenly, she didn't want to get on that plane.

Her mouth went dry, but her fingers moved smoothly as she carefully put the needles back on what was left. Three lines. Three out of nine.

Exhaling, she ran her fingers across the first row of knits and purls, feeling the sporadic purls as dots and dashes.

HARRY LENORD

Harry? She knew him. He worked out of the Seattle office.

GINA TRECHER

Shit, that was Harry's drafter. It was a list, and most of it was gone.

BILL IS CORRUPT.

Peri's breath caught, and it was as if the world turned sideways. *Bill is corrupt?* My God, her world was falling apart, and if she couldn't trust Bill, she couldn't trust anyone.

Slowly Peri pulled the last three lines of the message out and into oblivion. Fingers winding it back on the ball, she sent her eyes over the terminal as options flashed through her. Were they people to contact? Avoid? One thing was sure: she wasn't getting on the plane.

Giving her security detail a bland smile, she

stuffed the needles and yarn into her carry-on and took out her phone. Her first delight at the new glass technology had waned somewhere between trying to find her address book and the look the saleswoman had given her when Allen had shown her how to use the purchase app. She thought it ridiculous that she could change her car's color but didn't know how to access her voicemail.

Muscle memory would eventually triumph, though, and she scrolled through the dialed numbers to see whom she'd been talking to. Her brow furrowed when she realized her mother's number wasn't on it. Allen had said she'd called her Friday. Her frown deepened at an odd exchange, and wondering if her mother had moved, she hit callback, flicking her short hair out of the way as she looked up at her and Allen's security. They weren't here to keep her safe. They were here to keep her from running.

"Top of Charlotte," a pleasant but recorded voice came through Peri's phone, and her focus blurred. *Silas mentioned Charlotte.* "Hours are four thirty p.m. to ten a.m., seven days a week. To make a reservation, please leave a callback number."

Pulse quickening, Peri hung up before the beep. Silas had said she'd been on a task. Her black eye put it about two days ago—Jack's and her last mission. She wanted to retrace her steps without Opti—without Allen. If Opti didn't know she'd guessed the location of her last task, they wouldn't look for her there right away. *Maybe.*

Peri exhaled, casual as she shoved her phone in a pants pocket, not her purse. She was ditching the bag, but the phone she'd keep a while longer. Her wallet was already in her back pocket. She'd miss her purse, but walking off with it would raise red flags.

Eyes scanning the terminal, she quickly marked three women. All were her size, traveling alone, and at different gates. And thanks to the airline cramming too many flights into too little space, they'd all be boarding within thirty minutes of each other.

She wasn't getting on that plane. Allen wasn't her anchor. Her anchor was dead. A snarky alliance operative named Silas had more answers than she did. Charlotte might tell her something, but first she had to get them looking everywhere but where she was going.

An announcement came over the speaker that her flight would preboard in twenty minutes. Peri looked at her clean palm, fingers curling over it. She'd left her necklace pen at Allen's, at his insistence. The trip was supposed to be down-time, not a task, he'd said. *I'm a trusting idiot.*

The security guard chatting across from her brought her head up, and she smiled at Allen as he wove through the scattered luggage, two cups of blessed caffeine in his hands. Allen had been a perfect gentleman last night, sleeping on his couch and making her breakfast when she got up late. He might not be her anchor, but he'd been someone's—he had the pampering down.

"Here you go, Peri. Half a pump of caramel syrup. Just how you like it."

The cup was warm in her hand, and she took a careful sip. *Just how I like it?* she thought, deciding that, yes, this was good, making her wonder if Bill had found her diary already and was coaching Allen. The more comfortable she was, the more likely she'd believe their story. And she was becoming convinced it was a story. She'd seen Bill's thread of anger-driven fear last night. He needed something from her. The names she'd just destroyed, perhaps? Chances were good the original was still somewhere.

The three security people were getting uptight about the increasing press of passengers, and Peri unclenched her jaw when one of the women she'd been watching suddenly stood. Trundling her luggage behind her, she headed for the bathroom.

Crap. Why couldn't it have been the one with the Dries van Noten coat? "Watch my things?" she asked Allen as if they were the *best* of friends, and he nodded, oblivious. "Be right back," she added, making a point to set her purse beside him as she waited for the woman guard to stand. There was no way they were going to let her out of their sight, even to use the facilities.

"Sorry," Peri said to the female guard, regret almost a pain as she left the jacket and snappy cap beside Allen. "I hate plane commodes."

The guard looked to be just out of college, especially in the civvies she had on, but her Opti-boot-camp haircut gave her away. Peri hoped she wouldn't follow her in. Unless the woman had undergone additional training before joining Opti's security, her self-defense would be limited. Even so, downing anyone with a single blow was chancy.

Peri's gut tightened and she swung her arms as she followed the woman in the blah brown coat into the bathroom. Sure enough, her escort followed her in. Peri scanned the corners to find the cameras, and then turned to go into the first half of the bathroom while the woman in the brown coat wrangled her luggage the other way. She had a few moments to act—that was it.

Her side of the bathroom had a woman at the hand dryer. Peri grabbed a bunch of brown paper and soaked it into a soggy mess, using it to pat her neck and cool herself. Finally the woman at the dryer left. From the other wing of the bathroom, a toilet flushed.

Peri moved. With a decisive gesture, she flung the wad of paper at the camera in the corner with a strong sideways throw. It hit with a splat and stuck. Turning a hundred eighty degrees, she tucked her right leg and pivoted on her left. The guard's eyes widened. She reached for her absent gun, and Peri's right foot connected with her head. Crying out, the woman fell back into the stalls, legs and arms flailing. Peri followed her in, grabbing her hair and slamming her head down on the metal piping.

She quit moving. Peri backed up, breathless. A soft splat told her the wad of paper had fallen. Chances were good that no one would investigate if she could get the woman's legs tucked into the stall in time.

"Sorry," Peri whispered as she pulled the guard into an undignified, slumped, seated position, locking the door and rolling into the adjacent stall. Brushing herself off, she shook out her hair and strode boldly out and over to the other side of the bathroom. *If she was lucky . . .*

She was.

"What was that?" the woman said as she primped at the mirror. Her coat was off and draped over the raised handle of her rolling bag. Her purse was on the tiny shelf.

A pair of feet moved in one of the stalls. She didn't have time to take care of the camera. "I am so sorry," she said, grabbing her fist with her other hand and swinging her elbow into the side of the woman's head. The woman cried out as Peri struck, reaching for the sink as Peri followed it up with a punch to her jaw.

"Hey!" the woman coming out of a stall

exclaimed, but the first woman was down and Peri crouched beside her, feeling her pockets for her ticket. She hated this. These people were not criminals, but she needed the three minutes of disorientation this would give her.

"Boarding pass!" Peri demanded as she stood from her crouch, the woman's pass in hand, and the next woman coming into the bathroom changed her mind and fled. "Give me your boarding pass!" Peri said again, and the woman backed up into the stall, her face white.

"Take it!" she said, throwing it at Peri.

Peri scooped it up. Now Opti would focus on two flights. Grabbing the handle of the first woman's bag, she walked out of the bathroom.

"Stop her!" the woman in the bathroom shouted. "Someone call 911!"

She had ten seconds—tops. A wash of panic hit her as she realized she was committed and on her own. If they caught her now, she'd be incarcerated in an Opti jail forever.

I need a coat before I get to baggage claim, she thought, her fast pace fitting right in as she hustled down the hallway. Wadding the tickets up, she threw them away. There was a commotion behind her, an argument between two passengers, and she took a quick right into an open restaurant. Passing a table, she lifted the nearby unattended coat. It was scratchy with nylon, but it was long and the color was right. She picked up a man's hat at a food kiosk. Five seconds later she was back in the hallway. They'd be missed, but all she had to do was go faster than the uproar, and people usually wasted time trying to get someone to help them instead of taking action. Allen wouldn't make that mistake. She'd seen it in his eyes last night.

Adrenaline pounded through her when the "Mr. All-on" page went out, telling airport personnel to check in and watch for anything unusual. That was why she'd taken the tickets. They'd shut everything down if they thought she was catching another flight. Dealing with angry passengers would give her more time to get out of the airport. It was a trap with many holes, and she was going out the front door.

The woman's borrowed luggage was of higher quality than hers, holding a straight line as she trundled down the moving walkway, heading for baggage claim. Head lowered, she avoided the electric cart with six uniforms on it speeding past. Her phone hummed from a back pocket, and she shut it down when she recognized Bill's number.

But her cool façade was wearing thin. Staring dead ahead, she strode by the security gate. Someone else's cheap perfume rose from the borrowed coat, sticking in her throat. Clusters of suits and ties were refastening shoes and gathering belongings. She dodged around a family with a stroller. Baggage claim was down an escalator, and from there she'd be gone. She'd probably been on camera since popping that poor woman in the bathroom. The escalator would be one of the first records they looked at, seeing as everything funneled through it.

And yet she smiled as she imagined Allen, or maybe Bill, jammed into some trashy back room among half-empty coffee cups and wadded-up bags of chips, scanning security tapes to find her. By the time they looked, it'd be too late for anything but figuring out how she'd done it. The hat wasn't going to help much longer.

That would, though, she thought as she spotted a family headed for baggage, struggling with two kids in a twin stroller and two more trailing behind.

"Need some help?" Peri said, and the harried woman glanced up, her suspicion evaporating as she saw Peri's apparent innocence and free hand. "I can take a bag," she added, and the woman handed Peri hers.

"Thank you so much," the woman said as she grabbed the hand of the smallest child. "I'm not flying again until they have their driver's licenses."

"Where did you come in from?" Peri asked as she tucked in behind them to become part of a family instead of a single woman on her own.

"Boston," she said, her accent heavy as she got on the escalator and sighed. "It's my granddad's birthday. Maybe his last one. Or I'd never fly out here with all of them."

They descended slowly, the kids trying to walk backward while holding on to the moving handrail. At the base of the escalator, a pair of industrial boots turned into a set of thick blue trousers. There was a weapon holstered to the man's waist, and Peri looked away before she and the family got low enough for the guy in the blue to see a face.

"Your shoe is untied," she said, dropping down to the little girl beside her, and the mother badgered her to stand still, worried Peri wouldn't finish before they got to the end of the escalator. Peri's fingers fumbled, and the moving steps began to sink level. She could see his boots, and heart pounding, she stood, turning to grab the rolling bag. Looking back as if worried it might catch, she stepped off the escalator in the wake of the noisy family.

Heart in her throat, she almost cried out when that stupid rolling bag snagged, but the guard was on his cell phone. She'd made it. "Do you have it from here?" Peri asked the woman as she shoved the bag's handle at her. "My carousel is the other direction." Not waiting for an answer, she walked away. A quick glance at her watch: she'd been alone for almost four minutes. The glass doors were just ahead.

But then her breath caught and she made a sharp right turn. *Allen.* Somehow he'd gotten down here before her, phone to his ear and watching everyone. *Damn it all to hell and back.*

Fingers shaking, Peri got in line at the coffee hut, hoping her borrowed, off-the-rack coat and black slacks would make her invisible among the businesspeople. She'd seen his wiry strength and scars last night. He was bigger than she was, and she had no doubt he'd use it to his advantage. If she had to fight, she wanted a cup of hot coffee in hand.

"I can help who's next!" the barista called, and she stepped forward, ordering a venti. She had cash, but she turned her phone back on and used it instead, knowing it would pop up on their security in about fifteen minutes. She'd either be in Opti's custody or long gone by then. There was a pen by the register, and she took it, keeping it in her hand to gouge with if needed.

She edged to the pickup counter, going still when Allen's pacing brought him close. Freedom was a glass door away. No matter what happened next, she was gaining that curb. If she could do it without him seeing her, all the better.

"I don't know, *Bill*," he said into his phone, clearly irate. "She was complacent enough this morning. I grounded everything, but she's gone. I doubt a plane was her goal, but we're watching to see if she tries to exchange it for another flight. I'm at baggage claim."

Her order came up, and she took her large coffee, wishing he'd look the other way.

"To see if she's going to walk out the front door.

Why do you think?" Allen snapped, then abruptly ended the call. "What an ass," he added softly, and then their eyes met.

Allen's lips parted. "Hey!" he exclaimed, hesitating when she ambled forward to meet him. The world waited behind double glass doors, and she was tired of being afraid.

"This is for lying to me!" Peri shouted, squeezing the cup to make the lid pop off, and then tossing the contents at him.

He ducked, coming up angry as the scalding liquid nicked him, but her foot was already swinging. He blocked the first kick, and screaming, she backed him up onto the door's sensor pad with two front kicks that never landed. Cooler air blew in, smelling of exhaust and icy pavement.

"And this is for making me think I trusted you!" she shouted, grabbing a suitcase off a cart and throwing it at him with a cry of frustration.

Allen shifted out of its way, and Peri lunged forward, grabbing his arm to swing him into the unbreakable glass doors. He hit with a satisfying thud, groaning as he slid down—out cold. Cars had stopped, and she stood over him, breathing hard. "It was a very bad vacation," she said to the man whose suitcase she'd thrown, and he nervously smiled, clearly trying to stay out of it.

Chin lifted, Peri strode out, crossing the road and making cars stop. A shuttle was leaving, and she swung onto it. She jerked, shocked, at the top of the stairs when she realized there was no driver, then hit the SAME key to input wherever the previous passenger had. It pulled away even before she'd found a seat.

"You forget three years and everything changes," she whispered. The shakes started right about then. She was alone. For the first time in five years, she was completely alone, and she felt the pen in her pocket for reassurance. What if she drafted? She'd never know what had happened. Enough blank spots in her memory, and she'd go insane.

"What are you doing, Peri?" she whispered. But she knew. She was running for control of her life, for the answers to what had happened in Charlotte, for the knowledge of whether she was a dirty operative, or if just her anchor had been.

Fingers trembling, Peri took off her watch and shoved it between the seat and the backrest. She had a feeling that Jack had given it to her and it probably had a tracker in it. Her phone, too, was suspect; popping open the side of it, she took the wafer-thin, glass SIM card out and dropped the phone under the seat. The wallpaper of a desert sunrise didn't mean anything to her, but she was sure she'd taken it.

Exhaling with what sounded almost like a sob, she leaned her head against the cold window, feeling the bus shift and jerk as it worked its way past passenger pickup, gathering people as it went. Someone was probably going to a hotel, and from there, she could get a bus ticket to Charlotte. That's where the answers were.

But she pulled to a full, adrenaline-pounding stiffness when out the window of the bus she saw a familiar face.

"Silas," she breathed, and the man in an exquisitely cut brown jacket leaning against the pylon met her eyes, not smiling as he folded up his paper and let it drop to the planter beside him. She tensed, but the bus jerked back into motion, and her heart pounded when he crossed the road and headed into the airport.

He knew about Charlotte—had told her it was her last task. He'd know that's where she was going.

Great.

CHAPTER
THIRTEEN

Silas got out of the cab, his hand going to his head when he thought he'd left his hat behind, only to find it right where it belonged. Checking the street addresses against the list of Charlotte's Internet cafés on his phone, he crossed the street, hand raised to stop a slow-moving car.

Electric bikes darted unnervingly around him, and he eyed an erratic, low-flying drone, relaxing as he decided it was a courier and therefore not a threat. He was in university territory, and his high-end coat was getting noticed. *She'll know I'm not a student anyway,* he thought as he took his tie off and stuffed it in his coat pocket.

It had been almost twenty-four hours, and if he didn't locate her soon, Opti might find her first. She'd done a fair job of muddling her destination, but they weren't stupid. Once they ruled out her apartment, they'd realize she'd bucked her deep conditioning against being alone and focus on the obvious: the city her last task had been in. He figured she'd ditch her phone and search for both answers and anonymity at an Internet-access café, but after finding nothing at the three that were closest to the bus station and claimed to have gen-three glass technology, he was starting to wonder if she'd instead gone to the library and their slower system.

Either way, his window was closing. Opti might know her conditioning, but he knew her soul, and he was counting on that to keep him one step ahead of them.

"University Dregs," he whispered, feet scuffing to a halt as he looked past the crackling e-board shorting out and into the modern if sparsely decorated café full of students soaking up the free hotspot. "Thank God," he whispered, seeing her sitting alone at a small glass table, that same black coat he'd seen her steal at the airport draped over her shoulders. Her head was bent low over the glass screen built into the top, a ceramic mug of coffee and that man's hat beside her. Even as he watched, she tapped a new phrase into the search engine and hit the ENTER key with enough force to make the screen phase and her coffee ripple. Clearly things weren't going well, and she ran her hand through her short hair in a gesture of frustration as she looked up.

Her expression blanked when she realized two young men across the store were gesturing for her attention. Her model's cheekbones, long neck, perfect complexion, and toned dancer's body had gotten her noticed, and he shook his head in memory when that full sweet smile of hers blossomed with just the right amount of annoyance to convince without ticking them off. Falling against each other, they dramatically pretended to be crushed.

Okay. He'd found her. Getting her to trust him wasn't going to happen, but he knew Peri would risk a lot if she was hungry, tired, and dirty. She looked all three.

Taking a deep breath, he entered, head down as he went to the to-go counter and out of her direct sight instead of ordering from the store tablets at the tables. Peri looked half starved, and he added a muffin to his medium, straight-up black coffee, taking it in a metallic-footed store mug instead of a to-go cup. Turning, he unbuttoned his coat in the warmth and noise. Peri was scrolling through a list of recent local crimes, choosing one before sitting back and sipping her coffee while the screen loaded. She looked frustrated and—so well hidden he almost missed it—scared out of her mind.

What am I doing? he asked himself as the barista put his paper-wrapped muffin on the counter; peeved, he vowed she wasn't going to get one bite. She'd made her choice. He wasn't her anchor to coddle her, reinforcing the pap that Opti filled her head with that she deserved it by right.

And yet, seeing her last night, numb and in shock from something she didn't recall, had shaken him. She was so rare, so fragile in her uniqueness—one in a hundred thousand able to twist time, and even more rare in having the skill set and drive to use it. It had been a painful relief when she'd gotten snarky, hiding her fear that she'd been cut adrift again. Even more obvious was that she didn't know him.

Closing his eyes, he exhaled to calm himself, not wanting to add to Peri's mood. She looked as irate as he felt, tapping the store-supplied stylus against the touch screen with a frustrated quickness. She hadn't changed at all—just as moody and irritating as ever. Her paranoia would be in overdrive—for good reason. He couldn't simply walk up to her and tell her they had to work together to end the very organization she depended upon. She'd never believe him.

Silas's jaw clenched when someone knocked into her. And then he stiffened when, with a snap, the room reset and the last four seconds replayed, Peri adroitly shifting in her chair at the right instant to remain untouched. Time caught up, meshed, and he shook himself, a cold feeling slipping through him when Peri, oblivious to the skip-hop, leaned forward to read the screen.

Uneasy, he pushed off from the counter. He'd watched her jump three times to escape the airport. It was doubtful she even knew she had drafted. Her mind was flirting with collapse, and that he felt responsible bothered him. It had been too large a task; too much of her life had needed to be erased.

It was her choice, he reminded himself, but he still felt betrayed as he came closer, halting just within her range of sight and waiting to be noticed. Power and recognition meant more to her than he liked, but her determined drive had drawn him regardless. Even now, years later, he could feel it, and his jaw clenched.

As if sensing it, she looked up, her hazel eyes and long lashes vivid against the heavy eyeliner she'd used to muddle any facial recognition software. Her shock melted into a quickly quashed panic. She was afraid of him. "You," she said, eyes darting to the perimeter for others even as she blanked her screen. "What are you doing here?"

"It's just me. I'm alone. You don't have to run."

"You're alliance, aren't you?" she asked. Nodding, Silas set his coffee down, the electrical field in the base engaging the table's heating circuits with an audible click. Her eyes were determinedly not on the muffin, but they lingered on his tablet tucked under an arm, and he set it tauntingly on the table between them. Immediately her gaze rose from it, traveling over his pressed shirt tucked into his high-end jeans, then dropping to his leather boots and belt, and finally his coat. Her eyebrows arched in question; he shifted his coat so she could see he had no weapon.

"I do so love the scent of imported cashmere," she said. "Armani?"

He dropped his hat on the table, annoyed that she'd found the one nerve he had and stomped on it. So he was a clotheshorse. So what? "So you'll understand if you dump your coffee on me like you did Allen why I'll throw mine in your face," he warned as he took the hard-backed chair across from her. Still she said nothing, staring at him with that assessing gaze, and he ran a hand over his short-cropped hair to smooth it in unease.

"I should have gone to the library," she muttered.

But she hadn't run, and Silas took a sip of coffee, relieved. "I think this is what you're looking for," he said, hitting a few buttons on his tablet to bring up a news story. "Go on. Read it," he said, pushing it toward her. "I'm not stalling. The alliance doesn't know I'm here."

"No?" Suspicious, she used her stylus to drag it over, and he swallowed hard when she flicked her bangs in a gesture so familiar that Silas felt an unwelcome flash of hurt. Eyes darting, she read the highlights about the security guard and CEO found dead two days ago. It was being called a botched robbery, but it was how the guard had died that he wanted her to see.

Her signature killing style was all over it.

Peri's fingers were trembling by the time she got to the end. "Is there any doubt why the alliance is trying to put an end to Opti?" he said lightly.

Her eyes flicked up, and he spitefully took a bite of muffin, corralling the crumbs onto the scrap of wax paper. Her stomach growled, and he wondered why he was being so nasty—except that it had been a long, hard year when she'd left.

"He must have killed me first," she said, her words almost lost in the surrounding conversations. "I don't kill anyone unless they kill me first."

"Whatever helps you sleep at night," he said.

Peri's eyes narrowed. "Did you call the police? How far behind is the alliance?"

He licked his fingers, elbows on the table as he leaned in close enough that she could smell the sugar on his breath. "I already said I'm here alone. But as for Opti?" He shrugged.

"You're not afraid I'll draft and run?" she said, eyebrows high.

He had to get her out of here. Clearly the enticement of food wasn't going to do it—even half starved as she was—but the lure of knowledge might. "You won't risk forgetting this." Confident, he took his tablet back and tucked it into an inside coat pocket.

She watched it go, and his pulse quickened as he saw her calculate the risk of making a scene in the busy café. "I could just leave and look it up later."

He nodded as if considering it, then went cold in the sudden realization that he'd made a mistake. He shouldn't be here. He should have let someone else do it. But no one knew her better, that she was like a wild horse: canny, indomitable—and likely to run at the clink of a stone. "Go ahead," he said, calling her bluff. "Make both our days."

Expression cross, she flopped back into the chair to stare at him, probably trying to figure out why he was here. There was a nasty-looking pen by her hand, and he watched as she shifted her fingers and drew it close. "I'm not a dirty agent," she said, chin lifted.

"Then why did you run away?"

"It seemed like a good idea at the time." Her eyes avoided his. "They think I'm corrupt. I'm going to prove I'm not."

He snorted, sucking muffin crumbs out of his teeth as if he had all the time in the world. "Anyone who can do what you do is dirty."

Eyes narrowed, she leaned toward him. "I work for the government. I am a soldier."

Silas flicked a look at her hands, carefully flat on the table. The pen was gone, hidden somewhere. She'd never come with him unless she felt in control, and he looked at the ceiling, rocking his chair back on two legs. "Sure you are."

Even expecting it, he jumped when she reached out, grabbed him by the coat, and yanked the chair down on all fours. "I am a soldier," she growled. "Say it."

Her hand gripped him just under his chin, both soft and strong at the same time. "Okay, you're a soldier."

Satisfied, she let go.

"A corrupt soldier who hires herself out to the highest bidder," he added, not liking that people had noticed and were watching.

"I might lose memories, but my morals don't change," she said. "I wouldn't do a dirty job now, so I didn't then." But her eyes became crafty, worrying him. "You need my help."

Grunting, Silas put his arms on the table. Damn, he'd forgotten how good she was. "Something happened up there," he said, tapping his coat where the tablet lay. "I want to know what. I think you do, too."

"I'm not helping you," she said. "You're trying to shut Opti down. We do a lot of good."

"For the Billion by Thirty club, sure, but not for me," he said with a bitter laugh. "Not for that guy at the counter. Opti is going down regardless of what I find. If you're corrupt, you're going down with it. If you're not, I'm the only one who can help you clear your name. Help me, and maybe you'll survive. Maybe walk away. Live your life."

She didn't move, but he could see the thoughts sift through her, and he chuckled. "You think you can use me and lose me?" he said, and she flushed. "Go ahead and try. But keep this in mind, Peri Reed. I *knew* where you were going. I *know* what you need, and *I* can take you wherever your intuition leads you."

"So why are you talking to me?" she said bitingly.

Right to the point, he thought, fiddling with his coffee to make the heating circuits click on and off, until she noticed and he quit. "I, ah, need your help to get up there," he admitted. "I don't have your skills."

Peri's eyebrows rose. "You seriously think I'm going to *work* with you? Right after you told me you think I'm corrupt and a joke?"

"I never said you were a joke."

"You said I wasn't a soldier," she said. "I can't work with you. You're too tall to be subtle and you'll scream like a little boy at the first hint of trouble."

Brow furrowing, Silas looked her up and down, crossing his arms to make his biceps bulge. "I can take care of myself."

"You will slow . . . me . . . down," she said, her finger tapping the table in time with her words. "Yeah, I see your pretty muscles, but I bet you can't run a mile without throwing up."

His lip twitched. He wasn't built for speed, and he always felt like a hulk next to her slim quickness—even if his mind was as dexterous as hers. More so, maybe. "I'll keep up."

She leaned in, daring him. "I'd be surprised if you've ever seen the inside of a firing range, Mr. Muscles. I. Can't. Use. You."

Peeved, Silas leaned to within inches of her, his breath held as he quashed the thought that her eyes, a deep hazel that could morph into green depending on the light and her mood, were what had first attracted him to her—and they hadn't changed. "I'm actually pretty good with a weapon, but I'm not the one in trouble, Ms. Reed. You've been drafting, and you don't even know it."

She jerked back, her sudden flash of angst making him almost regret his words. Face white, she scanned the noisy coffeehouse. "I have not," she said, but her hands were under the table, probably holding that pen of hers like the security blanket it was.

"Yes, you have," he said. "I wasn't lying when I said I used to work for Opti."

Peri fixed him with a tight stare. "You trained to be an Opti anchor? You took Opti training and then left them to work for the alliance? Are you kidding me?"

Silas forced his hands to unclench. "Most of us at the alliance worked for Opti at some point. Until we realized it was corrupt to the core and left."

"You washed out," she said, and his eyes darted to hers.

"I quit," he said tightly.

She was looking at him in distrust, but under it he could see her desperate need. He'd been playing on all the wrong triggers. She needed him like she needed a knife and a pistol. She needed him like a black suit and a fast car. He was a tool, a safety net. And right now, seeing the fear in the back of her eyes, he knew she'd do anything to keep him from walking out that door.

"Prove it," she challenged him, but he could tell she badly wanted him to succeed.

"What, here?" he said, his attention traveling over the noisy throng.

Peri bit her bottom lip. "You don't have to bring it back, just tell me where I drafted. What did I forget?"

He almost had her, and he ran a quick hand over his hair as if thinking it over.

"Fine," she said, and she stood, shocking him even as she wavered. "This conversation is over. Can I have your tablet, please?"

She stuck her hand out, expecting him to give it to her, but she froze when he took her hand in his instead. "You were seen leaving the bathroom," he said, and she stared at him, fear in her eyes as his voice took on the singsong pattern of an anchor bringing back a memory. "It took three guards, but they got you down, and then you jumped. In the draft, you tripped a businessman into another to distract security and avoid them. That was right before you stole the coat. They caught you again at the top of the escalator until you drafted and hid at the jewelry stand until the family with the stroller showed up and you went downstairs with them."

Slowly Peri sat, her hand loose in his grip.

"It took me a few minutes to get downstairs, but the next time you drafted was when Allen saw you at the coffee counter."

Clearly scared, she pulled her hand away. "I didn't draft at the coffee counter."

"It was tiny," he said, pity reaching his voice despite his intentions. "A skip, if you like, turning away at just the right moment in the draft so he didn't see you. Just now, before I sat down, you skipped about three seconds so that kid in the corner who looks like he hasn't shaved in a week wouldn't bump you. Peri, you escaped Opti.

You're good, but it would have been impossible without drafting, and you know it."

It was hard to tear her down like this, especially knowing how fragile she was, and Silas felt like an ass as he took in her pale face. "If you're lying . . . ," she threatened.

His anger was gone, sponged away by her fear. "Where are you staying? I'll bring all three jumps back. If you like what you see, we can work together. If you still don't trust me—"

"Trust has nothing to do with it," she interrupted. "You want to shut down Opti."

"Trust has everything to do with it," he said bitterly, and her eyes dropped. "Finding out what happened up there is the only way you're going to clear your name. What happens after that is secondary. Let's go."

Chin lifted, she looked at him. "I haven't said I'd work with you."

"Not with your lips, no."

She grimaced, clearly thinking. "I don't have a place yet," she said softly.

He had her, maybe not for anything longer than an hour, but he had her. He stood. "I do." Feeling light-headed, Silas took up his hat and started for the door. Her Opti conditioning never to be alone would get her moving faster than anything else. Still, it didn't feel as good as he thought it would when she closed out her session on her borrowed Internet link and got to her feet.

"Why are you helping me?" she asked as she shrugged into her coat, that ugly, man's hat already on her head.

Silas's teeth clenched. "I'm not helping you. I'm getting the job done."

Together they wove through the busy tables, and he fought with himself not to clear the way for her. He wasn't her damned anchor, and this association would last only until he got what he wanted. She paused at the door to drop her mug in the wash bin, and he leaned over her as he set his mug beside hers, breathing in her scent, almost hidden under stale fear and worry, to whisper, "That, and I'm impressed at how you continue to function with minimal drafts. Not bad, Peri. Not bad at all."

Blinking, she looked up at him, the slight praise clearly meaning more than it should. "It's patently obvious you don't like me, Silas, but I'm not corrupt. And I'm the only way you're ever going to find out what really happened, so how about lightening up a little."

He smiled bitterly as he pushed open the door. "I could say the same thing."

Her head was up as she went out before him, and he belatedly realized he'd opened the door for her, a common enough courtesy, but one he'd vowed he wouldn't do. The cold wind blew up from the street, and she hunched deeper into that coat she'd stolen. "This is very bad for my asthma," she whispered.

"Excuse me?" he blurted, the phrase from their past shaking him to his core. *She still uses it? Maybe there is something left after all.*

But her eyes held only confusion. "Um. I just say that . . . sometimes," she muttered, her melancholy deepening.

Hunching into his coat, he pointed up the street. Silent, she fell into step beside him, clearly not realizing that she'd lengthened her steps into matching his suddenly slower pace so they would strike the same beat even if she was a good eight inches shorter.

God almighty, he thought, trying to shift his pace back to his normal length and failing. She was beside him, and yet not, missing a man she didn't remember, one who had lied to her for three years, mourning him even if she had killed him.

And he was going to try to bring that back?

CHAPTER FOURTEEN

Silas's hotel room was in one of Charlotte's high-rises, twenty-fourth floor, corner suite. The elegance of the elevator alone had made Peri feel like a homeless woman, still dressed in her traveling black slacks and that woman's borrowed, no, *stolen* coat, and a hat that smelled of its previous owner. She knew she wasn't smelling that great either after sixteen hours on a bus. The couple in the elevator with them hadn't said a word, with their perfume, cologne, and expensive jewelry. No one could make you feel inferior without your permission, but she was usually the one in the upscale fashions, and the knockoff coat wasn't doing it for her—not when Silas had the real thing, reminding her of black cars and laughter over sparkling wine.

Getting to his room and finding that it had all the niceties did almost as much to relax her as the shower she'd insisted on taking before letting him near her again. She was still hungry, but at least the caked eyeliner was gone and she didn't stink. Even better, the steam had gotten most of the wrinkles out of her clothes. A real anchor would have gone downstairs to the boutique and purchased something else for her to wear, but washing her underwear and socks in the sink would do—for now.

Clean and dressed, her feet in hotel-supplied slippers, and her wet hair bumping about her ears, Peri sat in a cushy chair away from the window and tried not to think about the thin sandwich she'd gotten out of a vending machine eight hours ago. She was confident that damp clothes weren't her usual attire when defragmenting memories, but sitting in a strange man's hotel room wearing nothing but a robe wasn't going to happen. The blinds were angled to block most of the light bouncing in off the neighboring tower and her head rested on a pillow smelling of new fabric. Silas's fingers pushed at her temples with firm, professional strength. Clearly his claim to be an anchor was valid.

His comment yesterday about blind trust bothered her. She'd been a fool, not just for walking away with Allen, but for working with Jack for three years and never suspecting they were doing non-Opti-sanctioned jobs, ignorant of enough that she fell in love with the man. Because even though she couldn't remember him, there was an ache.

"This would go faster if you unclenched your jaw," Silas said drily, and Peri forced her shoulders down. His touch on her temples was not invasive, but her mind was too full.

"How long has it been since you've done this?" she countered.

"None of your business."

Peri exhaled in a long, slow sound. That he smelled like leather and his fingers felt like a cool ribbon of water somehow wasn't helping. "I don't think you were ever in Opti."

"I was there," he growled. "How can I be expected to work when you won't relax?"

"How can I relax when I'm *starving!*" she exclaimed.

His fingers pulled away and she opened her eyes to see him stomping across the blind-darkened room to the bed. Shoulders hunched in anger, he picked up the bedside phone. "I swore I wasn't going to do this," he said, punching a number with savage ferocity. "I was *not* going to do this!" he added, glaring at her as he brandished the receiver.

Sitting up, Peri finger-combed her damp hair, more peeved than curious.

"Hi," he said flatly as someone on the other end picked up. "This is Silas Denier in Twenty-four thirty-five. Can I have two strawberry milkshakes and a plate of fries sent up? If you can get them here in ten minutes, there's a twenty in it for you." Setting the phone back in the cradle with a dull crack, he sat on the bed and stared at the wall.

I love milkshakes and fries. Guilt swam up, and she shoved it aside. "Thank you," she said softly. "I don't have any money to pay you back."

Wiping a hand over his chin, he said, "I've noticed that about you."

He was angry about things she had no control over. "I didn't know I was running until—"

"Until what?"

Until I destroyed half the message I'd left myself? Until I found out Bill was corrupt? That I might be, too? "I didn't actually plan this, okay?" she said, her damp fingers smelling of hotel shampoo.

Silas turned, his empty expression taking her aback. "I'm not your slave. Got it?"

"Slave!" Her headache returned full force. "Is

that what you think anchors are? No wonder you washed out." Ticked, she put her feet up on the coffee table.

He rose and began to pace, his agitation far more than a plate of fries and two shakes deserved. "I'm *not* going to make your coffee, wait on you, or rub your feet. As soon as I know what happened in that office, we are *done*. Understand?"

Sniffing, Peri brushed at her clothes. "You have the personality of an armadillo. You say I'm corrupt—without proof—dangling the truth before me, accessible only if I help you bring down everything I believe in. Forgive me for having a hard time letting you into my mind."

Hand over his mouth in frustration, he turned to face her. "You're right. I'm sorry," he said as his hand dropped. "I have no evidence that you're corrupt. You're probably a very nice person. Someone who only kills people who kill her first."

And his apology started so nicely, too. "That's as good as it's going to get, huh?"

"Yup." Silas bobbed his head, the golden light leaking around the blinds, casting stripes on him. Her gaze, drawn by the glow, traveled up his narrow waist to the hint of hair showing from behind his not-so-pressed-anymore shirt. Her eyes rose farther to his strong jaw—currently clenched in anger. The hint of stubble made him look . . . more than accessible. Familiar, almost.

"You know what I'd really like to know?" she

said, watching the way the sun moved around him, catching the stubble on his jaw and making him glow.

"What?" he said flatly, his thoughts clearly on something else.

"If Ridley Scott ever finished his *Blade Runner* sequel."

He started, the blank wonder on his face giving her pause. "Ah, yes, he did." Mood softened, he sat down. "It was really good."

"Mmmm." Her focus went past him, distant. "I wonder if I saw it," she mused.

"I've got an idea," he said, jolting her from her reverie as he came back and pushed her feet off the coffee table to sit right in front of her. "Give me a foot," he said, holding out a hand.

Suspicious, she eyed him from under her bangs. "You just said—"

He reached for one, taking the slipper off and letting it drop. "I was speaking metaphorically," he said, and she stifled a shiver at the feeling of his hands around her bare foot. "It's a relaxation technique that's helpful with antisocial people who don't like to be touched, a mix of reflexology and Swedish massage."

"I like being touched. Just not by you," she said, but he'd begun twisting his hands around her foot to make it ache wonderfully, and she didn't pull away, even when he rubbed his thumb along the arch and she had to bite her lip to stop herself from releasing a groan. She wouldn't give him the satisfaction.

"I can get rid of your headache," he said, head down over her feet. "Promise."

She hadn't told him about the headache, but what he was doing felt really good. Not altogether trusting it, she eased into the chair to stare at the high ceiling.

"Okay," he said as his touch became firmer. "Let's see where you're hiding your tension."

"Ow!" she cried, jerking when his thumb ran along the side of her foot. "Not so hard!"

But he grabbed her ankle and pulled it back. "That's your back and hips. If I can loosen those up, I'll have a chance at your headache. Just relax. Deep breaths in through your nose and out through your mouth. Haven't you ever had a massage?"

"Not like this," she said, and he actually smiled. It was real, and finding comfort in that, she closed her eyes. The more she relaxed, the better it felt. Slowly the muscles in her back eased, and then her neck . . . and finally her shoulders.

Silas took up her other foot, the expected jolt of pain quickly dulling as the muscles lost their tension. "Thank you," she said when his pressure-point work shifted to a more relaxing motion. She wasn't an idiot. She knew everything was connected, and if she was too uptight to let him touch her face and shoulders, this worked.

"Okay." Silas's voice was low with a new confidence. "Tell me about your spot."

Peri's eyes opened, the lazy lassitude she was drifting in vanishing. "Excuse me?"

His hands kept moving with a firm, decisive motion. "Your safe spot," he said. "The place you go in your mind to find peace."

Reassured, she closed her eyes. "Oh. I've never had to practice that. My anchors can usually bring everything back without a problem."

He pinched a nerve, and she jerked. "Ow?" she said, not pulling away because she probably deserved it.

"This isn't a recall technique," he said. "It's to bring you to a centered position."

He sounded like a psychologist, which was both reassuring and unnerving. "What branch of Opti did you wash out of?" she asked. There was no answer, but his pressure on her foot didn't change. "Silas, what branch?"

"I didn't wash out. I quit." His thumb ran up the outside arch of her foot again to show that all the tension was gone. "Find a spot. Tell me what you liked about it. How you felt there."

Fine. She was willing to do almost anything if he'd keep rubbing her feet. Her headache was almost gone. "Can I pick a person instead?"

His motion on her foot hesitated. "Ah, no."

She held her breath, exhaling when she had an idea. "When I was a kid, I spent a few summers at

215

my grandparents' farm. They had a couple of trees right in the middle of one of their fields where there was an old graveyard. Just a few faded markers. Couldn't even read them. But it was peaceful, and the wind was sweet." Peri smiled, and the last of her headache vanished. Maybe there was more to this than she gave him credit for.

"What did it smell like?"

Her reluctance to tell him something so personal vanished at his logic. The triggers of scent and touch were important in making a successful connection between a drafter and an anchor, and so she was willing to give him more and see where it went.

"The earth was both hard from roots and loamy between them," she said, fingers moving as if she could feel the black soil. "The bark was smooth to the touch and detailed in grays. I could be alone there, just me and the sun and the wind, and like the world, it smelled like dry dirt down low, and like freedom when I climbed into the leafy green."

She was totally relaxed, even if recalling the scent of the dirt seemed to stick in her.

"Centered and still," Silas said, no longer working pressure points, but maintaining a gentle touch to tell her he was there, listening. "Peri?"

"Mmmm?"

"Do you want to try to remember the airport?"

"Sure." She could do that, and she cracked an

eye to see the bands of the noon light on the ceiling. The TV had gone on in the room next door, and the drone of sound was comforting.

"You were anxious," he said, and she closed her eyes to deepen the connection so as to let him in. "Now you're calm and nothing can touch you, but then, you were anxious."

Though unable to remember the precise recall technique used by her last anchor, she'd worked with enough professionals through the years to know what to do—and she relaxed.

"You had a coffee and you sipped it to allay suspicions," he said, and Peri fastened on the memory that she still retained, shoving away the concern that he'd been spying on her even then. "You set it down when the woman you'd marked went to the bathroom. The planes were starting to board. You were ready to act."

In her thoughts, she was in the sun, but she knew she'd sat in the shade at the airport. She could smell the wind and dirt, taste the caramel from the coffee Allen had brought her, but it mixed with bitter, expensive chocolate. A flight announcement echoed in her memory, and the flash of a white face in the haze of a holographic monitor came and went.

The memories of several events were meshing. Silas's calming techniques were not mixing well with her last anchor's, but she could do this, and she focused on the known impressions of the airport, pulse quickening when Silas's confidence suddenly congealed about her conviction. He had found her fully, his presence in her mind professionally light but certain as they began to share the same vision, each leading the other. He'd found her mind with unusual quickness, settling in with a cool detachment that she appreciated, but if he had once been an Opti psychologist, he'd have the knack. Satisfied, she slipped deeper into the light trance.

"Safe now," he soothed as if she might be afraid, "but you were in danger, and you had a plan. A guard went with you."

A flash of a man's pale face lit by a monitor came and went again, and Peri shoved it aside in favor of crowds of people and rolling bags. "I went in first," she said, taking up the narration as she felt wisps of unrealized fragments gathering in the background of her mind. It was almost as if Peri could sense Silas ordering them, seeing them before she did. "I had to wait for a woman to leave, but it gave me time to throw a wad of paper at the camera."

She caught the scent of the hotel shampoo and the cloying dust from the grove. *No, from the carpet.* She frowned as the image of the underside of a bed intruded, drawn by the conflicting sensations of clean hair and dirty carpet. The warp and weft was unforgivably matted, but where her fingers were splayed open over it, it was dusty and uncrushed. Her palm lay open in welcome. A crumpled sock lay at the edge of shadow and golden light, a blue button beside it. It was a talisman, and she worried she'd forget it. The fragments didn't mesh with the fading impressions of the airport. They didn't fit, and she sensed Silas's rising concern.

"I knocked the guard into a stall," Peri said, forcing her thoughts from the contented feeling the image of the sock under the bed filled her with. "I followed her in and hit her head on the pipe."

The expected empty ache of missing memories thickened, a morass of conflicting images. Instead of a crowded airport, Peri saw a flash of pure gold light from under a door across a matted carpet. It didn't fit, and her heart hurt as more fragments intruded, scaring her. "Silas . . . ," she whispered, and she felt him take her hands as his presence in her strengthened.

"This isn't a draft fragment. It's just forgotten," he whispered as he saw it, too. "Peri, where are you?"

"I'm safe!" she half moaned, her chest clenching in grief as she gripped his hands. She was safe. In her lost memory, the golden light fell over her skin. Her robe was almost off and the warmth of a body she knew and loved was above her. Love and a pleasant exhaustion suffused her. *It's Jack,* she groaned in her thoughts, and Jack smiled down at her, the glow in his eyes telling her that he loved her.

"Jack!" Peri cried as she jerked upright. Pain lanced through her and Silas gasped when she pushed him from her mind and she was again alone in her thoughts.

Grief-stricken, she stared at Silas as he knelt before her, seeing his pity and full understanding as the memory of Jack's and her love came cascading back. Jack was dead. Allen had said so. Silas had said the same. She had loved him, and he was gone forever because . . . *she'd killed him.*

"Oh God . . . ," she moaned, pulling her feet up onto the chair and holding her knees to herself. The jolt of shoving Silas out of her mind was a bitter slap, and the black of her traveling clothes shocked through her, her thoughts expecting the white robe Jack had brought from home. Angry, she pushed Silas's hands away, curling up in the chair and hiding her face. It had been a memory, not a draft that needed fragmenting, and it hurt.

"Shhhh," he said, putting his arms around her anyway. "Let it go, Peri. Let it go."

"You bastard," she said between her gasping breaths as the scent of leather grew heady. "You knew I'd remember that."

"No, I didn't," he said, and she looked up, the lump in her throat hurting. "I'm so sorry," he added, the knowing reflected in his eyes telling her he'd seen it all, and she hated him for it. "I was trying to bring back your drafts at the airport. I had no idea this would happen. You shouldn't be able to remember anything about Jack."

Peri got a clean breath in, then another. "You're an Opti psychologist," she managed. "Are you working for them? Is this some sick way of trying to bring my three years back?"

He shook his head. "No. I really am with the alliance. I left Opti a long time ago. I don't believe in what they do. The lies they tell you."

Peri dropped her eyes. Her life was a misery. "They don't allow drafters to leave. Ever."

She felt cold when Silas pulled away. "You always have a choice," he said, and she closed her eyes, the image of Jack swimming up anew. She had only that one memory, but tied to it was three years of emotion. *I loved him.*

"That was Jack?" Silas said, awkward as he knelt before her. "Blond hair? Blue eyes?"

An entire person reduced to a description of hair and eyes. She nodded, thinking it was unfair to remember love but not remember how she had found it or how it had ended.

Silas rocked to his feet. "This is incredible," he breathed, his focus distant.

"Jack was not corrupt!" she exclaimed, not knowing why she was defending him when she herself didn't believe his innocence.

"I don't care," he said, and when her eyes widened in outrage, he added, "Okay, I do, but,

Peri, listen"—he dropped back down and took one of her hands—"you shouldn't be able to remember him at all," he said eagerly. "It was a memory knot, and you untangled it, not me."

Memory knot! Fear pushed out the heartache. "We're done here."

Scared, she stood, and Silas lurched backward out of her way. Spotting her socks drying on the windowsill, she scooped them up. They were still damp, but they were all she had, and grief hammered at her as she sat on the bed and pulled them on, first one, then the other.

"You're okay," Silas said, shoulders hunched in excitement. "I know Opti has told you that memory knots are like rats fleeing a sinking boat, but they aren't. It's just your mind trying to recover something."

"Something that might drive me to MEP," she said, not liking the feel of damp wool.

"But it was a real memory," he protested. "Not a draft to be fragmented or solidified."

"I know. I was there!" she exclaimed, uncomfortable that he'd seen her depth of emotion.

"Don't you get it?" he said, eyes bright. "It was gone. Three years, you said. But if I can help return a memory to you that I didn't see once, I can do it again. With enough clues, I can bring back everything that happened in that office," he said, pointing at nothing.

Peri licked her lips. Jack and she had made love

and she'd been happy. One day later, she had killed him. One of them was a dirty operative. Allen said it had been Jack, but what if it had been her and they'd erased the knowledge? *Would I feel better or worse if it was me?* "You saw Jack. In my thoughts. What else did you see?"

His eyes dropped. "That you loved him."

She was silent. That's all she had seen as well—just enough to hurt her. Fingers slow, Peri reached for her boots. Silas had arranged them neatly by the edge of the bed, right where she'd look for them.

"We need to get into that office," Silas said, his voice low but determined. "If we have something to build a memory on, we can find out the truth."

When has truth ever meant anything? The zippers of her boots sounded loud as she pulled them up. Her toes were uncomfortable in her damp socks, and she was reluctant to put that woman's coat on. "That isn't normal. You being able to fix a memory you didn't see, I mean."

"Not that fast, no, but we do it all the time with new drafters," he said, sounding like a psychiatrist. "You must have wanted to remember, hence the memory knot."

"It was not a memory knot," she protested, but his head was down over his phone.

"I need to make a call. I want you to meet someone."

Uneasy, Peri reached for the coat. "One of your

alliance friends?" she said bitterly as she shoved her arms in. *I want to remember that I loved the man I killed? Right.*

Silas hesitated, cell phone in hand as he saw she had her coat on. "Where are you going?"

She didn't know, but she couldn't stay here. Jack was dead, and she could hardly breathe.

They both turned at the soft knock on the door and the muffled "Room service."

"There's potential here, Peri, more than I've seen in five years. At least stay until you've eaten," he said as he put his phone in a back pocket and strode to the door.

Peri's stomach rumbled at the thought of food, and she fell back down in the chair, rubbing the blue upholstery and feeling a matted, dirty maroon carpet instead. *Where did we make love? What city were we in?* She closed her eyes so they wouldn't well up. She felt drained, exhausted, aching with the knowledge of Jack. There'd been a button under the bed. It was a talisman—she'd felt the pull to it even in the memory. It was probably in her apartment. If she had access to it, she might be able to recover the memory of that night, with or without Jack. That's why drafters made talismans in the first place.

"Coming," Silas said as he moved a chair to make room for a rolling table. "I've got a spot by the window," he said as he unlocked the door and pulled it open.

Peri's head snapped up when Silas cried out, falling back to crash into the closet door and slide to the floor. Eyes wide, he plucked a red-fletched dart from his shoulder.

Allen stood in the hallway, black curls swinging as his dart gun shifted to her. Behind him were three men, the cart with their fries and milk-shakes pushed to the side.

Gasping, she rolled to hide behind the chair.

"Got her!" Peri heard a man say, and on her hands and knees, Peri looked at the red-fletched dart stuck in her arm. Horrified, she yanked it out, relieved that the thick coat had absorbed its length. She was untouched.

"How did you find her?" Silas groaned. And then his air puffed out as someone kicked him. The dart was probably a massive muscle relaxant to keep her from drafting and make her easier to catch.

"Peri?" Allen's steps were silent on the carpet. "We don't have to do it this way."

"You lied to me!" she exclaimed from behind the chair, then wondered if she should pretend to have been hit. "Jack isn't corrupt. You are. You and Bill!" But if Jack wasn't corrupt, that meant she was.

"We're trying to help you," Allen said, and Peri looked under the chair to see his dress shoes moving across the room. Four men, and only a questionable assist from Silas. She desperately didn't want to draft. She'd left her pen on the bathroom counter, and Peri frowned, glad she was wearing boots; she wouldn't break her foot slamming it into thick male skulls.

Peri stretched to reach the tray under the empty ice bucket on the desk. There was a soft thump and Silas groaned. He was still at the door, propping it open by the sound of it. "Get him in the van," Allen said, and she rose up with her tray, screaming.

The two men pulling Silas into the hall dropped him to fumble for their dart guns. The third man got a shot off, and she deflected it, howling as she front-kicked his middle, then spun to hit the side of his face with her boot as he conveniently dropped it down within easy reach. His weapon was there for the taking, and Peri yanked it from his slack grasp, dropping to the floor to avoid the volley of darts.

One scored on her coat, and she left it there as she shot at them. They both jumped for the doorway, falling over Silas and out into the hall.

"I'm trying to help!" Allen shouted, hands upraised.

"Yeah, right," she said, then threw the gun to Silas. He caught it like a field agent, and she smiled, eyes fixed on Allen's as there was a sudden commotion in the hallway, then silence.

"And don't come back!" Silas shouted, making her smile even wider.

"How did you find me?" Peri asked, watching the man who'd tried to shoot her as she moved closer to Allen—and Allen backed up, hands upraised and eyes wide under his curly black hair. His long face was even longer in alarm. "How?" she barked.

Silas found his feet and leaned heavily against the doorframe. "We have to go," he panted.

She held out her hand, and he threw the gun back. Allen moved while it was in the air, and she went after him instead, letting the gun hit the floor.

"You lied to me!" she exclaimed, arm going numb as Allen blocked her punch.

"Just . . . listen," Allen pleaded, and she planted a vicious side kick on his knee.

Mouth open in a silent cry, he went down, clutching it. Peri back-kicked the guard grasping for the dart gun, then she reached for Allen's arm as he shakily went for whatever was in his belt holster.

"No one lies to me," she snarled, and broke his fingers. At least three.

Allen crumpled, white-faced and staring at her in shock as he cradled his hand close.

"We have to go," Silas said. "Now."

Peri hauled Allen up by his shirtfront and pushed him against the bed. "I couldn't have killed Jack," she said, shaking inside. "I loved him."

"Peri . . . ," Silas breathed from the doorway. "Please."

She spun away, adrenaline pounding through her as she kicked the dart gun farther from the guard. Snatching up Silas's coat, she tucked a shoulder under his armpit. They staggered into the hallway and the door shut behind them with an absurd click.

Damn it, I forgot my pen. Peri took a breath—looked one way, then the other. Silas was heavy, and they had a long way to go. "That'll work," she said, leading him to the rolling table. She went to push everything off it, and Silas snatched a frosted glass just before it hit the edge. She felt sick as dishes crashed to the floor. A door down the hall opened, then quickly shut.

"You're hungry," he breathed, clearly hurting as he carefully levered himself onto the table. "God bless it, what are they putting in their darts? Here. Drink it in the elevator."

"Thanks." Peri got the cart moving. "Please tell me you have your wallet."

"Yep." His head was bowed, one hand on his middle, the other clutching his coat.

The wind from their passage shifted her hair. She felt good, even with the ache of Jack in her. She was doing something and she wasn't alone. "Did I draft?"

"Nope." He looked up, sweat on his brow. "You're kind of scary, you know that?"

Peri felt a twist in her, part heartache, part unknown. "Saving her anchor's ass is what a drafter does," she said. "It sort of makes up for the coffee-in-the-morning thing."

He laughed, choking it off when his face pinched in pain. Peri's smile faded.

Jack . . .

CHAPTER
FIFTEEN

Charlotte's premier mall had an astounding amount of weekend traffic. The food court was just inside the two-story-tall window entry, and Peri liked that she could watch the main entrance and the central convergence of the three wings at the same time. And whereas Peri would've preferred a quieter spot to get lost in while they regrouped, there was food and potentially some clothes. She'd told Silas he was a genius for suggesting it even though the thought to go to the mall had occurred to her, too.

No need to tell him that, though. Not after he'd bought her dinner. Watching his thick fingers spin through the at-table ordering pad with the dexterity of a fourteen-year-old had more than surprised her. The way he'd flirted with the server on skates bringing it out had set her back. Even the simply prepared but flavorful rice and fish he'd ordered had gone a long way toward reassuring her that she was not going to die today.

That was an hour ago. Across the way, the two-story arcade popped and whistled, and as Silas bargained with the man at the nearby phone kiosk, she watched four guys with military cuts on the live-play deck, battling aliens with a team from South Africa. She wasn't sure how she knew they wouldn't be able to get off-planet without the keymaster who lived in the swamp, but it was all she could do not to go over, jump on the interface, and tell them. *Jack, maybe?* she thought, tarnishing her good mood. Had she really killed her anchor? *Did he really shoot me first?*

No longer hungry, Peri set down her chopsticks and broke open the fortune cookie. It was stale, the sweet biscuit flat as she snapped it between her teeth and read the fortune. *The heart is stronger than the intellect,* she mused, wadding it up and flicking it across the table to land against Silas's empty cup.

Yeah, okay, she thought, watching Silas with that salesman, his very clothes flashing logos and discount codes. Since leaving the hotel, Silas had been silent and brooding, but he *had* bought her dinner. Sighing, Peri looked at the plastic knife before slipping it into her empty boot sheath like a child's promise—heady with intent but weak on follow-through.

Finally Silas shook the man's hand, a new bag in

his grip as he wove impatiently around three giggling girls dressed in full Japanese schoolgirl charm, their green hair matching their swirls of face paint designed to thwart facial recognition scanners. *Not a bad idea.* A phone would be great, but she wasn't leaving without new underwear—even if she had to steal it off a mannequin—which might be difficult seeing as they were all holographic simules.

"Better?" he asked as he sat down and shook his head at the three girls now singing what had to be the latest Hatsune Miku single at the top of their lungs. The interactive mannequins within their earshot began to sing along, the simules' attire shifting to something the tweens might buy.

Peri crumpled up the nearly useless napkin and dropped it on the leftover rice. "Very much so. Thank you," she said, meaning it down to her still-damp socks. "It was a little heavy on the lemon, but not bad. They probably added it after cooking instead of before. It's an easy mistake to make."

"Since when do you cook?" he asked, almost laughing.

Affront flashed through her and her eyes came back from the dusky parking lot. "I cook all the time," she said, embarrassed to admit that she didn't remember cooking anything, but clearly the knowledge was there. Sandy had once suggested she explore her new kitchen as a way to relax.

Clearly she had. But why had Silas assumed she couldn't?

He shrugged contritely, and not liking the silence, Peri said, "Mind if I borrow your phone and get some underwear?"

"Sure," he said, his attention caught by the flashing ads on the servers bussing the tables, fast on their in-line skates. "Your sweater is looking a little tired, too. Can I see your phone first?"

"My sweater?" She looked down at it, not believing what he'd just said, and his neck reddened.

"It's, ah, not very practical," he amended, and she slurped the last of the orange juice from the glass of ice in a sound of disbelief. "Phone, please?"

"I ditched it in Detroit," she said sourly. *I'm not supposed to cook and my sweater is a little tired? It's Donna Karan.* But, on second thought, he was right about the sweater.

"Really?" He took a glass phone out of the bag and pushed it to her, the purchase apps lighting up as it found the table's ordering system. "Good thing I got you a new one, then."

Suddenly feeling grungy, she reached for it, wishing he'd gotten a smartphone instead. This new glass technology was fun, but her learning curve was shallow. At least she knew how to turn it on. That Silas was with her brought a weird mix of guilt, gratitude, and discomfort. "Thanks," she said as she took her SIM card from her wallet and flipped the phone over. "I'm still going to need your phone. If I tap my bank, they'll know where I am."

"Whoa, whoa, whoa, is that from your old phone?" She nodded, and he held out his hand, his expression both irate and relieved. "May I?"

She handed it over, shocked when he snapped it in two. "Hey!" she shouted, then lowered her voice, not liking that people had turned. "You can't track SIM cards," she said as he dropped the broken card into his empty cup. "That was my only link to my past three years!"

"Opti gave it to you?" he asked, voice as angry as hers.

Ticked, she slumped into her chair, her new resolve to stop snapping at Silas being tested. She didn't have much left, and he'd thrown it away as if it had meant nothing.

"Look, I'm sorry," Silas said as her peeved silence grew. "I know the names and numbers were important, but don't you have a diary? Every drafter I've met does, hidden somewhere."

Frustrated, she rubbed her fingers into her temples. Even if she found her diary, she wasn't sure she'd trust it now, written in her own handwriting or not. "You can't track a SIM card," she said again, but he was dead serious, and a sliver of worry cooled her anger.

"Maybe." His gaze went distant behind her.

She'd accuse him of girl-watching, but she was doing the same thing as she scanned the floor for Allen or Bill—or anyone who looked too perfect. "It takes a while to zero in on a tracker. Even if you're tagged, we probably have some time." His eyes flicked to hers. "Seeing as you broke Allen's kneecap and fingers."

She winced at his accusing tone, remembering Allen's face pale under his black curls when she snapped them. "Fingers, yes. Kneecap . . . I didn't hit him that hard. Forgive me if I didn't want to end up in the back of a white panel van."

Silas held up a hand in acknowledgment, and she relaxed. "Yeah. I got that part. Here."

Her emotions swirled as he reached for his wallet and took out a handful of bills, making her feel as if she was at the mall with her mom. *Holy crap, my mom*. Allen had said she'd called her last week. She didn't remember it, and the need to hear her mother's voice almost hurt.

"I'd rather you use cash," Silas said as she punched in her mother's number. It probably hadn't changed. "Get yourself outfitted for light travel. And I mean light." He did a double take, realizing the phone was to her ear. "What are you doing?"

"I'm calling my mom."

"Are you crazy?" he blurted, reaching for it.

He pulled it from her ear, but she refused to let go, and they both held the phone over the middle of the table, neither one giving in. Peri could hear a woman's voice on the end of the connection, and her face warmed. "You like that hand?" Peri said tightly. "You want to keep it?"

There was no easy way for Opti to track them down through her mother, especially through a new phone, and knowing it, Silas let go. Mollified, Peri lifted her chin and brought it to her ear. "Hi, I'm Belle Marshal," Peri said, using the name of one of her mother's longtime friends. "Can I talk to Caroline Reed, please? I can hold."

"I'm sorry," the voice on the other end said. "Mrs. Reed doesn't have phone privileges."

Peri's lips parted in surprise. "Yes she does. I talked to her last week," she said, and across from her, Silas grimaced.

"No," the woman said again. "She hasn't had a phone for over a year now. Who is this?"

Breath shaking on her exhale, Peri hung up. "Allen said I talked to her on Friday."

"He lied," Silas said sourly. "Everyone lies to keep you content and happy."

Her eyes flicked up. "Funny. It only makes me pissed." She hadn't talked to her mother in over a year? A feeling of having been remiss slithered over her as Silas set a small stack of hundreds on the table. *That's right. I need to go shopping.* But her earlier enthusiasm was gone. "You want me to pick you up anything?" she said as she stood, wanting to get away from his pity.

Still subdued, he shrugged. "You first. If no one shows, I might get a new toothbrush. If your phone rings, leave and meet me at the car dealership. The big one with the tent."

Taking the cash, she jammed it into her pants pocket. "What if I draft?" she said, still trying to wrap her head around her mother. "It's not hard to lose ten minutes."

Nodding, Silas took the pen from his breast pocket and clicked it open. He reached for her hand, and she let him take it. Even though she'd thought to do the same thing to herself, it still felt degrading when he wrote CAR DEALERSHIP on her palm. It both tickled and hurt, and she made a fist to hide it when he let go.

"Brilliant," she said sarcastically as she left her hat and coat on the back of the chair.

Silas hunched over the dirty plates. "You've got ten minutes."

"I can't outfit myself in ten minutes. I can barely buy underwear in ten minutes, and I need a new coat, pair of pants. And a sweater, apparently."

"Fine!" His brow furrowed as he began piling the remnants of dinner on top of each other. "Take my ten minutes as well. I don't need anything like Ms. Princess does."

"Yeah? You see those shoes falling?" she said in a huff, but her eyes jerked to Silas's. Why had she said that? He seemed as surprised as she was, but then he shrugged.

"Don't worry about it," he said, his mood clearly soured. "It's a, ah . . . Jack thing."

He was lying, about what she couldn't tell. "A *Jack* thing?" she said, hand on the table.

Avoiding her, he focused on the arcade behind her. "The asthma comment means you don't remember crap but it's easier to say that than 'I don't know.' Shoes falling is probably you warning me that it's not over yet. Like waiting for the second shoe to drop?"

"A Jack thing," she said flatly, and when he stayed silent, she grabbed that ugly hat of hers and walked away. She'd spent the last three years with Jack. She knew she'd loved him. How long was it going to hurt when things like that kept popping out of her mouth? *I hate psychologists,* she thought as she shoved the man's hat in the trash and continued on.

Feeling Silas's eyes on her, she put a little extra wiggle in her step, not wanting him to know how shaken she was, but when she looked back, he was on the phone, arguing with someone— probably about her. Peri's steps slowed as her anger faltered. Despite the difficulty he'd had this afternoon simply getting her to relax, he was one of the most talented anchors she'd worked with, Opti's best trainers included. Cavana had taken almost a month to rebuild a draft he hadn't seen; Silas had done it in one session.

But we both knew what we were doing, she

thought, wondering if that was the difference as she glanced at her palm and Silas's cramped, somehow familiar handwriting. Every passing moment made her less prone to forget where they were going to meet. She had six hundred bucks in her pocket and a serious lack of wardrobe. *Easy peasy.*

The next twenty minutes spent in retail therapy went almost as far as dinner in restoring her mood, and using the 3-D image simulator to try on six outfits and a new coat simultaneously made it painless. It took longer to find a manager to accept the cash payment, and after waving good-bye to the bemused but happy salesclerks, Peri trundled her new carry-on filled with a week's clothes back into the corridor. Her boots clunked, and her fingers played with her new felt pen on a necklace. It was made of plastic and chintzy, but it felt right and gave her a sense of security.

Her smile faded when she saw Silas stand up from a nearby bench and make a slow, hands-in-pockets beeline for her. Peri's fingers twitched for a knife that wasn't there. Heart pounding, she scanned the mall, seeing only kids wandering around not buying anything.

"You bought a roller bag?" he asked, lips quirked as he eyed it.

"You said light," she snipped back, but it was obvious something was up. "What is it?" she said as he came even with her.

Saying nothing, he took her new coat from her, and then the roller bag. She let it go by force of habit before mentally kicking herself. "I can pull a roller bag," she said, reaching for it, but he shifted it smoothly to his other hand, out of her reach.

"Opti has a field force here," he said.

Peri's breath hissed in, habit keeping her moving forward, not a bobble in her pace, not one furtive look behind her. "No," she breathed. "Bill?" she asked, smiling as if nothing was wrong. If Opti was here, they were watching them this very instant.

Silas looped an arm in hers and slowed her even more. "Not that I've seen. Just Allen. Him and about half a dozen operatives dressed like salesmen and secretaries. I've been watching them watch you. I should have known you're chipped."

A slimy feeling slipped down her spine. "Excuse you! I'm *not* chipped like a dog."

"Then how did they find you so fast?"

"Maybe you called them?" she said, knowing it was untrue, and he snorted. Somehow she managed to keep her free hand swinging lightly, her gaze fixed on the macaroon shop at the end of the hall as she went through her assets to find she had almost nothing. *I'm chipped? My own people chipped me?*

"They knew exactly where you were when they rolled in," Silas said. "The mall cops are gone, but

I think Opti would rather collect us in the parking lot. That's why I didn't call you."

Us. He said us. The fish and rice sat heavy in her. Opti was after her, and she was relying on a man who wanted to see the end of everything she found any worth in, who was helping her only until he got what he needed to end Opti. Who was going to shut down the cyberterrorists if Opti was gone? Find the lost planes? Kill the sadistic dictators?

But right now, he was all she had. "Thank you," she whispered, shoving her panic down. "Don't let me leave my luggage behind in the fight. It cost more than the rest of my clothes put together. If we go far enough, fast enough, they will lose time zeroing in on me."

"You want to fight?" he said as if disappointed. "Even if we could get out of here, we have to extract that chip or they'll just find us again. I've got this under control."

"I have a chip in me, and you tell me you've got this under control?" she said pleasantly, her teeth bared at him as she smiled for the passing people. There were two Opti agents by an escalator, and Silas's grip tightened again.

"I can get it out of you," he said, his anger not directed at her for once. "We can do it here. It's all set up. All I need from you is a little trust."

That phone call, she mused, searching her intuition, but it was as if she didn't have any.

Nothing. She was coming up empty. She had to trust him. Or rather, she had to trust her gut, and her gut was saying he wasn't lying to her, even if logic said he was. "Okay," she said, and he exhaled. "But I'm not so good at trusting others."

"I've noticed." His lips twisted wryly, and he turned them down a hallway. "Keep walking. A man named Squirrel is waiting for you in the women's bathroom."

Peri's doubts rushed back. "Squirrel?" Was he serious?

"We all have lives outside of this," he said, his grip pinching her elbow. "He looks like a janitor, okay? Just go in, and he'll take the chip out."

"Just like that? You want me to go into a bathroom and let a *janitor* cut me open?"

Silas slowed to a stop, and she stared at him. Did he have any idea what he was asking of her? The bathrooms were next to the main entrance, and there were people there, people watching them without watching.

"I'd take you to his office, but not when you're chipped. Peri, please. Squirrel and I go a long way back. He's a good man."

"Tell me his real name, then," she demanded as she counted the agents. Six? Seven? She was twenty yards from the door, twenty from the bathroom, and nothing felt real anymore.

"No can do. But I'll come in with you if it will make you feel better."

There was a CLOSED banner across the bath-room entry, the door propped open with a wooden wedge. Two men and her alone in a bathroom? "No. I can do this," she said. *Great. What if I draft? What if I forget and run out of the bathroom and give Allen a huge hug?*

Silas sighed and handed Peri her coat. "Thank you," he said. "I'll see you in five minutes." Snatching up her wrist, he rubbed a thumb on her palm over the words he'd written, smearing them. She nodded, cold, as she understood what he was saying. He might not be there when she came out. She'd have to get to the dealership on her own. *Screw it. I can do this.*

"Don't forget my luggage," she said, and then, chin high, she strode toward the bathroom. One of the men by the main door was talking to himself in a whisper, and she fixed her gaze past him, pace never faltering. She couldn't resist a quick look back as she ducked under the tape cordoning off the bathroom. Silas was on a bench, slouched and feet spread wide as if waiting.

"Bathroom is closed," a wiry man with dread-locks and dark skin said as her boots clunked on the chipped tile. "Don't they teach you how to read at that high school of yours? Get out. I'm not going to lose my job because you have to pee."

"Squirrel?" she whispered, not liking how pale her face was in the mirror's reflection.

Immediately the late-thirties man sighed as he

propped his mop up against the dented janitor cart. Hands on his hips, he made a show of looking her up and down. His eyes were scary-bright, and she didn't like how they lingered on her black eye. "You're smaller than I thought you'd be," he said, his accent marking him as from the South, maybe Louisiana.

"Uh, sorry?" she fumbled, not liking that the janitor cart was stained from chemicals and covered with torn stickers. She liked it even less when he opened up an old toolbox, but was reassured when she saw packets of clean bandages and doctor stuff. Peri came closer. His hands were scrubbed to a soft pink, and they were smooth, not the hands of a janitor. The door was open, but Silas would let them know if someone was going to come in.

"You work for the alliance," she said, alarmed when he lifted a panel and brought out a wand. "How do I know you're not chipping me?"

Expression wry, he handed her a hand mirror. "You can watch. Stand still. Arms out."

She put her coat down, noticing that he'd dried the sinks when she draped it over one. "What is that?" she asked when he ran the wand over her.

"It's a chip finder from my office," he said, and she almost turned until he grunted at her to stand still. "I'm a vet in my other life."

Peri frowned as he wanded her back. "Opti doesn't chip their personnel like *dogs*."

"Uh-huh," the man said, and the wand beeped.

No. Shocked, she pulled the hand mirror up, turning her back to the row of mirrors. Her heart pounded, and the ugly feeling of betrayal slid through her. It was high up on her shoulder, where she'd had a mole removed four years ago. They'd chipped her.

"Well, at least it's not in your ass. Can you slip your sweater down a little?"

She spun, horrified, and he ducked his head, smiling. "I know what I'm doing," he said as he put the wand away and snapped on a pair of purple gloves. "I've got a license to practice medicine. It's the vet degree that's fake. It's easier to get regulated meds as a vet. You can watch. That's why I gave you the mirror."

Feeling the urgency to her core, she slipped her sweater farther down her shoulder. The mirror shook in her grip, and she used both hands. She'd been chipped, and that bothered her more than anything she'd learned in the last day.

White-faced, she stared at her reflection. His hands were warm on her back, his pressure firm as he palpated the skin. She saw it in his eyes when he found it, his gaze meeting hers through the reflection past his swinging dreadlocks. "You've done this before?" she asked when he took a scalpel from its wrapper.

"Unfortunately, yes." Brow furrowed, he touched her back again, swabbing it down to make a cold spot. "Sorry, but there isn't time to numb it."

She nodded, and then her breath caught as he cut. Her stomach clenched, and she watched the blood flow. The pain was tolerable even as he pressed on it.

"Tell me if you get woozy," he said. "It's not a big cut, but people are funny. Lots of pressure now."

Her teeth clenched as he pushed as if trying to get a sliver out. The hand mirror shook when something white and red slid out of her, the size of a grain of rice. Moving fast, he grasped it with a wad of gauze. "Here," he said, extending it to her. "You going to pass out?"

"No." Her shoulder throbbed, then burned as he cleansed it. The gauze was in her grip, the stark red and white riveting.

"You okay?"

His voice was kind. Peri set the gauze on the shelf under the mirror to tug her sweater back into place. The tape over it made a bump, alien and reminding her of what they'd done. Bill had *chipped* her. "I'm fine," she said, but inside she was reeling, not from the cut or the blood, but in the realization that if Silas had been right about this, maybe he was right about everything else.

"We'll send them on a chase," the man said as he collected his things. "All part of the service. Liz will be here in a second, so don't hit her, okay? You might pull your tape off."

Pulse fast, she leaned against the sink. Her

world was coming apart, and there was no one to catch her. *How did this happen?* The chip sat on the shelf, and she checked her phone. Five minutes. It seemed longer, and she gathered her coat to leave, the need to run strong.

"Whoa, hold on," the man said as she headed for the door. "Wait until Liz gets here. How long since you've eaten?"

Liz? Bet that's not her real name, either. "Just a few minutes ago."

"Mall food," he said in disgust. "Did you sleep last night?"

"On the bus," she said as a dark-haired woman wearing a bright blue nylon coat walked in. Her eyes were exaggerated with swirls of soot to confuse the facial recognition software, and Peri's brow furrowed. It would be hard to match that with what Squirrel had in his cart.

"Hi, Squirrel," the woman said brightly, her expression souring when she saw Peri. "You'd better be worth it," she said as she belligerently handed Peri a stick of body paint.

"That's enough," the man said sharply, and Peri clicked the soot stick open, leaning into the mirror to apply it. "If you don't want to help, you shouldn't have come."

"Oh, I'll help, but I'm doing this for Silas, not her." The woman shrugged out of her blue coat and handed it to Peri when she straightened, looking for approval. "I owe him."

But the approval never came, and Peri stiffened when the woman snatched up Peri's new coat with an appreciative sound. "If you hurt Silas, I'll be all over you like a rabid dog," Liz said, settling into Peri's coat with a smile. "Oh, this is nice. If they catch you, I'm keeping it."

"I saved his life once," Peri said. "I'll do it again." *Am I really that short?* she wondered as she slipped the soot stick into a pocket to keep, but their heights were nearly identical.

"Yeah, from a dart he got protecting you. Walk for me. Didn't you have a hat?"

"I threw it away." Seeing her logic, Peri paced before the sinks.

"I think I'll leave out the pained hunch," Liz said drily. "Where's the chip?"

Squirrel had put it in a tiny specimen bag, bloody gauze and all, and taking it, the small woman dropped it into a pocket. "Put on my hat and coat and go," she said, pointing to the door. "They're getting antsy. Don't look at Silas when you leave. You think you can do that?"

Liz snorted when the doctor helped her into the blue coat, and Peri's jaw clenched as she put on the rough, knitted blue-and-white stocking cap, thinking the pompom tassel ridiculous. "Thank you," Peri said when Squirrel adjusted the nylon monstrosity about her.

"Don't thank us," he said, smiling wryly. "We're trying to close you down."

Maybe that wasn't such a bad thing. Peri didn't know anymore. Pace slow, she held her head up so she wouldn't look as if she was hurting.

But she was. She'd never felt so alone.

"What do you think?" Peri heard Liz say as she hesitated at the door by the CLOSED banner, out of their sight and not yet in the hallway.

"I think you need to lighten up," the man said. "And I think that Silas needs to get over it and do his job."

"His job?" Liz scoffed. "What do you expect? He hates drafters."

"He does not hate drafters," came Squirrel's quick, angry answer. "That woman is half starved and emotionally ready to crack, and much of it's his fault. He knows the barriers to self-sufficiency that Opti instills in their drafters, and him trying to force her to break them when she has no resources isn't helping anyone, least of all her. He has a job to do, and if he doesn't start doing it, we're going to lose everything, Peri included."

Her back against the wall, Peri froze, caught between two worlds on the threshold of a scummy bathroom, Opti on one side, the alliance on the other, both of them lying to her. Instilled barriers to self-sufficiency? Was he saying she'd been conditioned to think she needed someone else to survive? It was undeniable that she was used to being part of a team, but that didn't mean she couldn't function alone!

But then she thought of Silas's giving her money, buying her food, his room where she'd recuperated. Even worse, the possible MEP that lurked after every traumatic draft if she didn't have someone to fill in the holes. Heart pounding, she gripped her borrowed nylon coat close about her. If Opti was here, she'd never get into that upstairs office. She had to know what had happened that night, not look at a cleaned-up crime scene. She had to find the button she'd seen in her memory of Jack. It was a talisman, and it held a memory. It held the truth.

"This is our best shot in five years at bringing Opti down, and he's blowing it because he doesn't want to buy her dinner?" the man said, and Peri felt the blood rush to her face. "That's a load. Tell Silas to suck it up and do his job. He can do this for the week it's going to take."

Angry, Peri pulled the CLOSED banner down, letting it fall to the floor as she left. Head high, she strode quickly into the mall, ignoring everything and everyone. She didn't see Silas as she passed the Opti personnel more intent on a vid screen and chip than what was in front of their faces. It was a mistake they wouldn't make twice.

Her hand was in a fist, hiding the words that would bring them together in case she forgot. She wasn't going to the dealership.

She was going home.

CHAPTER
SIXTEEN

Silas reclined against the hard mall bench, his long legs stretched out and his ankles crossed as he waited for Peri. His head was thrown back, and his hat covered most of his face, allowing him to watch the restroom and front entry without looking obvious about it. It had been only a few minutes, but they all felt like hours.

Fidgeting, he pulled himself out of his slouch when he saw Liz mince into the bathroom. The three suits pretending to catch a smoke in the vestibule began discussing their options, and his eyes flicked to the arcade, drawn by a burst of realistic gunplay. *Hurry up, Howard,* he thought, twitching his coat tighter about his shoulders. It might take his old friend longer to get Peri to trust him than for him to take the chip out. Trust was going to make or break everything, and everything was screaming for him to move and move fast.

Fran had called him while Peri was shopping, tracking him down through his request for Howard, the alliance's cleaner. The shortsighted woman had told him to cut Peri loose so Opti could pick her up, scrub her down, and start the game again. But the information was there in Peri's head. All he had to do was convince Peri to let him see it. Fran had given him one more chance, but if this failed, it was done, and Silas's worry deepened as more agents gathered in ones and twos, pulled in from the outskirts. They were getting ready for a push. Time was up.

"Thank God," he whispered when he spotted Peri from the corner of his eye. She was almost unrecognizable in that blue nylon coat and Liz's white-and-blue-striped knit hat pulled down over her head. She looked smaller, more vulnerable, in the more casual clothes. He could tell she was shaken; every ounce of her usual confidence was gone. The grace, though, remained, and he wondered what might have happened if she had never fallen from that playground swing and had become the dancer she had intended.

But she is a dancer, he reminded himself. She danced with death, and if she didn't keep up, the bastard would win.

Breath held, he watched the men at the door ignore her, focused on a tablet and presumably the tracker. She gave them a backward sniff as she passed them, pushing open the glass doors—and was gone.

Bold as brass, he thought in relief and checked his watch. He and Liz would lead them through the mall and out the south entrance to leave the tracker on a bus before doubling back. Peri would probably be test-driving the latest model from Detroit. The woman did like her cars.

Not so fast, he thought, standing when he saw Liz striding through the food court. Peri never walked that quickly even when she was late, firm in the conviction that if you were important enough, they'd wait. Liz's arms swung too far, her hips swaying not quite enough. The coat Peri had bought hung on her a bit loose; her shoulders weren't wide enough to carry off the high fashion. The grace Peri held was missing, but no one else seemed to notice. Every single Opti agent was focused on her, and his pulse quickened as he swung Peri's roller bag around as she approached.

"My God," Liz said as she halted before him, beaming up at him in excitement. "The woman is a nightmare."

Silas's jaw clenched. *True.* "She's complicated," he said, hand on her shoulder to point her in the direction of the south entrance.

Liz flicked a glance behind them, disguising it with a tug to her new coat. "Yeah? You like paranoid, sarcastic basket cases who can kill a man with a ballpoint pen?"

"I like you, don't I? South entrance is our best bet."

"Where the construction is? Got it." Liz fell into step with him, and he couldn't help but notice that her pace was shorter than Peri's. It took effort to shorten his stride to meet it. Funny how it had never seemed like a chore with Peri. "I can't believe you're still carting her luggage," Liz said, almost obnoxiously cheerful against the weight of his concern. "All the way from Detroit."

"She just bought it. It was my idea," he said, not sure why he felt the need to defend her, when Liz got an *Oh my God!* look on her face. "She hadn't seen her closet in two days," he added, and Liz's expression darkened.

"Okay, two days is a long time," Liz said as they wove their way through the crowd to the south entrance. "But she bought a *suitcase.* How much did you give her?"

"Stop." Silas warmed. Two hundred would have sufficed, but six had made her happy.

"Howard says you need to start acting more like an anchor and less like a dumped boyfriend," she said, voice tight. "Personally, I think you need to stop acting like her doormat."

"I said, *Stop,*" he repeated, not liking the number of Opti people at the south entrance: three, and one was on the phone calling for reinforcements. "When it gets sticky, you're to run."

"I didn't agree to this so I could run at the first sign of trouble."

It was all he could do not to give her a shake to wake up. This wasn't a game. "You will run," he said tightly. "I can't keep both of us free."

"I can take care of myself," she said, and his bad mood cracked. It was exactly what Peri would have said.

"Let me get the door," he said as she quickened her pace. "Peri always waits."

"She is *such* a princess."

Liz rolled her eyes and dropped back, and Silas hesitated. "Yes. She is," he said, and Liz's expression went sour again.

He pushed the door open, and they walked out into the early dusk. Silas scanned the area, wondering if the chain-link-fenced area under construction might hold some promise. Liz was silent, her chin lifting as she picked out the agents one by one.

"I see three," he said, the roller bag thumping on the rough pavement.

"Five," she corrected. "And more coming. Shit, who do they think she is? Superwoman?"

"Yep," he said, pulse quickening. "Incoming at two, five, and eight."

"Huh." Liz's pace had shortened, and he gave up on trying to meet it. "I thought we would have gotten a little farther."

"I'm surprised we got out the door." Silas met the eyes of the closest three, warning them before the fight even started. "I'll plow your road. They won't shoot to kill." *Not her, anyway.*

"Silas . . ."

"Watch out for darts." The three closest agents were almost on them. "Run!" he shouted, shoving her forward.

Crying out in frustration, Liz went. Silas

whipped Peri's luggage around like a hammer throw, grinning madly as he winged it at the man Liz was headed for. It hit him square on, and the man fell, grunting as he fumbled for her foot and missed.

"Keep going!" Silas shouted, then spun, affronted when a dart hit the back of his leg.

"God bless it," he muttered as he pulled it out. His leg was going numb, but he could still stand on it. At least they weren't shooting bullets.

"I said no drugs!" Allen's voice came over one of the agents' radios, and they warily circled him as if he were a lion, waiting for more backup. "No drugs! I can't interrogate an unconscious man. Good God! Isn't there anyone out there higher than a brown belt?"

Allen, Silas thought, changing his plans. He'd let himself get caught. He wanted to talk to him. His smile grew as the three agents looked uneasily among themselves. Alive and undrugged? He didn't have any such constraint, and he threw the dart away, flexing his hands in anticipation. "You heard the man," he said, scuffing the pavement for purchase. "Who's first?"

But no one volunteered, and finally Silas bellowed, rushing the smallest.

Silas hit his middle like a linebacker, stealing his air and sending him flying. He spun for the next, and they were on him, forcing him to the ground. He twisted, but someone had his arm, yanking it up and back in a submission hold. Two more landed on his legs.

"Cuff him!" someone shouted, and Silas grimaced at the feel of steel ratcheting about one wrist. Twisting, Silas flung the man away.

"Keep him down!" someone else demanded, and Silas's air huffed out as two more men fell on him. One got a face full of elbow, but then they got his other arm, twisting it back with the first and fastening them together.

"Get off me!" he demanded, and in a breath, they seemed to vanish.

Shocked, he twisted, managing to get himself seated upright. Six men all in black suits ringed him. One had a bloody nose, another a red face as he still struggled to breathe. All of them were angry, their nice black suits mussed with dirt and oil.

His own nose was bleeding, and he wiped it on his shoulder, staying put when one of them shoved him to stay down. Silas followed their attention to Allen, who was hobbling forward between the parked cars, awkward and slow with his right hand bandaged and a crutch to ease the weight on his damaged left knee. Bound in cuffs, Silas's hands clenched, and his skull began to throb.

"He's got one dart in him," the tallest man said, almost panting as Allen limped to a halt and looked Silas up and down. "Sorry, sir."

Allen's brow lifted in amusement as he took in

the men trying to put themselves back together. "Don't worry about it," he said, while Silas seethed. "It hardly slowed him down." Allen scanned the parking lot, other agents keeping the curious onlookers moving. "Can you stand?" he asked Silas.

"Fuck you," Silas said softly, his chin hurting where it had hit the pavement.

Allen chuckled. "Get him up," he said confidently, and two men yanked him, stumbling, to his feet. "I want his phone. Wallet. Everything. Where's the van?"

Silas stood stoically while they searched him. If they were focusing on him, they were not looking for Peri, and a curious feeling of anxious satisfaction coursed through him as Allen step-scuffed on his crutch to a nearby agent to find out what was taking the pickup van so long.

"Booted?" Allen echoed, clearly peeved as a shopper tried to get it all on YouTube, complaining when an agent took the phone and snapped it. "We cleared it with the local cops!"

"Yes, sir," someone said. "It's got a VigilantVigilante sticker on it. I have a car coming."

"Seriously?" Frowning, Allen shifted his gaze from the mall to the nearby construction trailer. "I don't want this plastered on the Net. Someone open that up. Denier, move, or we'll move you."

Silas slowly started for the construction office,

his hands bound behind him. The chain-link fence door rattled open, and Silas eyed the gun on Allen's hip. He'd take that when he left, and he waited patiently as an agent darted up the metal steps and into the dirty single-wide.

"In," Allen prompted when the agent stuck his head out and proclaimed it clear.

Silas went, his pace stiff, and he gave the agent at the steps a look to back off as he managed them himself. His mood darkened when he found the ceiling predictably low and the furnishings covered in the expected filth and grime—but his clothes were ruined already.

"Put him there," Allen said, and two agents shoved Silas into the rolling chair before the messy desk, going farther to tether his cuffs to an immovable, fireproof file cabinet with a long, plastic-coated wire. Silas leaned back as much as he could, his hands fisted behind him.

"We're tracking the woman," one man said, and Allen sighed as he rested his rump against the top of the desk. "She's heading east," he added, showing him on the tablet. "Mobile, and moving fast."

Allen glanced at it. "Don't bother," he said as he got his phone from a back pocket and started flicking through the apps. "It's not Reed."

Shit.

"Sir?" the agent asked, his tablet drooping until Silas could see it was a map of the city.

"It's not her," Allen repeated, smug as he met Silas's eyes. "Is it."

Which means Peri is still free, but his elation quickly reverted to worry. How long would she wait? An hour? The trailer was only a short walk from the dealership.

"Out," Allen demanded as the trailer shifted when two more men tried to come in, and they retreated. "You." Allen handed one of the remaining three agents Silas's phone and wallet. "Go thank the mall security. Tell them we have our suspects and we'll be out of their hair in five minutes." Brow creased in pain, he turned to the remaining agents. "You two go find the car and *make sure it gets here in five minutes!*" he shouted. "Not ten. Not six. Five!"

They headed for the open door, and Allen clicked open his radio. "I'm in the construction trailer on the south end," he said sourly. "Give me a forty-foot perimeter around it. Now."

Eyes fixed on Silas, he pulled his handgun from the holster and set it on the desk, sighing in relief. Still the agents hesitated, and Allen waved at them, shooing them out. "Go on," he demanded. "He's cuffed and tied to a five-hundred-pound cabinet."

Slowly they retreated, talking even as they shut the door behind them.

"You slimy son of a bitch," Silas intoned, not liking the changes in his *old friend.*

"Shut up," Allen said as he turned off his radio.

"How could you do that to her?" Silas whispered, leaning as far forward as he could. He'd almost blown it when Allen had walked into Opti's med building, posing as her anchor. He might look the part, with his lanky, athletic body, but Allen's defrag techniques weren't good enough. How he'd worked himself so high in Opti's ranks so fast was more than suspicious.

"I said"—Allen set his phone where Silas could see the live, hijacked mall security video focused on the trailer—"shut up a moment."

Silas was silent, his pulse throbbing against the new scrape on his face, and they watched the men surrounding the trailer fall back to a comfortable forty feet. The changes in Allen went deeper than the bandages. There was a little more maturity across the shoulders, and his black curls were cut shorter. Pain had made his long face even longer, but he was as fit and scar-marked as ever. The safety glasses were the same black plastic. Silas knew he used them to keep women away—birth-control frames, he called them. Not that Allen didn't like women, but he treated them like his next big hill to be conquered—at his preference.

"Seriously, are you okay?" Allen said, shoulders slumping to show how much he hurt. Clearly he was avoiding the pain meds, a reasonable precaution seeing as they interfered with the ability to recognize drafts. "They didn't hit you too hard, eh?"

Wet and filthy from the parking lot, Silas eyed Allen, gaze lingering on his Opti pin. "You are . . . a son of a bitch."

Allen's expression hardened. "We have five minutes. You want to spend it telling me how much of an ass I am, or do you want to figure out how we can fix this?"

"I was there," Silas said flatly, anger growing. "Ready to extract her. She had everything we needed to end this, and you *scrub* her? Why didn't anyone tell me?"

Allen looked out the grimy window. "Maybe because you drove Matt's van into the Detroit River?"

"Don't get cute with me, you little pissant."

"I scrubbed her to save her life," Allen reiterated, his attention coming back to him, but Silas thought there was far too much guilt in it. "You were already in transit before it happened. There was no way to tell you. And there's still a chance to end this. Fran wants you to cut her loose, and I agree. She needs to come back to Opti to finish it."

"You scrubbed her because you finally had her with you!" Silas accused, satisfied he was right when Allen flushed.

"I had to." Allen slid from the desk. "Good God, Silas. She was *dying*. Dying in my arms and wouldn't draft. Bill knows she is an alliance sleeper agent. He's probably known since day one. If I had taken less than three years, they would have suspected me."

Maybe. Silas eased back as he recalled how low the odds had been when they'd started this five years ago. "Bill doesn't know who she is," he muttered.

"He does." Allen carefully stretched his damaged knee. "That's why Jack kept scrubbing her to keep her oblivious and productive."

"Like you," Silas said bitterly.

"Not like me." Allen frowned, eyes drifting to nothing. "The idiot shot her to get her to draft, and with her intuition—"

"She never would have accepted him, scrub or not." Silas's focus blurred, his shoulders aching from being pulled back too tightly. Peri was a pain in the ass, demanding and particular, but he trusted her intuition more than most people's facts, and there was no one he'd rather have watching his back in a tight spot. Even now.

His eyes flicked up to Allen. *Especially now.*

"So you let her kill him," Silas accused. "When there was no one else to be her anchor."

Allen's expression sharpened. "I did it in the hopes that with closure we could play this out to the end." He pulled himself up stiffly, weight on his good leg. "The government knows Opti is rife with corruption, but they need Opti like bread needs flour. They tasked Bill to find it, which of course he did, using the opportunity to modify the list so as to keep his game going. Peri found out she was on the original and responded in her usual style."

Silas nodded, the drying blood on his face pulling. And in the aftermath, she'd drafted and forgot everything. "Where does that leave us?"

Allen pushed his glasses up. "Bill has the list, but Jack kept the original chip with everyone's names on it for insurance. Bill has already ripped their apartment apart looking for it. It's not in her Mantis or the hotel they stopped in, and neither Peri nor Jack would have destroyed it. Has Peri said anything about it?"

Silas snorted, his cuffs catching as he leaned back. "No. But she wouldn't know, since you wiped her clear back to her first Opti anchor.

"I think you've gone native," Silas accused. "I think you like where you are, what you do, playing both sides. I think you like that Peri knows you and not me."

Allen hunched, angry. "And that's why you're buying her dinner, outfitting her for travel, refusing to cut her loose when Fran told you to send her back in? Peri doesn't know anything, and I'm this close," he said, his finger and thumb a mere inch apart. "If I can get Peri back and working, I can find who's funding Bill. I've got a shot at finding how far it goes. I know the idea was she'd be the one to break it, but I can finish it and we can all go home."

Silas squinted at him, cheekbone throbbing. He never could decide when Allen was lying. He'd always relied on Peri to tell him. His eyes flicked to Allen's broken fingers and damaged knee. *No reason to change that now.*

"That woman does not like to be lied to," Silas said, gaze rising to find Allen's waiting.

"Tell me about it," the tired man said around a sigh. "You think I did this to be with Peri? Every time I touch her I'm scared to death I'll trigger a wisp I didn't fragment. She knows I'm lying to her, just not about what."

Allen is worried about leftover fragments, and the only things she remembers about me are a few inside jokes about asthma and shoes. Silas's suspicions tightened.

Fingers fumbling, Allen searched a pocket of his suit coat, holding up a theme book before setting it on the desk. "I haven't gone native, but I'm starting to wonder about Peri."

"You read her diary?" Silas's lip curled.

"It was either me or Bill," he said. "I told him it would help me convince her I'm her anchor, but I went through it to find evidence of Opti's corruption. Something we could use."

"And?"

Allen shook his head. "Nothing. If she kept track of her findings, it was somewhere else."

This was going nowhere. He had to get out of here. She wouldn't wait forever.

"She's changed, Silas," Allen said, bringing him back to the cruddy little construction trailer. "Her diary? She enjoys what she does a little too much. We don't know what's going on in her head apart from what she tells us and what we can piece together. What's to say she's not working for Bill to find the head of the alliance and assassinate the top people?"

"Are you insane?" But she'd killed people before, even if she didn't remember it.

"Just be careful," Allen said. "I'm telling you, she's not the same woman."

Remembering Peri's off-the-cuff comment about the fish, Silas huffed, "Tell me about it. When did the woman learn how to cook?"

Clearly relieved at the change of subject, Allen smiled. "Haven't you heard? Bill made it an Opti-sanctioned stress relief. She's gotten good, from what I hear."

"And you're eager to eat it up, eh?" he said. "Move right in where Jack stepped out. She made you sleep on the couch, didn't she? That's all you're going to get."

Allen's face darkened. "*I'm* not the one who tried to convince her to wash out. I supported her and her idea to bring down Opti. I still do."

Silas leaned in, his arms hurting. "You're after the glory, Allen. That's all you ever wanted, and you played on that need in her like it was an addiction needing to be fed because you couldn't do it alone. You used her. Convinced her it was possible."

"It was possible," Allen protested, and Silas's eyes narrowed at the guilt. "It still is."

"You *used* her," Silas pushed. "And now her mind is so full of holes that the traumatic draft you forced on her is going to ooze right through and drive her mad. This is your fault."

"This is *not* my fault." Allen stood, white-faced. "She wanted to do it. She knew the risks."

"You encouraged her," Silas accused. "*You* erased the year we trained for it."

"You agreed to it." Allen began to pace in his odd step-scuff motion, pain only making him more agitated. "You were there with me, making sure I got everything."

"To try to keep her alive!" he shouted back.

Allen hobbled closer. "She's gone," he said flatly. "She left five years ago. She chose to make a difference, but there's nothing left of her. Let it go, Silas."

Silas forced his jaw to unclench. "She is waiting for me right now. Get these cuffs off me."

Allen straightened, eyes furtive. "Ah, you helped her escape. I can't let you go."

Silas's lips parted. "She's waiting. Uncuff me, give me your gun. Tell them I hit you."

"Where is she?"

Silas said nothing. Allen turned away and Silas jerked at his cuffs, making the smaller man jump.

"She's one bad draft away from a MEP," Silas said. "That crapfest at the bar is already trying to manifest itself. I untangled three potential memory knots just getting her to relax yesterday. She's going to snarl up if she's left alone."

"So tell me where she is so we can take care of her."

Take care of her? He meant another memory wipe. Pissed, Silas fumbled for the tether and gave it a yank. It pulled tight against the heavy cabinet and held firm. He didn't trust Allen anymore, and his pulse quickened until his face throbbed. "Don't do this, Allen."

"They trust me," Allen said, suddenly in a hurry as he looked at his phone. "Tell me where she is, or nothing happens."

"Don't do this," Silas warned, and Allen jumped when he tried to stand, failing, stopped by the cuffs. "Allen."

"I'm sorry," he whispered, eyes on the grimy windows as the sound of approaching agents grew louder. Lips pressed, he tucked Peri's diary back behind his coat. "I'll make sure you get a chance to read this. I think she's beyond recall. All we can do is bring Opti down."

"Allen!" Silas exclaimed, furious as Allen hobbled to the door.

"Where's my car!" Allen shoved the door open and hobbled down the stairs.

The door shut, and, fuming, Silas yanked at his

cuffs to no avail. Allen was lying. Peri knew it, or at least her subconscious did, otherwise why would she break his fingers and fracture his knee? He had to get out of here. Warn her. It was never meant to go on this long. He needed to get her out before everything she'd been was gone.

But he couldn't even get out of his chair, and with a groan of frustration, he fell back, stymied and brooding. Allen had always been a tricky bastard, even when the two had been the best of friends. Nice to know some things never changed.

CHAPTER
SEVENTEEN

Peri walked quickly across a student dorm parking lot, uncomfortable in Liz's cheap, blue nylon coat and trying to look as if she knew where she was going. She knew what she was looking for, just not where it was. An early-model beater wouldn't have a security system or computer that could be LoJacked, and taken from here, it might not be missed for days.

It was starting to mist and the temp was dropping as it grew dusky. Clammy and cold, it was an ugly night in Charlotte. She fingered the long-handled screwdriver in her pocket that she'd lifted from the garage she'd passed. The lime-green two-door with the torn cloth top was a good bet. If she was lucky, it would be unlocked.

She was.

Smiling, Peri yanked the handle up and slid in as if she owned the ugly thing. It clearly belonged to a guy; there were shark's teeth hanging from the rearview mirror, and silhouetted, naked-girl floor mats.

And it stinks of aftershave, she thought, nose wrinkling as she slipped her boot off and hammered at the steering column until it cracked. She'd been jumping buses for almost half an hour, putting a fair amount of distance between her and the mall. The nylon coat rasped as she moved, and she thought longingly of the coat she'd left behind, not to mention everything else. If she'd even guessed she'd be looking to hot-wire a car, she'd have bought a knife instead of socks. At least she had clean underwear on and a few bucks in her wallet.

And a phone, she thought as her back pocket began to hum.

Guilt rose. She'd just walked out on Silas—no explanation, no nothing—but Liz's unforgiving assessment of her burned. She was good at her job. She was not helpless alone.

Frustrated, Peri yanked at the broken casing around the column until it pulled free with a loud snap of plastic. Sucking on the edge of a pinched finger, she wiggled the phone out. She didn't have to look at the number; only one person would be calling her. Hitting ACCEPT, she put it to her ear.

"Peri." Allen's low voice filtered out, the state-of-the-art technology catching every nuance in his anger.

Eyes flicking, she looked in the rearview mirror, then locked both doors, her shoulder tape pulling when she leaned across the long bench seat. *Jeez. No power anything.* "Hi, Allen." She reached for the tumbler, bringing it—and the attached wires—out into the dimming light. If she was lucky, all she'd need would be the screwdriver. "How's the hand?"

"Taped. It's the knee that bothers me the most. Tore my ACL. I'll be up and in a Flexicast as soon as the swelling goes down."

"Ouch, that's a bitch." There was no background noise. She couldn't tell if he was in a hospital room or a surveillance van.

"I've had worse, but usually a bike or parachute is involved. Running was a mistake."

Phone tucked awkwardly between her shoulder and ear, she tried turning the tumbler, getting nothing. *Why can it never be easy?* "So I guess you have Silas if you're talking on his phone." It was all going to fall apart fast if she couldn't get this thing started.

"Oh, yes." It was smug. "It's a shame I wasn't there, or we might have you as well. No one moves like you, Peri."

That plastic knife was less than useless, and she leaned, shoulder protesting, to rifle through the cluttered glove box for something to cut and strip the wires with. He was drawing this out, meaning the call was being tracked. She thought the best they could do would be to find the tower she was using, but she could be wrong. "Why are we talking?" she asked to cover the noise of pulling everything onto the floor. A jackknife glinted, and she snatched it up, brushing the grit off before snapping it open. *Gold!*

"Just sharing good news," he said, and she heard background radio chatter. *Great. He's in a surveillance van.* "But it's not good for you. If it was my decision, I'd let you twist in the wind, but Bill thinks we can scrub you clean and start again. So here I am."

"Scrub?" The word sounded foreign, and an ugly thought pinged through her—Opti could control how much she lost when she drafted? They had lied to her. Even worse, the anger now lifting through her was too old for her not to have known this before. *Allen took three years from me. I should have busted his jaw, not his knee.*

Ticked, she found the starter wires, following them down from the tumbler until she had enough to strip the ends and twist them together.

"Personally, I think you're more trouble than you're worth," Allen said. "But if I work this right, I get the best of both worlds, attached to a high-profile drafter and the chance to screw you every night."

That was nasty, and she awkwardly held the phone to her ear as she touched the starter wires together, wincing as the engine turned over. It wasn't the jolt so much as the burst of radio that startled her, and she dropped the phone to turn it down.

"Thanks to you, Bill has an alliance representative willing to testify that you're corrupt," Allen was saying when she got the phone back to her ear, oblivious that she'd dropped him. "Where are you, Peri? We can protect you."

Like I'd tell you? "Silas doesn't believe I'm corrupt." The car was running, but three years' worth of lost memories or not, she could tell it had been a long time since she'd hot-wired a car. Again, her anchor had probably done it on the rare occasions it was necessary. *I am so stupid.*

"Believe?" Allen said, and she closed the vents to let the car warm up. "That's a funny word, *believe*. Right now he *believes* you set him up. He *believes* that you knew all along that Opti is corrupt to its core and that you were a part of it. A nasty little mole working your way up the alliance rank and file to get close enough to take out the top alliance operatives."

Her face went cold. Opti was corrupt. She'd probably figured it out before her jump at Overdraft and Allen had *scrubbed* her. Bill,

Allen . . . Jack? Oh God, she *had* killed him. She might not remember it, but if she'd found out he was dirty, she might have killed him. Silas had told her the truth. *And I left him.*

"We're going to let him escape soon," Allen was saying, but Peri hardly heard him, struggling to take it in. "He's going to use you to bring Opti down." He laughed. It wasn't a nice sound. "You have to love his innocence. You can't shut Opti down. Too many high-profile bank accounts want us right where we are. Hell, the government wouldn't be able to wipe their asses without us. But if you bring yourself in and work with us to remove the last couple of days—"

"You can go to hell and die," she said. "In that order." The need to move was almost an ache, but the phone was too small to reliably hold between her ear and shoulder, leaving her one hand to drive. She couldn't effectively drive stick with one hand in stop-and-go city traffic.

"That's what I told Bill you'd say," he said, not at all regretful. "Think about it, Peri. If you run, every cop from here to both borders will be looking for you. You're not that good on your own. The same patterns that keep you sane will be what we'll find you with. It's not your fault. We made you that way. Sooner or later, you'll slip up and be brought down, tried, and put away as the corrupt Opti agent who killed her own anchor to hide her guilt."

"You can't expose Opti," she said, and he laughed. "The public would demand an end to all of us if they knew what we can do."

"Which is why your special abilities won't be hinted at. You are hereby a homegrown assassin, Peri, a member of a government-funded special forces group belonging to a military project that has been alive since the forties, because we say so. We've got the paperwork to prove it. Ninety-five percent of it is true. It's not as if we haven't had to start from scratch before."

I am no one's scapegoat. Frustrated, she pulled her knitted cap off and tossed it aside.

"Opti will survive, but one way you'll be in jail for the rest of your life, and the other will have you with me, oblivious and happy, doing what you like to do. What you're good at."

"I need some time to decide."

"You don't have any!" Allen shouted. "I need an answer. Before my pain meds kick in!"

Stymied, she didn't say anything. She wasn't going back to be a dog doing tricks for them, wiped to ignorance every time she figured it out. *How long? How many times?*

Allen's voice was satisfied as he said, "I'll take that as a no. See you soon, Peri."

The phone connection broke, and she turned it off. The car was still sitting in the middle of the dorm parking lot. Leaning to the floor, she pushed through the mess until she found a pen and a yellow receipt from a tire place. She jotted down Silas's cell number, then shoved the yellow paper in her pocket. She'd ditch the phone when she got on the expressway.

I don't remember ever driving my Mantis, she thought suddenly and in regret, grimacing at the AM/FM radio and the filthy clutter strewn over the age-torn vinyl seats. According to the literature, she could start her Mantis from a hundred feet away using the fob or her phone. It would cut out if anyone not registered sat in the driver's seat. It came with a lifetime SiriusXM radio subscription. It could do zero to sixty in three point two seconds. The warming engine went *barrummm!* when she started it, to make her insides feel good—and she was driving this piece of crap?

Sighing, she put it into drive. Okay, she had a car, but getting to Detroit and that button didn't seem important anymore. Heart pounding, she headed for the exit. A few miles ought to put her under a different tower, give her some margin of security. She couldn't allow herself to believe Allen. Her gut said that Silas was too smart to believe him, too.

"Sooner or later I'm going to slip up, huh?" Peri muttered as she swung onto the road, deciding it was better to be angry than afraid. She wouldn't get caught. She was a professional, damn it. She might not remember everything, but she had skills.

But her greatest asset was also her greatest liability, and she wouldn't have an anchor to bring her memory back the next time she drafted. She needed Silas.

"Vets," she said, deciding to stop and eat while she did her research. "I need to find a vet who specializes in squirrels." Hands shaking, she hit the gas, wanting to see what the big, over-indulgent, American-made engine could do.

CHAPTER
EIGHTEEN

"**A** squirrel," Peri said, pitching her voice high and doing a good impression of being panicked as she held the shoebox she'd found in a Dumpster and tilted it to make the rocks it held scrabble like claws. "I accidentally hit her. I couldn't leave her there, and your ad says you handle exotic animals."

The twentysomething woman behind the counter dubiously eyed the box, then Peri's worn but professional attire behind that nasty blue coat and ugly blue-and-white-striped hat. "Yes, ma'am, but domestic animals, like lizards and birds. We've never seen a squirrel."

Peri leaned on the counter, not really having to fake her distress. "You have to help me. Her leg looks broken. Maybe she has babies! She let me pick her up okay. She's really tame." Peri shifted the rocks. In the back, dogs barked, and she stifled a shiver. *Why don't I like dogs?*

The woman stood, uncertain. "I'll see if I can find him," she said, going to the back.

Exhaling, Peri retreated into the reception area, smiling wanly at the second receptionist who was separating the "bring your pet in for a visit" cards the printer was spewing out. The diploma on the wall said Howard Lamms—which would be better than Squirrel, but not much. *God save me from amateurs,* she thought, her tension returning threefold.

Earlier, she'd grabbed a quick and lonely meal at a sandwich shop, where she'd borrowed an actual phone book—she hadn't seen one since she was a little girl—to scope out the vets in a fifteen-mile radius. From there she'd prioritized them by how many doctors each had on staff under the assumption that if "Squirrel" was stealing meds, he wouldn't want a partner around to have to explain things to.

Peri was currently standing with her box of rocks in the third office she'd tried. She didn't have a lot of hope, but there were six more addresses on her list with multiple doctors if this last one didn't pan out. She felt naked for having wiped off the anti-facial-recognition smut, but using it outside of large public places garnered more unwanted notice than not. It didn't help that it'd gotten dark, but what bothered her most was that Allen was filling Silas with lies that were easier to believe than her truth.

A door slammed, and adrenaline surged as she heard a familiar voice shout, "Susie, will you take Buddy for his walk? The auto walker has gone fritzy again. I can't keep the stupid thing . . ." Howard's voice trailed off as he came around the archway, looking professional in a white lab coat, dreadlocks pulled back. "Flying . . ." He set a leash-draped drone on the counter and stared at her.

"Please. I need your help," Peri said. "Something awful happened."

"She has a squirrel, Doctor," the receptionist with him said, and the silence stretched as disbelief, curiosity, and finally mistrust came over him.

"I'll take a look," he finally said, and relief filled her. "Exam room three. We can skip weighing her in. Has she *bitten* anyone? We might have to *put her down* to check for rabies."

"No, she's really very sweet-tempered." Peri lurched into motion, the rocks sliding as she passed the front desk and entered a short hallway. "Just in a bad place and misunderstood."

Howard held a door open for her. "Trying to help a wild animal rarely works out. The safest thing would be to turn her over to the proper authorities."

"They'd kill her," Peri said, meeting his eyes as she passed by him. "And she doesn't mean any harm."

"Wild animals seldom do," he said sourly.

The door shut, and Peri carelessly set the box of rocks on the exam table.

"Are you crazy?" Howard almost hissed, snatching up a wand and coming at her.

"Hey!" she exclaimed, then lowered her voice as he ran it over her. "You already took the chip out. I'm clean."

"You could have been rechipped and forgotten it."

"I haven't drafted," she said as he set the wand down, beads in his hair clinking.

"You sure?"

"Pretty sure," she said, and his eyebrows rose as he saw her doubt. "Wait," she said as he pointed at the door for her to leave. "Opti has Silas. They caught him." Howard's mouth dropped, and she looked away, ashamed. "I ditched him to go back to Detroit, but Allen called me as I was hot-wiring a car, and now . . ." *What am I doing?* He'd never believe her.

"You stole a car?" he said as if that was the only thing that registered.

"You're worried about a stupid car?" she said, then frowned at the shadow of feet passing at the thick crack under the door. "Allen admitted that Opti is rife with corruption," she whispered.

"Him. Bill." *Jack?* "Allen told Silas that I set him up to be captured—that I'm in on it. They're going to *let* him escape, knowing he'll use the lies Allen is filling him with to try to shut Opti down and make me the fall guy. But Opti won't go down; it's too big. They're going to frame me for everything to give the corruption in Opti the chance to bury itself deeper. Howard, you've got to help me."

"How do you know my name?" the man asked, his dark eyes suddenly threatening.

"It's on your vet certificate in the office," she said, and Howard dropped back, grimacing.

"Allen admitted Bill is corrupt?"

She nodded, breathless, and then they both turned at the knock on the door. Not wanting anyone to come in, Peri ran a hand along the counter, knocking things over and making noise. "She got away! Oh God. I'm so sorry!" she shouted.

Howard stared, then added, "Give us a few minutes, Anne. I'll call you if I need help."

They waited until Anne's footsteps shushed away, her loud conversation with the other girl up front both complaining and excited. "You're not afraid anymore," Howard said as he gathered a handful of cotton-tipped swabs she'd spilled.

"I don't have a tracking chip in me anymore. It's amazing how that can boost a person's confidence." Peri frowned. "Please. I have to get Silas back before they fill his head with lies."

Eyes averted, Howard tapped the swabs on the counter and returned them to the container, brow furrowed as he pushed the jar to the wall. He looked different in his white lab coat, but his hands were the same. He wasn't a large man, but he had a big presence. "I don't know what you think I can do," he finally said.

"You don't care that he's being held?" Peri said, aghast. "Lied to? Manipulated?"

"Of course I do, but he knew the risk. We all want to see Opti shut down. But I don't care if you fall with it. And neither does Silas."

Peri sucked her teeth. Lame, it was lame and cowardly. "Listen to me, little man," she said, and Howard started in affront. "Who do you think keeps terrorists out of U.S. airspace, gets the guns to oil-friendly rebels, and cleans the crap off your favorite politician? Too many people want Opti, depend on it to keep downtown America buying technology they don't need, and that the alliance is trying to shut it down is starting to piss me off! They will shred the files, fire the secretary, and open it back up again calling it something else with the public thinking we are the Green Berets or SEAL Team Six B or some other special ops group. But I'll be *damned* if I let Bill be in charge of it. I'm *not* corrupt, and the Opti I worked for isn't either."

"Yeah?" Howard had his arms over his chest, clearly not liking the *little man* comment.

"I don't need to explain myself to you," she said. *Coming here was a mistake.* "Are you going to help me rescue Silas or not?"

He leaned back against the counter, thinking. "What do you want?"

It wasn't an agreement, just a question. "Funding." He snorted, and she warmed. "Equipment to free Silas, and a ride to Detroit for the talisman I made of the night where this all started. Silas can help me re-create the memory tied to it, and with that, the truth comes out."

"Your talismans," he said flatly, beads clinking as he shook his head. "They're nothing but paperweights with your past anchor dead."

Peri's chest clenched, but she used the grief, mutating it to anger. "Silas defragmented one of my memories. One he'd never seen. If he did that once, he can do it again. The talisman will help." Howard's lips parted in disbelief, and she made a fist in frustration. "Are you going to help me or not?"

There was a knock on the door, and Peri held his eyes. "Doctor?" the vet tech called, and Howard grimaced.

"Don't open the door!" he said sourly. "I've got her cornered." He leaned over the table, his brow furrowed. "Anchors can't defragment memories they haven't witnessed."

"Opti does it all the time with new drafters. It isn't impossible, just really hard and time-consuming." But it hadn't been either of those things when Silas had done it. "Something happened in the Global Genetics office. Going there and looking at the chalk outline won't help. I need Silas and my talisman. I need to remember."

Clearly unhappy, Howard took his out-of-date smartphone from a pocket and checked the screen. "I never agreed with Silas's plan to use you to gain information."

"Thank you."

The phone went dark and he stuffed it away. "That wasn't a compliment. I thought it was a stupid idea that would hurt him more. I only supported it because he needed to face his grief, not hide from it." Seeming to have decided something, Howard pushed the jar of swabs from the counter. Peri jumped, startled even though she'd been expecting the harsh noise. "Anne is such a snoop," he muttered.

Frustrated, Peri splayed her hands on the exam table. "I need a vehicle that won't be called in as stolen, a few thousand dollars. Maybe a good throwing knife."

"A few thousand dollars?" Howard echoed, his eyes wide.

"And a toothbrush. I'd kill for a toothbrush."

Squinting, he rubbed his forehead as if in pain. "Get your squirrel," he said as he turned to a drawer and pulled out a spool of gauze.

"You'll help?" she asked as he wrapped his hand.

"I don't know yet. Keep your mouth shut and come with me." He opened the door, looking taller on the threshold.

Peri grabbed the box, tucking it under her arm as she paced after him. But she nearly ran into him when he stopped short, a flustered Anne before him. "Get room three cleaned up," he said, his words clipped. "Cancel my appointments. I'm going to Emergency."

The woman's eyes were large. "Are you okay?"

"Just a nip," he said as he bodily moved her out of his way. "But I want it taken care of now." Turning, he glared at Peri. "Let's go. And keep that box closed, will you?"

Head down and box tucked tighter under her arm, she followed him.

"Squirrels!" Howard shouted as he grabbed his coat from the rack behind the desk. "Sure, I'll take a look. Susan, take a memo. No more squirrels!"

"Are you okay?" the second receptionist wanted to know, already on the phone.

"Ask me tomorrow." Howard stiff-armed the glass door open. Hardly breathing, Peri followed him out into the dark. Lights were coming on in the lot, and the nearby traffic seemed to glow from the mist. Howard stood with his hands on his hips as he looked at the green monster she'd driven in on. "You *stole* that piece of crap?"

"You can't hot-wire a new model," she said in

affront. "They have chips and things. If I had taken a Lexus, I wouldn't have gotten ten minutes down the road before getting busted by the cops." Gratitude filled her, and she hesitated. "Thank you."

"I haven't said I'll help yet." He was moving again, and Peri hustled after him. "That's my van," he said, the vehicle flashing its lights when he pointed a fob at it.

She jogged to the passenger side. The no-windows thing it had going made her uneasy, and she hesitated, fingers on the handle. "What does your gut say?" she whispered, cold in the mist, and then in a flash of decision, she lifted the latch and got in, squirrel-rocks sliding.

Howard was already behind the wheel, coat in the back, key in the ignition, when she flopped into the seat. The van was cluttered with a mish-mash of boxes. Peri tossed the shoebox to the floor with the rest and put her seat belt on.

Distracted, Howard said, "The fact that you trust me does not instill me with confidence."

Peri nudged a take-out bag away from her foot. "My gut is usually right." Something felt off, even though everything was going the way she wanted it to.

"So is mine," he said, starting the van. "Go sit in the back and look at the door, princess, so I don't have to knock you out, or cover your eyes, or anything else dumb like that."

Seriously? But he wasn't moving, and she finally undid her belt and picked her way awkwardly through the clutter until she sat on a pile of clean but frayed towels. They were for the animals, she guessed, and her bad feeling grew when he put the van in gear and crept to the entrance, brakes squeaking as he halted for traffic. "Where are we going?" she asked, not expecting an answer.

"Safe house. I'm passing the buck." His face was silhouetted in the lights from the passing cars as he waited for a gap in traffic. He looked angry, and his hands tapped the wheel impatiently. Muttering under his breath, he slammed the van into park when the light at the corner turned and his chance to drive away vanished. He stared out the window, then pulled the scrunchie from his dreadlocks and tossed it to the dash to sit with the three others. Turning to her, he said, "I want to know something. What did Silas defragment for you that he'd never seen?"

Peri licked her lips, feeling lost in the back of his van. "That I loved Jack," she said, not knowing if it would help or damn her. She looked away, blinking fast. Government agents didn't cry, even when they were lost, alone, and fighting their own people.

Nonplussed, he turned to the front and put the van in drive, griping at the car that didn't slow down when he gunned it into the street. Miserable, Peri propped herself up against the rocking van, hating how relieved she was that someone was willing to help her.

"You treacherous bitch!" Howard yelled, and she eyed him, thinking he had some serious road rage, but he was looking at her. "You lied to me, and I bought it!"

"What?"

Peri's eyes widened when she looked out the front window. Cop lights, red and blue, were coming up the road. Instinct made her reach for her pen pendant, but there was nothing to write.

"I should have known!" Howard shouted, dreadlocks swinging. "Silas warned me you were slippery as slime mold."

"Howard, you took the chip out, and Silas bought me a new phone they can't track. I'm telling you, it's not me." Cops. Opti wouldn't be so obvious, but they might use the local police to drive them into a trap. "I found your address in fifteen minutes knowing only that you worked as a vet and had a thing for squirrels," she said calmly. "Maybe Silas let something slip. Or maybe they just *followed* your sorry ass back here, Mr. Janitor. I saved you by getting you out. See?" she said as the cop cars squealed past the van, lights still flashing. "They aren't following us. They're headed to your office."

Howard's anger was replaced by stone-cold fear. "I can't go back."

Peri moved into the front seat, scrunching low to

keep out of sight. "It sucks, doesn't it." They had to get off this road. There were traffic lights every block, and they were making zero time in the rush hour.

Howard's teeth clenched, and the glow from the oncoming cars glinted on his beads. "They'll have my address, everything."

You catch on fast, Doctor. "We have to ditch this van. They'll put an APB on it as soon as they see it's not in the lot. Mass transit is fifty-fifty as long as it's aboveground. Anything below always has cameras, and I'm tired of face paint."

"The van." Howard's grip on the wheel tightened. "They'll be looking for it."

Peri sighed. "Yep. We need to ditch it. Sorry."

He glared at her, then back to the road. "If I find out you're responsible for this . . ."

Ticked, she sat up. "If that's what you think, then stop the van right now and let me out. I'll walk away and you'll never see me again." Damn it, this wasn't going well.

Howard abruptly jerked the van to the right, wheeling into an abandoned tire place and lurching to a halt. Weeds were thick at the edges, and a gully sank behind the building, rising to more weeds. About a half mile back, a big-box store glowed in the mist. Shocked, Peri stared at him. "Come on," he said as he snatched up his coat. "We're going to have to walk."

Her relief was so thick, she could almost taste it.

He wasn't abandoning her. "You believe me?" she said as she scanned the van for anything useful.

He was already outside, taking his lab coat off to show his brown slacks and a knitted vest over a stark white shirt. All he needed was a bow tie. Squinting at the mist, he shrugged his coat on and pulled his collar up, clearly disliking the rain. "Believe you? No, but Silas trusted you. We'll go through the empty lot and pick up a bus at the superstore. We're skipping the safe house and going straight to the alliance. Someone else is going to have to decide what to do with you. I'm done."

He slammed the door shut. She didn't have time to search the van for anything to help their flight, so she got out and hustled to catch up. His back was bowed, and his office shoes were already wet and muddy. "I'm sorry," she said, meaning it, but he never met her eyes even as he helped her down the ravine and across the shallow ditch of water.

It was going to be a long night.

CHAPTER NINETEEN

Peri stood sideways in the bus's aisle, two bags of food in her hand as she waited for the heavyset woman ahead of her to finish draping her coat over her seat back and sit down. It was after midnight, and the chartered bus full of over-dressed, excited women had finally settled as the complimentary wine and late hour took their toll. She'd jumped at the chance to make a food run when the BING bus had pulled off the interstate for a fifteen-minute comfort break. The choice had been tacos, burgers, or subs. The subs won, hands down.

Finally the woman put her butt in the seat and Peri edged past. It felt good to get up and move around, but Howard had been sleeping when she'd left, and she wasn't sure how he'd handle waking up and finding her gone.

The bus jerked into motion, and she easily caught her balance. Sure enough, she spotted Howard's horrified expression in the shifting streetlights. Their eyes met and she held up the bags of food in explanation. Relief cascaded over him, quickly followed by guilt.

Swaying with the motion of the bus, she continued past several rows of open, plush seats to get to where they'd retreated to try to distance themselves from the tour group.

"I didn't know what you wanted, so I got you a steak hoagie on whole wheat," she said as she sat, her voice betraying her slight annoyance.

Eyes wide, he shifted in the indulgent seat to tuck his phone away. "I thought you'd left."

She extended him a bag, arm stiff. "I asked for your help, remember?"

Sheepish, he took it, bag crackling as he opened it up and looked inside. "That was before my cover was blown. Thanks."

"Bottled water . . ." She handed him one that had been tucked under her arm, and he took it, closing out the complimentary Web link and lowering his tray table. "And your choice." She opened her bag and brought out the chips. "Salt and vinegar, or black pepper."

Howard smiled weakly, his face seeming to vanish as the bus lurched onto the service road and into a more certain dark. "Black pepper?" he asked, and she handed it over.

That he hadn't trusted her rankled, and Peri sat silent beside him at the back of the bus, lips pressed as she arranged her sandwich and chips on the fold-down table. She left the courtesy light off, but the ambient light from the monitors, currently muted and showing the late news, was enough to see his continued embarrassment. Apparently Asia's borders were closed, anyone trying to break the containment being shot on sight and dragged away by workers in hazmat suits. Peri thought it disturbing that no one seemed to care. Perhaps it was an ongoing thing she'd forgotten. She hadn't been able to find any Twinkies the last couple of days, either.

"I left you a note," she finally said, and he winced.

"I didn't see it," he said, clearly lying. "Thank you for the sandwich."

"Uh-huh," she said drily, the snap of the breaking seal on her water sounding loud.

Howard seemed to shrink in on himself. "I'm sorry," he started, and she cut him off, hand waving as she swallowed.

"Don't worry about it," she said when she came up for air. "I'm the bad guy, remember?"

"I never—" he said in affront, and she eyed him sharply as she recapped her bottle. "Fine, maybe I did," he amended, looking at his sandwich forlornly. "But can you blame me?"

"Eat your steak, Howard," she said flatly.

Immediately he picked it up. "Opti is a mercenary task force," he said around his full mouth. "The only thing keeping them from being classified as a terrorist group is that they're on the government's payroll." He swallowed. "Among others."

"I'm taking my black-pepper chips back," she said, plucking them from his tray.

Howard chuckled, dark hands securely wrapped around his hoagie. "You do what you need to do, but you can't tell me that Opti didn't help that power plant melt down in the Middle East last year."

"Why on earth would Opti blow up a power plant?" she asked, her voice hardly audible over the bus, roaring to get up the entrance ramp. The bus darkened further, cocooning them.

"To put an end to the religious extremists slaughtering reporters and medical relief workers." Hardly more than a shadow, Howard hunched over his tray as his sandwich threatened to fall apart. "Millions displaced, thousands dead. Acres of newly arable land wasted. It's a shame. The world lost a lot of history, too. Only so much of it could be trucked out ahead of time under the excuse of lending it to a museum."

She didn't remember, and for the first time, it bothered her. "Accidents do happen."

Howard's dark fingers stood out against his hoagie as her eyes adjusted, and he set his sandwich down. "They've done it before. Chernobyl ring a bell?"

Peri frowned and broke a piece of bacon off her BLT. "You're mistaken."

"Am I?"

The salty bacon tasted flat. Again, doubt trickled through her, her blind loyalty wearing thin. "What about Opti breaking up that credit card–strip hacker ring? Millions of dollars caught before it was funneled overseas. And Stanza-gate. You really think that wack job should set policy? How about finding that plane that went down in the Alps? Rescuing all those people before they started eating each other."

Howard's brow furrowed in thought. "That was three years ago."

"Well, it seems like yesterday to me," she said defensively, and Howard adroitly snatched his chips back, his faint look of pity-laced understanding irritating her.

Opening the packet, he leaned close. "I hate to break it to you, but the strip fraud was a front, paid for by the Billion by Thirty club to force that nifty new banking app on your phone into play. Opti found the Alps plane because they were the ones who downed it trying to keep a defector from going over to the wrong side. I'll give you Stanza-gate, though. The guy was crazy."

"Yeah, we should just let the world go to hell," she grumbled. "Free choice and all."

"That's not what this is about." He hesitated, the lights from the oncoming traffic making the furrows on his brow look deep. "Okay, the alliance is trying to shut Opti down, but not the work that drafters and anchors do. We *need* the terrorists stopped, the flesh-trafficking rings ended, and the power-hungry extremist governments held in check. And sure, the alliance isn't so much the green tree-huggers that we don't understand why sometimes it's better if someone dies early or innocents suffer for the greater good. What the alliance believes is that it shouldn't be a handful of wealthy families who both dictate and benefit, telling the rest of humanity that they did them a favor and to be happy with their new toys and don't ask who paid for them and how."

Peri pushed her food away, her appetite gone. She wasn't so innocent as to believe that there was a right or wrong answer, either. But Opti *had* rescued that plane. They *had* saved the taxpayers millions of dollars. *And murdered a politician before he could strong-arm a series of laws into legislation that would set the U.S. back a hundred years.*

But even she had a problem if the real benefit Opti was serving might be only the interests of those who could pay for the miracle of changing time.

"Jesus, Howard, how did you ever get mixed up in this?" she said softly, not really expecting an answer.

Digging to the bottom of his chip bag, Howard chuckled. "A woman."

"See a man in trouble, look no farther than the woman beside him," she said, saluting him with her water bottle.

"No. It was Silas," Howard added as he shook the crumbs from his chip bag into his palm. "I was a tutor in college, and I met Silas when he came over to pick up one of my clients. We found we liked the same football team, started hanging out, watching the games. He got drunk one night, staggering drunk over a girl I'd never heard him talk about before. I took him home." Howard crumpled the chip bag and threw it away. "The entire ride he debated with himself the moral responsibilities of how much someone should sacrifice for their beliefs and the responsibility of those who love them. He told me this fantastic story about what if people could jump back a few seconds and rewrite a mistake but in the doing, forgot it."

Peri met his eyes, glad it was dark. "Drafters."

He pushed his crumbs into a tiny pile. "I found out about anchors and drafters. Found out that Opti was a for-hire service. The rich get richer, the poor get cheese off a truck. The alliance was my chance to be more than I am, I suppose. Put my actions where my mouth is. You don't always have to have a reason other than the need to do what's right. And it was exciting to know that there really are people who can do what you do and to be a part of that." He shrugged. "Why does anyone do anything?"

A smile crossed Peri's face. *Why indeed?*

"How about you?" Howard asked, and she reached to pluck a chip off his starched white shirt.

"I fell off a swing," she said, not wanting to talk about it. "Would you mind if I sat across the aisle to catch a few z's?"

"No, go on," he said, gaze falling to her untouched sandwich. "Are you going to eat that?"

She shook her head, smiling as he shifted it to his tray. "Wake me up before we get there, okay?" she asked, and when he nodded, she took her water and moved to the other side of the bus.

The seat was cool as she settled into it, but it wasn't the temperature or the cold window she rested her head upon that made her shiver. Eyes open, she stared at the passing lights, her mind full as she weighed the last couple of days against what she'd known her entire adult life. She wasn't sure if remembering those three missing years would make any difference.

Opti was both more and less than she had thought: more involved and insidious than she had believed, and less moral and transparent than she had ever imagined. The alliance couldn't be as ineffective and laughable as she had been told—not if it attracted people like Howard, people risking their lives not for revenge or money, but because it was the right thing to do.

Peri shivered again, pressed against the side of the cold bus.

She couldn't believe Opti was entirely corrupt—because if it was, it meant she was, too.

CHAPTER
TWENTY

Peri stepped off the charter bus, the ugly blue coat over her arm as she blinked in the clear, early sun. Howard was tight behind her, almost running into her as he took her elbow and edged her out of the way of the excited passengers. Eyes closed, she took a deep breath to push out the lingering, mild paranoia of being trapped in a bus with women who *did not shut up.*

Silas was being lied to about her, and that bothered her more than she'd like to admit. Exhaling, she opened her eyes. People dressed with an overdone flair mingled with those in jeans and tees in a noisy throng, all walking the paved path to Churchill Downs. The track was closed for the season, but the venue could apparently still be rented out, and Peri squinted at the woman on the blond horse welcoming everyone to the Run for the Hearts charity race.

An announcer blared over the noise of the leaving bus, and the woman wheeled her horse around, making it prance in place as the crowd before her cheered. A small jet roared nearby in takeoff, and Peri noted it. Not far away. Not far at all. Mid-sky, several low-Q news drones hummed over the track getting footage, and she lowered her head as one buzzed the parking lot for a shot of the arriving fans. Black cars lined the shade at the outskirts of the lot, their drivers catching a smoke or clustered around tablets. Most of the vehicles were late-model—probably rentals with drivers—but there were enough *real* cars to make her run a hand over her rumpled sweater. She'd fit in better with a big hat and jewelry. *Black pearls,* she thought, not knowing why. It was an odd mix of wealth and commonality bound together by the love of horses. That Howard's contact was among the throng wasn't encouraging.

"That way." Howard pointed to a narrow

sawdust path that led away from the track, and she pushed herself into motion, relishing the chance to move. A flicker of mistrust rose as they passed the sign stating they were headed for the platinum campsites, but her gut said Howard was being honest with her. His mood had softened this morning, and she had the growing suspicion that he felt she needed rescuing.

"It's up on the right," Howard said, head down over his phone as three girls in skirts too short and heels too tall passed them going the other way. "It's about time she answered my text."

"Gawwd," one of the girls drawled. "Did you see her black eye?"

Oh, yeah. I forgot about that. Giving her hair a fluff, she lifted her chin. *It is what it is.*

Howard's pace slowed as they entered the campsites and he began casting about. Huge RVs were spaced haphazardly under old trees. A number of them had golf carts parked in front. Others had tents with alfresco eating more lavish than most restaurants offered inside. There was a permanent pool and spa, and horses were clearly welcome, judging by the number of places available to tie them up or water them down. Millionaires camping out. Go figure.

"There," he said, exhaling in relief, and Peri followed his pointing finger to one of the more elaborate campsites under a banner reading JACQUARD EQUINES. A blond woman in a black evening dress sat in the cabana-like lounge area, her laptop and tablet open and in use. An overdone silk derby hat crowned by a veil and an enormous magnolia blossom rested on the table beside an untouched julep, unnoticed as she talked on her glass phone. But it was the multiple dishes on the roof of the RV that captured Peri's attention. This was the alliance? She'd been expecting something backroom and slick with sunglass-wearing security. This felt like home.

Seeing them, the woman stood, her conversation continuing as she came forward. She moved confidently, smoothing her long blond hair, which had been mussed by the hat. Peri eyed her low-heeled sandals in approval—stylish but still good to run in. Her dress was modestly high at the bodice, but it clung to accentuate her femininity. Even her jewelry was perfect, simple enough to keep her from sliding into the ranks of partygoers but saying "money" nonetheless. It was clearly a cultivated look, both elegant and in charge.

"Hi, can I help you?" she said with a slight drawl, phone call ending as her gaze ran over Peri before returning to Howard. And then her eyes widened. "Oh. My. Gawd! Howard!" she exclaimed, her southern drawl strengthening. "I haven't seen you since my freshman year!"

"Taf." Howard grinned, grunting in surprise when she yanked him into an enthusiastic hug. Her hair shifted to show a butterfly tattoo, and then she pushed back, beaming. "Wow, you look fabulous. I should have changed my major. How's life been treating you?"

"Great! I work for one of the big hospitals planning their events. I'm using up all my vacation days to help my mom out on this, but God help her, she needed it. How about you? You got your license, right? I bet you're why my mom is in such a state. Lord love a duck, you know better than to bother her when she's fund-raising."

"Yeah. About that." Flushed, Howard dropped back, his eyes darting to Peri to include her. "Taf, I'd like you to meet Peri Reed. Peri, this is Taf Jacquard. We met at school. I was pre-med. I think Taf was going for her MRS degree. How many majors did you have, anyway?"

MRS degree, as in Mrs. . . . Peri took the woman's hand, surprised at how firm it was.

"Just one," Taf said, giving him a mock punch as she let go of Peri. "I'm a marketing events coordinator, which means I can plan one hell of a party for six or sixty thousand. Nice to meet you. It's Taffeta, actually, but call me Taf."

"Pleasure," Peri said, forcing her smile to stay undimmed as Taf checked out her scuffed boots, wrinkled slacks, and ugly coat. At least she didn't say anything about her black eye.

"Is your mom around?" Howard asked, fidgeting. "She's expecting us. I think."

"Sure. Come on up and sit down," Taf said, and

then louder to the aide hovering near the cabana, "Find out where my mom is, will you?" The aide murmured something, and Taf barked, "Then

text her! The woman has her phone grafted to her ass." All smiles, Taf turned back to them. "You want something to drink? It might take a minute. She's got an entire group flying in from LA, and she's trying to cram in as much as she can before they get here."

Peri eyed the cabana in anticipation, but before they could move, Taf sighed at the sound of hoofbeats. "Speak of the devil and she will appear," she said, a tired resolve in her voice. Peri caught a flash of irritation on the young woman's face, and then it was gone.

"Hoo . . . boy." Howard backed up when an arch-necked, light-blond mare high-stepped into the campsite. "I really don't like horses."

"Then you came to the wrong spot," Taf said as two men in stable livery came out from behind the RV to take the animal's head.

It was the woman from the parking lot, and Peri refused to retreat as the horse shied. "I've never seen a horse that color before," she said, thinking it had almost a metallic sheen.

Taf eased up beside her, so close Peri could smell her expensive perfume. "It's an Akhal-Teke gold. I think she spent more on it than on my entire education."

"*She's* our *contact!*" Peri blurted, eyeing the

woman in her velvet blazer and vibrant cravat. The dappled light caught the diamond-encrusted broach of a horse head, and her short, blond hair was bound up under a small but eye-catching derby hat. She looked like a politician's wife with too much money and not enough to do. But then Peri spotted the security men behind the RV coming forward. An unsettled feeling crept into her, curling around twice before settling into the pit of her soul like a bad dog.

The woman dismounted, graceful from practice. Taking off her hat and gloves, she handed them to one of the men. "Howard," she said, eyes bright and color in her cheeks that makeup couldn't hide. Her riding boots, unlike everything else, were well worn, and Peri looked for a whip, thinking it wouldn't be out of place. "Your text was nebulous, to say the least. You'd better have a good explanation. This isn't a good time."

"Is it ever?" he said, shaking hands with her, but the woman never took her eyes off Peri.

Taf had shifted to make room, ultimately ending closer to Peri than to her mother. "Mother, this is Peri Reed," she said formally, a stilted smile in place, and Peri shifted her coat to stick her hand out. "Peri, this is my mother, Fran Jacquard."

"Pleasure," Fran said, motioning her security forward.

"Hey!" Peri exclaimed when one took her hat and coat, and the other patted her down.

"Seriously?" Taf complained. "Howard wouldn't bring her here if she wasn't clean."

"Mistakes happen." Sculpted eyebrows high, Fran waved off the guard when he showed her the jackknife she'd taken from that beat two-door car she'd hot-wired.

"Peri is clean," Howard grumped as the security guys dropped back. "It's what I do."

"Good, then." Fran stood before Peri, her sharp attention making Peri stiffen. So she was dirty and smelled like a bus. She'd been working three days straight. "I understand you have something for us?" Fran prompted, and Howard shifted from foot to foot, making the beads in his dreadlocks clink.

"Ah, actually . . . ," he hedged, "we don't quite have it yet. That's why we're here."

Fran turned to him, but Peri was wondering what the *it* was they were talking about. Taf, too, looked out of the loop. "It what?" Peri asked, feeling ignored.

Fran leaned toward Howard, her expression twisting up in irritation. "Howard," she said softly. "What is she *doing* here if she doesn't have what we need to close Opti down?"

Oh, that *it,* Peri thought. "Mrs. Jacquard, Opti has Silas Denier. He works for you, yes?"

Fran's attention shifted. "And you do not," Fran said as Howard exhaled in relief.

Peri's eyes slitted. Pulse fast, she scanned the area for a fast way out. The horse had been led away, and the nearby golf carts might or might not be faster than someone running. They couldn't outrun bullets, though. Coming here suddenly felt like a mistake, but she'd never left a man behind before, and she wasn't going to start now—even if it was Silas.

"Peri thinks Silas can bring back a memory that proves Opti is corrupt," Howard pleaded.

"And prove I'm not," Peri added.

"Opti *is* corrupt," Fran said, motioning for her security to back off. "All of it."

"*I'm* not corrupt," Peri said, working to keep her temper. Pissing off her alliance contact wouldn't help. "And I'm not a scapegoat," she added, feeling vulnerable under the woman's accusing eye. "Silas can help me remember what happened at Global Genetics." *What if I remember more? What if he brings it all back? Do I want to remember Jack's death?*

Asking for things was not unusual for Peri. She did it all the time and usually got what she wanted. But asking a group that was hell-bent on destroying everything she believed in was chancy—even if her success might mean a realization of everything they wanted. At this point, it was hard to argue that Opti was not rife with corruption. All she wanted was to clear her name.

And yet, Fran's expression as she stared at Peri made her feel . . . guilty.

"This is counterproductive," Peri said, trying for

a firmer tone. "Every moment spent talking this over makes it harder to retrieve Silas. I need him to reconstruct what happened up in that office. You want to know who's corrupt? So do I. But it isn't me. Silas can bring it back."

"An anchor can't defragment a memory he or she didn't witness," Fran said quickly.

"Yes they can." Peri warmed as she recalled Silas's hotel room, his cool thoughts in hers.

Howard inched closer, his knitted vest looking tired next to Fran's high style. "I talked to Silas yesterday. He's been *working* with her," he said, and Peri wondered at the emphasis he put on the word. "He's already had some success bringing back her past anchor. If he can do that—"

"The one she killed, right?" Fran interrupted, and Taf's lips parted in surprise.

"Why are we still talking about this?" Peri said in disbelief. "I'm trying to help."

"To help yourself." Fran frowned, clearly undecided. "Isn't that why you're here?"

"I'm here because I need to know the truth," Peri said, her pulse quickening.

Fran sighed. "Don't we all," she said, then jumped when the phone on her hip vibrated. "How nice. Their plane came in early," she said sourly as she took a look. "I have to go, but you are coming with me. You can explain on the way."

Peri didn't move, gaze sliding from her dirty clothes to Taf's understated elegance. Howard, too, looked uncomfortable, and he scrubbed a hand over his thick bristles making a dark shadow on his face. "Ahh, I know half-beards are in these days, but I could really use a shower before going to your box, Fran."

Fran jerked to a halt, grimacing. "I don't have time for this."

Excuse me?

"Mom." Taf put a hand on Peri's shoulder. "Go do what you need to do. Take Howard. He can wash up at the jockey showers. I'll give Peri something of mine to wear. We'll meet you there in twenty minutes. You can get your guests settled, and then we can talk."

Shower? Peri's impulse to walk and keep going faltered. "You have something that might fit me?" she asked, and Taf nodded, eyes bright. "You are a lifesaver. I've been wearing this for three days." She knew that if they got Howard alone he might dish the dirt, but she hadn't done anything in the last three days that she'd do differently—given the chance.

"Howard?" Fran prompted, and the man took both of Peri's hands, surprising her.

"You'll be okay?" he asked, the depth of question in his brown eyes startling.

"Y'all go along, Howie," Taf drawled cheerfully. "I've got this."

But he didn't leave until Peri nodded. Somehow it made her feel even more vulnerable.

"I *told* you to lose that accent, Taf," Fran said as she and Howard got into one of the golf carts, and Taf frowned.

"I don't know what they're worried about," Peri said drily when Fran told her security to stay with Peri. "They took my jackknife."

"Come on," Taf said, her voice tight and accent almost nil as she tugged at Peri's elbow. "I've got something that will go fabulously with your skin tone."

"I'd be happy with just something to cover my black eye, thanks," she said distantly, following her up to the permanent decking that the RV was parked against. Taf was still smiling, but the tension between her and her mother was easy to see, old and deep.

The shower was surprisingly decadent for something on wheels, and Peri indulged until the water went cold, appreciating the expensive soap and shampoo. After some talk about the non-functionality of the first painted-on dress that Taf had picked out, Peri settled into skintight white jeans and a black blazer with a white silk button-down shirt underneath. There was even a matching derby hat, and taking the glitzy black-and-silver monstrosity in hand, she left the tiny bathroom vestibule and went into the main space.

Taf looked up from her laptop, her face lighting up. "Wow, you look better in that than I ever did.

It's a little casual for the races, but damn, girl! You look good!"

Flushing in pleasure, Peri spun to show it off. "You don't think the hat is too much?"

"No." Standing, Taf all but pushed her down into one of the cushy chairs. "Sit."

Flustered, Peri sat, watching Taf through the mirror as she pinned the hat in place. She'd never had many girlfriends. It was easier to drive potential friends away than have them think she was stupid when she couldn't remember what they'd done together last week. "Thank you," Peri said softly, not knowing what to make of the attention. "You're not going to get in trouble about the pants, are you?" They were Fran's, seeing as Taf had legs the size of toothpicks.

"What is she going to do? Ground me?" Taf took the hatpin from between her teeth, carefully wedging it to hold the hat on. "Sorry about my mom. She's intense. Here. Try this on your eye."

"Don't worry about it," Peri said as she popped open the compact and used her finger to dab the makeup around her eye to find it was a good match. "My mom is worse. *Bless her heart,*" she added in a thick southern drawl to make Taf chuckle. "She wanted me to be a dancer," she said, not knowing why she was opening up to Taf, except that they both had overbearing, controlling mothers. "I took all the classes, spent my summers at dance camps, blah, blah, blah."

"My mom just wants me to be married," Taf said as she closed down her laptop.

Peri laughed at the dry humor she'd put in her voice, but Howard's crack about the MRS degree now made sense. "You're one hell of an event organizer," Peri said as she spun around to find Taf slumped into the cushions. "What did you minor in?"

"Business," Taf said glumly.

Which was clearly not her first love. "What *else* did you minor in?" she prompted.

Taf's eyes flicked up and away. "All kinds of things," she said, clearly avoiding the issue. "My mom thought it was a waste of time, but I've got almost-minors in half a dozen studies."

So she wouldn't have to graduate, Peri thought, completely understanding. It was far easier to avoid a domineering mother than to stand up to someone you loved. And Taf did love her mother. "Taf. You can't live your life on what your mother wants," she said, and Taf looked up, shocked. "So it's a hassle standing up to her. So she might cut you off. It's your life. She already got your first twenty years. Don't give her your second. By then, it's too late."

Her lips pressed, making Peri wonder if she'd gone too far. But then Taf stood and held out a matching shawl. "We'd better get going."

Yep, she'd gone too far. Peri took the shawl from her, feeling depressed. "Thanks."

Taf's pensive silence held all the way up the sawdust-packed path to the track, giving Peri time to stew over the stone-faced guards accompanying them in the golf cart. All around was colorful, early-spring attire, and the men were taking the rare opportunity to flaunt pinstripes and flamboyant colors as much as the women. Big hats, mint juleps, and outrageous ties made Peri think she should have gone with Taf's first instinct of the short red dress.

The silence continued to grow as the cart driver took a service road leading to the back of the main building, the cinder block painted a dull yellow and lined with one-way doors probably leading to kitchens and service areas. From the unseen track, a bugle sounded to bring the stragglers in. A rising exhalation from the stands rose into a roar.

If Peri had been trying to get away, it would have been a perfect spot to act—quiet and unobtrusive, and the bodies wouldn't be found until after the race. But she wasn't, and the rising adrenaline broke over her with nowhere to go. Her pulse quickened as she got out of the cart.

"Down the hall, through the doors, and up the stairway," Taf directed, and Peri halted.

"Taf. I'm sorry I said what I did about your mother," Peri said, and Taf jerked as if slapped. "It was out of place, and none of my business."

Taf almost smiled, reaching out to give Peri's

elbow a squeeze. "No," she said softly, leading her forward to the double steel doors. "You're right. I need to grow a pair."

"That's not what I meant," Peri said. "You're not a coward. She's your mother."

"Exactly." Taf gestured Peri should go first, and feeling even more unsettled, Peri followed the first security man through the twin service doors. The sound of people laughing grew loud long before she saw them, and Peri balked when they turned a corner and the hall opened onto a huge room overlooking the track.

"That way," Taf said, pointing out the staircase, and Peri nodded. It was a fabulous southern affair, complete with a woman in full southern belle regalia at the base of it, her accent charming as she checked names on a list before allowing access to the second floor. Two men in servant livery waited to reject any unwanted visitors if needed. Haves were being parted from the have-nots, and Peri's tension spiked. But the organizer of the event wouldn't be in the stands.

"Go right on up, Ms. Jacquard," the woman said, drawling Taf's name into four syllables.

The noise muted as they rose, and the soft strains of a piano became more obvious. The wood floor was varnished to a hard black. "That's ours," Taf said, indicating an elaborate door, and Peri slowed as she entered the sprawling observation room.

The floor-to-ceiling windows were expansive, and the comfortable seating was arranged like a living room, with coffee tables and plush pillows. Older women in bright colors mingled with thin women in tight black who threw their heads back to show off their necks when they laughed, mimicking those downstairs but in a higher tax bracket. The piano was live and the food in tiny portions. Overlooking it all was Fran.

Seeing them, she excused herself from her guests, the group clearly from LA with their cool façades. "Taf, a word," she said in greeting, then turned to Peri. "You can sit if you want."

"Why, thank you very much," Peri said sarcastically, and Fran gave her a double glance, her expression inscrutable. Feeling as if she belonged, Peri eased down into the plush cushions of a chair with its back to the wall, where she could see everything. It was the nicest thing she'd sat in for three days, and she stretched her arms out along the back of it to make the space hers. From across the room, a man smiled and started over, but he jerked to a red-eared halt when the security men who had accompanied them in took up positions to either side of her.

"No sense of adventure," she said around a sigh, then beamed at the servers offering her hors d'oeuvres. Happy, she heaped a little plate high. Mouth full of foie gras, she beckoned over the man with the champagne. "Thank you very,

very much," she said as she took a glass, and he inclined his head, eyes bright.

"Howard!" she called, seeing him at a window, looking like an awkward wallflower in his new suit and tie. His dreadlocks were pulled back in a ponytail, showing off the elegance of his face but still looking exotic. His face was damp from a quick shave. "You wash up good," she said as he came over, giving her security a glance before gingerly sitting down in the chair beside her.

"I could say the same for you," he answered, but his brow was pinched.

"What did you tell her?" she asked, suddenly concerned.

"Nothing you wouldn't want me to." His eyes were on Taf arguing with her mother. "I don't know, Peri. Something doesn't feel right. There's too much talk going on."

"Yeah. I'm smelling what we're stepping in, too." Peri settled back to wait, the rich food not sitting well. Everything was achingly, wonderfully familiar, but her intuition was telling her to leave. It was only her need for their help in freeing Silas that kept her unmoving. That, and Tweedle-dumb and Tweedledumber beside her.

"Taf, enough!" Fran said loudly, then forcibly eased her features into a pleasant expression. Taf, beside her, was pissed.

"They're posting!" Fran called cheerfully. "Everyone to the windows!"

The excitement rose. Drinks were set down, and the little clusters of chatting people turned into a mob at the windows as personal space vanished in the thrill of the race.

Peri set her drink down, standing up as Fran strode to her. "I've got a moment. You, come with me," Fran said brusquely. "Taf, you and Howard can watch the race."

"I don't want to watch the race," Taf said, arms crossed over her middle.

Howard looked between the two women in unease. "Ah, if it's all the same to you, ma'am, I'd like to stay with Peri."

Fran glanced at her security. Peri stiffened as adrenaline poured through the cracks of her conviction. "Watch the race," Fran said tightly. "We're just going into the kitchen."

Peri eyed the swinging door the servers had been going in and out. *Something has changed.* "Go ahead, Howard. I'll be okay," she said, not liking the determined slant to his lips.

"There. See?" Fran said brightly, actually taking Peri's elbow and turning her away. "Everything is fine."

But it wasn't fine, and the only reason Peri had agreed to leave the room was so that Howard and Taf would be out of the line of fire. "What do you have for me?" she asked as she followed Fran into the kitchen.

It was full of men with weapons.

Someone touched her, going down when Peri swiftly broke his wrist. Head swiveling, she fell into a ready stance, but it was too late as safeties clicked off. She could draft, but she might lose the last half hour—forever.

"Mother!" Taf exclaimed as she burst in behind them, and in that instant, Peri was wrestled to the ground, her air huffing out as her hands were painfully yanked behind her and secured with the smooth feel of plastic. *Damn it all to hell.*

"Where's the audio binder?" Fran said tersely. "Well, get it on her. And the blindfold."

Peri struggled as someone's knee went to the small of her back. "I'm trying to help you!" she shouted, closing her eyes to block the grayish-purple color of the bag imprinting on her mind. But she gave up when a heavy hand pinned her face to the floor and a soft foam insert was jammed inexpertly into her ear. Her pulse hammered as an irritating whine filled half her hearing. It was over. She could close her eyes to block the color, but the precise hum of 741 MHz of sound could not be surmounted—and it worked instantaneously.

"Mom! What are you doing?" Taf said loudly.

"You don't think her request was the only one on the table, do you?" Fran said, and Peri went cold, sitting up when the two men pinning her to the tile floor shoved off her. "Why should we risk anything when Opti will give us Silas in exchange for her?"

Excuse me? "They're going to scrub me!" Peri said, her hands behind her back and a bag over her head. "I'm not corrupt! They're going to wipe me back to ignorance, and I'll never find out what happened!"

"Get her out of here."

Peri heard the door open as the excitement from the crowd grew loud. She was yanked to her feet, and the entire room seemed to shake with noise. She thought of Howard with the black feeling of betrayal, but he hadn't known. If he had, her intuition would have pinged on him and she never would have come in. They'd used him.

"She came to us for help," Taf said bitterly. "I can't believe you're doing this."

"Let me handle this, Taffeta. You've not earned the right for your voice to be heard," Fran said. "Go plan something."

"This is wrong and you know it," Taf protested. "Howard? Howard!" she called, but it was too late, and Peri stumbled, disoriented, when they shoved her into motion. The numbing hum between her ears was getting worse, even as her feet treaded on hard floors and the sound of the people downstairs became loud.

"Get her out of here," Fran repeated, her confidence irritating. "And don't take that hood off until she's been drugged at least twenty minutes."

Peri tensed, stifling a gasp when she was picked up in a fireman's carry, the steps jarring as they wove through several hallways, the sound of the piano and people going faint. This wasn't the end of it. Not by a long shot. But as the elevator began to descend, Peri wondered how she'd ever get out of this.

She was adrift and needed an anchor.

—————CHAPTER—————
TWENTY-ONE

Knees to her chest, Peri leaned against the side of the panel van to stay upright as they took a corner. She hated panel vans. That she'd been shackled, drugged, and thrown into the back of one was not changing her opinion. At least the bag was off her head. They'd left the audio binder in, though, and the monochromatic hum was set too high, giving her a mild headache. She was reasonably confident they were heading to the airport she'd noticed earlier. And they knew what they were doing, too, seeing as the drug they'd hit her with an hour ago was a mild muscle relaxant and a depressant all in one.

An attention-getting *ping* came from the front of the van, and Peri shifted to a kneel, leaning to watch the two men scramble to see whose phone it was.

"Oh God. It's Dragon Lady," the driver said. "You answer it."

"It's your phone," the other said, ducking when the driver smacked him. "What the hell!"

"Answer my phone. I'm driving."

"Hit me again, and I'll pound you," the second threatened even as he reached for it.

There was a rough spot in the wall where a screw protruded, but it wasn't enough to fray the plastic they'd bound her hands with, and Peri scooted to a new spot.

"Yes, ma'am. Yes, ma'am. Five minutes. Yes, ma'am, I'm writing it down."

Peri froze when the phone beeped. "What a control freak," the man said. "She wanted to remind us that they're still at hangar three."

"Shut up!" the driver said. "She's not supposed to know where we're going."

"Like she can't tell we're at the airport?" the other said. "The jets kind of give it away."

Yes, the jets did kind of give it away, and Peri struggled for balance when they took a turn onto what was probably a service road.

"Holy shit!" someone exclaimed, and Peri tensed when the van swerved again and the other man began shrieking, "Turn! Turn! She's coming right for us!"

The tires hop-skipped. Peri gasped, rolling to the front of the van. Her head hit the back of the seat as tires screeched, and they stopped in three seconds flat.

For a moment, the om of sound between her

ears was the only noise. Peri's heart pounded and she heard a groan. The van was tilted forward. Adrenaline made a spot of clarity in her drugged state, and she felt as if she'd been sleeping. She could smell propellant, and she panicked before she realized the airbags had deployed.

"O-o-o-ow . . . ," a man groaned, and Peri tried to move, cataloging new hurts. "She ran us right off the road. Jeff, you all right?"

"Yeah," came a softer voice. "I think I'm going to puke. Is the woman okay?"

No, the woman isn't okay, she thought when the driver leaned to check.

"Back off!" she shouted as he reached for her, and he jerked away in surprise.

"She's alive," the guy said, settling back in his seat.

Her head was throbbing, and either the audio binder, the drugs, or hitting the back of the seat with her head was making her nauseated. There was a rush of cooler air, and both men turned to the front window. "Hey, you'd better have good insurance—" the driver started, and then Peri froze at the click of a safety releasing.

"Y'all do anything I don't like, and I'll pop you!" Taf shouted, and Peri's head snapped up. "You think my mother's a bitch, I'm her devil spawn. Hands up. Out of the van. Now!"

"What is she—ow!" the second man said, and

Peri pulled herself together as the back of the van squeaked open. *Howard?*

"Peri, are you okay?" Howard said, awkward as he levered himself into the slanted back end. She blinked at the bright sun, the light hurting her eyes. They were in a ditch, the empty road stretching behind them at a weird angle.

"Both of you men get out!" Taf yelled from the front of the van. "Get over here. Move!"

Howard's eyes were creased in concern, and she croaked, "I'll live."

Relief crossed his expression. "Does your neck hurt? Can you move everything?"

"If you're rescuing me, I can run a marathon." Peri clumsily got to her knees, her hands still bound behind her.

"Let me get that," he said, reaching to cut her hands free. The cuffs released with a snap, and she hissed at the pain. Fingers numb from the lack of circulation, she fumbled for the audio binder. Blessed silence replaced the irritating hum. Renewed, she took a deep breath. "Thanks," she whispered, wondering why he was here, helping her again.

Taf's voice came from outside the van. "Howard? If she's okay, we gotta go."

Howard slid to the back, hand extended to help her. Strength seemed to rush to fill her as she took it, and she crab-walked out, surprised at the faint vertigo.

Taf was pointing a big-ass rifle at two men kneeling beside the front wheel. The driver's-side fender was wrapped around a tree. Their hands were laced atop their heads, and they looked like assassination victims. Across the road was a 1954 Ford F100 truck, tricked out and painted a bright red. A part of Peri wondered how she knew what make and year it was, but she did.

"Sorry about that," Taf was saying, but she was talking to Peri, not to the men. "I didn't know what else to do other than play chicken with them. You okay?"

Taf had changed into black slacks and top, blond hair pulled back in a ponytail and a leather duster furling about her boots. Peri didn't like that she looked like a younger version of herself on a good day. "Ask me tomorrow," she said, knowing the real aches wouldn't start until then. "Your mom is calling every five minutes," Peri added, leaning on Howard as she limped forward. "Get their phones."

"Phones. Now!" Taf barked. "Easy . . . ," she warned when their hands dropped. "I never liked you, Wade. Give me an excuse."

Peri looked up the empty road for signs of trouble, knowing they likely had only moments. The vintage truck was clearly their way out of here. It was half in the ditch, but it was a muscle car, by God, even if someone had prettified it with flames; a ditch wasn't an issue.

"Throw 'em," Taf said, and two phones thumped at her feet. "Good," she said, the shotgun never wavering as she pulled two sets of cuffs from her pocket and tossed them to the two men. "Put them on."

Peri was starting to wonder about Taf. Where was she getting this stuff? "Thank you," Peri said as Howard helped her across the road. "Why are you doing this?"

Howard supported her with a professional surety. "You aren't the only one being spoon-fed lies," he said tightly. "Taf planned it. She can do more than parties. Are you okay to drive? You look a little spacey. You're going to want to ditch it before you go too far, but it will get you out of here. You don't know what they gave you, do you?"

"Muscle relaxant?" she guessed. Her shoulder hurt, and she hoped she found a bottle of aspirin or, better yet, tequila before the adrenaline wore off. "I'm good. I can drive."

From behind the van, Taf shouted, "Cuff yourselves to the van. The van!" And then Peri spun, heart pounding at the thunder of the rifle firing. *Shit*.

"Taf!" Howard cried, but the young woman was sauntering to them, ponytail swinging, looking sharp with that duster furling around her ankles, the open rifle draped over her arm and smoking as she dropped a new shell in. The two men were white-faced but fine, the van spewing a pink fluid.

Taf smiled as she tossed her bangs out of her eyes. "I wasn't going to shoot them. Scared the crap out of them though, huh?"

Taf laughed, as Peri sagged in relief and staggered to the truck. "Nice escape vehicle," she said, thinking it was a sweet ride, even if it was not inconspicuous. And in a ditch.

Howard was already moving to the back of the truck. "I'll push. Get in."

"You like it?" Taf said cheerfully. "It belongs to a friend of mine. Can you drive a stick?"

Peri lifted the latch, smiling at the sound of money behind the small click. "Jack's better at it than me, but yes," she said, then froze as the thought burst against the top of her brain. *Jack's better at it than me,* she thought again, though there was no memory to accompany it.

Her smooth step up faltered at the pain, but she managed it. "I appreciate this," she said as she started the engine, relishing the overindulgent *brum* of sound. "How close is the airport?"

Howard stood up from where he'd been leaning over the tailgate. "Uh . . . why?"

"Silas. If that's where the exchange is, that's where I'm going."

Taf's smile fell and she caught Peri's closing door. "I did not risk cracking up Jamie's ride so my mother could catch you again."

Peri tugged at the door, and Taf yanked it out of

her grip. Sighing, Peri looked up from her stinging fingers. "I know I said to stop letting your mother control your life, but this isn't what I meant."

Taf smirked. "Funny. That's what I heard."

The truck shifted, and Peri looked across the long bench seat as Howard got in. "Get out of the truck, Howard."

Eyes down, he flushed. "Taf is a big girl. She can push. You're going to need help getting Silas." His eyebrows bunched. "He's my friend. Maybe I should drive. You look a little green."

Still between the door and the body, Taf crossed her arms over her middle. "I am *not* pushing a truck out of a *ditch*."

I'm going to go crazy. "Ah, guys? I appreciate this, but this is a bad idea. You're a vet," Peri said to Howard, "and you plan events," she added, not liking the headstrong woman's frown. "This is secret agent stuff.

"Ow!" Peri yelped as Taf shoved her to the middle of the truck.

"Get over." Taf dropped her rifle next to the seat and wiggled that tiny butt of hers into place. "I can get us out of a ditch," she said, reaching for the gearshift.

"This isn't a game," Peri said as Taf started rocking the truck and Peri's head began to throb. "People die. Sometimes I'm the one who kills them."

Howard held the chicken strap, grinning to show his white teeth. "Only the bad ones."

Taf shrieked in delight as the wheels caught on the last roll, and spitting dirt out the back, they regained the road. "Got it!" she shouted, and the engine thrummed as she floored it.

This is not happening.

"I almost-minored in evasive driving," Taf said, performing a neat three-point turn and heading back the way they'd come. Peri looked behind them in the rearview mirror to see the two men cuffed to the van. They had maybe five minutes, max.

"There is no such thing as a minor in evasive driving," Peri said. "I appreciate you both wanting to help, but this is a bad idea." Howard probed Peri's head, and she jerked away. "Do you mind?"

"You have a nasty lump," he said. "How's your light sensitivity?"

"Fine," she lied. Taf was fiddling with the state-of-the-art sound system, and Peri smacked her hand. "I *said* this isn't a game. They're at hangar three."

"Got it. No tunes." Taf popped her gum as if this was a most excellent adventure.

Peri gripped the dash, gut tightening when Taf skimmed a pothole. "Okay, you can drive," she admitted. "But you stay in the truck. Both of you."

They didn't stay in the truck. They followed her, whispering all the way to the rear door of hangar three, and they didn't quiet down until Peri threatened to shove Taf's rifle up the ass of the next person who opened their mouth. It had been at least an hour since she'd been injected, and she didn't know yet with what. She might not be able to draft yet. *Just as well.*

Waving them back, Peri busted the lock on the small entry door, and when no one came to check out the slight noise, she slipped inside.

"Stay here and watch the truck!" Peri hissed at Howard when he tried to follow, but Taf had already inched past Peri and was creeping along the far wall of the building toward the sound of an argument. Giving up, Peri motioned for Howard to stay behind her, and with more help than she wanted, she followed Taf to a pallet of freight.

The hangar door was open and the light streamed in to show a small single-engine plane sitting cockeyed to a black car. She could feel the heat of the engine from where she crouched, and Peri's eyes narrowed when she saw Allen sitting on the rolling stair pulled up to the plane. His leg was in a Flexicast, his hand bandaged. He was having a hard time using his phone. Peri didn't feel sorry about it. *You stole three years of my life.*

Fran stood at the car, clearly frustrated. She had one strong-armed man with her, the guy clearly trying to stay out of her way. Things were not going well in the land of prisoner exchange. The small size of the plane was good, limiting the number of people Peri would have to deal with.

If Fran had one man, then Allen probably had one man as well. *In the plane?*

One of the borrowed phones in Taf's pocket began to hum. Her eyes wide, she smacked a hand to cover it, but they were too distant for the soft sound to carry.

"They should be here by now," Fran said, phone to her ear.

Allen shifted his weight, clearly uncomfortable. "You lost her."

Fran ended her call, peeved. "They aren't answering because I keep calling."

"I told you not to confuse forgetfulness with stupidity," Allen said. "She's extremely intelligent. Did you use the audio binder? Give her the Amneoset?"

"Of course I did," Fran said, and Peri's flush at his "intelligent" comment vanished. At least she knew the drug was almost out of her system. Amneoset metabolized in an hour.

"I want to see Silas," Fran demanded. "I have only your word that he's in there."

"Then show me Peri Reed," Allen said, clearly hurting. He wasn't taking his meds, probably because painkillers interfered with his ability to recognize twin timelines. *Maybe that's why Jack liked to drink,* she mused. Her face blanked as the thought swirled in her; then she shoved the heartache away. Silas was in that plane, and she had a job to do.

"John!" Fran barked, and Peri jumped. "Retrace our route and see what's keeping them."

The man bolted into motion, the car door slamming shut and the engine loud as it started in the echoing space. Peri frantically waved for Taf to stay put. *Where does she think she's going?* Howard stopped her, and they began arguing in hushed tones. Peri's eye twitched. She should have shot them both in the foot.

Allen whistled to get the pilot's attention, limping away from the stair and craning his neck to see into the cockpit, but it wasn't nearly far enough away to let her sneak onto the plane. "Tell the tower we're leaving," he demanded, and Fran frowned, hands on her hips. The car was backing up to the wide door. Things were deteriorating fast.

"What about the exchange?" Fran stalked forward. "I want Silas."

"And I want Reed, but you lost her."

Peri's eyes fixed on the plane. Silas was on it. If they left now, she'd never find him.

"You don't know that. Give me five minutes to figure out what's going on," Fran said.

Allen hobbled forward, his expression creased in mistrust. "Five minutes," he said, gesturing behind him to the plane. "But my man goes with yours."

Fran shouted at the car, and it stopped. Peri's heart pounded when a man thumped down the plane's stair, a pistol in his unsnapped shoulder harness. He didn't look like a pilot.

"Go with him," Allen said brusquely. "If by some miracle you find her, call me and keep your distance. I don't want to lose her again."

Fran huffed. "I haven't lost her."

The man hustled to the car and got in. Slowly the car accelerated, and it was gone. Grimacing, Allen hobbled to the plane. Fran was right behind him. Peri was betting they both had weapons or they wouldn't have sent their people away. Fewer people meant fewer witnesses.

"Taf, give me your rifle," Peri whispered, her hand extended behind her. Howard made a small noise, and she turned, eyes widening when she saw that Taf was gone. "Where's Taf?"

Finger shaking, Howard pointed across the hangar. Peri's face went cold as she followed his gaze. "Oh no . . . ," she whispered. Taf's slim form was slipping along the wall.

Howard edged closer, beads faintly clinking. "I couldn't stop her," he whispered. "She's going to distract them for you so you can get Silas out of the plane."

Damn it all to hell. Peri's gut clenched when Taf boldly stepped out into the light, boots clunking. Fran spun and Allen froze, their backs to the plane. "Hey, Mom," Taf said, her feet spread wide and her stance confident as she hit the southern drawl hard.

"Mom?" Allen questioned, and Peri crept closer.

"This is my daughter," Fran said drily, not scared nearly enough by her crazy-ass daughter holding a rifle. "She's not supposed to be here."

"Things change," Taf said. "I can tell you what your stooges will find. Want some spoilers?" she mocked.

Fran punched buttons on her phone. Taf's pocket began to hum and the older woman became livid with anger. Allen laughed.

"What did you do?" Fran exclaimed, stalking forward until Taf cocked the rifle.

My God, is she going to shoot her mom? Peri thought, remembering the temptation once or twice herself.

"I'm fixing to stop wasting your time and my life," Taf said, as satisfied as her mother was angry, but she'd drawn them far enough from the plane, and Peri gave Howard a look to stay before slinking forward. She crept up the stairs, trying not to shift the plane's weight as she eased aboard. Relief was a surprising wash through her when she found Silas bound and gagged in a seat. Finger to her lips, she smiled at his glare. His eyes were angry but clear. New bruises and scrapes showed they'd beaten him, but he wasn't drugged.

Hunched under the low ceiling, Peri held up two fingers, eyebrows high in question. He shook his head, nodding when she held up one. *One man,* she thought, following his glance to the cockpit.

Shouldn't be difficult. Peri slowly drew out the bottle of wine chilling in the ice bucket. *Rosé? Really?* Allen had no sense of style.

The shifting ice caught the pilot's attention, and he shoved his man-on-man magazine out of sight. "Should I tell the tower we're staying?" he said, so frantic to hide his magazine that he didn't even notice she wasn't Allen until their eyes met. Almost sorry for the guy, she smacked him with the cold, wet bottle, wincing at the reverberation shaking up her arm.

"Never hide who you are," Peri said as she backed out. Five minutes. He'd be up and bitching in five. She hadn't hit him that hard.

Peri dropped the bottle back in the slush, hands cold but feeling cocky in the relief of doing what she was good at. Hunched from the low ceiling, she returned to Silas. He was waiting impatiently, bound hands held up before him. Still smiling, she knelt before him and pulled the gag away. "Hi," she said as she started on the knots. "Can you move fast?"

"What are you doing here?" he whispered, and she glanced up, fingers faltering on the rope. "Wearing *that?* Are you crazy?"

"Ah, it's called rescuing your ass in style?" Peri said, flushing as she saw that her skintight white jeans were now smeared with grease and dirt. "I'm a soldier, remember? I don't leave anyone behind."

His expression went empty, then resolute. Fran's angry "You did what!" echoed. Flustered, Peri gave up on his hands and moved to his feet. He didn't need his hands to run.

"Peri is long gone," she could hear Taf saying, and Peri began to sweat, fingers fumbling. "I gave her a car and she's reached the mountains by now. Good luck with that."

The knots weren't budging. Probably because he'd been trying to get free and had instead tightened them into immovable chunks. "There's a red truck out the back of the building. Keys in the ignition," Peri said as she puffed a strand of hair out of her eyes. "Good Lord, what did you do to these knots?" *Amateurs.*

Silas winced. "Ah, check the bathroom. One of them was using a knife to trim his nails."

"Thanks for sharing." Peri got up. The thing was eight inches long, and she decided to keep it despite the gauche camo pattern on the hilt. In three seconds, he was free; in four, she was sliding the knife away, almost shivering at the sound as it slipped into her boot sheath.

"Find her!" Allen shouted, and she joined Silas at the window to see Allen on the phone. So far, Taf's was the only gun showing, and Peri prayed it would stay that way. Clearly pissed, Allen ended his call. "Your *daughter* ran them off the road," he said tightly. "Where is Peri headed? Detroit or Charlotte?" he asked Taf.

"She said something about Cuba," Taf said with a simper.

Peri peeked down the stairs. Silas rubbed his legs, clearly pained. Too bad she didn't know how to fly, or they could back out of here and just go. The engine was still ticking-hot.

"Tell me, or I'll shoot your mother," Allen threatened, and Peri's brow furrowed. She didn't want to have to draft to save anyone's life, but she knew she'd do it.

But Taf shifted the barrel of her weapon to Allen, as cool as if she'd done this a thousand times before. "Ya'll just do that," she said in a thick accent, convincing Peri at least. "My momma is a bitch, but you make one move and I'll plug you myself. I'm from the South, sugar, and I kill my own snakes."

Silas's breath was tickling her neck, and she stifled a quiver when he said, "Allen is playing us both."

Do we have to do this right now? "Tell me about it," she said tersely. "I was on my way to Detroit when I realized they had you. Allen is a liar. I didn't turn you in."

"Turn me in? Allen picked me up before I could meet you." Silas's gaze went distant, and he scrubbed a hand over his face. "You ditched me," he said, and Peri grimaced. "You had no intention of meeting me at that dealership."

"Can we maybe do this *after* we escape?" she

whispered in frustration. "I'm sorry, okay? You're right. I left you, but I didn't know they were going to pick you up, and when I found out they had, I came back. What do you think I was doing at the alliance?"

"Having drinks, by the looks of it," he snarked, and she sighed in exasperation. Why was he stomping all over her high?

The sound of Taf's rifle echoed like a cannon. Adrenaline was a jolt, and Peri shoved Silas back from the door and into safety. Taf was shooting again?

"Peri! Let's go!" Taf shouted roughly, and Peri's breath fogged up the window. Allen was on the cement, his hand clamped about his foot, blood seeping around his fingers.

"You shot him!" Fran stared aghast at her daughter. "Are you crazy?"

"I shot his foot. He was going to kill me! Gawd, Mom. You think I should have just let him? And I'll be damned before I let you railroad another innocent woman."

"Innocent?" Fran laughed, and the cold sound tripped down Peri's spine. "Don't be naive, my dear. Give me the gun, and for God's sake, drop the accent."

"I am not ashamed of who I am!" Taf shouted, face red. "Peri? We gotta go!"

Before she really gets pissed, Peri thought, shoving Silas to the door.

"You involved Taffy?" Silas grimaced over his shoulder at her. "She's just a girl!"

"The woman's name is Taf, and she's rescuing us," Peri said. "And shooting at people. At the same time." He stared at her, and she gestured to the stairs. "Who do you think planned my escape? Listen to the woman with the rifle and move your ass!"

Silas fell into motion. Allen stared at them as they limped down the stairs. Howard gestured for them to hurry, half hidden by a pallet of freight. This was so messed up. How many people did it take to rescue one man?

"Howard?" Silas exclaimed in shock. "What are you doing here?"

Peri sighed, wondering the same thing. Her feet hit the concrete in a last lurch, the jarring sensation traveling all the way up to her skull. Hunched, she waved Taf to join them. Taf jogged forward, yelling at her mother to stay where she was, but Fran was still in shock, torn between yelling at her daughter and seeing if Allen was okay. Ashen, Allen held his bloody foot, silent as he watched them flee.

"You okay?" Taf said, eyes bright as she held Allen's Glock out to her. "Silas?"

"He can move." Frustrated, Peri took the handgun and pushed Taf toward the back door. Howard had tucked his shoulder under Silas's arm, and Taf walked backward to make sure her mom didn't follow.

"Don't believe her, Silas," Allen shouted, his voice holding equal amounts of anger and pain. "You'll never know the truth! She doesn't even know it herself. I read her diary. I know how easy it's become for her to kill."

Peri's face went cold, her pace faltering. *He saw my diary?*

"We will find you!" Allen called out, still on the floor, a small puddle of blood around his foot. "We know everything you'll do, Peri. We trained you!"

This was going to give her nightmares. Taf walked backward beside Peri, the young woman's long coat furling like the heroine's in a sci-fi flick, her rifle pointed at the floor, but neither Allen nor her mom was moving.

"You trust her?" Peri heard Silas ask Howard, and her jaw clenched.

"I don't know," Howard said. "But coming back for you was her idea."

"Taf, you are cut off! You hear me?" Fran exclaimed.

"Yeah, I know," Taf said, a hint of the depth of her bitterness showing.

"Taf!" Fran shouted as they got to the back door and light spilled in.

Peri stood a shaky watch with Taf as Howard got Silas to the truck. Silas wasn't moving well, his wide shoulders hunched in pain, and Peri was worried.

"You first," Taf said, motioning for Peri to go. Silas was already in the truck, pained and crunched into the door. Behind her, the security door slammed. Taf stomped past her, the young woman's head down and the rifle held in a white-knuckled grip. A frustrated female cry echoed in the hangar.

And even though she couldn't stand the woman, Peri knew exactly how Fran felt.

CHAPTER

TWENTY-TWO

The small room was warm from body heat, and the reek of Howard's solder overpowered the scent of the hot chocolate Silas had brought back for her from the nearby coffeehouse—along with something for everyone—when he'd gone in search of an honest-to-God paper newspaper. Nose wrinkled, Peri sipped at the cooling drink, levering herself out of the faded chair to nuke it in the microwave. Silas looked up from where he was kneeling over the coffee table with Howard. Styrofoam and plastic bags littered the floor, and Silas gave her a quick smile before Howard recaptured his attention with a request to hold something.

The large man was clearly glad she'd relaxed enough to finally eat. She hadn't let them stop except for gas and snacks on the drive back to Detroit, eager to get to a safe house—one that wasn't tied to Opti *or* the alliance.

Peri set the hot chocolate in the microwave, started it up, and waited beside the small efficiency sink while it spun. The bachelor apartment was a welcome spot of security. Even Opti didn't know she had it, Peri having bought the entire building on her eighteenth birthday during the great exodus for five hundred bucks and a promise to renovate. Which she had. It was in someone else's name and attached to an offshore bank account that paid expenses accrued. The rent from the comic book shop downstairs kept everything even with inflation. It had been almost five years since the last visit—that she remembered—but Joe downstairs had been glad to see her, selling her a couple of rare Superwoman comics she'd been looking for to round out her collection. She was a good landlord, easy on the rent, and quick to upgrade the technology that let Joe stay competitive.

It was supposed to have been an investment, but she'd bought it because it was set right downtown in a neighborhood that had never undergone the modernization the rest of the city enjoyed. That, and she liked comics. Here, Detroit showed her past with stone and steel, bad parking, authentic ethnic restaurants, beggar musicians on corners, and shopfronts pushed right up to the street. It was noisy and cramped, and Peri felt good that she'd helped save it, even if it was only a few blocks long and there were more electric Sity bikes than cars now.

There was only one window that overlooked a parking lot and the adjacent street. The old rug did little to cover the scratched floorboards, and the muted voices filtering up from below were comforting in their predominantly male tenor. The furnishings were worn and mismatched, and Peri smiled as she remembered buying them at a secondhand shop simply because it would irritate her mother. Smile widening, Peri looked at her bright red fingernails as she dried her hands. She'd done a lot back then simply because her mother wouldn't like it. Still did, apparently.

The microwave dinged, and Peri took the hot chocolate to the window to watch the dark street for Taf, currently out getting Howard a circuit. Silas had agreed to help Peri get her talisman and bring back what had happened at Global Genetics, but there was a reluctance in him, a big "however" that kept tweaking her confidence—and it was beginning to get on her nerves.

It might be that Opti car at her apartment in Lloyd Park. Breaking in, immobilizing, and leaving before Opti could react might be an issue, but the five thousand under the silverware caddy meant she had more resources and didn't have to rely on Silas anymore. *Maybe that's what is bothering him,* she thought, sipping her drink as

Silas jumped, jerking his finger away from Howard's motherboard and scowling.

"Taf is back," she said, and Howard looked up, brightening.

"Good. I could use her little fingers," he said, but Peri didn't think it was just her hands he was glad to see. Thinking their past must be thicker than she'd first thought, Peri shifted the blind to keep the young woman in sight. Even lit by streetlight and the oncoming cars, she was the picture of privilege, a blond goddess with that swagger of hers and a little bag dangling from her hand. She fit right in with the other Motown shoppers. Letting the blind fall, Peri listened to the guys downstairs flirt with her, and then the creaking of her steps on the stairs. There was no way up them except noisy.

Bright-eyed and cheerful, Taf strode in, looking sharp in her "rescue attire." Peri rubbed ruefully at her new jeans. They'd gone shopping this morning, but remembering what Allen had said about the ease of finding her, she'd left every-thing she liked on the rack. The faded fabric and sweater felt untidy, but since "not her" had been her goal, it would do.

"I think I got what you wanted, Howie," Taf said as she shoved Silas farther down the table and upended the bag. "Smartphone-to-glass compatible chips. Gawwd, these things are expensive. They were going to charge me full price until I poured on the southern charm. That and I paid cash. This town *loves* its cash."

Yes, it does, Peri thought, hot mug in hand as she sat at the kitchen table before the half-knitted scarf she'd found tucked among the throw cushions.

"That's it. Thanks," Howard said as he ripped the plastic off, and pleased, Taf took her coat off and slipped in where Silas had been. Seeing her ponytail inches from his dreadlocks made Peri smile. They were so unlike, but they complemented each other perfectly.

Shoulders bunching, Silas stood, looking massive next to Taf's petite bounciness. Clearly the odd man out, he went to the dusty shelves to eye the titles of the books and movies.

"Howard and I will swing by your apartment tonight to see if Opti is still there," Silas said as he pushed the button on the SS *Enterprise* model to make Spock tell him to live long and prosper.

Peri's brow furrowed. She didn't like him touching her stuff. "Don't bother. They aren't going anywhere," she said as she set her knitting down and joined Silas. "Getting in might be an issue."

Howard hissed in pain, shaking his hand as the smell of solder rose again, and Taf laughed. "Taf and I can help," he said, glaring at her mirth. "Distract them. Draw them off."

"And have you end up in an Opti cell?" Peri protested. "No. We'll find another way."

Taf snorted as she used a pencil to hold something for Howard to solder. "We won't get caught. I know someone in Detroit with a sweet bike. Totally uncatchable."

Howard looked up, blinking. "I've never driven a bike before."

"And that's not going to change," Taf said. "You sit behind me, dreadlock man. Real men don't mind their women driving."

Silas frowned. "No," Peri said, agreeing with him. "No one is going to be a distraction. Opti kills people," she added. *Opti kills people. I kill people.*

"What the blazes are we here for, then?" Taf complained.

"Extraction." Peri plucked the picture of twelve ten-year-olds in tutus out of Silas's hand before he picked her out of the group, setting it next to the autographed picture of Putin riding a Photoshopped bear where it belonged. "Three g's, and an r: Get in, get the info, get out, relocate." They weren't her words, but *Jack's*. She didn't remember—she just knew.

"Extraction?" Taf sighed. "I can do more than drive. I can shoot, too. All us debutantes learn how to shoot before we get our first push-up bras."

"Extraction is where someone who almost minored in evasive driving belongs," Howard said, his head low over his work, and Silas snorted.

"You've got the entire Buffy series on disk?" he said, and Peri flushed, embarrassed to admit she didn't remember watching them. The feeling that she loved the people on the covers was undeniable, though.

"Oh, cool. Let's watch a few tonight," Taf said, looking at the dusty Blu-ray player under the obsolete gen-one glass monitor beside the TV. "It works, doesn't it?"

"Sure, right after we sneak into Peri's apartment, outwit the government-funded bad guys, and save the world," Silas grumped as he fiddled with the biker's cap on her Goth American Girl doll. "Maybe we can stop to pick up popcorn on the way."

"You don't have to be so snide about it," Peri muttered, suddenly not liking that she'd brought them here. Her comic book apartment had been a refuge from her mother's demands since she was eighteen, filled with the things she loved and wanted never to forget. It had always felt like a tree clubhouse to her, and Silas was poking about like it was a junk shop.

"Sorry," he said, expression blank as he turned to go into the open kitchen.

Brow furrowed, she straightened the commemorative coffee table book of Princess Diana's royal wedding. The sucking sound of the freezer opening turned her around, and her lips parted when he took out a box of Thin Mints.

"God bless it, will you get out of my stuff!" she exclaimed, and Silas spun, eyes wide.

Taf made a long "Oooo, you're in trouble . . . ," laughing when Howard shushed her.

"You've got like six boxes in there," Silas said indignantly, and Howard gave Taf a nudge to be quiet when she opened her mouth again.

"Fine, go ahead." Peri stomped back to the kitchen table. "But put them on a plate so we can all eat them."

"Sure, Peri," he said reasonably, but she was still peeved. Her unfinished scarf was stretched out over the table, and she studied the irregular bands of red, orange, and gold, trying to figure out what she'd been trying to do so she could finish it off. Knitting was supposed to be relaxing, but not with Silas bumping about in her kitchen.

"Ah, why do you have comic books in your wine fridge?" he asked.

Jaw tight, she ignored him. "Be careful with those," she said when he reached for a blue glass plate, and his motions became exaggerated as he shook the frozen Girl Scout cookies onto it and set it down precisely between them. "They're antique," she added, not knowing for sure.

"You know what? I need another circuit to finish this," Howard said suddenly as he stood and stretched. "You want to come with me before they close, Taf?"

"What, now?" Taf appreciatively eyed Howard's

stretched body. "This is just getting good. What are we making, anyway?"

"Bug detector," he said as he collapsed in on himself. "A-a-a-and . . . it works," he added as he picked it up and waved it over Taf and a light on it glowed.

"I am not bugged," the woman said indignantly, but Silas, who had sat down across from Peri at the kitchen table with his paper newspaper, had taken an interest, too.

"She's clean," Howard said as Taf smacked his thigh and eased up to sit on the couch. "It lights up at any outgoing ping, like from a cell phone."

"I know I'm clean. Gawwd!" Taf drawled as Howard beamed over three squares of plastic he had been working on.

"A quick tweak to the GPS on my phone, and we'll have traceable bugs," he added as he set it clattering on the table. "If we can get one of these on Allen, we'd know when he comes within half a mile. Or we can drop them like bread crumbs to find our way back somewhere or to each other if we get separated."

Fingers smoothing the yarn, Peri said, "If this vet thing doesn't work out, you could always open an Electronics Hut."

Howard chuckled as he put his coat on. "Sure. Taf, you can make coffee, right? I could use you and your dozen almost-minors for security. You're amazing with a rifle."

"Thank you, Howard. You say the sweetest things!" Taf purred, bounding up to give him a little peck on the cheek.

Silas sighed, rattling his paper as Howard blushed, his dark skin taking on a pinkish hue.

"Speaking of shooting people, I need to pick up some more shells." Taf reached for her coat. "Do we have time to stop?"

"Sure, I don't see why not."

"Ah . . . you aren't carrying a gun tonight," Peri started when Taf picked up her purse.

"Excuse me, boys and girls?" Silas said, paper flat against the table. Suddenly Peri felt like they were the parents of two hooligans eager for a night of chaos and gunpowder.

"We'll bring back pizza," Howard said as he pushed Taf to the door.

"I'm sick of pizza," Taf complained. "I want Cantonese."

"Fine. Whatever," he said. "Let's get out of here before they think of a reason for us not to go." And then the door shut and Taf's voice filled the stairway as they creaked downstairs.

Peri glanced at Silas, pretty sure Howard and Taf hadn't left for circuits and shells. They hadn't even set up an alternate meeting place in case of trouble. She wasn't used to working with more than one person, and she was making mistakes. "I don't like them out on their own," she said, to fill the new silence.

"Me either." Silas shook his paper again. He'd taken time to shave and shower in the tiny bathroom while she and Taf had been shopping, and his thick short hair was sticking straight up, an unruly, charming mess without product. Peri couldn't help but wonder what it would feel like on her fingertips. *Silk, maybe.*

Sensation plinked through her, and, disconcerted, she put her attention firmly on her yarn. "This isn't going to be easy," she muttered. "Opti is already at my apartment. I'm going to have to fight my way in, or out, or both. We should have left them in Kentucky."

"But you don't mind me coming," he said flatly from behind his paper.

"Actually, I do, but I need an anchor," she said. "I'll keep you alive. Promise."

"Maybe I don't want that assurance."

Peri squinted at the paper between them. "It comes with the job. Deal with it." She was starting to figure this out. Someone he'd loved had died to save him. *Not my business,* she thought as she laid the scarf out and tried to find a pattern in the stripes, but a growing ire at Silas was percolating through her. "I need you, Silas, but you're not a piece of firmware."

"I know that."

That paper was starting to tick her off. "Silas," she said softly. "Quit with the girly 'if you cared, you'd figure it out' crap. Tell me what's bothering you, or leave the baggage on the curb."

His big hands gripped the paper, making it crackle as he lowered it. His strong jaw was tight and his shoulders were so stiff they pulled at his shirt. His lips twitched as a thought flitted through him, and something in her fluttered, a memory, almost. "Your pattern is off," he said.

"Silas!" she shouted, and there was a long "Oooooo" from the store below, followed by laughter.

Still holding the paper, Silas leaned across the table. "Listen to me, Peri Reed," he said as he took a frozen cookie. "My bad mood is none of your business. Besides, your pattern *is* off. Why don't you fix it? It's not me that's bothering you, it's your asinine, anal need for perfection." He snapped through the cookie and leaned back, eyes holding his anger.

"It is not," she said, hiding her irritation behind a sip of hot chocolate. But then she looked at the yarn in her lap. "Damn it, Silas. Now it's going to bug me forever."

He lifted the paper back up between them. "So fix it. We've got time, princess."

"Don't call me that," she said, glumly brushing the pattern. She hadn't even known the autumn-shaded scarf existed until this morning, and it rankled her that he knew the error bugged her. Not only bugged her, but enough that, yes, she'd fix it. Sighing, she pulled the yarn off the needle.

"I'm going to fix it. I was just making sure I hadn't coded something into the pattern first. The last time I unraveled a project I didn't remember starting, I destroyed a list of names."

Silas jerked, the soft rattle of the paper making a shiver cross over her. He slowly lowered the paper, and Peri took in his white face, not knowing what she'd said. "I'm going to fix it?" she prompted, and Silas's chair creaked as he leaned forward.

"Do you remember them?" he said, brow creased.

Warning flags snapped in the wind of her imagination at his intensity. "The names? No," she lied, not knowing why except that knowledge was power, and he was agitated. "Why?"

Silas sputtered, pushing back to gesture at nothing. "Allen asked me about a list of corrupt Opti agents that Jack got hold of in Charlotte. He's desperate for it. It was the only thing Opti pressed me for, wanting to know if you knew of it. Which I think is stupid because they were the ones who scrubbed you."

Harry and Gina are corrupt? Cold, she recalled the nine rows of knits and purls she'd pulled out in the airport. How many of her other friends had been on it? Well, not friends exactly, but they were all she had.

"Bill thinks the original chip is still alive," Silas said, pulling her attention back. "Do you know where Jack might have hidden it? If we can find it, then all this ends. It ends, Peri."

Her eyes flicked up at the determination in his voice. *Why are you only telling me this now?* she thought as mistrust flashed through her. "Jack doesn't retain sensitive information," she lied. She'd obviously not only seen the list, but knitted the information into a scarf. "How will a list of corrupt agents bring Bill down? Is he on it?" she asked, remembering the last phrase, *Bill is corrupt.*

"I doubt it, but he's already submitted a fake list of corrupt Opti agents to protect his own stable, and if the real list gets out, he's done." Silas's hands clenched, the man clearly anxious. "You must know where Jack hides things. Right?"

Head down, she pulled out a row of stitches. Not anymore, she didn't.

"Sorry," Silas apologized. "It's just that I've been working on this for five years, and we're so close. Jack wouldn't have had time to stash it anywhere but your apartment."

Peri nodded, the yarn making a kinked mass of red in her lap as she pulled off more. Her Mantis had a safe, but Opti knew and would have looked. Putting the information in an off-site data storage unit was out. They were too easy to find and hack into. That's why she'd knitted the information into her scarf. The knitted list was gone, but if Bill was looking for the original, it probably still existed.

And though her hiding things wasn't a good idea, she did have a few cubbies she could check. They were going there for her talisman anyway.

"Please," Silas said, startling her when he reached across the cookies and took her hand, stopping her from pulling off more yarn. "Help me find that list, and I'll help you get your memory back. Whatever you want."

"Just the fragment from Charlotte," she said, uneasy. "I don't want to know anything more about Jack than that."

"Okay. Good." His hand slipped from hers, and Silas stood, hesitating as if not knowing what to do with himself. His eyes went from the door to the window. He took out his phone, clearly wanting to text Howard or Taf.

Frowning, Peri pulled the last of the red off the scarf, the kinked yarn in her lap looking like the insides of an exotic insect. She reached for a cookie, the scent of the chocolate suddenly turning her stomach. In a wave of vertigo, the red yarn at her middle became a blood-soaked wad. Jack's face, pale from pain and blood loss, flashed across her mind.

A thump from the bathroom jerked her head up, and she froze when a suntanned, manicured hand pushed open the door. Her pulse hammered, and she stared past Silas.

Jack?

She dropped the cookie to the floor, heart

pounding as Jack smiled at her from around the bathroom door, his blond hair tousled and his stubble thick the way she liked it. His tie was loosened and his white dress shirt was a brilliant bloodred at his middle, but his eyes all but danced. "Don't ask about things you're not going to like the answers to, Peri. Questions are bad for your asthma."

She blinked, hand clenched on the bare needle. She didn't even remember picking it up, but there it was, set to gouge as she stared at the bathroom. The door was closed. No one was there. Silas was looking at her over his phone as if she had lobsters coming out of her ears. Clearly he hadn't seen Jack. She was hallucinating.

Oh God, I'm going to MEP. She'd forgotten something so traumatic that her mind was fighting to recover it. If she couldn't get a clean defrag, the hallucinations would get worse until she couldn't tell reality from fantasy. She'd go insane by way of daydreams. *How long? How long until I can't function?*

Silas retrieved the cookie, setting it down with an accusing snap. "Thirty-second rule."

"Thank you." Hands shaking, she smoothed the yarn, not seeing it. She was hallucinating the man she'd killed. She was losing it. Big-time.

Making an appraising *"mmmm,"* Silas settled across from her, his hands laced over his middle as if waiting for something. "So how's it going?"

His voice held too much guile to be referring to her knitting. *Great. I think he knows.* "Fine." Peri pulled out another row, her fear growing as the two colors tangled. "I'm trying to decide how to access my apartment," she adlibbed. "Unless I moved it, I have a key downstairs in case I get locked out." *Don't look at the bathroom. There's nothing there. Crap, I'm sweating.* "What's the weather supposed to be tomorrow?"

Silas set his phone to vibrate and put it on the table. "How bad are the hallucinations?"

She lifted her chin, refusing to look at the bathroom. "Hallucination, not hallucinations. There is no plural."

"I thought so." A thick hand scrubbed his clean-shaven face. "We have a problem."

"We?" Her heart thudded. "I'm fine."

His gaze held pity when he looked up. "They're going to get worse."

Hating her flush, she met his gaze unblinkingly. "I'll deal with it."

"Peri, I can help. Let me try to render something."

Worried, she looked at the yarn in her lap as if the answer lay tangled there. "No," she whispered. The last time he'd been in her head, she'd remembered Jack.

"I won't lead you anywhere you don't want to go," he said as he leaned across the table, eyes showing his shared worry. "I know you don't want to remember what happened, but if you don't let your mind work through this, it will . . . impair your ability."

Peri had a feeling he'd been going to say it would drive her crazy, because if she didn't find a way to deal with it, it would. "No," she said firmly, then, "Yes. No." Her eyes closed.

"What if you have a vision tonight of something that's not there and make a mistake?" he asked. "At least let me help you untangle any memory knots that might be snarling."

Memory knots. Shit. He was right, but she was scared, and she stiffened when he stood and moved to stand behind her. "Memory knots are dangerous," she said, jumping when his big hands landed lightly on her shoulders.

Silas chuckled, leaning to put his face inches from hers. "Only if you ignore them. Now, tell me this isn't better," he said as he pressed his thumbs into the tension.

Oh, God. That feels good. "Better," she whispered, her eyes closing as her head dropped forward over the spilled yarn. "I don't want to remember Jack."

"That's fine," he said as the strength in his hands eased, and she cracked an eye.

"You're so full of psychiatric bull."

He laughed, the sound relaxing her more than his fingers. His pressure on her was familiar, soothing, and utterly professional. Her body remembered this and was clicking over to what it needed to do, taking her mind with it whether she wanted it to or not. "Please don't make me remember," she whispered, a wisp of fear coloring her thoughts.

"I won't. I promise. Just relax."

She sighed as he found every knot of stress and eased it away. Peri tensed when Jack's pale face flashed into her upper thoughts, then exhaled when she felt Silas dip into her mind and set it aside. He didn't fragment it, he set it aside. Impressed, she relaxed more deeply, trusting him. Silas was probably the best in his generation. Why he'd left Opti was a mystery.

"Find your safe spot," he whispered, and she drowsed, remembering him doing this before. "You can sleep there." Sleep would be a blessing, and knowing that her "safe spot" would be free of Jack, of Opti, of everything, she turned her thoughts to her grandparents' farm, feeling herself fall asleep high in her tree, the wind smelling of bees and sun in her hair. . . .

Until she realized it was winter and the leaves were gone. She reached for a dead branch; her fingers were stained with blood. Frightened, she looked down to see Jack lying below her in the yellow fields, the long, sparse grass waving to touch his face creased in pain. A scarf she had knitted was wadded up and pressed to his abdomen, red and soaked with blood. Dagazes decorated it. Panic stirred.

"I'm sorry," Jack whispered in her dream, blood at the corner of his lips. "I don't want you to remember me like this."

Suddenly she realized the branch she was holding was really a rifle. Tears spotted it. She was crying. Had she shot him?

"I love you, Peri," Jack said. "I'm sorry I wasn't stronger."

"Jack!" she shouted, horrified, as she dropped from the tree. Her feet landed on the scuffed wood of a dance floor, not the loamy lumps of earth. The air stank of gunpowder, and her ears were ringing. Blood covered her hands as she reached for Jack, but his eyes were empty. He was dead—dead on the floor of Overdraft.

Peri snorted awake, jerking violently. Her yarn was in a pile on the table, and beyond it was Silas working with his phone, the empty cookie plate beside him. He met her gaze, clearly startled. "Did I draft?"

"No, you fell asleep sitting at the table." He looked at his phone. "Fifteen minutes ago."

Her heart was pounding. Sitting up, Peri put her elbows on the table and hid her face in her hands. "I dreamed about Jack. I shot him. I shot him at Overdraft. I killed my own anchor." *I don't want to remember this. But if I don't, I'm going to go crazy.*

Silas shifted, his shoes scuffing the faded linoleum. "It was a dream, not a fragment. Peri, please let me render something back before this gets worse."

Maybe he's right. Peri wiped a hand under her eyes, exhausted and drained. But what if she had been the corrupt one and she'd killed him to keep it quiet? Sniffing, she wiped a hand under her eye again. *Doesn't this place have any tissues?*

Silas reached across the table and took her hand. "Let me help you remember."

His fingers among hers were rough, and she jerked away when they were suddenly red with blood, her mind painting them with a memory she didn't want to realize. Silas stared at her as her heart thudded. She was hallucinating, and he knew it. She couldn't work like this. She had to find out, no matter how much it scared her.

"You're right," she said suddenly. "I need to go to Overdraft."

"Now?" Silas leaned back, a hand running over his hair in worry.

"Yes, now. You're the one who just said I needed to remember." She had to go now, before she chickened out, and she stood, striding over to snatch up the coat Taf had picked out for her.

"I meant with careful exploration techniques, not dumping your psyche into a morass of confusion. I don't know if I can defragment something that emotionally charged all at once. You might get nothing back, or I might fix something that really didn't happen."

Pulse racing, she checked the safety on Allen's Glock, then the one on Taf's rifle. "If we're going to find that list, I need to know what happened last week. I need something real." She looked over the room for more assets, finding only Silas. Breathless, Peri peeked through the blinds: people walking, Sity bikes weaving through cars, the homeless man on the corner playing music, two low-Q drones monitoring traffic.

"And you're right. I need to render something, or I'm going to go crazy," she said, still scanning the street. "And then how will you get your damn list? You can text Howard and Taf where we are. It's Sunday. No one will be at Overdraft until tomorrow. Coming?"

Silas stared at her. Her stomach was in knots, the feelings of fear and exuberance a tight slurry of emotion. She was going to get some answers, whether she liked them or not.

Finally he gestured helplessly and stood. "Okay. I get Taf's rifle, though."

—————— CHAPTER —————— TWENTY-THREE

Cold, Peri shoved her hands deep into the pockets of her coat with the sour realization that the black jacket was the fourth one she'd had in as many days. Silas was working at the lock of Overdraft's rear door, and she wished he'd hurry up about it. They were in back, where the deliveries came in and obnoxious drunks went out, since it was less obvious than the main door. The CLOSED DUE TO ILLNESS sign at the front was better than the cops' DON'T CROSS banner she'd expected. Opti was good on details.

"Are you sure there's no alarm?" Silas's brow was furrowed and his fingers were red from the cold. She thought they should just kick the door in, but they could try it his way.

"There wasn't one three years ago." Peri leaned back against the Dumpster wall and scanned the service area. The security lights were coming on, humming just off her hated 741 MHz. She was getting the weirdest sensation. She knew that she'd been here only a few days ago, but her last memory was of summer. The snow flurries and gray nothingness were disconcerting. The gas station across the street was a different vendor than she remembered, and the coffee place at the end of the strip was new. Sometimes it was easier to pretend that she'd been gone for the time she'd lost and was coming back after an extended trip.

"Got it," Silas finally said as he picked up Taf's rifle, and she pushed away from the wall, toes cold and dread filling her. Tense in anticipation, she followed him in.

It was dark, the door to the huge walk-in cooler to one side, an unused time clock on the other. The smell of beer-soaked wood was strong, and she shivered when Silas closed the door behind them. Allen's Glock was an uncomfortable bump in her sock, easy to reach if she was pinned to the floor.

Silas pulled, then pushed on the fire door, grunting in surprise when it shifted four inches and clanged to a padlocked stop. "It's illegal to chain fire doors like that," he said, but Peri stared at the cold gray links as if they were important. Her nose wrinkled, and she thought she smelled gunpowder. It wasn't coming from their borrowed weapons.

Silas reached inside to find the lock, and Peri impatiently pulled him out of the way. "Give me a second," she said, wedging a crowbar in place. Her hands fisted, and then she smacked it with a side kick that expended all her frustration. Shock reverberated up her leg and she stumbled, but the lock snapped and the door swung inward. Her entire leg had gone numb, but she didn't care.

Silas grabbed her elbow as she regained her balance. "Feel better?" he said drily.

"We don't have time for you to pick another lock," she muttered, and with a last look at the dangling chain, she limped into the bar.

The glow from the Juke'sBox and lotto console made weird shadows, and the gaming lounge was a pit of darkness that somehow still reeked of testosterone. She passed it, feeling odd being here when no one else was around. The automatic floor cleaner was stuck against the stage, clicking as it tried to reset. Peri's gaze lingered on the mirror behind the bar, but she didn't know why. Her chest hurt as the need to remember became an ache.

"Cold in here," Silas said, his nose wrinkled as he set down Taf's rifle.

"And dark," she added, frowning when she realized her hands were in her pockets so she wouldn't leave prints. With a resolute frown, she went to the Juke'sBox screen and planted a big kiss on it, making sure all her fingers and thumbs pressed the glass.

Silas was staring when she turned around. "I assume there's a reason for that?"

"I want Allen to know I was here." She kept looking at the front door. No . . . not the front door—the solitary chair sitting beside it. Frustration made her antsy. She knew what she had to do, but not how to start. It was like the first time in bed with someone, awkward and having all the urgency of needing to get on with it before someone's parents walked in. It would probably be as satisfying as that, too—as in not at all.

Silas swung a chair from a table and set it before the black hole of the fireplace in invitation. Peri's heart hammered. "Give me a second," she said, scanning for something that spoke to her other than the padlock and the chair beside the front door. The scratched floor before the stage pulled her. It was a trigger. She'd seen it in her dream.

The image of Jack, white from blood loss and pressing a red scarf to his gut, surfaced. Peri stared at the parquet. It would be hard if she lay down on it, like a gym floor. There'd be a layer of wax that she could rub aside to find the smooth finish below. Her stomach knotted, and she turned away. Did she want to remember?

"Peri?"

"I can't believe I'm trying to render a memory with a memory knot," she said, feeling ill.

Feet scuffing, he crossed the room to her. "I'm sorry. If you don't want to—"

"That's why I'm here, Doctor," Peri said sharply, not liking that he'd baby her. She was an Opti agent, damn it. She could take it.

But her grief had grown heavy. She had to find the root of the corruption to clear her name. The answer was here—somewhere between the scratched floor and dark timbers. *I need more triggers,* she thought as she closed her eyes. She needed the smell of gunpowder, the feel of a smooth rifle stock in her grip, the sticky sensation of blood on her hands. Stiffening, she rubbed her fingers together. She'd been cold that night. Her coat had been on the bar.

Her eyes opened, and she looked at the blood in her cuticles as the disorientation of a fragmented memory trying to reassert itself wafted through her.

"Don't force it," Silas said, looking helpless and glum. "Take your time."

"I don't have time!" she exclaimed, then gasped, dropping to a kneel and fumbling for her Glock when Allen walked in the locked front door. There was snow in the parking lot behind him, and lights from the traffic. Nodding to her, he sat down in the chair beside the door and brushed the snow from his black curls before pushing his glasses back up his nose.

Hallucination, she thought as she started to shake, unable to drop her gun or look away.

"Peri?" Silas hadn't moved, his cautious glance at the door convincing Peri it was her imagination, even as Sandy set a cup of coffee on the bar and tossed a rag over her shoulder.

"We're going to have to get that furry orange mouse-eating bug back into your apartment. We could have lost you on your 'evaluation mission,'" the small woman said, and Peri stood, shifting her aim to her. Frank was there, too, and her face twisted in pained confusion.

"Here you go, sweet pea," the huge man said as he set a cup of coffee on the bar. "Something to warm you up."

Trembling, Peri closed her eyes. *They are not here. I am hallucinating.*

Her eyes flashed open when Silas put a hand atop hers, holding the Glock. "You okay?"

The bar was empty, the apparitions chased away

by his touch. Scared, Peri turned the weapon upside down and extended it to him. "I don't care what I find out, I've got to try." She looked at Silas. "Unless Allen really is sitting by the door and Frank and Sandy are tending bar."

"No." Silas set the pistol on the low stage. "Sweet Jesus. You should have—"

"What?" Peri said flatly as she pushed her fingers into her forehead. "Come to you sooner, Dr. Denier?" *How can anyone get a clean defragment from this?* Arms around her middle, she paced to the chair he'd pulled out and sat down in a huff. "Do your thing," she said belligerently.

Silas frowned. "Your attitude is counterproductive to success."

"You think?" she said as he came up behind her. Scared that this would work, and terrified it wouldn't, she closed her eyes. Immediately they began to dart from side to side. Her mind was desperate for her to recall, pushing for it. A sliver of fear colored everything. If she had enough triggers to open the gates, everything might pour through unchecked. It would be up to Silas to make sense of it, order it into a logical flow. If he couldn't, she might never recover.

"Oh, Peri," he whispered, his fingers cold as they found her temples. "We waited too long. Can you give me a few solid things to work with?"

"Other than blood on the floor and Jack with his stomach spilling out?" she said sarcastically.

"I'm going to go out on a limb and say Allen was here. Frank and Sandy, too."

The tension in her shoulders hurt when Silas moved his fingers there, following the lines of muscle and nerves, using pressure points to overstimulate the endings and make them relax. "I don't know Frank and Sandy," he said. "Who am I looking for?"

Interesting, Peri thought. Anchors used what they already knew to start a defrag, but maybe they did more than rebuild a memory from their own recollections, also using the drafter's latent ones. It had always felt as if she could feel an anchor's emotions twining in hers.

"Frank is Anglo-Saxon," Peri said, wondering about her sudden tension when she recalled him. "Looks like a pro wrestler. He dresses like a bouncer in a polo shirt. Sandy is an Asian princess in jeans and a black chemise. They run the bar." Peri's eyelid cracked, and she looked at the shadowed mirror behind the bar. "They're my psychologists," she added.

"Go with it," he murmured, and her eyes shut as his fingers became more gentle, finding the trigger points under her eyes, pressing until the tension eased. "You came to Overdraft with Jack. Something went wrong. Jack was upset."

It was an unconscionably vague place to start, but Peri settled deeper into the light trance. Jack was upset, guilty, maybe. Exhaling through her mouth, she felt the chill soak into her. She could see Jack's worry in her thoughts, a familiar stranger standing at the stage with Frank. There was a ladder beside them. Jack looked guilty. She was angry.

I was angry with him. Did I shoot him?

"Shhhh," Silas murmured. "Don't guess. See it. The ladder. Why was it there?"

His words shocked through her. She hadn't said anything about a ladder. Silas was seeing what she was, and the confidence from that allowed her to sink deeper—remember more.

"Frank was fixing the sound system," she said when the memory surfaced, and Silas's touch became a gentle hint. Images of Frank slipped through, bits and pieces from a hundred meetings with him, all meshed into one. She felt Silas with her, cycling the multitude of visions down to a single moment of Frank and Jack beside the ladder. She was with Sandy at the bar. Peri breathed deep, smelling the bitter scent of Overdraft coffee and polish. This was right. She could do this.

Sandy flicked her hair back. "You always remember, you just don't recall."

Peri twitched. Memories were returning, dragging the feelings of betrayal and fear with them. Bill had given them a new task right after she'd lost six weeks in Charlotte. They were sending them out the day after they'd come back.

Why hadn't Sandy cared? She was her psychologist!

"You're safe now," Silas whispered. "Nothing can touch you here."

But fear serrated her synapses when a memory of Sandy rose. *"Life isn't fair. Love is not real. I'm doing you a fucking favor!"* Sandy shrieked.

Her heart pounded, and she felt Silas's confidence as he gathered the memory to him, not fragmenting it but setting it aside as true. A new one took its place of Jack's face, white from shock, his expression bunched in pain as he lay on a yellow scratched floor. She knelt with him, her hands holding his stomach in. *No!* she thought, heartache making it hard to breathe.

She didn't want to see this. Everything spun in a nauseating blur until Jack wasn't on the floor, but standing beside her, the ladder next to them. Relieved, she let herself remember.

"Sandy doesn't care we lost our downtime. Neither does Frank. They're our psychologists, for God's sake."

Shock darted through her, magnified by Silas's emotions twining with hers. Frank and Sandy? They were corrupt? Her own psychologists?

"I'm not a mercenary. I don't kill for money," Peri shouted, wiggling in Frank's grip as Jack levered himself up on the low stage, his middle covered in blood. But he wasn't dying, and Peri stared as the sound of Velcro ripped

through the air and he took the body armor off.

"If you're not doing it for money, then you're doing it for kicks," Jack said. "Admit you like it. The thrill, knowing that you might have to kill someone to survive. The sense of superiority you get from it. Otherwise it wouldn't have taken you this long to figure things out."

That's not true, she thought. Betrayal was an acidic blanket, burning both Peri and Silas. Bill was corrupt. Jack was part of it. He'd been lying to her. Her entire world was a lie.

But Silas was gathering the memory up, making room for more. It hurt, and Silas's fingers spasmed as Peri clenched in pain. She looked down, focus wavering as she saw she was shot in the chest. Something had happened. She'd been shot.

By Jack . . .

He stood by the door to Overdraft, his Glock in his grip. Peri's fingers were warm and wet when she touched them to her chest, and she coughed, scared when it came out bloody. The floor was hard against her back as she looked up at the ceiling. Not again.

"Jump." Jack holstered his weapon and stood over her. "Go on and draft. I like you better when you're stupid."

Peri knew she wasn't dying in Overdraft. She sensed Silas sifting through the swirling morass, frustrated as he tried to organize it. He didn't need to pull the memories from her anymore. They were bunching up on each other, fighting to be realized. Groaning, she slipped out of the chair and hit the floor. Silas followed her down, wrapping his arms around her to keep her connected.

Suddenly it wasn't Silas's arms around her, but Allen's. She could draft and forget for a chance to kill Jack, or die.

"I'm not dying for her," Jack said, backing to the door.

Allen's lips quirked. "How about it?"

"You'll wipe me down to nothing," she groaned. *"Use me."*

"Someone will. You'll never remember Jack, but I'll give you the chance to shoot him before you forget."

"No," Peri moaned as she realized she'd done this to herself. She'd let Allen scrub her for the chance to kill the man she'd loved. What kind of a monster was she?

And then Silas caught and saved the memory as another pushed into its place. She could feel his heartache mirroring hers, building on it, making it hard to think.

"We're in a draft!" Frank shouted. *"Twenty seconds and she's done! Sandy, get down!"*

Jack backed to the door, his bloody hands outstretched. "Babe, let me explain!"

"There are no words," she said, *and with an*

unhealthy amount of satisfaction, she pulled the rifle up and shot him in the back as he ran.

Another fragment layered over it, wrong and out of place, making her dizzy.

"I told you she was verging on one of her epiphanies," Sandy said as Allen one-handedly caught the keys that Frank tossed him, locking the front door before pulling a chair from a table and sitting, his feet spread wide and stance alert but casual.

Agony pulsed through Peri as a memory rose from the rest, out of synch and dizzying.

"Love!" Sandy shrieked. "There is no such thing as love!"

Teeth clenched, Peri threw her knife at her. She wanted her to shut up.

Sandy twisted to avoid it, crashing into the mirror behind the bar, shattering it as she fell.

Peri moaned as Silas destroyed the memory since the mirror was clearly intact, but more memories ran in its place, a confusing blur until Silas fastened on one.

"Hey, I gave her a clean memory," Jack said, and she hated him more than anyone in her life. "Do you know how hard it is to fragment an entire person? Make a realistic timeline from two?"

Groaning, Peri tried to get away, but it was a trap of her own making, and Silas was failing. He couldn't control it. Numb, Peri existed in a haze as images passed faster and furious. Silas couldn't catch them, and it was going to drown her in insanity.

But as she sat on the floor and shook, she didn't think she cared anymore. Jack was dying on the floor and she couldn't save him. Then it was her on the floor, Allen holding her head from the scratched boards, and she wanted Jack dead. She wanted him dead!

"Make it stop!" Peri screamed, but nothing touched her ears. Silas's arms around her jerked, and he looked up when the glass in the front door shattered. A dark hand snaked in, looking for the lock. Dazed, Peri stared at it, wondering if she was alive. She was on the floor. Silas was wrapped around her as if he could keep her from falling apart by his touch alone. He hadn't known what to fragment, and now they were both there, two timelines fighting for supremacy, driving her insane.

"Thank God you told me where you were," Howard said as he tumbled in, the light gray in the parking lot behind him. "Opti is two minutes behind us."

She was hallucinating again. Howard couldn't really be here.

"Silas!" the imaginary man shouted as he rushed forward and grabbed Silas's shoulder. "We have to go! Pick her up!"

Peri's breath came in with a heave when Silas stood, scooping her up in one move. "Where's Taf?" Silas said raggedly.

"We got a car. Another friend of hers. Come on!"

Peri shook. They'd been interrupted mid-defrag, and she was dying. Howard held the door, and the flush of cool air struck Peri with the suddenness of a slap.

"What happened?" Howard said, pacing beside them to the car.

Silas's lips pressed. "I tried to defragment something I shouldn't have."

Peri's chest hurt as she felt her breath come and go. Around and around the memories spun. There was nowhere to hide, and she shook, going into shock.

"What's wrong with Peri?" Taf said from behind the wheel as the two of them got Peri into the backseat.

"Just go!" someone yelled, and the car lurched into motion, going too fast for even an empty parking lot. Dazed and unable to separate reality from memory, Peri breathed in the scent of Silas as he held her in the backseat. She looked at her hands, wondering where the blood was. The sky was gray. The ground was gray. She was gray, stuck between the two. She loved Jack. She'd killed Jack. Everything was all at once. Where there had been a hole in her memory, there was now overwhelming confusion and loss, married to images that made no sense. She couldn't handle two realities. If she could, she'd be an anchor.

"Is she going to be okay?" Howard addressed Silas worriedly.

"I don't know," Silas said grimly. But as Peri tried to remember how to move her lungs in order to breathe, she doubted if okay was anything she would ever be again.

CHAPTER
TWENTY-FOUR

Silas watched Peri breathe, amazed her mind was still fighting even as it was fraying right before him. Both timelines held information they needed: who'd betrayed her and how deep the corruption went. He had fragmented almost nothing, believing he could hold it all until he had the entire two lines. But the memories had come too fast and adhered too quickly—and though the two time-lines weren't yet coherent, she had them both now. The more they fell into place, the more unstable she'd become. She was trembling, full into a memory overdraft, which was a nice way of saying he'd screwed up, leaving her mind to destroy itself.

"Turn left," Silas whispered, his voice just louder than the car's engine. They'd been interrupted, and he didn't know what to destroy, what to fix. And she was in agony. *Damn you, Allen. I blame you.* "It's the third one up. Stone walkway," he said.

"I see it," Taf said, and Silas held Peri closer to minimize the jostling as Taf drove them through the high-end subdivision. He could feel Peri's thoughts circling as she tried to organize the memories he'd unearthed. Her pain and betrayal resonated in him as if they were his own. It was the pain that was keeping her sane right now, the desire for revenge. She couldn't allow others to believe they wouldn't be held accountable for what they'd done. But it was only a matter of time until Peri got everything in the right place. Grief wouldn't be a strong enough emotion to hold her together then.

"Peri?" he whispered when he realized her shaking had stopped. "Stay with me."

"Is she okay?" Howard said from up front, and her eyelids flickered.

"No." Silas's voice was ragged as his thumb brushed the hair from her cheek. "Peri, can you hear me?"

Her breath came in as a wheezing, pained sound, and he fastened on it. She could hear him, even lost in the twin timelines her mind was stuck on. If he could mute them both to where the present was stronger than the past, he might be able to stave off the inevitable. But for how long? "Hang on," he whispered, seeing Karley's two-story home, gray in the snow and porch lights. "Concentrate on what you hear. I'm not letting you go."

His heart leapt when her narrow chin quivered.

She'd heard him, and he held her tighter. My God, she was stronger than he'd ever given her credit for.

"Drop me at the curb," Silas said, scooting to the door with Peri still in his arms. "I don't want a second tire track in the drive. Ditch the car and come back. Karley will be more likely to let me in if you're not with me."

What am I doing, bringing Peri here? But he had no choice, ex-wife or not.

"Silas . . . ," Howard protested, even as he got out to help.

The sudden cold was bitter. Lurching, he got out with her in his arms, her weight hardly anything. Pale and fragile-looking, she opened her eyes, but he could tell she wasn't seeing the gray and white snow above them.

"Stay with Taf," Silas said, and Howard reluctantly dropped back. "Karley will help me. She doesn't like me, but she'll help me, if only to tell me how stupid I am."

"You're sure about this?"

He nodded, his desperation growing. Not knowing what to do, he started up the steep drive, staying within the tire track to minimize evidence of his presence. Howard got back into the car, but they didn't drive away, and Silas frowned as he used his elbow to ring the doorbell. She had to be home. There was only one set of tracks in the light snow.

"I can fix this, Peri," he whispered. "Hang on just a little more. I'll make it go away." His fear began to shift to anger. Jack had used her, used her love to blind her, the very man who'd once held her sanity and soul. She'd been right to shoot him.

Her eyes fluttered, unseeing as the door swung in and light spilled over them.

"Karley," Silas said to the late-thirties woman standing in the glow from inside the cavernous, ostentatious house. She was still dressed from an early dinner out, lipstick faded from the glass of whatever she'd been drinking, heels off, purse on the table by the door. Frowning, she put a manicured hand on her cocked hip, showing off her legs under her professional suit dress. Her brown hair was pulled back in a clip that made her look both severe and elegant. "I need your help," Silas said when Karley leaned to look past him to the car running at the curb.

"Of course you do," she said, eyes coming back to Peri.

"They're not staying," Silas added, and Karley laughed bitterly.

"Neither are you. Opti has already been here looking for you. I'm not doing this again."

"This isn't about me!" he said as the door began to close. "I tried to defragment something and it got out of control. We were interrupted, and she's in overdraft. I can't take her to Emergency. Opti wants to wipe her, and she's got the end to this buried in her mind. It's not too late to pull her out. I just need a quiet room."

Guilt kept his eyes firmly on hers. He'd learned the knack of lying to the women he loved early on. There had to be a way to save both Peri and the memories she held. He just didn't know how to do it yet.

"Why do you do this to me?" Karley leaned closer, moved by Peri's dire appearance, if not by his words.

"Please," he said again, begging. "This isn't about me. She needs help."

Karley made an ugly sound, but the door was still open. "All right. Hurry up," she finally said, looking past him at the car and waving it off. "Get in here. How confident are you that you weren't followed? Are you clean?"

The warmth and muffled sound of a well-furnished home enfolded him, pushing aside the images of blood and hard yellow floor that were leaking into his awareness. Peri was trying. She was fighting for her sanity even if her eyes were shut and she shook as if she'd been beaten.

"Howard brought us," Silas said as the door clicked shut. "We're clean. As for being followed? Who knows."

"You are a bundle of good news, Silas. Nothing's changed there. Put her on the couch."

He knelt before the couch in the lavish living room, his chest clenching when Peri reached for him as she felt herself drop. She wasn't as lost as he thought, and his indecision became almost unbearable. The hell with the information. He had to save her. Fingers trembling, he folded her hands over her chest, never letting go as he pushed the hair from her eyes.

Karley leaned close over them both, her lips pressed into a thin line as she professionally evaluated Peri's state. The smell of hairspray grew strong, and he held his breath, praying Karley wouldn't say it was too late. She'd always given up too easily. On everything.

"How long ago did it happen?" she asked, her tone holding that cold lilt he hated.

"Twenty minutes." Karley straightened up, and he breathed easier.

"I meant, how long ago was the draft you tried to render?" she asked pointedly.

"Four days." Guilt sank its teeth in another inch, and he tugged the TV blanket up over her. "She was starting to hallucinate. I thought it was worth the risk."

"She was hallucinating within four days?" Karley's voice was raised in anger. "Are you blind or intentionally being an idiot? It must have been highly traumatic to cause hallucinations after only *four days*. Where's her anchor?"

Silas glared up at her, wanting to stand but unwilling to let go of Peri. "She killed him," he said drily.

Head shaking, Karley picked up her short glass of ice and something clear. Hand on one hip, she stood before the oversize flat screen currently displaying the house's security. "That was the memory you tried to defragment? Her killing her anchor?"

Frustrated, he fixed the blanket tighter under Peri's chin. "Part of it."

"And you wonder why you lost control?" Karley's professional outrage began to show. "No wonder Opti threw you out. What could she possibly know worth risking her mental stability for?"

"Opti didn't throw me out. I quit." He stood, bitter and not wanting to add to Peri's already swirling emotions. "There's no way I could've kept control of what I unearthed. The rewrite was intertwined with the original like hair in a dreadlock."

Karley pointed at him with her glass, ice clinking. "What does she know that's worth risking her sanity for?"

He stiffened. "I need a quiet place to piece her back together. Are you going to help me, or should I go to a Motel 6?"

"You left her with two timelines, didn't you?" Setting her glass on the mantel, Karley waited, anger pulling her eyebrows together when he said nothing. "You are an idiot. Drafters can't handle two timelines. That's why they forget them! And you *left* them there?"

"I'm trying to *help her,*" Silas snapped, slumping when Karley made a frustrated *Well?* gesture. "Peri has information about the corruption in Opti. It goes deeper than Bill. I didn't fragment anything yet because both timelines hold the proof."

"Oh, my God. Bill?" Karley sat down, her anger replaced by shock. "Isn't he her handler?"

Silas nodded. "It gets better. He was the one tasked with finding the corruption. He sent Peri and her anchor to get a list of bad agents so he could modify it before reporting them. Peri found out, killed her anchor. But the original list is still live somewhere. If we can find it before Bill does, we can end this."

And if not, everything lost will have been for nothing, he thought. "Peri and I have a good working connection," he said, and Karley's head snapped up, eyes bright in warning. "I successfully untangled a memory knot created by Allen's wipe."

"Damn it, Silas, those things are dangerous," Karley said in exasperation.

"No they're not," he said, his frustration at an old argument getting the best of him. "Opti uses fear to control drafters. Fear that unresolved timelines will cause madness. Fear of being alone so their leash holders are always there. Fear that they can't do without anchors when they can. They filled her head with lies to make her helpless."

Karley shook her head. "Even the best drafter will go insane with twin timelines."

His pulse quickened at the truth of that. "I can hide them under enough distractions that she can live with it. We'd have our proof."

"Silas."

"I can do this!" he said loudly, then glanced at Peri and lowered his voice. She'd regained enough motor control to curl into a fetal position, and guilt made him feel ill. If he didn't hide the twin lines well enough, she'd ferret them out and go mad before his eyes. He couldn't watch another drafter go mad like that. Not again.

Karley rose fast, her indecision obvious. They'd been married for three years, and hiding his fear from her was impossible. "It can't be done," she said, touching his shoulder. "I'm sorry."

"All I need is a quiet room," he said pointedly, and Peri flinched. But that was a good sign, even as he sensed the memories in her tumbling over themselves. "I can't leave her like this, and I can't fragment everything she worked so hard to uncover. But I can get the information and keep her sane."

His jaw clenched at the pity in his ex-wife's eyes. "It's one or the other. She's not Summer. You can't save her."

Silas's gut twisted as Peri picked up on his sudden grief and moaned. "Summer is gone,"

Silas said. "I know I can do both. Are you going to help me or not?"

Brow furrowed, Karley strode to the fireplace. She took a drink, ice clinking. "I can't believe I'm doing this," she said, angry at herself as she gave in. "You can stay until morning. Then you're gone, whether she's conscious or not. Sane or dead. You understand? So you'd better impress the hell out of me and fix this, Doctor."

His breath came fast and he dropped to a kneel to gather Peri to him. She was so light, hardly there, and he found his feet with a new determination even as his fear shook itself and became that much stronger. "Thank you," he said, and Peri's eyes opened, scanning the ceiling before she choked and closed them. The fear of being left alone shocked through him—Peri's emotion was resonating in him.

"Upstairs," Karley was saying over her shoulder as she walked to the stairway between the living room and kitchen. "You don't happen to know her safe place, do you?"

He tried to smile when Peri's wandering, unseeing eyes found his, and his hope leapt when she clutched at his arm. "Don't leave me alone," she slurred.

It was a clear, coherent thought, and his heart soared as he followed Karley. "Thank God you're still here," he whispered, eyes on hers. "It's going to be okay. I won't leave you until there's somewhere safe beyond the confusion."

Her breath came in a heave. Tears were spilling from her as she nodded, and her eyes closed again as if the sights and colors hurt. "Please hurry."

"She's still cognizant," Silas whispered as Karley opened a door at the top of the stairs, and he watched Peri's face for any sign of pain when he lowered her gently to the bed. Her long lashes rested on her pale cheeks, making her look lost among the faded colors of the room. Gently he brushed back her black hair making stark lines on the white pillow, and she shook, feeling it. "I need coffee. Can you get me some coffee?"

Karley nodded, lips pursed in disapproval as she left and shut the door behind her.

"Silas!" Peri cried out at the soft click, and he took her hand as he knelt beside the bed to put his face near hers. Her eyes opened, but he knew she wasn't seeing him. She was seeing Jack, and an unknown horror sheened her eyes as she moaned and closed them. She was sliding back into the chaos of memories Silas had unearthed.

There was no way to separate them, but he didn't have to. Steeling himself against the grief and betrayal, he opened his mind again, reliving everything with her, studying it in detail as she cried, shaking between the covers. But he wouldn't let her relive them alone, and as he shuffled and aligned, piecing everything together by using the fall of shadows and tiny details that she'd never focused on, he realized how he was going to hide her twin memories in plain sight. When he was done, she'd be able to rest her mind from the horror in the scent of polish, the darkness of the beams, the glint of the Juke'sBox, and the almost-subliminal hum of the bar's gaming lounge.

Slowly he shifted the memory of Jack dying, blurring it until the only thing that mattered was the shine on the floor. He tweaked Peri's savage rage while shooting Jack, down to the glint of light on a nearby shot glass. He blurred the voices until the hum of the floor cleaner was all she heard. Allen restraining her as she sold her memory for the chance to kill Jack became less important than the pinch of her boot, something she'd never noticed.

He fragmented what he could, but the twin lines were there still, muted until they and the incongruities they fostered wouldn't be noticed, blurring everything into a monochrome that would let her sleep.

And finally, she found it.

Shaking from the effort, Silas opened his eyes. For a long moment he studied her slender fingers twined in his. *Delicate, but strong,* he thought as he looked at his blocky knuckles beside hers. He listened to her breathe, thinking the smooth sound was the most beautiful thing he'd ever heard. But everything he'd done would last only until her intuition picked away at it. She was too smart to allow such deception, even when she knew it was to save her life.

But that was not what pained him, even as she slept exhausted before him. As he'd sifted through her thoughts, aligning and hiding them, he saw within her that Allen might be right. She'd willingly become what they needed for this task, but she liked who she was, the power she held. Tricking death and walking away to a fast car and cocktails at thirty-four thousand feet had addicted her to the high of being bulletproof, to the point where she might not abandon it when the task was finished. The elegance and grace she wrapped herself in was a mask to hide the ugly truth. She'd become that which was needed, perhaps too thoroughly to come back from.

He found he didn't care.

But he wasn't done yet, and he closed his eyes and slipped into her mind again. He had to hobble her intuition in such a way that it would give her freedom as well as safety.

That his fix was going to involve Jack, the man she'd grown to love and then hate, was probably a fitting punishment for his own sins.

CHAPTER
TWENTY-FIVE

The sound of a hushed argument pulled Peri from a deep, dreamless sleep. She stretched, eyes closed and luxuriating in a pleasant ache and the sensation of clean sheets on her bare skin. It was like skinny-dipping, and she sighed, not wanting to wake up.

"If you aren't out of my house in five minutes, I'm calling Opti and I'll have them here in ten!" a woman was saying, her voice familiar, but there was no face swimming up from Peri's memory to go with it. She was comfortable, and her mind was as clear as if she'd just finished a task. To get up was too much work for too little payoff.

"Touch that phone, and I'll shoot you," a higher voice whispered, and Peri frowned at Taf's anger. "Peri isn't hurting you."

There was a soft thump, and then Howard said, "Ma'am. Don't make me tie you up."

Peri's eyes opened. The room was bright with sun and richly decorated in colors she liked. It was morning, and she didn't have a stitch of clothing on. Someone must have taken her clothes off, because she never slept that freely. *Maybe I drafted?* But there was no recall itch in her mind, none of the unease that an unfragmented draft usually left her with. Frowning, she tried to remember how she'd gotten naked in a nice room like this.

The sound of an unseen door opening pulled Peri upright, and she tugged the sheet to cover herself. There was a glass of water on the night-stand, and she gulped it down in one go, then wiped a drop from her chin.

"You're going to wake her. Can you do this downstairs?" Silas said in a hushed whisper.

Peri took a breath to call out, choking on it when a movement in the corner drew her eyes. Heart pounding, she tightened her grip on her empty glass and stared at Jack, sitting in the corner in a pressed suit and tie, just the right amount of stubble, a heat-filled glint in his eyes. *It didn't work.* She was still hallucinating.

"Hi, babe," he said, and Peri closed her eyes, willing the vision to leave.

"Go away," she whispered, eyes flashing open when he cleared his throat. "You aren't real," she said, glancing at the door and the hushed argument beyond it in the hall.

Jack put an ankle on his knee and loosened his tie to look indescribably attractive. "At least you can think again," he said, and a sliver of panic slid through her. *Fudge on a stick, they're starting to interact with me.*

"She's going to call Opti," Taf said from the hall, her exclamation a whisper.

Silas sighed. "Karley isn't going to call Opti. All of you get away from Peri's door before you wake her up."

"She *will* wake up, right?" the unknown woman said, but at least now Peri had a name.

Taf gasped, and Howard shushed her. "Of course she will," Silas said. "I was able to do a few things last night."

Do a few things? Peri's gaze flicked from the door back to Jack. Her shoulders slumped as he wiggled his fingers at her, grinning madly. "Go away," she whispered, setting the glass down so she wouldn't throw it at him. "You're not real. You're *not* real. I killed you. You're dead!" She didn't remember a thing from Overdraft, but that's what everyone had said she'd done. Every time she tried to remember it, it sort of . . . slipped away. The anger, though, the sense of outright betrayal at something she couldn't recall—that was real. And if she felt that much betrayal, then she had probably loved him. *For God's sake, why can't I ever find a nice man?*

"You're right. I'm not real," Jack said, and her eyes narrowed.

From the hallway, Howard said, "Jeez, Silas. You look like hell. You want a coffee?"

"Yeah. Thanks," he said, and Jack rolled his eyes and made a *blah, blah, blah* gesture.

"Did it work?" Karley asked, halfway down the stairs from the sound of it.

"I won't know until she wakes up. Mental scaffolds are not magic pills."

Peri stiffened when Jack found her under-wear laid out on a chair and held it up, eyebrows waggling. "Put that down," she whispered. "Go away. You're a hallucination."

Jack obediently set it down. "True. But I'm going to keep you sane if it kills you."

"You call this sane!" Peri shouted, then covered her mouth and looked at the door.

The thumping on the stairs halted. "I think she's up," Silas said, and Peri winced when the muted thunder of multiple ascending footsteps turned into silence, and then a hesitant knock. "Peri?"

Sheet held tight, Peri looked at Jack to keep his mouth shut, then the door. "Come in."

Silas poked his head in, disheveled and stubbly. His hair was even worse, but somehow it made him charmingly accessible. "Um," he started, clearly not seeing Jack in the corner. "How do you feel? You look better."

Jack wrinkled his nose at Peri, and her heart pounded. "I *look* better?" she exclaimed. She was crazy. She'd trusted him, and now she was crazy. "I'm blue-lined insane!"

"Not if you're yelling at me, you're not." Silas came all the way in, and Taf and Howard looked in around the door. It was only his relieved expression that kept her quiet when a woman she didn't recognize pushed in past Taf and Howard. That, and she was still naked. The woman was dressed for the office, and she looked irate. *Karley?* Peri guessed.

"I'm still hallucinating," Peri whispered, and Jack popped his cheek with a finger. She hated it when he did that, but she wasn't going to look at him.

Silas flushed as the woman cleared her throat in rebuke. "Yes, I know," he said, rubbing a hand over his stubble. Turning to the door, he said, "Can we have a few minutes? Get your stuff ready. We'll be leaving within the hour."

Taf gave Peri a thumbs-up, her relief obvious. "I'm glad you're okay."

"Me too," Howard said, then yelped when Taf yanked him into the hallway. Their voices grew faint, and the confusion of last night whispered at the edges of her awareness. She frowned at Silas, knowing he'd done something, judging by his tension and Karley's impatience.

It must be her house, Peri thought, wishing someone would introduce them.

Silas gave Karley a look as if asking her to leave, but she shut the door, feet planted firmly on the white throw rug. "I want to know if it worked," she said.

"What worked?" Peri asked suspiciously, and Jack blew her a kiss.

"I'm your bag of magic rocks, babe," Jack said,

and she stifled her pique that he'd use a phrase from their past so glibly.

The woman arched her eyebrows mockingly, and when Silas remained uncomfortably silent, she said, "Hi, I'm Karley. Silas's ex-wife. Silas was part of an experimental Opti program whose goal was creating fake memories for drafters."

Peri looked at Silas. "What did you do to me?" Seeing his guilt, Peri turned to Karley. "What did he do to me?" she said, louder.

From the corner, Jack said, "I'm going to keep you sane, Peri."

Silas gingerly sat at the foot of the bed. "The idea was to provide drafters with a cushion when they lost large chunks of their lives," he said. "Give them temporary memories until they'd built up enough new ones to feel comfortable again. I quit when Opti began experimenting with giving drafters memories designed to make them react in a specific way."

"As in making them corrupt," Peri accused.

"I did say I quit." A flicker of anger crossed him. "It was only supposed to help."

It would explain how he'd helped her rebuild a memory he'd never witnessed. At least her hallucinations weren't bleeding anymore. "What did you do to me?"

Silas looked at Karley, then her. "Why don't you ask Jack?"

She hesitated as Jack stood, stretched, and

ambled forward, a grin on his face as he tightened his tie as if getting ready for work.

"He's here, isn't he?" Silas said, his eyes wide. "Damn it. If he's not, it didn't work."

"Jack is dead," Peri said, stifling a shiver when Jack leaned close, blowing on the skin below her ear.

"What is real, anyway, babe?"

Okay, she was filled with feelings of betrayal, but how could she be angry at a hallucination in John Lobb shoes and an Armani suit?

Karley shifted her weight and looked at her watch, impatient in her makeup, heels, and dress jacket. "Peri, will you just ask Jack? I have to be at work in forty minutes, and I want all of you out of here before I leave."

Jack gestured as if in invitation, and at Silas's encouraging nod, Peri cautiously faced Jack, not liking that no one else could see him but they all knew he was there . . . leaning casually against the dresser, perfect in the sun and dancing motes of dust. *And I killed him.*

"Jack?" she said, feeling stupid. "What's going on?"

Jack beamed, but his bad-boy charms that had probably once attracted her felt tired. "I'm a spit-ball of psychiatric bullshit. Silas melded me to your intuition so that any time you begin thinking about those twin timelines he left crashing about in your skull, I can distract you." He leaned close, and she froze as the scent of his aftershave sifted through her. "But, like your intuition, I will show up any . . . time . . . I want," he whispered.

Fear spun her to Silas. "You left twin timelines in me!"

"Peri, it's okay," Silas soothed as he reached out.

"Fragment them!" Frantic, she pushed his hands away. "Fragment them now!"

But he caught her wrists, bringing her to a frightened stillness. "If I do, everything we've worked to achieve for the last five years is gone. We need what's in your head to clear your name and bring Opti down. You're okay. Just relax and breathe. You're not insane."

Not yet, anyway. Peri looked down at his grip around her wrists. "I can't believe you did this," she said. But he was right. The confusion was gone. The conflict of emotions she'd been dealing with the last few days had settled into a faint ember burn. She hated Jack, enough to kill him, apparently. Sandy, Bill, and Frank, too, were on her new shit list. But when she tried to remember why, she was . . . distracted before her mind could . . . circle back and recollect.

It was the oddest sensation, and Peri pulled out of Silas's hold. "Well, I guess Jack's right then," she muttered, and Silas nervously stood.

"About what?" he asked.

"That he's a spitball of psychiatric bullshit."

Karley laughed long and loud, and somehow it made Peri feel better. "Oh, I like that," the polished woman said as she glanced at her watch. "Nicely done," she added as she gave Silas a peck on the cheek. "I didn't think it was possible. Now, get out of my house."

"It's just a Band-Aid," Silas said, still uneasy. Peri wasn't happy, either. "You have to be really careful until you get a few days of base memories. I don't want you to risk drafting."

"So why am I seeing Jack?" she demanded as the hallucination began arranging her underwear again. "And how can he answer me? Talk back and everything?" Silas had saved her, but she felt fragile, as if a sneeze might destroy everything.

Silas's brow eased. "Think of him like a mental cop on the corner. I needed the flexibility and awareness your intuition would give, and it manifests as a hallucination because disembodied voices in your head can lead to, ah, more problems."

"I'll bet." It made sense, but she still felt like his personal science project. "Why Jack?" she asked. Just saying his name felt slimy, her cooling hatred toward him tempered with hints of past tasks, of danger shared, of good times—before it fell apart.

"You'd rather it be your mom?" Silas said, and her eyes widened as the horror of that slid through her. "They're the only two people you listen to."

"Jack is fine," she said. "But I don't trust either one of them."

Silas stood, and Karley edged toward the door. "I said listen to, not trust." Silas's eyes crinkled at the corners. "I know this is hard," he said, his voice low. "But if I destroyed both timelines, we'd have no way to clear your name or bring Opti down."

Tired, Peri put her forehead on her drawn-up knees. It was hard to be angry with him, even if it was unconscionable for an anchor to leave twin timelines in a drafter. He was right; she was alive. "How long until you can fragment one of them?" she asked, her words muffled.

"It depends on how long it takes to, ah, find that original list."

She lifted her head, a faint sense of purpose growing. "It has to be in my apartment. We can do it tonight." Peri wanted this done, and done fast. Silas's patch job was just that.

Karley was on her way out, but she hesitated on the threshold, shaking her head at Silas's inquiring glance. *No? Did she just tell him no?*

"Not yet," Silas said, and Jack, forgotten in the corner, laughed quietly as Peri's eyes narrowed. "You need to build some memories before you can risk your mental state. I don't know what will happen if you draft. You can stay here with Howard and Taf."

"You are all leaving." Karley pointed at the unseen front door. "Right now."

Peri began to get out of bed, hesitating when the

sheets rubbed her bare skin. "You need your list. I need my talismans. They can give me the cushion I need. Keep me from a MEP." Her heart pounded as she said what they were all thinking, none of them saying.

"It's not worth the risk, especially if all we have to do is wait a few weeks." Silas pushed Karley out the door, the woman protesting hotly.

"I'm not waiting a few weeks!" Peri exclaimed. "Besides, it's a little late to be flying the flag of not wanting to stress my mental state."

"Opti is camped out at your apartment. We wait." Silas had a hand on Karley's arm, forestalling her complaints. "We'll get you some new IDs to keep you off Opti's radar. You need at least three months of solid memories before you can risk another draft. You're going over the bridge this afternoon."

I'm not going to hide out in Canada, either. "What do Taf and Howard think about this?"

"I'm sure they'll agree," he said calmly.

"Last time I checked, that was doctor-speak for you've not told them yet," Peri said, and Karley chuckled and went downstairs.

Sighing, Silas came back in. "I don't want to risk it," he said, his concern obvious. "Add an unexpected jump to what you're running with, and you might go into MEP. We have time."

She frowned, thinking he was being overly cautious. The answers were right there, and she wasn't waiting three months to ransack her own apartment.

"Silas!" Karley shouted from downstairs. "Let her get dressed! I have to go to work!"

An old irritation pinched his brow. "Coming!" he shouted out the door, then softer, to her, "Your clothes have been washed and are on the chair."

"Thank you." Waking up naked was a small price to pay for clean clothes.

"I'll see you downstairs, then." Silas shut the door behind him with a soft click. From the hall came a muffled "Karley, did you throw out all my clothes?"

Peri listened to the garbled response, and when Silas's steps were gone, she turned to Jack. "Where did you stash that list?" she asked hesitantly, thinking it was stupid talking to a hallucination who knew nothing more than she did. But there was no way she was going to hide for three months. Not when she had an apartment with five years of talismans just a drive away.

"You don't know, sweetheart," Jack said. "If you did, I'd tell you. But it has to be in the apartment. Get me in there, and I can probably find it."

That didn't make her feel as good as she thought it would, and she slid out from between the sheets, grimacing when Jack made a wolf whistle. It was just a hallucination, but thanks to a thousand forgotten memories, it was going to act just like

Jack would, and damn her if she didn't start to understand why she'd blinded herself for three years. He was perfect.

A perfect mistake, she amended as she pointed at the chair for him to put her panties back down so she could pick them up. "Jack, what do you think about Silas?"

Jack snorted. "You think he's a mistake, too, babe," Jack said, which made sense since, as her intuition, he wouldn't know anything she didn't already.

But it was still nice hearing Jack say it.

CHAPTER
TWENTY-SIX

"**C**anada?" Taf's hand extended out the car's window to Silas, who was standing resolutely on the curb, fake IDs in hand. The short spring coat he'd gotten from Karley was open to show his pinstripe shirt and tie. Karley, apparently, hadn't thrown anything away. The tips of his hair from under his hat shifted in the faint breeze off the river, and his freshly shaven face was reddened from more than the cold. Angry, he wouldn't look at Peri, stewing in the backseat.

"We can't go to Canada. Peri needs her talismans," Taf complained as she took Howard's new ID and passed it over. "And what about the list? It's our ticket back into the alliance. We can do this. Peri is fine!"

"Fine" was a relative term, but compared to the comatose, confused state she'd been in last night, yes, Peri was fine—and not happy about Silas's argument because it made her feel vulnerable and she was tired of feeling like a porcelain princess. She, Taf, and Howard had already come up with a rough plan to access her apartment. It had evolved in the scant hour when Silas had been arranging their new IDs. It didn't involve let's-do-nothing Silas. Slipping him was step one.

Silas squinted down the street. It was noisy with early-morning deliveries and pedestrians, and he pulled his hat lower when a harmless, low-Q drone hummed over the parked cars. "Opti is camped out at her apartment," he said as he handed in a second package. Taf took it, glanced at it, then handed it to Peri in the back. "We can try in a few weeks when they aren't as attentive."

Sara Washington? Couldn't he come up with something better? Peri thought sourly as she eyed her new ID. Getting the pictures off their phones turned into passable IDs had been more difficult than it needed to be, since Silas had insisted on the enhanced driver's license that functioned as a passport for ground travel between Michigan and Canada. *All the better to hide you, my dear.*

"Who put you in charge?" Taf protested. "It's over 'cause you say so? Bull cookies! We need to do this before Opti finds the list themselves."

Peri kicked at the back of Taf's seat. In the front, Howard leaned across the center console. "Peri needs some time to recover," he said, squinting meaningfully. "You're going to hurt her feelings if you don't *shut up*."

Taf hesitated, then exhaled. "Fine. I like snow. Canada might be nice."

"You're coming with me," Silas said, and Peri exchanged a worried look with Howard through the rearview mirror. "Howard can get Peri settled."

"Whoa. Wait a moment. Where are you going?" Taf protested as Silas opened her door.

"*We* are going back to the alliance to try to clear up a few misconceptions," he muttered. "They don't like that I'm withholding you from them."

Scooting across the long backseat, Peri rested the flats of her arms on the open window and leaned out to the curb as Taf shut her door, jerking it right out of Silas's grip. "You're going to the alliance?" Peri asked as she looked for a lie. Explaining to the alliance what had happened wasn't a bad idea, but it might just be a ruse allowing him to search her apartment without her.

"I am *not* going back," Taf muttered, a flush creeping up the back of her neck. "My mother can just eat green eggs and fart. She was going to give you to Opti," she said, locking her door when Silas tried to open it again. "My *mother!*"

"So come back with me and explain to them why that was a bad idea." Silas's dress shoes scraped the salt-rimed sidewalk. "Out. Come on. Time to do the grown-up thing and talk to your mom. Howard can get Peri across the bridge."

It was a good plan, but Peri's eyes narrowed as she read Silas's tells: the slight hunch to his shoulders, the tightness of his lips, the way he was swallowing his words. Damn it, Silas knew. He knew she was going to make a play for her apartment with or without him and was chipping away at her resources.

"Silas . . . ," Taf complained.

"Just go," Howard grumbled, and after a long moment, the young woman got out in a huff. Peri tried to find a neutral expression so as not to look as if her plan was coming apart.

"I'm sorry for having put your mental health at risk for a chance to bring Opti down," Silas said, and she snorted at his apparent sincerity. "I have to talk to the alliance before they start coming for us. Me. But don't hesitate to call if you have any issues with, ah, your intuition. I'll contact you in a week. It's not over. I'll be back."

"I don't know why you think me being there is going to help," Taf said as she zipped up her leather jacket and stuffed her hands in her pockets. "I pointed my daddy's rifle at her."

"But you didn't shoot her," Silas said, almost smiling.

"True."

Peri jumped, startled, when Jack, coming straight from her subconscious, lifted the handle of the backseat door on the street and slid in next to her. "Silas is a good liar. Almost as good as me," Jack said as he slammed the door and settled himself behind Howard—which was really weird, since the car door never really opened and the wind never truly gusted, even if she had a sudden chill and had to tuck her hair back. It was her mind inventing a way for him to be there, and it was kind of freaking her out.

"Thanks, Howard." Silas extended his hand into the car, and Howard leaned to take it. The two shook. "Get her across the bridge. I'll call you when I know something."

"Will do. Thanks."

Silas put his hands in his pockets, shoulders hunched and neck red. "I'll call you in a week, okay?" he said to Peri, eyes pinched and asking for forgiveness. "We need to work on a more permanent solution. I just need to take care of this. I'm not abandoning you."

But it felt as if he was.

He waited for a moment, and when Peri said nothing, he reluctantly turned away.

Her heart thumped and she reached out after him. Embarrassed by her impulse, she pulled herself back, clenched hands jammed in her lap. She didn't need Silas's help. Taf would be sorely missed, though.

His hands still on the wheel, Howard sighed. Scooting to the middle, Peri leaned over the console. "This is going to be harder without Taf."

"Don't worry about Taf," he said, his words slow. "She'll get four hours down the road and ditch him." He put the car into drive. "She'll be back."

"You sure?"

Howard nodded. "She got out of the car way too easy."

Not only that, but she'd left without much of a good-bye. Yep, she'd be back—if she could. Still unsure, Peri watched Silas and Taf cross the street ahead of them to reach the bus stop. Silas's long, slow pace looked odd next to Taf's fast click-clack in her boots. "Run him over, Howie. Just run him over," she said. "He's right in the middle of the street."

"Ah-h-h, he means well." Howard pulled out, sighing when Taf enthusiastically waved and turned away. It felt wrong leaving her to make her way back to them, and Peri slumped in the backseat to watch the shopfronts and foot traffic slide by. It bothered Jack, too, seeing as he was cleaning under his nails with the camo knife she had picked up at the airport. She hated it when he did that, and she fought the urge to tweak the imaginary knife away and throw it out the window.

I'm not depressed because Silas left, she told herself. His reasoning to wait was sound, but she couldn't help but feel abandoned. He was an anchor—and she was adrift.

"You'd better hope Taf doesn't show," Jack said, and she checked to see the knife still in her boot sheath. "Even Howard is too much. You're going to get them killed."

Guilt swam up, and she sat straighter.

"You think you feel guilty now, wait until they're dead," Jack added.

Peri stared out the window, ignoring him. She was in charge of the task, and it was her responsibility to give her team members no more than what they were capable of. But part of her hoped Taf couldn't make it back. She was too enthusiastic, too optimistic, clearly never having known real loss, and Peri wanted to keep it that way.

"Will you be okay on your own for the morning?" Peri asked as she divided her plan into low- and high-risk tasks. "I need to find out about the men Opti has on my apartment."

"Our apartment," Jack said, and she unclenched her hands.

"There're always empty flats in the building across the street. We can set you up in one of them so you can do surveillance on my building,"

Peri added, looking behind them when they slipped through a yellow light. Howard would be out of sight, out of Opti's mind. "Do you have enough for a set of binoculars?" she asked, reaching for the bills she'd taken from under her silverware caddy.

Howard's beads clinked as he nodded, and she settled back. "Good. Even if the blinds are pulled in my apartment, you can watch who goes in the building and make a guess as to how many agents are in there."

"If you're watching your apartment, Opti will be too. Once I know their schedule, I can play janitor and sweep the hallways for evidence of monitoring," he offered.

"Good thinking." The thrill of the task was bringing her alive, and she leaned between the seats to avoid Jack's disapproving frown. "Just make sure to cover those dreadlocks. They know what you look like now. Take a right here. I'm going to walk the area to see where they put the foot men. That will keep me busy until about three. Once you get outfitted, find an empty apartment. They're listed online. Text me the number around three fifteen. If I don't show up by three thirty, get out and meet me at the coffeehouse where we had breakfast. If you get itchy, just go. If Silas shows up, go. I'll be fine."

Jack slowly scratched the stubble at his jawline—a show of nerves, her sketchy memory said. Howard seemed good with it, but she didn't like Jack manifesting her worry. "I'll bring dinner," Peri said, pointing for Howard to take another right into a residential area, quiet on a Monday morning. "I need some paper and a pen. Can you pick some up while you're out? We'll need a final sketch of where Opti is, how to avoid them, and where to stash the bodies."

That last came out of her mouth without thought, her head jerking up to find Howard's brow furrowed. Jack cleared his throat. "This is a bad idea, babe. You know it."

"I'm sorry," Peri said, and Howard flashed her a nervous smile. "I'm doing the prep work to minimize conflict, but—"

"We're good," Howard interrupted, but it had been too fast, and Peri's sense of guilt dampened her mood. Jack was playing cat's cradle with a string of pearls, the black spheres clinking with the sound of an abacus. She didn't need him to tell her this was a bad idea, and she threw the gloves Karley had given her at him. They made a soft plop as they hit the seat . . . and he was gone.

Lips parted, Peri cautiously stretched across the backseat of the car to pick them up. "If you have any doubts, tell me now," she said, and Howard shook his head.

"Taf is not going to let this go," he said, clearly concerned as his grip tightened on the wheel. "Where she goes, I go."

So his drive to do what's right isn't entirely his own, she thought, then started when she figured it out. "Taf's the student you were tutoring when you met Silas, wasn't she?"

"Yes, ma'am," Howard said, his worried smile going wistful.

"Do you love her?" she asked, needing to know before she put either of them in harm's way, and his smile faded.

"I'm afraid to, but yes. I just don't want to be the man she uses to punish her mother."

Deciding they were far enough out, Peri put on her gloves. "You aren't," she said, leaning over the seat to give him a kiss on the cheek. "Why don't you drop me here?"

The car's brakes squeaked as he stopped, and Howard was smiling when she got out. "See you about three thirty," he said, and she gave him a little wave and walked away. Howard pulled up to the stop sign ahead of her, turned, and was gone.

Head down, she started for her apartment, vowing nothing was going to happen to either of them.

CHAPTER
TWENTY-SEVEN

It was edging toward midnight when Peri stood at the dark window of the empty apartment across from her building, munching on Chinese take-out as she half-listened to Howard and Taf talking in the master suite. True to Howard's prediction, Taf had showed up, and she envied their banter as they ate their rice and fried meat. It was obvious that Taf had come back more for Howard than for her. Peri had to keep them both safe.

Her recon to find where the Opti agents were positioned had been successful, and she'd easily spotted the expected three teams stationed around the building in the standard Opti triangle formation. According to Howard's intel, an additional two Opti agents were wandering the halls as security guards, a third probably in her apartment, since Howard hadn't seen him since he'd arrived. The agent at the concierge's desk made four on-site, and there were two in the van at the curb.

It was Howard's opinion that everyone wired, which could work for them, with a little effort, especially since Howard had located Opti's off-site observatory post three stories up from the room she was now standing in, eating cold Chinese food from a take-out box. After three hours of watching the black Opti van almost beneath her feet at the curb, she decided it was worth the risk to try to take out the monitoring room. It would be a grand place to leave Howard—relatively safe and out of the way.

It's a nice apartment, even with the lousy view, Peri thought as she dug through the vegetables to get to something other than tiny corn and broccoli. Open floor plan, nice fixtures. But most people liked the view of Detroit poking up from the new green spaces, all connected by the visually pleasing, raised magnetic rail. This no-view suite was probably hard to keep rented.

Jack was sitting on the floor beside the ceiling-to-floor window, his back against the wall and his legs stretched out, eyes closed as if waiting for a task to begin. She was getting accustomed to him popping in, but if she ever saw Silas again, she was going to smack him. Seeing her mother there giving her advice in her lordly tone, her hair perfect and her fingers playing with her jewelry, might have been preferable to a sexy man in a Dolce & Gabbana suit who had betrayed not only her, but her love for him.

Digging into a water chestnut, Peri crunched through it, an unexpected pang running through her. She and her mother hadn't been on the best of terms when she'd left. It was sort of too late to fix, but maybe she could find closure for herself. *God help me, but if I survive this, I'm going to visit her,* she thought, and Jack opened his eyes and stretched.

Leaning to look down the front of the building, Peri watched two suits leave, the men making eye contact with the black Opti van before getting into their black car and driving off, headlights shining. They weren't the same two who'd gotten out of it five minutes ago. Shift change, perhaps?

"Howard?" Peri called softly, and she heard him grunt. In half a moment, he came in from the back bedroom rubbing his dreadlocks and moving slow, stiff from the floor.

"Is it time?" he asked.

"Yes." Her pulse quickened, and she set the take-out box down to shake her hands out. "I'd rather do this at four in the morning, but midnight is close enough. As long as we stay out of the square, we'll be clear of people."

Yawning, Taf came out from the back room, her hair mussed. "You sure?"

"Absolutely." Peri did a double take, realizing only now that Taf's butterfly tattoo glowed in the dark. Taking the felt pen she'd been using to sketch the apartment, she stuck it in her boot sheath next to that awful camo knife. *Mightier than the sword,* she thought drily. "This is a quiet neighborhood where gunshots are mistaken for transformers on the telephone poles blowing. That's why I wanted to live here." *Even before Jack,* she thought, then started when she realized

411

Jack was eating from the box she'd set down, picking through the vegetables with chopsticks from Overdraft. The box was steaming now, and he was dressed in task black, looking good enough to pin to the floor.

Unhappy, Peri ran a hand across her jeans. The lack of her usual polish bothered her. An untidy thief was lowbrow. A well-dressed one was classy, ending up in the chief's office instead of the local lockup with hookers and sullen shoplifters.

Jack pointed his chopsticks at her. "Don't involve them. They'll get hurt."

But what choice did she have? "Okay," she said, hands clapping once. "Slight change of plan. Taf? Howard and I are going to go upstairs and take out the Opti observatory post."

"We are?"

Peri nodded. "If everyone is wired, having you there to monitor and misdirect will widen my window tremendously."

Taf reached for her rifle, her lips pressed tight. "I'm coming with you."

Jack cleared his throat, but Peri was ahead of him; taking the rifle out of Taf's hand, she gave it to Howard. "Taf, you're a crack shot, but a better driver, and you don't put your driver in a place where she doesn't have a car."

"But," she started, and Peri shook her head.

"I don't want us caught because we don't have an exit plan," Peri interrupted, and the younger woman slumped in resolve. Behind her, Howard exhaled in relief. "Once Howard is set, I'll go in. Taf, you keep watch on the stairwell. When I turn the light on in my apartment, I want you to leave. Howard, you too. Both of you take the car and park it at the restaurant I indicated on the map. You'll be able to see my apartment from there, and it will give you a clean run to the front to pick me up when I signal by turning the light off again."

"Our apartment," Jack said, and her eye twitched. *Only because I invited you in, you prick.*

"I'm not doing anything," Taf complained, and Peri stretched, enjoying the sensation of her body coming alive.

"That's why I like this plan." Peri looked up from her lunge, hoping Taf could see her smile in the gloom. "I say we have a seventy percent chance of getting away clean. Ten if you're not behind the wheel. I'll probably be coming out hot. I need you ready."

That made the woman smile, and Howard gave Taf a relieved kiss and a squeeze, while Jack set the take-out box aside and stood, his dark expression saying he knew her estimation was grossly overgenerous. Why was it harder to listen to her intuition when it had Jack's face?

Deciding against her coat, she tucked Allen's borrowed Glock in her waistband. Alone, she tried not to watch as Howard finally let Taf go. "See you in an hour," he said, his voice soft, arms falling from her reluctantly, and the young woman nodded, head down. *See a woman in trouble, look no farther than the man beside her.*

Taf's unhappy smile met Peri's own, and Howard jiggled on his feet, nervous as he looked at the rifle, then gave it to Taf. God help her, she hated this. They weren't helpless, but seeing them risking their lives to bring the corrupt fraction of Opti to light was giving her a bad feeling. She was trained for this. They were not.

But she had little choice. Hoping Jack would stay behind, she headed out with Howard tight behind her. He was breathing fast, and she eyed him as she hit the button for the elevator.

"You got a plan for this, right?" Howard said as the little green arrow lit.

The doors slid aside, and Peri grimaced at Jack already in there, waiting for her. "Going up?" he said slyly, and she stepped inside, ignoring him.

"Um, Peri?" Howard said, dark eyes wide as she pushed the button for the sixth floor.

"You keep the first man I down on the floor, and I'll take what's beyond him," she said.

"Sure." Howard licked his lips. "But we only have one gun."

Guns. Why was it always about guns? "You can have it," she said, giving it to him as the doors opened and she padded out into the hall. *602 . . . 604 . . . 606.* Her gut tightened, and she motioned for him to stay back from the door. "Tell them you forgot the keys," she whispered as she stood sideways to it and pounded aggressively on the door. "And don't touch the man I bring down. He'll probably know something hinky to turn the tables on you."

For cripes' sake. It's like Self-Defense 101. What else haven't I told him?

Howard's eyes widened, and she motioned for him to say something. "Ah, I forgot the keys!" he blurted, then dropped back when Peri waved him off again.

"Are you shitting me?" someone inside said, and Peri found her balance. "Christ almighty, Jason, I swear you'd forget your balls if your girlfriend didn't have them already."

The door opened. Peri stepped in front of him, hands free as she grabbed his arm and tucked into him. He knew enough martial arts to go with it, and he flipped over her, his breath whooshing out as he hit the floor in the hall. Still holding his hand, she gave a twist, and he screamed as she snapped his wrist. That would keep Howard safe—at least from one direction.

"Hands where I can see them!" she shouted, taking his pistol from his holster as she jumped over him and ran into the unfurnished living room. A second man was getting up from a folding chair, barbecue wings going everywhere as he lunged to the bank of equipment.

Peri shot the floor, hearing the slug bury itself in

the cement and bits of wood splintering out. The man skidded to a stop, hands in the air. From the hall, a pained groan filtered in. "Howard! Get him in here! Kick him if he doesn't move on his own. Don't touch him!" She wasn't going to take for granted that because they'd caught them off-guard they were sloppy. Opti hadn't expected her to be here, not really. "Howard!"

"You heard the lady. Inside," Howard said, and Peri motioned for them to stand in the barren kitchen. The man who'd answered the door looked pale enough to pass out, and Peri relaxed a notch—until she saw the restraining equipment on the counter, ugly with its needles and drugs. Preventing a draft was easy. Holding an agent trained in the art of escape was not.

Fine, she thought as she shoved two bottles and a handful of syringes into her pocket. If they were going to use it on her, she had no qualm about using it on them.

"Move," she snarled as one tested the waters. "Both of you in the bathroom. Now!"

Howard looked peaked, but not as shaky as the man with the broken wrist when they shuffled into the bathroom. Sure, Howard was an agent, but if the alliance was anything like Opti, cleaners and tech guys seldom saw real action.

"Good. Lock yourselves to the piping." Peri tossed in two pairs of cuffs from the counter.

Howard started to follow, and she pulled him

back from a potential turnaround until the cuffs clinked. They'd put them on their ankles. That was fine. They'd be going to sleep shortly.

"Okay." Peri took Howard's pistol and handed him two syringes and a bottle. "*Now* you can sedate them."

Howard's eyes flicked to the bottle in his hand. "I'm not sure of the dosage."

"Every field agent knows how to pick handcuffs given enough time. Our other option is to shoot them," she said, and Howard winced, rolling the bottle to read what it was.

"I'll, ah, use the dog dosage," he said. "You're, what, about two German shepherds?"

"Don't get between me and them," she said as she stood in the tub with her Glock pointed to make sure they stayed polite while Howard put them under. Not a twinge of guilt assailed her. The only reason the drugs were here was to use on her.

They went down slow, the one with the broken wrist fighting it until finally his shoulders eased and his breathing grew steady. "Nicely done," Peri said as they stood over the fallen Opti agents, Howard a little wide-eyed, as if he still didn't believe what they'd done. "How long until they wake up?"

"Few hours?" he guessed as he followed her out and shut the door.

It would be enough. Anticipation spiked as she helped herself to another pair of cuffs.

"Here." Howard came forward with a wire. "Take this. I'll do what I can."

"Thanks," she said. It was one-way, but she appreciated it nevertheless. "If things go wrong, promise me you'll get Taf and go. I mean it." His brow pinched, and Peri frowned. "Howard, please," she said, feeling vulnerable for some reason. "I know you think I'm in over my head, but this is what I do. This is who I am. I need your help, but not at the expense of putting you and Taf where you're going to find yourself somewhere you're not prepared to be. I like you here," she said, gesturing at the bank of equipment and sensing he felt at home there. "I like Taf behind the wheel, even if her driving scares the crap out of me. Promise me you'll take her and leave if things go wrong. I don't want you showing up at my apartment. Okay? If it goes bad, let it go bad and get yourself out."

The door clicked open, and she spun, relaxing when it was only Jack. "We gotta go, babe," he said, and she put a hand on Howard's arm to convince him she wasn't jumping at shadows, even if she was. The door snicked shut, never really having moved at all.

"Please?" she asked again, and Howard nodded, clearly not happy.

"We'll do it your way," he said wryly.

"Thanks." Smiling, Peri felt the wire he'd given her, loosely coiled and tucked in a pocket.

"They have Electronic Huts in Canada, don't they?"

Finally his grim look eased, and he waved her off. She looked back to see Howard settle himself amid the switches and monitors, Allen's old Glock within his easy reach. After checking to make sure the door would lock, she shut it gently behind her.

Jack paced beside her as she jogged to the stairway. "He looks right there."

"He does, yes," she said, trying not to imagine him dead as she wove her way downstairs and out through the back entrance to settle among the recycle bins. She desperately didn't want to draft, even if it was becoming easier to work without the security of an anchor. What did anyone really need to know, anyway?

But if anything happened to Howard or Taf, she vowed she'd never forget.

———————CHAPTER———————
TWENTY-EIGHT

What if I draft? Will the patch job hold?

Quashing her angst, Peri crept to the Opti van at the curb. Howard would handle any electronic fallout, and having the way plowed for her escape would be worth it, especially if it made Taf safer. Besides, she had the power of drugs now.

The clear spark of adrenaline pushed out the

lingering worry as she paused in the black shadow of the building to fill three syringes, wedging them through the fabric of her shirt like pins to keep them handy and out of the way. Grabbing a rag from the Dumpster, she jogged to the back of the running van and, after wadding the cloth into a ball, jammed it into the tailpipe, holding it there with her foot.

Jack slid to a bright-eyed stop beside her, causing her to almost shriek in surprise.

"What are you doing here?" she whispered, feeling foolish talking to nothing.

He wrinkled his nose and crouched beside her. "I've got your back, Peri. I always will."

That bothered her, but she wasn't going to argue with herself. Finally the running engine choked into silence, and she touched the syringes lined up on her sleeve like soldiers. Her tension spiked when the passenger-side door opened. "I don't know crap about cars, Tony," the one inside said as his companion got out, and she smiled when the hood popped up. *Perfect.* "You look."

Peri dropped facedown on the pavement. "Office shoes," she whispered, spotting them at the front of the van. This should be easy.

"Okay, try it now!" Tony called, and the engine whirred and chunked, and died.

Motions slow and even, Peri tried the back door, elated to find it unlocked. *Idiots.* She slipped inside, praying the man behind the wheel wouldn't notice the flush of air. On cat feet, she crept up to him, Glock in hand. The hood of the van filled the front window, and adrenaline sang as she slipped behind the driver and put the muzzle of the weapon to his neck. Messy. A gunshot to the neck was messy, and you didn't ever come back from it.

"Ahhh, shit," the man breathed, his hands coming up from the wheel. He didn't care if she was caught or not—at least, not enough to risk his life.

Peri smiled. "Good man. Be ready for a poke. I'm going to put you down nice and easy. If you move or open your mouth, it's going to be a bullet through your neck instead. 'Kay?"

He nodded, grunting when she took one of the syringes and jammed it into his bicep.

"Chuck, try it again!" Tony called, and she reached over him to turn the key. The engine choked to life before failing. "Hell if I know," Peri heard Tony mutter, and she lowered her pistol. Chuck was out, pulse strong and steady. Heart pounding, she tucked her weapon away, taking Chuck's hat before grabbing another syringe and boldly getting out the passenger-side door.

"I hate computerized cars," Tony was saying. "Better call it in and get a new van out—hey!" he managed to yell before she was on him. He lurched backward, avoiding her front kick.

Tony's eyes went bright in recognition, eager as he came at her. She blocked, pain racing to her spine. She grabbed the next blow, spinning around and getting behind him to yank his footing out from under him with a swift kick to his knee. He went down laughing, which was just insulting, and she forced him to stay there, tugging his arm up behind his back until he stopped.

"Ow! Reed," he said, his nose bleeding from the fall and Opti pin catching the street light. "You are so caught."

"Say good night, Tony."

He yelped when she jammed her second syringe in his ass, but she had his arm twisted, and he gave up fast. She sat on him a little longer to be sure, the van's bulk and the shadows hiding them. Exhaling, she stood and rolled him under the van and out of sight. Turning, she waved at Taf and Howard before she gentled the hood down and crossed the street. Jack was waiting for her at the entrance, and she scooped up Chuck's hat in passing, putting an extra sassy sway to her hips as she put it on her head in case Opti had tied into the building's facial recognition cameras.

"Nice of you to give me room to work," Peri said, and Jack inclined his head.

"Nice to see you can do something on your own," he said back, and she strode in, head down as she cleared the front door.

The enormous rock and silk flower arrangement by the entryway hadn't changed, and Peri shoved the four-foot-high vase over, snatching up her spare apartment card even before the heavy plaster hit the floor. *That was easy.*

The man behind the concierge's desk looked up at the crash. *This might be harder.*

"Reed is in the building," he said into his two-way, telling Peri no one knew yet that Howard was up in Suite 606. Smiling, she tucked her card down her blouse. "No closer, Reed," he said, dart gun pointed at her, and she threw Chuck's hat at him.

His eyes shifted and she dove to get below the angle of the desk. Her air huffed out as she hit the wall of the desk—

And suddenly—she wasn't pressed against the desk, but standing over him, three feet from where she'd landed and in the middle of the lobby.

Shocked, Peri looked down at the unconscious man, not knowing how he'd gotten that way or how she'd moved across the room. The dart gun was in her hand. An empty syringe was jammed into his leg. *Damn it! I've drafted!*

Scared, she smacked her hand against her boot sheath to find her knife still there. Then she looked at her palm for a note she hadn't written, her fingers closing into a fist as she listened to the silence and waited for the nightmare to begin. Her heart pounded. *Nothing.* Slowly her fist opened as she exhaled. She was okay. Silas's patch job had held through a draft—this time. "Jack?" she breathed, anxious for an answer. Her head hurt as if someone had yanked on her hair. Strands of it were drifting to the floor.

Gasping, she fell into a defensive crouch when Jack stood up from behind the desk. "You drafted," he said, grim-faced. "Move. It doesn't matter if you don't remember."

"How long?" she whispered, grabbing the heels of the Opti agent and dragging him behind the desk.

Jack looked down at him and shrugged. "Hell, babe. I don't know. You didn't lose more than the draft, though. Thirty seconds?"

"How about that," she said, remembering what Allen had said about Opti being able to artificially scrub time from her when she drafted. *Damn it all to hell. It's true.*

A tinny voice calling her name pulled her to the square of black plastic kicked across the floor. It wasn't her original wire, and figuring it belonged to the man she'd just downed, Peri scooped it up as she went for the stairs. "Peri! Are you there?" It was Howard, and a second wash of relief took her.

"I'm fine." She put her back to the fire door and leaned into the stairwell, listening to Howard babble as she took a quick look up and down the hall. "Howard. Relax," she said, interrupting him. "I drafted, but I'm okay." Peri opened the door wider, and Jack went before her, taking the stairs two at a time until he waited at the fire door. "I'm going up now," she said. "Get Taf and leave.

Don't wait for me. I've really pissed them off. I'll see you over the border. Tell Silas I'm sorry and that his patch works."

"Peri, you can't do this alone. It's too dangerous—"

She didn't have time to convince him. Dropping the radio on the stairway, she stomped it into silence. Feeling his eyes on her through the scope, she went up the stairs and fished out her card key. It seemed stupid—needing a key to get into her own apartment—but she'd had the door reinforced and it would be easier to break a hole in the wall than to knock the door from the frame.

She ran down the hall, tapping her card key and turning the knob in a single fluid motion. There was no sound, and a ribbon of light showed from under the door. Images of a matted maroon carpet flashed in her thoughts. Shoving them aside, she went in.

She froze just inside the door. Lips parted, she stared at the brightly lit, demolished apartment as emotions fought to be recognized. Shock, dismay, heartache . . . anger. It didn't even look like her place. Everything was off the walls, her shelf where she put her talismans empty. Broken furniture and clothes made a pile in the middle of the room. The ceiling had been pulled down to expose the ductwork, and light fixtures dangled from wires to make the glow shine in weird patterns. The blinds had been jerked from the windows and piled in the corner, taking up an astounding amount of space. Blackout film had replaced them—blocking the view in, but not the view out—and Detroit glittered past the bare windows. Just as well she'd told Howard to leave. He'd never know if the lights were on or off.

"Change settings. Warm," she said softly, but there was no cheerful ding. Peri came in a step. Jack stood before the pile, his head bowed over a shattered picture. Even the plants had been uprooted, the dirt scattered and the vegetation abandoned to wilt and die. They'd destroyed her home, her security, the way she found herself after every draft.

"I'm sorry, babe," Jack said, and her anger at what they'd done grew heady, strong enough to taste it, sour in the pit of her belly. He had no right to tell her he was sorry. He was why her life was screwed up. But the sliding thump of sound from the bedroom brought her attention around.

"No weapons. They don't know you're here yet." Jack dropped the picture and lurched after her. "Watch your control. He didn't do this. Don't kill him, Peri."

"What do you care?" Peri snarled under her breath. Ticked, she shoved the bedroom door open, barely registering the savaged mattress and holes in the walls when she saw the man in a black suit standing before her dresser, holding up one of Jack's shirts as if measuring it for size.

"Hands *off!*" she yelled, launching herself at him.

She got one good front kick in that snapped his head back. She followed him as he fell backward, scoring a fist on his solar plexus. In uncaring rage, she punched him again, and he blocked it. Stinging tingles raced up her arm.

His foot came out, and she fell, her legs swept out from under her. She rolled, narrowly escaping his savage kick, and she kept rolling. Still on the floor, she lashed out, scooting backward and to her feet. With an eager smile, he grabbed her arm and swung her into the wall.

She hit it face-first, the breath knocked out of her as she staggered. His foot slammed into her chest and she slid to the floor.

Unable to breathe, she scuttled into the bathroom. She couldn't see straight, and finally she took in a breath, looking up to see the man leaning against the doorjamb, a hand to his chest and clearly laboring as well. An Opti-issue Glock lay behind him, totally out of reach.

"Reed's here," he said, panting into an electronic wristband; then he came at her, his hands stretched to grab. If he got a grip on her, she was done.

Shit. Peri stumbled into the bathroom, grunting as his weight slammed into her and pinned her face to the wall. Cat litter ground under her feet as she flung her head back into him.

He cried out, grip loosening. Peri dropped, her

hand reaching for her knife. He followed her down, pinning her neck to the floor with a wide, heavy hand, wedging the knife from her with the other. There was blood on him. She'd broken his nose.

"Peri, do something!" Jack shouted, and she grabbed a handful of cat litter and threw it at the sound of the man's grunting breath.

"Bitch!" he exclaimed, and his hand lifted. Peri dragged herself upright, grasping the lid to the toilet tank and swinging it at him. He was half-way to a stand, and it hit his head with a dull *thwap,* the weight of it spinning Peri full-circle to crash into the counter. Her hands went numb and the lid fell from her to break into two pieces. She slipped and went down, stifling a scream when her back hit the tub.

But the man was out cold, his cheek resting on a thin layer of cat litter soaking up the blood from his broken nose. A red lump showed at his hairline. Peri's eyes rose to find Jack. "I didn't like him touching your things," she said, the absurdity of it making her eyes wide.

Smiling, he held out a hand to help her stand. She lurched up, ignoring it as she took her knife back. Her chest hurt, and not because she'd taken a foot to it. She hated Jack, hated that it felt right with him beside her.

Shaking from adrenaline, Peri shoved her knife away and staggered into the living room.

Someone had to have heard that. She had to go. But as she looked at her life in a ten-by-eight-by-four-foot pile, she couldn't focus. "My talismans," she said, her anger growing as she saw a picture of Jack and herself in a desert, the coals of a fire behind them. She didn't remember it, but she looked happy. All of her memories were broken and lost. "Jack, where's the list? Did they find it?"

"I'm sorry, babe. I didn't know this would happen."

Frustration spun back into anger, and she rounded on him. "Where is it!" she shouted, her hands in fists as he picked up the silver frame and ran a finger down her pictured face. Tears pricked and she came close, wanting to take it from him but reluctant to break the illusion that he was holding it. For all she knew, the picture might not even exist. "Jack, where's the list?"

He looked up, tears in his eyes. "I don't think it's here."

Peri's breath came in fast. Had it all been for nothing? "They have it?"

"No." His gaze traveled over the destruction, clearly pained. "It's just not . . . here." Then: "You should have left. You waited too long. I'm sorry."

The sound of the door opening spun her around and Jack vanished. "Silas!" Peri exclaimed as he stumbled through the door. "I can explain."

Frightened, Silas caught his balance as Bill

strode in after him. Peri slid to a halt, only now seeing that Silas's hands were cuffed before him.

"Then he wasn't lying that you're here on your own. Curious," Bill said, looking menacing in his three-piece suit and expensive shoes, a gun pointed at one of Silas's kidneys. "If you jump, I shoot him in the new draft and he dies. Very fast." *Bill is an anchor?* It was the only way he'd know if there was a draft or not.

"I shouldn't have left you, Peri," Silas said, his eyes haunted. "I'm sorry."

From the hall, Allen's irate voice rose, saying, "Is she down?"

Bill smirked, pushing Silas deeper into the room. "He's afraid of you."

"Maybe he's the smarter man here," Peri said as two unremarkable men in suits came in. She prayed that Howard and Taf had left. It had gone wrong, so very wrong.

The prick of a dart striking the back of her neck made her yelp, and she yanked it out, the drug taking hold as a chalky taste covered her tongue. She gripped the dart like a knife, unable to draft now if she wanted to. She turned, seeing the man she'd downed in the bathroom lower his dart gun, blood dripping from his nose as he leaned against the wall.

"Whore," he breathed raggedly, and Peri backed to the bulletproof windows.

"Now, now," Bill said jovially. "No need to be

nasty. She's doing what we trained her to do. Ready to learn a new trick, Peri?"

Her boots ground on the spilled dirt from her plants. "Shove it up your ass."

Amused, Bill called loudly, "You can come in now, Allen. She can't draft."

Hunched awkwardly over a crutch, Allen peered in around the door. "She can still fight."

"True." Bill gestured to one of the men.

Adrenaline pounded through her as she spun. But it wasn't enough. The drug spilling through her muscles like honey slowed her, and she gasped, wide-eyed, as the man shoved her face-first to the floor. He knelt on her, and her air huffed out. She was helpless as he pinned her wrist to the floor with one hand and with the other forced her free arm behind her, wrenching it up until she cried out in pain and went limp. The dart fell to the floor and was kicked away, her knife taken.

Please don't dislocate it, please, she silently begged, as Silas protested. Her cheek pressed into the clutter, and a book she didn't remember reading was wedged under her shoulder. She clenched her jaw, refusing to let the tears of pain blur her vision. The picture of her and Jack in the desert mocked her. Dagazes decorated the silver frame, and she felt betrayed by the happy expressions in the photograph. They were gone now. Maybe they had never really existed.

"You're hurting her!" Silas exclaimed, and then her other wrist was cuffed to the first.

"Shut up," Bill said, and then, lightly, "How about it, Allen? You feel safe now?"

Allen glowered. "You keep misjudging her, and she's going to kill you."

Peri struggled to breathe, that man's knee still in the small of her back. She tensed at the scuff-pop of Allen hobbling closer. Working hard at it, he knelt down, and then she gasped as he pulled her head up by her hair so he could see her face.

"Hi, Peri," he said, his anger obvious in the slant of his eyes, and suddenly she hated his smooth-shaven features and his dark gaze behind his glasses. "We could have done things the easy way. But this has its own pleasures." Still holding her at an awkward angle, he looked at Bill. "She's been conditioned never to work alone. Where are the rest?"

Bill turned to one of the men at the door. "Gone," the man said, his expression suddenly worried. "We put all assets on Reed. You want me to send a car?"

"No. She's all I really need." Bill smiled at her, clearly pleased. "Aren't you, kiddo."

They got away, Peri thought, elated, and then Allen let her go.

Peri grunted as she turned the motion of her falling head into a bid for freedom. She twisted, and the man with his knee in her back sprang up and away. Allen scrambled backward, and she halted at a kneel, freezing when she heard the safeties click off. Her short hair was in her eyes, and she tossed her head, heart pounding. The drug was slowing her down, but she could still move.

"You think I won't remember this?" she intoned, eyes fixed on Bill as she stood. "I'll never accept Allen as my anchor."

Bill looked at Silas as if they'd already had this conversation. "No matter. We'll have this all fixed by tomorrow, thanks to Dr. Denier. We'll have you up and working in no time. I know it's what you love, and I'm going to give it all back to you."

"I'm not a part of this," Silas seethed. "They're using my techniques, perverting them." He glared at the man with the handgun who jabbed him to be quiet.

Bill checked his phone, nodding as if pleased. "By this time tomorrow, maybe the next day, you will be back to your usual self, and any latent memories that might surface will have Silas's face for Allen's actions. You know what your first task will be? Find and kill Silas. You'll enjoy it. Be driven to break the rules to do it."

"You can't do that," Peri said, but Bill's satisfaction said otherwise.

"We can." Bill checked his phone again before tucking it away. "But a little housecleaning will make it more effective. Allen?"

"Keep her off me," Allen muttered, and Peri's

chin lifted when the guy she'd knocked out in the bathroom stepped behind her, pulling her arms up until she flinched.

"Much of what Silas pioneered to buffer drafters from long-term memory loss has a wider potential in designing more efficient agents," Bill said.

"You mean brainwashed dolls," Peri accused, not liking Allen picking through the rubble of her life.

"If you like, but very dangerous dolls. It never lasted long with you, though."

Her breath came fast as Allen straightened with the picture of Jack and herself.

"We get around that by artificially scrubbing several weeks at the end of a draft, but *you* kept coming back from more and more difficult assignments intact, without a need to jump to survive them. Unfortunately, if you don't draft, we can't clean house. That's why we took matters into our own hands at Overdraft. It might have worked even then. But Jack screwed it up. He's not good enough for you anymore."

My God. How long have they been doing this? Is anyone at Opti not *corrupt?*

Allen pulled out the picture and let the frame drop to dent the wood floor. "If we destroy everything that links you to your past, you might never recall anything. It works best if you see the destruction." He turned to his cohorts, expression ugly. "Burning works."

She clenched her jaw when he folded the picture in two, knowing what was going to happen next. "New Year's, right?" Allen said. "I never liked Jack. He thought he was smarter than me. Guess not."

"Start with this," Bill said, tossing a loose-leaf journal to land at Allen's feet with a sliding hiss of sound. It was her diary—a year's worth at least.

"Bastard," she whispered as Allen tucked the photo in a pocket and began ripping pages out. "You're all bastards. I'm not going to forget this."

"Today should be no different from last week," Bill said, throwing a lighter to Allen.

Silas shrugged off his captor's hand. "Peri, I'm sorry!" he said, but she didn't know what for. It wasn't his fault. It was hers for having gotten caught. Her jaw clenched as Allen lit a corner of the book, the flame rising up on the outside, black smoke falling from the inner pages. He dropped it, and it flared before subsiding to a low burn that would choke itself if left alone. But he didn't leave it alone, adding torn pages one by one.

"Light it up," Bill said, a thick hand waving to encompass the entire apartment. Peri watched helplessly as men scampered like rats over the apartment, disconnecting the smoke alarms and bringing back more of her life to drop on the growing pile. The sliding doors to the balcony were retracted into the walls, and the smoke escaped, taking with it her desire to fight.

"There will be nothing left of your past, Peri,"

Bill said in the new chill sweeping in, and Peri bowed her head to the floor in grief. "I gave it to you, and now I'm taking it back. I'll give you a new one, a better one. You will accept the past we give you without question. You will take the jobs that Allen brings you, and you will never think twice about their validity."

"You bastard," Peri whispered. "You won't walk away from this. I promise you."

"No," he said, and she steeled herself when he reached out a fleshy ringed finger and touched her cheek. "I promise you," he said. "You should be glad you're my best or you would've ended up like poor Jack."

She seethed, coughing on the smoke as she knelt before him, and he turned to leave. Allen hesitated to follow. "You want me to save anything? Her clothes, maybe?" he asked.

Bill paused on the threshold, giving Silas a long look. "Just the cookbooks and yarn. I believe we still have that yarn bag she left at the airport." Turning, he smiled at Peri. "Mustn't let those Opti-approved obsessive-compulsive stress relievers go by the wayside. I like your hair long, though. Allen, implant the thought that she likes it that way."

"You can't do this!" she shouted, starting at the prick of another dart. A part of her was victorious— they were afraid of her—bound and darted, they were still afraid of her.

"Get him!" someone yelled, and she blinked the smoke from her eyes as she realized that Silas had shoved Allen down and run. He'd left her. Again.

"Let him go," Bill said, bringing everyone to a halt. "Finding him will be part of her conditioning. Someone called in the smoke. City services are on the way. Everyone out."

She was pulled to her feet, and she fought to stay where she was, with her past. Her shoulder burned as she fell on the heated picture frame, and she rolled from the flames. "Get off me!" she screamed when another dart struck her.

And then everything went blessedly away.

—— CHAPTER —— TWENTY-NINE

Waking up to a cat purring on your chest isn't the worst way to start the day. Peri had been drowsing the last half hour, listening to her upstairs neighbors move from the bathroom to the kitchen and finally to the parking lot six feet from the patio of her new Opti-issued apartment. When the doors of the couple's car had finally slammed and the battery-powered vehicle hummed away, she'd thought she might get a few more minutes of sleep.

But when a cat wants you up, you have no choice.

"Carnac!" Peri yelped when sharp nails made it through the covers, and the orange cat leapt from her, clawing her stomach even deeper. "Bossy cat!" she exclaimed, sitting up and pushing aside the covers, and then her nightshirt, to see the little red marks. Carnac stood by the open bedroom door, his tail switching and ears slantwise.

Immediately Peri relented, trilling to coax him back. The fickle cat jumped onto the bed, bumping his head under her hand in the hopes of some breakfast. "How's my old tom?" Peri said, breathing in his sweet-smelling kitty fur and fingering the ornate collar embroidered with red Xs and the name that she'd found him with.

The cat was the only thing that felt real to her, which was odd, since he was a stray she'd found hiding in the bushes outside her building, walking up to her and into her apartment as if he belonged. She loved him for it, all the while harboring hope that his real owners would never claim him. It felt good that the found-cat fliers she'd reluctantly put up last month were slowly being buried beneath band fliers and car-for-sale ads.

"Hungry?" Peri asked as she held him up to look him in the eye. The cat refused to make eye contact, but the purrs never ceased. She'd gotten a clean bill of health weeks ago from Opti's physical guys. Her psych review was this morning, and she wasn't sure how she felt. Excited, yes, but despite everyone's positive words, she still felt the cracks in her threatening to split wide open, even after six weeks.

Staring at the bathroom mirror, she fingered the tips of her shoulder-length hair, wondering why she'd ever cut it. It was taking forever to grow back out. But Allen liked it long. A smile flitted across her face as she thought of her anchor. His Flexicast was coming off today, timed perfectly with the psych eval. Allen had come out of their last task with a torn ACL, broken fingers, and a shot foot. It had been a bad task—everything had gone wrong.

Peri's jaw clenched as she started the shower, her hatred for the alliance operative who'd tried to kill them making her motions sharp as she stepped into the hot water and scrubbed her scalp. Silas Orion Denier. He'd tried to kill Allen. Saving him had taken every last scrap of memory of their three years together, and seeing Allen's hesitancy toward her, even now, hurt.

She lingered under the hot water, carefully feeling the odd burn on her shoulder. It was the only physical mark she had of the ordeal, and even that was fading. Opti hadn't found a lead on Silas yet, or at least, they hadn't told her of one. It rankled Peri that *Silas* was free, and she and Allen were struggling to put their lives back together.

Peri turned the water off and got out. The towel was rough, and after a token scrub at her hair, she wrapped it around herself and padded barefoot into the bedroom. Her life was coming together at the pace of a glacier thawing, but some of that might be her fault, since she'd insisted on moving from Opti's rehab to her own new apartment instead of sharing one with Allen. Bill hadn't been pleased, but when Allen had agreed she needed time, their handler had okayed her own place. Trouble was, now that she had it, she was reluctant to let it go.

Her frown deepened as she finger-combed her hair. Allen had defragmented what he could of the task, and the memory of Silas's smug smile when he pushed Allen through the window and then over the balcony of her old apartment still haunted her. There was a gap after that since Allen hadn't seen what happened, but the short of it was that Silas had escaped. That Opti wasn't doing anything to find him made her more than angry.

"Give me a sec, Carnac," she said, grabbing a pair of jeans and a black sweater, as the cat complained over his empty bowl. It was the only thing in her closet she liked. She dearly wanted to go shopping, but every time she set aside an afternoon, something came up. "What was I thinking?" she said as she held up a blue blouse with red flowers on it. Maybe she'd been channeling her mother when she'd bought all the stripes and patterns.

My boots are nice, though, she thought as she sat on the edge of the bed and pulled them to her knees. The dull ping of the doorbell sounded, and Carnac ran out, tail up straight. "Coming!" she shouted, looping her pendant pen around her neck before going into the living room. The blinds were closed at the patio door, and spotlights glowed on her shelf of talismans. None of them called to her. Even the picture of Allen and her standing before a sunrise over a beach last New Year's didn't reach her soul. It was depressing, but she couldn't let go of the hope that someday one of them would do its job and help her remember.

On the tips of her toes, Peri looked through the peephole to see Allen fidgeting, his dress shoes scuffing the carpet. She always wondered how many of the scars he had were because of her, but he wouldn't tell. *Maybe I should have dressed up,* she thought as she saw his black slacks and tie, but they were meeting at Overdraft. Why would she get dressed up to go to a bar at nine in the morning?

"Hi, Allen. You look sharp. Give me a sec and I'll put on some slacks," she said as she opened the door. His hair was tousled from the spring gusts, and the safety glasses reminded her of Clark Kent. She harbored a belief he wore them for the same reason: to hide his strength.

"Morning," he said, moving adroitly despite his cast to give her a quick kiss. "Don't change for me. I like the way you look in jeans. Ready?"

"Almost. I just need to feed Carnac."

"Why do you even *have* that cat?" he said, his good mood souring as his eyes lingered on her pendant, and she tucked it behind her sweater. "Haven't his owners called yet?"

Shrugging, she shut the door. "I like him. I hope they never do. He doesn't hog the covers, and| he doesn't eat my ice cream."

Allen shuffled to the breakfast bar, sighing as he levered his backside up onto a stool. Peri went to the kitchen, keenly feeling the distance between them. There was always space, and she didn't know why. Was it his guilt that she'd lost so much to save his life, or had the loss of memory changed her and he didn't love her anymore? She knew she and Allen had once had a good relationship by the heartache that flooded her when she thought about having lost it. She was trying. Allen was trying. But she still felt . . . broken.

"Peri, have you thought about moving back in with me?" he said, and she accidentally ripped the pouch all the way open, spilling it. "I wouldn't even mind the cat box," he said sourly.

"No," she said, trying to get the spilled cat food in the bowl. "Allen, I'm sorry," she said to ease the bite of her words. "I appreciate you not making a big deal about me moving out in the first place, and until I remember something more, it feels, I don't know." Allen made a face, and she gestured helplessly. "We need to do a few tasks together. That's all."

Gaze down, he picked at the edge of his cast. It had everyone's name on it but hers. She didn't know why she hadn't signed it. She was with him all the time, it seemed. "Psych keeps telling me to be patient," he said softly.

"Psych is right." Leaning over the counter, she gave him a kiss. His knobby-knuckled hand rose to caress her jawline, and her fingers slipped from his smooth-shaven face. Her eye twitched and she pulled up and away. "Let me clean this up and we can go."

"Sure."

She could feel him watching her as she wiped the counter down and washed her hands. "How come you never knit anymore?" Allen asked, and she looked up, startled.

"Ah, because it's spring?" she said, eyes going to her canvas bag tucked beside the couch. "It's not as if I need it." No, she didn't need the soft red scarf anymore, but clearly it bothered her that it wasn't finished yet, since it was still out.

"I like it when you knit," he said, and she came around the counter, looking for her purse.

"I'll finish it this weekend, then," she said as she found it and went to the front closet for her coat. *Good God, why did I buy a red coat? To match a scarf I haven't finished?* Her fingers on the smooth finish felt numb, and her focus blurred. The jacket smelled like real leather, but she didn't remember buying it, and she had her doubts.

"Why does Bill want to meet at Overdraft, anyway?" she said as she came out from behind the closet door. "Sandy always fills the Juke'sBox playlist with suicide country crap."

Allen laughed as he slid from the stool. "You'd rather go into Opti for a formal psych review? Give the guy a break. You're his best drafter and he doesn't want to push you."

Peri forced her shoulders down, but the fear of drafting settled like ice in her middle, and she had to fight to keep her hand from her pendant. "I suppose," she said dully. "Ready?"

"You want to drive?" he said, holding up his cast in explanation.

"Absolutely," she said as she headed for the door, eager to feel the smooth power of her Mantis around her.

A ground-floor apartment, she thought in dismay as she locked up. Even after a month, she didn't feel safe. She could not *believe* she'd let Allen talk her into it. It might have had something to do with that second-story balcony he'd fallen off.

The April morning air still held the dampness of last night's rain, and Peri paced to her car, hesitating with her hand on the handle for the car to recognize her and unlock. Allen hobbled to the other side. She liked driving, and the truth was, his cast made her nervous. Sliding in, she felt the car wake up around her, and for a moment, she felt good as she lost herself to the pavement and motion. Allen chatted about getting his cast off and the rehab to rebuild the muscle. He figured it would be at least a month before they got an assignment, and that was fine with her. She wanted some time to do her own research, research she hadn't told anyone about.

Her fingers gripping the wheel went tight, and she forced them to relax before Allen noticed. *Silas*. She wanted him dead, and she wanted to be the one to do it—needed to be the one to do it. It was his face that haunted her nightmares, and the growing urge to end his life filled her with more anticipation, more drive than she'd felt in the last six weeks.

Lost in thought, Peri nearly missed the turn into the strip mall where Overdraft was. The parking lot was almost empty, traffic moving fast just a few feet beyond. It was a cold, ugly place this early in the morning. A man in a tight-fitting overcoat stood under the overhang as if waiting for a ride, and she eyed him suspiciously.

"I don't see Bill's car," Allen said as he leaned forward to peer through the front window.

"He's always late," Peri said. "Or he might have walked it. He's been threatening to work out more. I saw him on the track last week."

Allen's reach for the handle hesitated. "Bill? On the track?"

She smirked at the mental image of the tall, somewhat prissy yet heavy man in Opti gray sweats lumbering after twentysomething athletes with their ponytails swinging and mouths going as they gossiped and jogged at the same time. Her smile faded. Where had all her friends gone? She had friends, didn't she?

"No, I was on the track—he was in with the belts practicing his martial arts," she finally said. Bill excelled at them, his extra mass adding to his proficiency rather than hindering it.

The man at the overhang was gone, but she didn't put her keys away, holding them between her fingers like claws as she got out. She was on edge, and she abruptly slowed to Allen's pace when she realized she'd left him behind.

"Peri." Allen pulled her to a stop at the front door. His eyes were pinched behind his glasses. "Hey, ah, you mind if I go down and get a couple of doughnuts?"

Peri's breath slipped out as she realigned her thinking. "Sandy wants me alone first?"

He smiled sheepishly, nodding. "Cream-filled? Jelly? What do you want?"

The mental image of red jelly oozing out made her ill. "Just a latte." She hadn't yet had her morning caffeine, and that way she'd be able to avoid Sandy's sludge.

His expression was relieved, but that wrinkle of concern was still there when he touched her shoulder. "One latte, skim milk. I'll be right back." He turned once as he walked away to make sure she was going in, and she waved, wondering why she felt so odd. He seemed afraid—not of what Sandy and Frank might say, but afraid of something nevertheless.

Shoving it to the back of her thoughts, Peri yanked open the door and went in, hesitating just inside as the door sealed her in the bar's warmth and dim lighting. The man she'd thought was waiting for a ride was sitting at the bar, his tailored overcoat carefully folded on the stool next to him. What he was wearing underneath was just as sharp, making her wonder who he was. Frank was tinkering with the floor sweeper, and Sandy was rolling silverware into napkins.

"Peri!" the dark-haired, petite woman said welcomingly. "Where's Allen?"

Unbuttoning her coat, she wiped off the damp of the street on the colorful entry rug. "He's next door getting breakfast so you can psychoanalyze me."

Frank tightened a screw. "Please tell me he's bringing coffee. Sandy just made a pot."

"Hey!" the small woman said tartly, but she was smiling as she came around the bar to give Peri a hug that felt both comforting and uneasy. She smelled like strawberries. Something niggled at her memory—an image of Sandy standing on the bar screaming, expression ugly with hatred. Peri stiffened and Sandy pushed back, her smile looking forced.

Frank set the sweeper on the floor, nudging it with a booted foot when it didn't move. At the tables, all the ordering pads blinked and reset as a sister restaurant updated their menu. "Stupid thing hasn't worked in six weeks," Frank muttered, kicking it to a corner, where it made a sad beep.

"Ah, Bill not here yet?" Peri said into the awkward silence.

"No," Sandy said cheerfully. "I wanted some time with you first. You know . . . girl talk. You want anything? We're technically open."

She shook her head, feeling a familiar pre-task tension in her gut. Avoiding the tables, she sat on the raised hearth, where she could see everyone. The logs stacked beside her looked old enough to crumble, and she picked at one, tossing the bark that flaked off into the unused cavern. "I'll wait for Allen's coffee," she said, hands clasping around her knees. "How's business?" she asked. Psych reviews sucked.

Sandy sat beside her, her thin but muscular ballerina legs stretched out and crossed at the ankles. "You know," she said lightly. "Same old, same old. Pay bills, listen to the gamehogs bitch about the college kids coming in to use the vid lounge. The only excitement is when one of you comes back. Still having nightmares about drafting with no one there to catch you?"

Peri shrugged, hoping that Sandy would believe

the coming lie. "No. I've been sleeping like a baby ever since getting that cat."

Sandy wrinkled her nose and pulled her legs under her. "Cats are nasty animals. I can't believe you took in a stray. He could have tapeworms and fleas."

"He wasn't a stray. He had a collar," she protested. "I had him vetted the first day, and until someone claims him, he's mine. He found me. Needed me."

Sandy made an unconvincing snort, and Peri flexed her fingers nervously. "Ah, that's actually something I wanted to ask you about."

Eyebrows high, Sandy faced her squarely. "Talk."

"Next time I go on task, I need a cat-sitter."

Sandy's eyes widened. "I thought you were going to spill. You want me to *cat-sit?*"

"Just . . . could you come over and feed him while Allen and I are out?" she asked, and Sandy made a face. "If we're out longer than two days, I mean," Peri pleaded.

Sighing, the small woman slumped in defeat. "Fine, okay," she said. "But only because it's you. I don't have to pet it or anything, right? And I'm not cleaning the cat box."

"Deal," Peri said, and the man at the bar watched them through the big mirror, causing Peri to wonder if they were being too loud. Frank had gone into the back room, and it was just them. *Is he an Opti psychologist?* she wondered. If so, why wasn't he being included? He certainly looked the part, well-dressed and professional, his short blond hair styled and a hint of stubble at his jaw. He felt familiar, but she'd been spending enough time with the "couch warriors" lately to be on a first-name basis with most of Opti's psycholo-gists. Maybe he was observing—which would explain why he was being ignored by everyone. She'd do the same.

"Peri, are you even listening to me?"

Embarrassed, she pulled her eyes from the man. "I'm sorry, what?"

Sandy's thin eyebrows were furrowed. "I said, cats steal the breath from babies."

Pitching her voice lower, Peri muttered, "Well, I'm not likely to have that problem, am I." It sounded bitter, even to her, and she wished she could take it back when Sandy reached for her hand. Peri stifled the urge to pull away, not wanting Sandy to think she was pining for a baby. A family. She wasn't. Not really. She'd made her choice a long time ago.

"It's not too late," Sandy said softly, and Peri refused to show any new emotion. "You have lots of time. Is that what's bothering you?"

Peri exhaled, deciding to come out with it if only to speed this up. "No," she said, meeting Sandy's eyes. "It's like half the people I know are gone, and the other half are treating me as if I'm going to break. As if they're afraid of what I might do, and I don't know why. Was I an ass-hat before I lost everything? Because that's the impression I'm getting."

"You were—are—*not* an ass-hat," Sandy said frankly, and the man at the bar snorted.

"Then what is it?" she whispered. "I have no friends but Allen, and even he's watching me as if I might suddenly—I don't know . . . go off on a nut and break his face."

"Allen has his own issues," Sandy said. "You might have lost everything, but he hasn't, and until he lets go of you in the past, he can't appreciate you in the now, much less the future."

Loss. It was a recurring theme in her nightmares. She had loved someone, and now love was gone. "I shouldn't have said anything. Now you'll be evaluating him."

"Oh, we've been doing that already," Sandy said drily. "I'll talk to him."

I bet you will, she thought sourly, looking up when Allen came in with a wash of light.

"Hello, ladies!" he called, the sun glinting on his dark curls as he hoisted a paper bag. "Frank!" he shouted, though the man was nowhere to be seen. "You want a doughnut?"

"Absofreakinglutely!" came a muffled shout, and Frank strode in from the back room, thick hands working over a towel.

Peri shifted on the hearth to make room for

everyone as Frank ambled over, but the large man took a nearby chair, turning it around and straddling it. Peri's eye twitched, and she dismissed it. Frank wasn't putting space between them because he was afraid she was going to flip out. He was a psychologist, for God's sake. But it still felt wrong, especially when Allen handed Peri her latte and sat beside Frank instead of her.

Allen ripped open the bag. "Mmmm, cream filling," Frank said as he took one, using a finger to catch the excess on his lips as he took a huge bite. "Thanks."

"Anyone want coffee?" Sandy asked, sitting back in a mild huff when both Frank and Allen vigorously shook their heads. "There is nothing wrong with my coffee," she grumbled, turning when the bar's door opened and Bill came in.

"Not when you're drunk, anyway," Frank said, laughing as she leaned across the space and smacked his thick leg.

"This is nice," Bill said as he smiled at them clustered around the empty fireplace.

"They're making fun of my coffee," Sandy complained. "My coffee is fine!"

"I agree. It tastes like it was ground this morning," Bill said, and Allen smiled at the old joke, wiping his hand free from powdered sugar and shifting to sit beside Peri. For the first time, Peri felt things were getting back to normal, and she glanced at the man at the bar. Even

Bill was ignoring him. He had to be an observer.

"So, how you doing, Allen?" Bill asked, and Allen glanced at Peri with a tentative smile.

"Better by the hour, Bill. Better by the hour," he said, and Peri warmed.

The man at the bar turned, sitting to face them with his arms over his chest and a disapproving expression.

"You'd better get a doughnut before they're gone, Peri," Sandy said, and Peri took one even though she wasn't hungry.

Finally Bill sat down, and Peri slowly exhaled. "Well, how is she?" Bill asked.

Sandy's entire demeanor shifted toward the professional. She looked at Frank, and he gestured for her to be forthright. Peri's heart thumped. "She's lying about her nightmares," Sandy said.

"I am not!"

Allen took her hand. "Peri, I'd never leave you."

Sandy made a tiny puff of sound. "It's not about you anchoring her, it's about her needing more backstory for her life. Shut up, Allen. I'll get to you in a minute. The nightmares aren't unusual. It's her wandering attention I'm concerned about."

"My attention is fine," Peri said, purposely not letting her gaze go to the man at the bar.

"And she hasn't mentioned it," Sandy said almost hesitantly, "but I think she still harbors a grudge against the alliance."

Peri worked to keep her breathing even so as not to show her anger. "Silas Denier almost killed Allen," Peri said, and Frank gave Bill a sideways look, his thick arms crossed over his chest. "And I'm supposed to pretend it didn't happen? Allen will heal, but my three years are gone, so, yes, I'm pissed. You going to put me in the hole because I'm pissed?"

Bill's eyebrows were raised, and Allen's hand slipped from hers in a silent rebuke. She'd probably just hurt her case for returning to active duty, but she didn't care.

"Just forget I said that," Peri said as she lifted her paper cup of hot milk and caffeine. "I'm fine. I'm happy. See?" She took a long drink, trying to minimize her anger while in front of three psychologists, her boss, and Allen.

"You are not *fine*," Sandy said, and the man at the bar nodded in agreement. "But moping around here isn't doing you any good. You need to go do something."

Breath catching, Peri looked up. *Is she serious?*

Allen beamed. "See, Bill? Sandy thinks it's a good idea. We need to get out of here. My cast comes off today. Give us something. I can do my physical therapy in the car."

Anticipation coursed through her as she looked at the faces around her, the first she'd felt in months. It felt good, so good.

"Hold up." Bill raised a thick hand. "Nothing

happens until I hear Frank and Sandy tell me she's good to draft."

Peri stifled a shiver when Sandy glanced at Frank, and when Frank nodded, Allen made a fist, pumping it once. "Yes-s-s-s!" he said softly.

"There's been minimal change in Peri's state these last few weeks," Sandy said. "I think the only way to shake things loose is to let her go. My larger concern is Allen."

Allen looked up, shocked, as he pushed his glasses back up his nose. "Me?"

"Yes, you." Sandy pointed an accusing finger at him. "You need to let go of the shared past you and Peri have. Your reactions are confusing her, causing more trouble than her missing memories. If you don't treat her as if she's trustworthy, she never will be."

Allen seemed to shrink down into himself under their hard gazes. "It's harder for me than you. I'm with her all the time."

Frank's hand twitched, and Sandy reached to still it. The man at the bar turned his back to them, and Peri wondered if more was being said than it seemed. "Allen, *you* are holding her back," Sandy said. "Peri is highly intuitive, and she knows you're not accepting her. Now, are you going to admit you have a problem and work with her to overcome it, or are you going to sit there and blame her for everything? She's trying. Are you?"

Miserable, Peri wondered if this was why she

hadn't felt accepted. Her anchor was sitting right next to her, but if he didn't trust her, then he wasn't there at all.

"I'm sorry," Allen said, and a lump swelled in her throat when he pulled her into a hug. "Peri, I'm so sorry. She's right. I've been treating you as if you're suddenly going to remember everything, and it just doesn't work like that." Peri let her head thump into him, breathing his scent and letting go of her fears. "Give me a chance," he whispered. "I just need some time."

Peri was smiling as he pushed back, but she dropped her gaze when he looked at her lips as if he was going to kiss her. *Not in front of Bill, Frank, and Sandy!*

"Okay," she said, feeling as if something had shifted. Everything seemed possible now. It had to get better.

"Ahh, hell," Frank said. "Give them something, Bill. Something that involves sun and very little clothing. They need to get out and find themselves."

"I just wanted to hear you say it." Bill reached behind his coat for a red-rimmed, short-life tablet and an envelope sporting Opti's logo.

"Where are we going?" Allen said as he took them.

Bill smiled at Peri's clearly eager expression. *Finally.* "Let me know if you're comfortable. Forgive me if it looks too easy, but Opti can survive you taking cream-puff tasks for a while. Besides, your knee is going to need several weeks of rehab."

Must be first-year stuff, she thought, leaning to look when Allen peeked past the flap to see boarding passes, then punched his Opti code into the tablet. It lit up, the small countdown at the top showing they had seventy-two hours before it scrambled its motherboard, destroying any electronic evidence of their task.

"Come on, Frank." Sandy stood to pull him into her wake. "Let the professionals get to work." She grinned at Peri. "It's good to see you where you belong, honey."

Peri's smile froze as Sandy's last word echoed in her mind. Sandy had called her *honey* before, but it hadn't been nice. Suddenly Peri realized Sandy had noticed, and she forced her expression to brighten until Sandy turned away. *Jeez, am I that paranoid?* Frank and Sandy were good people. She'd known them since her first days in Opti.

"First drink is on us when you get back," Frank said. "Knock 'em dead, Peri."

She took a breath to answer, hesitating when the guy at the bar slid from the stool to leave—head down as if depressed. Peri stifled a shiver, not knowing why. Small, positive noises came from Allen as he looked everything over. "This is nice," he said. "Bill, we'll take it."

Bill stood. "I'll leave you to it, then. Peri, do you

want us to move your things to Allen's while you're gone?"

"Sure," Peri said, vowing that she was going to make this work. The cold fact was that drafting came with the risk of losing memories, and it was only a matter of time before you lost a large chunk as she had. She had survived. Her relationship with Allen would, too. "Yes, please," Peri said, leaning over until she bumped Allen's shoulder and cast him a significant look. He gave her a preoccupied smile. At the bar, a flash of light intruded as the blond man left.

"Good!" Bill said, satisfaction—and maybe relief—etching his few wrinkles. "See you in a couple of days, kiddo."

"Yes, Dad," Allen said cheerfully, and then his gaze went past Bill to include Frank and Sandy. "Thank you. I think this is going to be better than I ever thought."

A warm feeling came over Peri, as if her life was finally oriented to the right place. Bill inclined his head, spinning on a heel to the door. She was going back to work, and it felt good.

"So . . . ," Peri drawled as Allen gathered everything into a pile. "Where are we going?"

"Not what are we doing?" he said, scanning a highlighted map.

Her hand touched the screen and it blanked, forcing him to look at her. "Where are the tickets to?"

Allen's expression went wary. "The West Coast. Why?"

Excitement stirred. West Coast. Opti wouldn't check on them until they were a day overdue. "You can get on that plane if you want, but I've got other plans."

Allen's brow furrowed. "Peri."

She leaned in, her voice hardening as she said, "I want the man who took three years of my memory and tried to kill you. I want Silas Denier. *He* is the reason I'm having nightmares, and as long as he lives, I'll never be able to." Heart pounding, she leaned back, watching Allen think it over. "I don't think you'll be able to, either."

Allen's long face was a bank of emotion. "I know where he is," Allen said, and her breath caught. "You aren't the only one who wants to see him in the ground and forgotten."

CHAPTER
THIRTY

Peri crouched amid the dry, waist-high grass, settling her weight onto her ankles in such a way that her feet wouldn't go to sleep or her legs tire. She could hold the position for hours, and anticipation trickled through her, bringing her alive as she studied the black silhouette of the abandoned building against the lighter darkness of the sky. Silas worked there. It was the only building standing within a mile, and looking away from Allen's shadow shifting about the foundations, she lifted her gaze to the tree above her, seeing the first stars among its dead branches.

In the near distance, the interstate made a dull-roar ribbon of light, but here, amid one of Detroit's deconstructed zones with the discarded fast-food wrappers and cigarette butts, it was utterly dark, the waning crescent of a moon giving no light. There was no electricity, no water. Everything that could be stripped had been. Everything not of historical value had been knocked down. New surveys had redrawn lines and sunk markers for parks, public transportation, and adequate parking. The bulldozers and train-car Dumpsters had come and gone, to leave the quiet stillness of waiting in the empty streets and vacant lots. Even the gangs avoided the deconstructed zones, needing something to break, deface, or steal.

But Peri liked the feeling of latent strength and endurance that lingered in the weedy gutters, especially when the occasional historical building was left to anchor the coming new development, the structure stabilized and wrapped with razor wire until enough backers could be found to turn the water and lights back on and the buses and new elevated tram brought life back to old Detroit.

Eastown, she thought as her eyes returned to the ugly stone and marble building behind the razor wire. The 1930s movie palace turned music arena had been little more than a crime trap and a place to get and use recreational drugs. Most of Eastown's elegance had been stripped by the time she'd stood among its blue musty seats and screamed with the rockers, but the ceiling had been exquisitely painted in a Neo-Renaissance style, and the common areas in marble had an elegance that couldn't be obscured by graffiti and misuse.

Silas, she thought, *won't be the first to die under the dome.*

As if her thought had pulled him, Allen's dark shadow darted from the broken edifice, his steps almost silent on the gritty street, then vanishing utterly as he found the ruined soil choked with bits of broken building and beer tabs from the seventies. In the distance, a drone passed between her and Detroit, illegal at this hour but too far away to be of concern.

"Well?" she asked when he joined her under the tree with his weight off his bad knee.

"Not bad. Some razor wire. But once we get past the chain-link fence, it's an easy in."

"Good." The feeling of being a team that had begun in Overdraft had strengthened, and Peri waited, easy, enjoying the sensation of coming action. Allen was almost a different person as he crouched beside her and used his night glasses to scan the top of the old building: his anxiety was gone, the hesitation. He had, she realized, the same drive to action that she did, the same need to prove to himself that he was capable. Together they were going to get the job done, Bill be damned.

"I'm glad you're here," she whispered, and he lowered the glasses, his eyes in the dusky light showing his surprise.

"I wouldn't have it any other way," he said, giving her hand a squeeze.

The need to apologize swam up, but she didn't know how to frame it. Instead, she lifted her gaze to the few stars that had braved Detroit's light pollution. "Orion is nice tonight," she said, remembering a sky so filled with stars they took her breath away—but not who had been with her or where they'd been. It was enough.

Sighing, he looked up. "You were always better than me at finding your way in the dark."

Her chest hurt with the need to make this work, to become whole again.

But then he shifted to ease the stress on his knee, and the moment was gone. "Shouldn't be long now," he said. "If we're lucky, we can make our flight. Bill will never know but for guessing at the obituaries."

She wanted this—wanted it badly—but still . . . "Did it ever occur to you that we're doing a non-Opti-sanctioned task?" she asked.

"One job on our own doesn't make us dirty." Allen turned to the interstate, the strip of glowing lights feeling as far away as the moon. "It's not as if we're doing it for money."

If you're not doing it for money, then you're doing it for kicks echoed in her thoughts, lingering to make her uncomfortable. "He's like a sliver I have to get out. Once he's dead, I can let it go and move on, but I don't feel like me. He took three years of my life and shoved you off a balcony. I need . . . *closure,*" she said sarcastically, thinking she sounded like Sandy.

"Let's make it fast, okay?" Allen said. "No talking. Not even 'You're being held accountable for what you did.' We do it and get out. He doesn't even need to know we're there until he's dying on the floor. Three minutes—in and out."

Peri nodded, her gaze on the black branches of the dead tree above them. "I can't believe he hasn't left the state, much less the city."

"Maybe he's calling us out." It had almost been a whisper, and Peri snorted. "I'm serious," Allen grumbled. "The alliance may have started an assassination corps."

Silas doesn't have the build, she thought, hunching down. A car was coming, the headlights bouncing across the abandoned streets marking the empty lots. "Right on time," Peri said. It was like an itch. If she could just do this one thing, the rest of her life would fall into place, she knew it. "Why does he do this at night? It's not like he's got to punch a clock."

"They only have one car, and the woman works at night," Allen said. "The guy with the dread-locks drops him off on the way to taking her to her mall job. He sits in the food court, soaking up the Internet until she's done, and then they pick Denier up on the way home. Until they come back, Denier is on his own."

And vulnerable. She jumped at the slamming of a car door as Silas got out. The darkness made Peri and Allen invisible. "See you later!" a woman called, and Silas half turned and waved at the car as it did a one-eighty and started back the way it had come.

"Let's give him a few minutes," Allen said.

Jaw clenched, Peri watched Silas unlock the thick padlock to get through the razor-wire fence. He left it unchained and used a second key to unlock one of the barricaded twin doors and slipped inside. Almost immediately the faint thrum of a generator rose. New light leaked out of the high glass windows that still remained.

Slowly Peri's mood shifted. She was inten-tionally going to kill someone. But the need to do something was almost unbearable. "I want this done," she whispered.

"Then let's go."

She stood, feeling exposed under the dead tree. In the distance, traffic sped in two lines of colored light—so many lives, and none of them would know what she did tonight. Steady, she touched her belt pack and then the Opti-issued Glock. The thrum of the generator echoed, hiding the tiny sounds of their soft-soled shoes on the old concrete. Allen was first to the razor-wire gate, carefully manipulating the chain so it wouldn't clank. She slipped in past him, then hesitated at the main door.

"Ready?" Allen whispered.

Anticipation was a sudden, bright wire snaking through her. Breath held, she scanned the fallow lots, the city looking like mountains. There, at the far end of the street, was a man. At least, she thought it was a man. Or was it a shadow. . . . Her eyes narrowed, and doubt made her hesitate.

"What is it?" Allen whispered, lips inches from her ear, and she shook her head.

"Nothing." Resolute, she shifted the door just enough to slip inside. Allen was right behind her as they entered the scarred lobby. Grit ground between her and the marble floor, the sound muffled by the drone of the nearby generator. Power cords snaked deeper into the building. Barren walls and gouged marble swept clean by hazmat teams had left a scoured beauty. She couldn't help but feel a kinship with the old building, a shell with only fragments and pieces left to rebuild itself, and her doubts pushed to the forefront. For the first time, she felt like a killer.

He has to die.

Peri's heart clenched in ache when she looked

past a dented, modern door and into the auditorium. There wasn't much left. The musty blue seats were gone, leaving only a massive, echoing space with barren walls, lorded over by the broken balcony. Most of the Neo-Renaissance carvings and relief had been chipped or were missing. Water had damaged the once polished wood, and the white marks where the rot had been cut out of the stage were stark in the bright lights hanging from scaffolding. But her skin tingled as she remembered the power of three thousand people crushed into space designed for half that, all of them living to the same sound for just that moment in perfect understanding.

A card table desk with a metal chair was dead center on the high stage. A laptop was open on it, looking like a prop in an apocalyptic play. The scent of rotted carpet mixed with the clean smell of cut wood. Her eyes rose, and she blinked fast. The dome was intact where the water from the leaking roof hadn't reached, the colors and gilt looking as bright as the day they'd been painted. *Eastown isn't gone yet, and neither am I.*

A scuff pulled her attention and the memory vanished.

It was Silas, oblivious to them as he strode from the backstage area. She hardly breathed as he scrambled up a short ladder with a flexi-glass to make an electronic rubbing from one of the engravings near the balcony. She didn't see a weapon, but that didn't mean there wasn't one.

This is the man who tried to kill Allen? she mused, recognizing his dark hair and muscular, body-building form, but having a hard time reconciling the calm, relaxed pleasure he was taking in restoring the old building with the savage, raging lunatic in her thoughts.

The click of Allen's safety jerked through her. "I'll do it," she said as she touched his arm, and Allen's brow furrowed. "Keep my exit open."

For a moment, she thought he was going to argue, but then he nodded.

The snap of her holster was more feel than sound, and Peri pulled her weapon, gut tightening as she strode down the bare cement steps to the front, then levered herself up onto the stage. She slowly stood, and it was there she hesitated as Silas turned, eyes widening.

"Peri," he breathed, and confusion stayed her—confusion at the relief and welcome in his voice. "You're all right," he said, flexi-glass in one hand, wide-faced stylus in the other.

"Don't move," she said coldly, and they both froze at the sound of the distant front door crashing into a wall.

"Silas?" a young woman's voice called, and Peri's mind fastened on it as familiar. "I've *told* you to lock the main door. We found tire tracks near the on-ramp, so Howie's going to stay with you tonight. Silas?"

Silas opened his mouth, but stayed silent as he tracked Allen bolting back to the lobby.

"Silas?" the woman called again, and then, "Holy crap! Howard!"

Silas jerked, and Peri motioned him to stay still. "Don't. Move," she said as the sound of a fight rose over the droning of the generator. She'd killed people before—some who deserved it less than this man. But it felt personal this time, and . . . wrong?

"They're lying to you." Silas edged off the ladder, hands raised. "Let me explain."

"Shut up," she demanded, her confusion growing even as her aim tightened. She wanted it to be over. She wanted the nagging noise in her head to go away. But as she stood on that stage amid the barren emptiness, she *couldn't pull the trigger.*

"Peri, wait," a new voice pleaded, and her eyes flicked to a blond man coming up the stage's stairs. Tense, she retreated so she could see both of them. It was the man from Overdraft, the one who had sat at the bar and observed, the one she'd thought might be with Opti's psych unit. *Shit. This is a test?*

"I can explain!" she exclaimed, her aim never shifting from Silas.

Distracted, she was too slow when Silas lunged for her. The flexi-glass hit her chest, and he had her, twisting her wrist until the Glock went off to blow a hole in the wall. Silas slammed her up against the marble wall. Crap. It had been a test. And she had failed it.

"Taf!" someone shouted, but Peri was seeing stars, her ears numb from the gun's shot.

"I'm sorry, Peri," Silas said, his fingers trying to pry the gun away as he pinned her to the wall. "I don't want to hurt you. If you would just listen."

"Get . . . off . . . ," she wheezed, twisting a foot behind Silas's and giving a yank.

They both went down. Silas yelped as they crashed into the hard wood, her on top of him.

"Will you hold still!" Silas said, and then suddenly she was facedown on the stage, her arms yanked behind her. "I'm trying to tell you something! Why do you never. Listen. To. *Me!*"

"You stole my life!" she shouted, hand still gripping the Glock but pinned to the floor. "Everything!" He was sitting on her. Allen wasn't here, and she desperately didn't want to draft. Teeth clenched, she struggled, never letting go of the gun even when her grip went numb.

"Remember your rule," Silas said, sounding more irate than afraid. "You never kill anyone unless they kill you first. I didn't kill you. I'm trying to help!"

How does he know my rule? "You tried to kill my anchor, you bastard!"

"Jack?" he said, and she gasped when the image of a smiling face, white from the light of a monitor, flashed through her. "I didn't kill Jack. You did."

Who the hell is Jack? Cheek pressed to the gritty wood, she puffed the hair from her eyes. "Not Jack. Allen."

"Allen wasn't your anchor." Silas's voice was full of doubt. "Jack was."

Again, she saw a smiling face in her thoughts, and the blond man from Overdraft inched into her peripheral vision, bending at the waist to wiggle his fingers at her as if to say hi.

The feeling was coming back into her hand, and her grip on the gun tightened. All she needed was an inch and it would be over. "You pushed Allen through a window," she seethed. "You threw him over the balcony. I *saw* you do it. I would've drafted but we were already in one, since you *shot him!*" She couldn't breathe, and she'd had it. "You over there by the table. Stop playing cute with me and get him off me! It's over. You won, you bastards."

"Oh-h-h-h-h. . . . Shit," Silas breathed.

Peri grunted in pain when Silas lifted her wrist and slammed it into the stage. Her grip opened and the gun spun away. Silas lunged for it, and she scrambled to her feet, skidding to a halt when he aimed the Glock at her. She could make a run for it, but at this range, he wouldn't miss. She'd probably end up drafting, and she backed up, rubbing her bruised wrist.

"Allen?" she called, and the silence was thick with the unknown. Lifting her chin, she glared at the blond man. "You guys are all dicks. Just let me kill him, and I'll be fine."

Breathing hard, Silas felt behind him and put the gun on the ladder. She watched, hungry for the feel of it in her grip. "Jack is here?" Silas said, his voice thick with wonder.

"You mean the Opti psych guy? Are you blind!" Peri exclaimed, pointing at the man.

"Oh, babe, this is so bad for your asthma. I don't think you should kill Silas anymore," the man said, and Peri's breath came in a heave. She knew his voice. She knew it!

"I'm so sorry, Peri," Silas said as if he'd never tried to kill her, never laid a hand on her. "Opti messed with your mind. That's not a real person. It's a hallucination I stabilized to keep you from going insane when you overdrafted while remembering Jack's death."

"Excuse me?"

Jack looked down, his fingers splayed over his Armani shirt. "Seriously? I'm not real?"

This is not happening. "Allen?" she called, and the woman who had dropped Silas off rushed into the auditorium.

"Is everyone okay?" the blond young woman called as she ran forward, ponytail swinging. A thin man with dreadlocks bolted after her, clearly trying to catch her before she made it to the stage. "Thank God you're here!" she called, a faint southern accent coming through.

"Stay back!" Silas warned, and the woman slid to a frightened halt. "She doesn't remember you, Taf. You're scaring her."

Scaring me? Peri thought, but the woman's expression had gone sad, and Silas's hand slowly dropped when the man chasing her pulled Taf back a few steps.

"Where's Allen?" Silas asked, looking nervous.

Immediately Taf brightened. "Out cold," she said, sounding as if she liked the fact. "The car is running. Are we taking her with us?"

Jack swung his head up, alarmed. "You touch me, and it will be the last thing you do," Peri threatened, and the thin man pushed Taf behind him. Allen's gun was tucked dangerously in his front pocket, and Peri eyed it, wanting it badly.

Silas glanced at his watch. "No. Opti tagged her."

"Opti doesn't chip their personnel like *dogs*," Peri said indignantly, and the guy in dreadlocks chuckled. "What's so funny, Sherlock?"

"That's exactly what you said the first time."

"Peri, just listen," Silas said, his broad shoulders hunched. "Opti used my research to give you false memories, but if you can see Jack, then that means they're starting to break apart."

Jack slowly sat back against the table. "That's me," he said, but no one looked at him. "At least, I'm pretty sure that's me."

Peri held her breath, trying not to hyper-ventilate. "I'm going crazy."

"No, you're becoming sane," Silas said. "We're going to leave in a minute, and you can tell Allen whatever you want."

"Oh, there's a good idea," the blonde said bitterly, and Peri couldn't help but admire her. "Give her right back to the people who brain-washed her."

"I never said she had to tell him the truth," Silas said. "It's up to Peri. And Jack, I guess."

Uneasy, Peri looked at the man in the suit, deciding she'd known him before she'd lost three years. "You're not an Opti psychologist? How come you were at the bar this morning?"

But Silas was moving, and she fell back to keep space between them. "Howard, will you and Taf wait in the car?" Silas said. "I need to talk to Peri alone."

"Sure," Howard said reluctantly, and the woman waved her fingers at her as they left.

Peri could hear their voices discussing her even before they got out the door. "You've got them well trained," Peri said, and Silas looked startled.

"I'm trying to help you," he said, sounding peeved, and she cocked her head when Jack cleared his throat in rebuke. "Okay, I'm trying to find out how far the corruption goes in Opti," Silas amended, neck reddening. "But I'm trying to help you, too."

"Opti isn't corrupt," she protested hotly, but doubt took her when Jack flicked his suit jacket aside and resettled himself on the card table. He was dressed better than Allen ever was, attractive with just the right amount of stubble and charm. *The perfect mistake . . .*

"Jack was your anchor until almost two months ago," he said. "You found out he'd been taking you on non-Opti tasks, then traded your memory of it for the chance to kill him."

Peri's eyes slid to Jack—who grinned at her like an idiot—then back to Silas. It sounded like something she might do.

"*This* Jack, the one here, is a hallucination. One I designed to keep you from going into overdraft when you tried to remember it."

"Liar!" she exclaimed. "I wouldn't kill my own anchor." But she had only Bill's and Allen's word that Allen had been her anchor the last three years, and doubt began to gnaw at her. *Shit. Who the hell am I?*

"You might if you found out he was working for Bill, not Opti," Silas said, looking toward the dented doors when a car horn blew. "They're both corrupt, and I'm not so sure about Allen anymore, either."

"So Allen is corrupt. I bet you didn't push him over my balcony, either?" She had meant it to be flip, but the man's entire expression became relieved.

"Exactly," he breathed, and her eyes flicked to the ladder and her gun still on it. "I was never in your apartment. At least, not that night."

"I'm not corrupt," Peri said hotly. "And neither is Allen."

"And yet you're both here killing a man for your own revenge," Silas said, and Peri's teeth clenched, the doubt becoming more sure. "I know your rules," Silas continued. "I know this isn't you. They implanted the suggestion for you to get rid of me. If you do it, it will reinforce their lies. Stay here when we leave. Opti will show up. I promise it. They want you to kill me."

"You can't give a drafter a false memory," she said, eyes going to the exit when Howard pushed the auditorium door open.

"Silas?" Howard looked worried. "We've got three cars with lights on the expressway."

"You can," Silas said, and Howard ducked back out. "That's why I quit Opti. But Jack is my idea, too. He's your intuition. Listen to him."

A hallucination? Peri looked at Jack, and he stared back, her uncertainty growing.

Grimacing, Silas pulled a creased photo from his pocket and set it on the ladder beside the gun. "Last February, you and I brought back a memory of Jack that I wasn't privy to. I lifted this from Allen before they torched your apartment at Lloyd Park, and I think this is what you remembered. I shouldn't have left you that night. I'm sorry. I thought the alliance would help if I could just talk to them. It was a mistake."

Peri blinked. *He should have been there with me?* But then her focus blurred. *Opti torched my apartment?* She hadn't moved because of a fire; she'd moved to get away from the memory of Allen being thrown off the balcony after going through the . . . bulletproof . . . window. *How can he go through a window that can't break?*

"Peri," Silas said, jerking her back to reality. "I need you to find a chip Jack hid. It's a list of Bill's corrupt drafters, and if you can get it to me, I can get you out. You'll be safe. The alliance needs a reason to trust you."

Breathless, Peri glanced at the picture, inching forward when Silas took the Glock and backed up. It was a photo of her and . . . "That's you," she said, looking at Jack, and he winced, nodding. "That's you and me—"

"In the outback, last New Year's," Jack finished, and her face went cold.

"My God. Who are you?" she said, staring at him, and he shrugged, bewildered.

"I don't know. But this guy trusts you, and Allen doesn't."

Vertigo took her as she realized it was true. "Hold still," she said, cautiously reaching out to Jack, then staggering when her hand passed through him. Heat flashed through her, and she felt unreal. "Shit, shit, shit . . . ," she mumbled, backing up with her hand gripping her pendant pen. "You're not real, and I'm going crazy."

"No. I told you, you're becoming sane," Silas said, and she stood there, shocked when he tossed the Glock to her and it hit her palm with a soft and certain thump.

"Oh, man . . . I'm a hallucination?" Jack put a dramatic hand to his chest. "This is very bad for my asthma."

Peri's heart pounded. She'd said that herself a hundred times. It meant she'd forgotten something, something important.

"Here's my number." Silas grabbed her hand and wrote it scrawling on her palm, ignoring the weapon in her other hand. "Find that list and I can get you out. If we can prove Opti is corrupt, it's all over. Isn't that what you want? For it to be over?"

He jumped from the stage, turning to look up at her. "Jack is your intuition, Peri. Trust him as you would trust yourself. He only knows what you do or suspect. He's not real."

Peri looked at Jack, and the man winced. "He's right. But that's okay, isn't it?"

"Oh, and in case you're wondering, you didn't draft." Silas turned and ran, his steps loud in the echoing space until the door squeaked shut. Peri took a shaky breath. Jack was looking at the picture, and she inched forward, not sure how to talk to a hallucination, especially one of a man she'd killed. "How did he know I was worried about drafting?" Peri wondered out loud.

"My guess is he's an anchor," Jack said.

She closed her hand to hide the number. Confused, Peri picked up the picture. She and Jack were standing before a fire gone to coals. She didn't remember it, but she felt centered as she looked at their tired, dirty, smiling faces. "This is not right," she whispered.

"You're telling me, babe."

They both looked to the exit at the unmistakable sound of cars screeching to a halt outside. She jumped, stuffing the photo down her shirt when the thunderous boom of the outer doors being flung open echoed.

"Peri?" came Bill's bellow over the calls of Opti forces.

"Back here," she whispered, wide eyes looking at the ink on her hand as if it were blood. "Here!" she called out louder, arms going up and dangling her Glock from a finger when a dozen Opti agents boiled into the auditorium through all three doors, screaming at her not to move. "It's just me," she griped as they swarmed over the space and then moved to the unseen back. The three remaining with her took the pistol and screamed at her some more. She ignored them, relieved when Bill strode in and told them in a very loud voice to back off.

"Peri!" the large man called as he strode onto the stage. "I knew it. I knew it! I never should have okayed you. Was this Allen's idea? Was it?"

Peri thought the real question was how Opti had known they were at Eastown. She took a breath to tell him what had happened, that the alliance had been here and claimed that he was corrupt and that he had filled her head with lies.

But then she fisted her hand, hiding the number. If Silas was lying, keeping silent would hurt no one. She thought it telling that she'd come here to kill Silas, but now . . . the feeling was utterly gone.

"Go ahead and put me in the hole, but yes!" she shouted. "Allen and I were going to off him, since no one at Opti *cares!* You got a problem with that, *fat boy?*"

Bill scowled when someone snickered and walked quickly away. "Did you get him?"

"No." Arms over her chest to hide the picture, Peri cocked her hip to keep her legs from trembling. "Allen's recon sucked. Denier's ride came back and surprised us. Has Allen always been this inept, or did Silas fracture his thinking bone, too?"

Bill laughed, and Peri stiffened when he put an arm around her shoulders and led her down the stage's stairs. "You are grounded, young lady," he said as they trekked up the incline and out to the lobby, bright with flashlights. "No California coastline for you. I want you back in Opti tonight. Bring your toothbrush."

"Bill," she protested, grimacing as Allen was toted

out between two Opti agents. "I don't need a full workup. I'll go in tomorrow morning. Promise."

Bill drew her to a stop just outside. Black Opti cars lined the street, their flashing lights and headlamps making an unreal glare. Agents rushed about to justify their presence, and Bill bodily shifted her so the light fell on her face. "You'll stay at Allen's?" he asked.

"Yes, I'll stay the night at Allen's," she said, temper bad as she stomped to the nearest car and got in the front seat, waiting for someone else to drive her. She didn't know what to believe, but there was one thing that was irrefutable. Jack had been dogging her steps the last five minutes, and Bill hadn't commented on him even once. Either she was crazy, or Silas was telling her the truth. That the truth meant she was crazy didn't make her feel any better.

The proof that Opti is corrupt is in my old apartment, she thought. She didn't want it to be true, but she had to find out.

"You can trust me, Peri," Jack said, and she jumped, swearing when she realized he was sitting in the backseat. "You loved me, once— before you killed me."

Frowning, she wiped at the ink on her palm to make it less obvious. Fingers curled to hide what was left, she put her fist to her mouth and stared out the window at Detroit's distant lights. *Oh yeah. That helps a lot.*

CHAPTER
THIRTY-ONE

Rain made the nearly empty streets shine under the streetlights as Silas waited in the dry shadows behind the massive pylons making up the grocery store's front façade. It was a questionable place to be this late at night amid the gum wrappers and empty nicotine caps, but Allen's car was parked in the nearly empty lot. This was the only place that carried Peri's cat's food that was open after midnight. Silas knew she'd sent Allen out for it twenty minutes ago. It was likely she'd wanted some time alone in the apartment to poke around, and a quest for cat food was an excellent excuse.

He had to talk to Allen, and though jimmying the door of Allen's Lexus and waiting there for him would have been less obtrusive, there was a perverse pleasure in lurking in the shadows. They'd have a quiet chat amid the dirt and cold brick. It would get his attention—make him listen. Peri's mental state was ready to crack, but his terse, one-sided conversation with Fran today had made one thing very clear. Until Allen vouched for her alliance loyalty, she'd be treated as a traitor—and Allen had flatly refused to give it.

Silas fidgeted in a slow anger, hands shoved deep in his pockets. Peri was vulnerable—because of her strength and abilities, not in spite of them. Some of this was his fault, but the Jack hallucination shouldn't have survived Allen's latest mental butchery. After seeing her shout at empty air and her expression change to horror as she realized her life was a lie, he knew the risk wasn't worth anything they could gain anymore. The task was over. They'd get their intel another way.

Leaning, Silas glanced inside to see Allen flirting with the old woman at the register. Slowly he dropped back, fingering the pistol in his coat pocket. He was having serious doubts about his old friend. Plausible deniability was a sword without a grip, and Silas had never liked the idea of sending her into Opti with no memory of her past, a double sleeper agent. He'd liked it even less when Allen had remained with her at Opti, dedicated to keeping her safe while she found what they needed. It didn't surprise him that Allen had somehow twisted things so that he would be the one to break the truth. Allen was all about the glory of the job, not caring much whom he hurt getting there. It was what attracted Peri to him in the first place.

Stress pulled his shoulders up as the twin glass doors, their e-boards flickering with the week's specials, slid open. Breath held, Silas strode out of the shadows. "We need to talk."

Allen's head snapped up, his brief shock

making Silas smile. "Jeez, Silas. You gave me a heart attack." He pushed his glasses back up his nose. "What are you doing?"

"Avoiding the bugs in your car," he said, shoving Allen to the shadows and pulling his gun out. "And deciding if I should pop you or not," he added when Allen's back hit the brick. "She could have killed me!"

Unperturbed, Allen looked past Silas's weapon to the rain-emptied parking lot. "You should get some sleep. You look like hell," he said, the bag with the cat food crackling in his grip as he started for the lot. Silas shoved him into the shadows again, and Allen looked up, peeved. "If she didn't shoot you the first second she saw you, she wasn't going to," he said tightly.

Silas's lips twisted. "I'm calling it. You're going to help me pull her out. Now. Tonight."

Allen's disgust snapped to disbelief. "I *wasn't* going to let her *kill you!*"

"This isn't about her pointing a gun at me," Silas whispered harshly, his grip on the Glock tight. "You think she's never done that before? I'm talking about ending this. We can't win, Allen. She's too fractured. Tell Fran she's clear so I can pull her out."

Allen's eyes slid to the gun. Three feet away, a cold spring rain hissed down, but here it was dry and dusty. "We have a real chance at this."

"Chance?" Silas gestured wildly. "There was

never any *chance*. We're *never* going to get what we sent her here for. She needs to be pulled out. Fixed."

Allen's focus sharpened. "Is that what this is about? Her not remembering you? Peri is not broken."

"You call what you made her into whole?"

"Hey! I did what I needed to do for both of us to survive," Allen said. "Bill trusts me. He doesn't like me, but he trusts me. I can salvage this."

Dropping back, Silas sent his gaze to his gun, and then he shoved it into his pocket. "She's falling apart."

"She's fine."

"She remembers Jack," Silas said, and Allen's expression went blank.

A woman was approaching, and Allen drew Silas deeper into the shadows. "How? There is nothing there. I'd swear to it," he whispered.

They were silent until the woman went in, never having seen them. Satisfaction lifted Silas's chin. His manipulations had held, had given Peri something to find the truth with. His fix never would have lasted if she hadn't trusted him. "I used the latent memory of Jack as a mental cop o prevent her going into MEP," Silas said. "Sort of an interactive hallucination."

Allen's lips parted. "And she knows it's fake?"

Silas nodded. "She does now. You can't keep her ignorant. Your false memories are flaking away like cheap paint. She knows you're lying to her. That's why she sent you out here for cat food. I hope you didn't leave anything you don't want her to find."

Allen pushed his glasses back up his narrow nose. "Nothing she would be surprised at. What did you tell her?"

"When you were out cold on the floor of Eastown?" Silas smirked. "Not much. But Jack is filling her in. Sandy had one thing right. You never forget, you just don't remember."

Silas jerked when Allen poked him with a stiff finger. "My life is in the open here, not yours," he said, eyes virulent behind his glasses. "What did you tell her about me?"

Silas smiled bitterly. "Everything except who you work for, because I don't know anymore. You keep saying Peri's gone native, but you're the one doing ugly things. I don't even remember why we agreed to this."

Uneasy, Allen shifted the grocery bag closer. "Because she was going to do it with or without us. Hell, Silas. You don't have to scare me. I'm scared enough already. I watched her fight what Opti did to her, is still doing. I had to remind myself she agreed to it when she was screaming at me, threatening to kill me. It took *three weeks* to turn her from a raving knot of defiance to what you saw walk into Eastown, and she's still shaky. You think I liked that?"

Silas stiffened. "She's everything you ever wanted. Proud of yourself?"

Allen's lip curled. "Will you get off your pity pony. There is nothing more I'd like to do than call Fran and tell her Peri is with us a hundred percent, but I can't tell where her loyalties are. I can't give her the green to come in. She likes who she is—a little too much."

"*You* like what she is."

"Shut up and listen to me. I'm telling you she likes who she is. I don't care if she's fighting it, she likes the power and ability, the status that Opti gives her. The feeling of superiority after every task. She enjoyed what she did with Jack, enjoyed it to the point where she ignored the lies and obvious incongruities until they were rubbed in her face. That's why they keep scrubbing her and starting over. She likes it. They know it. And *that's* why that Jack construct is still there. She won't let herself forget."

Silas backed up until a pylon hit his back. "She agreed to help the alliance fast enough."

"Which is the only reason I'm continuing with this farce. That, and we're in the best position we've been in for the last five years. You think I enjoyed stripping her down to nothing? Listening to her rave at me? Knowing I deserved it? She knew this might happen, and she agreed to it, but that doesn't make it any easier. Her core hasn't changed. But how she expresses it has."

Silas thought of the gun in his pocket, remembered the fear and determination in her eyes when she faced him across the stage and rediscovered how badly her world was messed up. "That's why I want to pull her out."

"We can't." Allen's eyes caught the overhead glow of the store's OPEN sign. "If we pull her out before it's done, the alliance will never trust her. She's gone too deep, becoming what she needed to be in order to survive. She has to give us Opti on a platter before anyone in the alliance will trust her to resume her full responsibilities. She either sees it to the end and makes the decision to side with the alliance—with her still oblivious about her beginnings—or she goes down with Opti. That goes for you, too."

"Me!"

Allen's chin lifted in anger. "Peri got a few points for freeing you, but *you* didn't take her back to the alliance. You ran off with her and the daughter of the head of the alliance, not to mention their best cleaner."

"So she could finish it," Silas said, remembering his fruitless conversations with Fran.

"Is that what you told Fran?" Allen said mockingly. "She buying it? All they see is you *not* doing what they sent you to do."

Silas's head thumped back against the hard brick. He had refused to bring Peri in as a traitor, yes, and now the alliance suspected him as well.

"You lost your cred." Allen glanced at the storefront and then the damp parking lot. "The alliance trusts me more than you. And unlike me, you don't have a golden parachute."

"Got this all figured out, huh?"

"Yup." He nodded, infuriating Silas. "You need to find another way. That list you set your sights on is gone. They couldn't find the chip, so they torched her apartment."

"You son of a bitch," Silas whispered. "You knew that was her ticket out. How could you let them burn it?"

"Let go of me," Allen said coldly, and Silas pushed the smaller man back, only then realizing he'd grabbed Allen's coat. "She can still clear her name," Allen said as he shifted his shoulders to get his coat straight. "It doesn't change anything."

"She gave her life for this," Silas said softly, not knowing how to help her anymore.

"We all did," Allen said flatly.

Silas's jaw clenched. To pull her out now would destroy her reputation and her future. He had no choice but to see it through, possible MEP or not. *Son of a bitch.* He hated feeling helpless. "She's going to kill you before this is over, Allen." *And if she doesn't, I will.*

"Maybe I deserve it," Allen said.

Silent, Silas turned and walked away, hands in his pockets and his head down against the light rain. "You think I'm misjudging our chances?"

Allen said, but Silas kept going. "You think I'd risk her life like this if I didn't think I could save her?"

But Silas hadn't been a coward for leaving Opti when Allen had continued as a double agent. He'd been a realist.

"I listened to you, Silas, now listen to me!" Allen shouted, and then more calmly, "Bill, before you have a cow for me leaving Peri alone, just listen. I'm at the store. She sent me out for cat food so she could search the place. I thought it might make her feel better, so I left."

Silas jerked to a halt and spun. Allen stood in the rain under the humming security light, cat food at his feet and phone to his ear.

"I don't mind her looking around," Allen said as Silas returned. "She'll relax more if she feels in control. Besides, I wanted to get out so I could talk to you. I have a doubt."

"About what?" Allen had angled the phone so Silas could hear Bill, his usually flamboyant voice flat through the tiny speaker.

It wasn't an inquiry, more of a suspicious warning.

"Ah, the memories your team implanted," Allen said. "I don't think they're holding."

"So get in there and tweak them," Bill demanded. "Did you think it would be easy?"

"Bill," Allen said, but Bill wasn't done yet.

"Sandy says it's your attitude that is holding her

back, and I'm tending to agree. Grow a pair, will you? I need you both in the field by next month."

"So sorry we're interfering with your bottom line," Allen said tightly, and Silas's mistrust flared. "Sandy was never hurt by her."

"Yes she was," Bill countered.

"That knife throw didn't even hit her. Besides, Sandy isn't sleeping with the bitch."

"And if you were, this might not be happening," Bill said, shocking Silas. "Get back to your apartment. It sounds as if she's taking the place apart, talking nonsense to her cat."

Silas met Allen's gaze. She wasn't talking to the cat. She was talking to Jack. "Look, I understand the closure she'd get by killing Silas," Allen said, "but seeing him might have jiggled something loose. She doesn't trust me."

"Do you blame her?" Bill said, his voice mocking. "I think it's a reasonable reaction. Silas's team came back. Interrupted her. She's right that your intel sucked. Maybe you're not up to her standards."

"The hell with you," Allen said, his anger too hot to be faked. "I didn't ask for this job."

"No. You only mishandled it so badly that you had to take it. Make it work. Get some ice cream and strawberries. She's a woman, Allen. Treat her like one. There's nothing wrong with her that a good screw won't fix."

Expression ugly, Allen ended the call and shoved his phone away. "Still think I don't know

490

what I'm doing?" he said bitterly. "Bill trusts me. That Peri doesn't is exactly why he does. I'm doing my job, so don't tell me you're ending it when *I'm* the one with the riskier, harder task here. Got it?"

Silas looked beyond him and into their past. "How much of that was a lie?"

Allen picked up the cat food. "If you're asking if I'm sleeping with her, I'm not."

Silas let that settle, not liking that it meant so much to him. "I'll give you two weeks."

"*You'll* give *me?* You are not in charge, Silas. I am."

Silas's fingers found the gun in his pocket, and he jerked back. "She's too close to a MEP. If this doesn't break in two weeks, I pull her out. I don't care if the alliance shuns her, ignores her, or puts a hit on her," he said as Allen frowned, knowing the threat was real. "Two weeks."

Turning, Silas stomped away into the rain.

CHAPTER
THIRTY-TWO

Allen's apartment was as much to Peri's liking as the things now hanging in her side of the closet, both a mishmash of colors and textures that had her wondering if Allen was color-blind. Somehow the professional polish exuded by his clothing had failed to make it to his decorating style. Maybe he was just eclectic in his taste.

Sighing, Peri sat on the leather ottoman before the gas log fireplace, Carnac on her lap as she watched an insurance commercial. She couldn't help but admire the Band-Aid-strewn guy on TV catching the kitchen drapes on fire when the homeowner tried to relight the pilot light with a match. He was having fun creating destruction with no thought of the consequences. Maybe she needed to be more like him.

The bell on Carnac's collar pinged as her nail hit it, and the cat jumped, his claws digging into her leg. He was jittery from having been jammed in a box for the trip over here. It was either that, or the garish, modern art paintings of blocks of color were getting to him, too.

Most of her stuff was still at her old apartment, and if things didn't improve fast, she was going to grab her toothbrush and her cat, and go home. The more time she put between her and the doubts that Silas had instilled, the more foolish and unlikely they seemed. If not for Jack, currently standing at her box of talismans beside the empty shelf, she might be doubting herself.

Maybe this is the first stages of MEP.

As if her thoughts had stimulated the hallucination, Jack turned, holding up a stuffed doll wearing a kimono. "Where, by the sweet fires of hell, did you get this?"

"Like I know?" She stood and brushed cat hair from her. That none of the things in that box held any real meaning was grating. Allen claimed it was because they hadn't defragmented the memories attached to them, but she had doubts— if Jack's poking around in them meant anything. Allen had cleared the shelf above the TV for her to display them, but she didn't have the heart for it. He'd only just left, and she was restless. The cat box had made it over here, but the cat's food hadn't, and so he'd gone out for some.

Peri wandered into the kitchen, cringing when she opened the fridge; she wasn't going to turn into Allen's mother and start cleaning. But the sight of three pouches of cat food stopped her cold. "I thought . . . ," she muttered, glancing at Carnac twining around her feet in the throes of starvation. "I'm sorry, Carnac. It was here all the time."

On the other side of the living room, Jack snickered. He was fingering a scrap of woven cloth that meant nothing to her. Now she remembered having put the pouches in there, and she grabbed one, opening a cupboard to find a saucer. The lapse wasn't like her, and uneasy, she put the remaining cat food in the pantry where it belonged.

"Give me a sec," she protested as she tore one open. The cat jumped onto the counter before she could put the bowl on the floor, and she laughed.

"Good grief, you're *not* starving," she said as she put first the bowl, then the cat on the floor. Carnac hunched into it, ignoring her last fondle behind his ears as she arranged the collar so the hourglass pattern was obvious.

They brought my knitting over, she thought, seeing the canvas bag beside the couch, and then she remembered telling Allen she was going to finish the scarf this weekend. "Why did I put the cat food in the fridge?" she said as she plopped on the couch.

Jack walked between her and the fireplace, startling her. "How else would you get Allen out of the apartment? Anything but cat food could wait until morning." He shuffled in her box of talismans. "He's driving you nuts."

She shrugged, liking Jack's idea better than the thought that she was so stressed she was gaslighting herself. "Yeah?" she muttered, wondering if the place was bugged. Maybe she should stop talking to Jack. *Jack, can you still hear me?* she thought.

"No," he said, confusing her. "Come look at this. You think this is real, or something Bill's wife picked up at a yard sale?"

"Oh. My. God. Talk about pegging your ugly meter." Peri levered herself up, becoming increasingly comfortable with the hallucination. Silas had said Jack betrayed her, but how could she be angry at a hallucination? What bothered her more was that Jack really wasn't holding the seashell with the mermaid stuck to it. It was still in the box, and she didn't want to know what kind of mental gymnastics her mind was doing to try to reconcile the difference.

Peri wouldn't take it until he put it down and her reality and her imagination became one. The garish thing felt dead when she picked it up. "This isn't mine," she said as she set it on the empty shelf. "I'd never pick something so gaudy as a talisman."

On sudden impulse, she pulled the picture of her and Jack out from inside her bra, unfolding it and propping it up against the shell. A slow smile crossed her face, and Jack put his hands into his pants pockets, rocking from heel to toe in satisfaction as they looked at it together. It felt right, but her smile faded as she recalled Howard and . . . Taf, was it? She hadn't remembered them, though it was obvious they remembered her. Taf, especially, seemed hurt that she'd forgotten them.

"It's okay, babe," Jack said as he shifted the picture so the crease down the middle wasn't so obvious. "You're too tense to remember what day it is. I used to have to wait almost twelve hours after you drafted before I could bring anything back. This is normal."

He wasn't really there, but it was comforting anyway. Maybe all it took was time.

"*That* looks like a real talisman," he added, his

hands on his hips as he looked at the bent picture. "Too bad Silas folded it. You want me to fix it?"

"You can do that?" she said, and he ran a finger down the picture, making it whole and unblemished in her mind.

Wow, she thought, an odd feeling spiraling up through her. Breath held, she picked it up, her mind having erased the fold to leave a pristine image. Her trembling finger traced her contented smile, and as she wished for that same peace to find her now, a memory of Jack and herself unfolded itself in her mind like a rose opening to the rain.

"Peri!" Jack exclaimed as she shuddered. The heat of a thousand summers slammed into her. Her heart pounded, and she heard the chanting of ancient words, felt the haze of raw alcohol fermented from the roots of plants she'd never seen before, smiled up at Jack in the contented lassitude of knowing that they were touching the ages, part of an endless circle.

It was a memory, a real memory, and she clutched the picture to herself. "Oh, Jack," she whispered, not wanting to open her eyes and see the cruel travesty that Silas had cursed her with. Jack was dead. She didn't remember how, or when, but she knew that she had loved him and he had been her anchor.

Allen was the imposter. Silas was telling the truth. It had to have been a memory knot, but instead of fear, it filled her with hope. Silas was right.

Jack . . .

Peri's eyes opened, and she sobbed once—only once—at the hallucination, his head bowed as if he was feeling the same pain. She'd killed him after finding out he'd lied to her for three entire years. It hurt looking at him—even if it really wasn't him. "You once loved me," he said softly as she propped the photo up with the reverence she reserved for her talismans.

Blinking fast, she nudged the photo straight. Allen was lying to her. Bill was lying to her. She wanted Silas to be telling her the truth, but that memories could not only be destroyed but created from nothing was almost too scary to think about. They could make her whatever they wanted. She had to get out of here before they made her into something she wasn't.

Suddenly she had to find out. "I have to get out of here," she whispered.

"How?" Jack sat down, dejected, feet spread wide. "Silas said you were tagged. If you leave, they'll just track you down."

Peri ran her fingers in a quick staccato across the shelf. "Time to do a scar tally," she said, pace fast as she strode to the bathroom.

Heart pounding, she waited for the light to flicker on. In a sudden flurry, Peri stripped down to her bra and panties, feet appreciating the heated tiles. The shoulder burn was the newest. That she had no memory of it was disturbing, especially when Silas claimed they'd burned her apartment. The scar on her knee was from learning how to ride a unicycle when she was twelve. The one on her forehead just below her hairline was from running into a door. The jagged punctures on her arm were from a guard dog. A long one on her thigh was a knife wound. Jennifer had been her anchor at the time and she'd been livid. But for the others, she didn't have a clue.

Fingers sliding from her skin, Peri's smile faded. There was a lump on her elbow that might or might not be a scar, and a tiny line on her shoulder, out of sight unless she used a mirror. "Well?" she asked the hallucination now standing dead center in the open doorway. The line on her shoulder was almost nonexistent, but it looked fairly new, and if they did it right, it wouldn't leave any scar worth seeing.

"I think me being dead is a real shame, babe."

Peri's eyes met his in the mirror. "Stop it. Is this it?"

He shook his head. "No. There's a newer one on your ass."

"No way!" Peri spun in a circle trying to see it. "How do you know?"

"You felt it in the tub," he said, and she thought back, remembering noticing a tiny bump the size of a rice grain the last time she took a soak.

"Are you kidding me?" she muttered, fingers palpating the smooth skin to find a hard knot. How was she going to get that out? She couldn't even see it.

"You could ask Silas. . . ."

Frustrated, she set the mirror down, yanked her panties back up, and grabbed Allen's robe hanging on a hook.

"Oh, babe," Jack protested as she tied it closed.

"I'm not running around his apartment naked," she said, tugging open a drawer and pawing through the masculine stuff to find a scalpel, razor blade, anything. She blinked at the two-pack of condoms, thinking it was better than finding drugs. Then she found the drugs, taking a moment to study what they were, first relieved, then concerned when they weren't recreational but medicinal, heavy hitters to put a person down fast.

No usable blade. She tried the kitchen next, pulling drawers out to expose the cavern behind them as she searched. She found the weapons cache behind the microwave, and she whistled, drawing Jack closer as she used a dishtowel to reach in and pull out the largest.

"That's a semiautomatic night-fire scout," the hallucination said, his gun envy showing.

"How do you know?" Peri said as she set it back in its cubby. "I don't know that."

"Your unconscious does," he said. "You must

have been listening when I made out my Christmas list."

Maybe I was, she thought as she struggled to put the microwave back in place. But now she was curious, and she began searching in earnest, her anger fueling her as she found weapon after weapon tucked away behind drawers and false-backed cupboards. Ten minutes later, Peri came up for air, evidence of her rummaging subtle apart from the soot spotting the hearth from her investigation of the flue. She'd found a passable emergency surgical kit in the laundry closet, but that was the least of her new treasures.

They never should have left me alone, she thought, as she took the kit and a roll of paper towels and returned to the bathroom. Her heart thudded as she slipped out of Allen's robe and carefully laid out what she needed.

Again Jack hovered in the doorway, brow pinched in concern. "Best to do it fast," he offered. "Pretend it's a dart. You've been hit with those before."

"I'll take your word for it." Peri awkwardly shifted her bare ass up onto the counter, twisting her torso to try to see. "Am I in the right spot?"

"Like I'd know?"

She sighed, feeling the muscle with one finger and holding the scalpel awkwardly between a finger and thumb. They were cramping up, but she held her breath and made a cut. Blood flowed, and she exhaled as she set the scalpel on a paper towel and grabbed an antiseptic wipe. She hissed as it met her skin, but the cut was bleeding like a stuck pig, and she quickly pulled several more paper towels free and applied pressure.

"Ah, babe . . ."

"Shut up," she muttered, feeling ill as she dabbed the blood until it slowed. Fingers squeezed her skin, her stomach lurching when a rice-size piece of something slid out.

Lip curled in distaste, she set the tiny chunk of electronics aside as she managed a wad of gauze and tape. The cut was small, but a regular Band-Aid wouldn't be enough. Only after she had Allen's robe around her again and checked to see that her blood was on nothing but the scalpel and the paper towels did she look to see what she'd pulled out.

"They gave me a goddamned butt bug," Peri said, nudging it with a finger before she cut another piece of surgical tape and stuck the bug to it.

"You did good, Peri. I'm proud of you."

Pissed, she looked up at Jack. He was sunburned now, his blond hair streaked as if from the desert and dirt on his nose. Resolute, Peri padded into the bedroom and taped the bug to the underside of the bed. Carnac was under there, his eyes big and scared from her taking everything apart, probably. Her butt hurt as she got up off the floor, but she was more angry than anything else.

Peri quickly returned to the bathroom to gather the evidence of her surgery and take it to the fireplace. It started with a whoosh, and she sat beside her box of treasures that were not hers. Carnac leapt up onto her lap, and she absently petted him. With the tracker out, she could move freely, but she'd have to remember to take it whenever she left so as to maintain the illusion it was still in her. "How am I going to fix this, Carnac?" Peri said, brow furrowed. "Who names a cat Carnac, anyway?" she added, a hand running all the way to the base of his tail.

And then her head snapped up. Jack had named him. Carnac was *their* cat.

"Jack?" she whispered, not seeing him, and he appeared in the kitchen with a bottle of wine in his hand. "You named Carnac, right?"

He nodded, and she gave the cat a hug. She knew it. She didn't know how, but she knew it. No one had claimed him. He had walked into her life as if he knew her because he did. He was *her* cat, and he was real. Those weren't hourglasses on his collar, they were dagazes.

Silas said something about a chip with corrupt Opti agents.

"Check his collar," Jack said, but she was already fingering the clasp. The little bell tinged to make Carnac jump away when the collar slipped free. "Opti couldn't find it because it was on the cat. It's the only thing that still exists from our apartment."

"My apartment," she muttered, standing up fast and slowing when her butt throbbed. There was a magnifying glass in the bathroom, and she turned the bathroom lights up high and angled it on the collar, looking for anything out of the ordinary.

Nothing. A feeling of desperation crept into her. Maybe it was hidden behind the embroidery, but she doubted it even as she felt for any telltale bump.

"The bell," Jack suggested, and she twisted it under the light. Her breath fogged the glass. Impatient, she wiped it clear with the cuff of Allen's robe.

"Something is stuck on the inside," she whispered. *A chip?* she thought, eyes widening as she saw that was exactly what it was.

She pulled back, vertigo washing through her as she felt her life spill through the cracks of the lies, settling into a new, unknown pattern. *My God. What if it's all true?* Peri's heart pounded, and she clenched the bell until it bit into her palm.

"It's probably encoded. Call Silas," Jack said as he took a sip of wine that didn't exist.

Her head dropped, and her hand slowly opened. She'd washed the ink off, but enough of a shadow remained to read it. To trust him was asking a lot.

"You don't trust him?" Jack asked, and she brought her head up, staring at the ceiling as if it held the answer.

"I'm going to have to," she whispered.

Jack turned to the door and her eyes widened at the sound of a car in the lot. Allen? He was back already?

"Shit," she whispered, panicking as she rushed to attach Carnac's bell to her key chain. Stuffing it back in her purse, she ran to the photo of her and Jack, a feeling of indecision filling her as she held it. There was nowhere she could keep it safe, and she couldn't risk it turning up and raising questions. "I'm sorry, Jack," she said as she dropped the photo into the fireplace and the flames licked the paper. *I'm so sorry. But I do have you. I can never forget you.*

"Hi, Allen!" Peri called out, turning with a smile as the front door opened. "You think I could have some space in the bathroom for my things? Two drawers, maybe?"

I can do this, she thought as he smiled back and held up a bag of cat food and ice cream. *Even without an anchor.*

CHAPTER
THIRTY-THREE

Peri held her phone to her ear as she sat at the kitchen bar and chased the last of the marshmallow clovers around the bowl. She'd always eaten the clovers last, ever since she was a little girl. *To give me luck for the day. And I need the* *luck,* she thought, listening with half her attention to the phone ring. She wanted to meet Silas and give him the chip, but contacting him would be tricky and she couldn't do it from her apartment.

Her phone had a bug in it, which was fine so long as she said the right thing. Allen was in the bedroom, drugged from his own pharmaceutical cache after she got him relaxed enough last night not to notice the needle. They were high-quality drugs and he'd wake with no headache, no bad taste, and no reason to check the levels of the tiny bottles. Good news was he'd be out for about four hours. Bad news was that the drugs were probably there to be used on her.

"Hello. Opti Health."

She slid off the stool. Carnac twined hopefully about her feet, and she set the bowl of sweet milk on the floor. "Ah, hi. This is Peri Reed. I'm calling for Allen Swift and myself," she said as she went to the window and peeked out the blind. "I'd like to switch our morning appointment to this afternoon. We had a late night, and he's got a headache the size of Montana."

The busy street was empty of any Opti presence, not even a drone. There was no need, not with that tracker telling them she was still in bed. She had to talk to Silas.

"Yes, ma'am. Three thirty, okay?" came the operator's voice, and Peri closed the blinds.

"Yes. We'll be there." Leaving her phone on the counter, she went to check on Allen.

"Sleep well, sweetheart," she whispered as she checked his pulse. "I'd bring you back a doughnut, but then you'd know I'd been gone." Turning, she looked at her reflection in the mirror, seeing the fatigue under the highlights and base. "Where's my effin' two weeks off, *Bill?*" she whispered as she touched up the heavy eyeliner trailing a good three inches off the sides of her eyes. It was overly dramatic for eight in the morning but, along with the artful cheekbone contouring, would change her face enough that the street cameras wouldn't tag her.

Satisfied, she tucked her pen pendant beneath her shirt and tugged the hem of the jacket she'd put on to try to hide a garish, flower-patterned top. Her eyes narrowed at her hair bumping about at her shoulders. Her mother would like it, but it needed to be cut, a liability in a fight.

Striding into the kitchen, she removed a drawer to reveal Allen's knives hidden behind it. She'd made her choice last night in her search, and she slipped the slimmest into her boot sheath. Purse over her shoulder, she checked to be sure the door would lock before she stepped into the hall. The air was pleasantly cool, and after a quick look up and down the hall, she wedged a fortune cookie slip between the door and the jamb, placing it a finger's span above the floor to tell her if anyone had entered or left while she was gone.

The streets were alive, and she enviously eyed the occasional steaming cup of coffee as she made her way to the elevated train. She hadn't slept well beside Allen. Inconsistencies kept pinging against the top of her brain. It wasn't so much what she remembered as what she didn't. She recalled eating a meal, but not buying the food to prepare it with. She remembered jogging in the park with Allen, but not where she'd gotten the shoes she'd been wearing. She could remember the movies they'd gone to see, but not waiting in line for the tickets or getting the popcorn she ate. They'd lied to her. The people she'd trusted her entire adult life had lied to her, filling her with memories and ideas that were not her own—and she was pissed.

It was a short ride to her old apartment at Lloyd Park, but as she got off the sky way, her steps faltered. Everything was familiar: the neon, the tidy streets, the commons with clusters of people enjoying the spring morning at the fountain. She knew what she'd see when she looked down the side streets, the trendy shops the same as they were five years ago. The feeling of coming home hit her, a sensation lacking in the rooms she was living in now. This was where she'd felt secure, knowing every side street and alley, every dress shop and boutique, every trendy restaurant. And it hurt.

"It's okay, babe," Jack said, seeming to take an extra-long step to suddenly be there.

"Yeah?" Startled, she sniffed back a tear, shocked to see it. "I always liked this neighborhood," she added as she turned to her old apartment.

"Me too. Ahh, I hate to say this, but you're being followed. Ever since the train."

Of course I am, she thought sourly, scrambling for a lie that Opti would believe and wondering where she'd slipped up.

But there was no fear, only anger. Eager for it, she took a quick left into an alley, putting her back to the wall and fishing out her pen. Cap between her teeth, she scrawled GO TO ALLEN'S to hide Silas's number in case she drafted. She didn't need an anchor. She could function alone.

Jack peeked around the corner as she recapped the pen and tucked it away. Hands in fists, she planted her feet firmly on the stained concrete. Masculine, fast-paced steps were coming, and she clenched her teeth so she wouldn't bite her lip.

Silent, she attacked as the man spun into the alley, planting her foot into his gut. He fell back with a surprised grunt, and she followed it with a fist to his chest, knocking him into the wall. Teeth clenched, she grabbed his shoulder and shoved him upright so she could see his face.

"Ow-w-w-w-w," Silas groaned, and shocked, she let him go.

"Silas?" Face warm, she backed up. Silas was

hunched over, his back to the brick wall; then he slid to the cold concrete to look like a mugged businessman in his dressy coat, pressed shirt, and tie. Silent electric cars and Sity bikes passed at the end of the alley, not seeing them.

"I didn't throw Allen over the balcony," he rasped, one hand on his middle, the other out in an attempt to placate. "Let me explain. God bless it, I think you cracked a rib."

Embarrassed, she winced. "I thought you were Opti. And I didn't hit you that hard."

He looked up, his eyes holding recrimination, and she belatedly reached to help him. He waved her off, refusing to take her hand as he pulled himself upright, expression sour as he brushed his coat off with short, angry motions.

"Hey, um, are you okay?" she said. "I'm sorry I hit you. Both times. You should know better than to follow me."

"It seemed like a good idea at the time." Silas felt his ribs. "What are you doing here? Jesus, you look like a pirate with all that eye makeup."

"It helps throw off the facial recognition," she said. "And I was looking for a clean phone to call you on." Her fingers curled to hide the message to herself. "There's one in the lobby of my old apartment, and they won't give me any guff about using it. I want asylum."

His gaze sharpened on her. "You believe me that Opti is corrupt?"

"Enough to be talking to you." Her heart thudded, her thoughts going to the bell on her key chain. "I think I found the chip you wanted." He had said it would end everything. She didn't care who was corrupt anymore—she just wanted out.

"I watched them burn your apartment." Silas's expression was thick with irritation as he looked out the top of the alley and into the bright sun. "I doubt what you found is what we need."

Peri's lip twitched . . . and then she let the anger go. Her talismans didn't matter anymore. Her past didn't matter anymore. "It was in the bell on my cat's collar. Jack gave me that cat. He's not a stray; he found me. I don't know why Opti let me keep him." Peri glanced at Silas, seeing a cautious hope. "Maybe they thought he was just a cat."

He went still in thought, then slowly put his arm in hers. Together they stepped out into the bright light and sporadic foot traffic. It was a beautiful spring morning, the wind off the nearby engineered lake cleanly lifting through her hair. Their feet struck the sidewalk in exactly the same cadence, and she wished she could enjoy it like everyone else shopping around her.

"You found the chip on your cat?"

His brow was high in disbelief, bothering her. "Yes. Last night while ransacking Allen's apartment looking for something to cut the LoJack out of my ass," she said, sarcasm thick. "And if you laugh, I'll hit you again. You said you'd give me asylum if I could find the chip. Well?"

"Mmmm," he said lightly, his pace never changing. "You owe me a coat."

His response took Peri by surprise. "I what?"

"Owe me a coat," he repeated, angling her across the busy commons to the shops and weaving around the dog walkers and couples having breakfast at the fountain. "This one has someone's slushy on it."

She leaned to look. "Sorry," she said, meaning it, and then a wide smile came over her as she saw where they were headed. "Mules?" she said, liking the upscale men's and women's clothier. "You got enough for this, pretty man?"

"You're paying," he said, reaching out to open the door for her as the simulated mannequins in the window "saw" and responded to them. "Besides, you need a cover story in case you get caught. You could buy yourself a new blouse. You *should* buy yourself a new blouse," he amended, and she looked down at the patterned monstrosity.

"Yeah," she said softly as the young woman in her skintight office dress rose from a round table covered in swatches and several open laptops. The boutique looked more like a redecorating store than a clothier, with drapes of fabric artfully arranged between the clusters of couches. A refreshment bar and two low stages were set in the center of the store, roughly dividing it into his and hers.

"Welcome to Sim's Mules. Can I help you?" the young woman said, and the older woman still at the round table returned to her work.

"I need a new coat," Silas said as he took his off and handed it to her. "She needs help," he added. "Lots of it."

Peri grimaced.

"Of course. I'm Kelly," she said as she handed the coat in turn to an assistant dressed to look like a behind-the-scenes prop man. Tsking, he took it to the center counter to clean it.

"If you'd like to step into the scanner, we can find your perfect fit," Kelly said, hiding a wince as Peri fingered an especially fine drape of rough silk. "We usually require an appointment, but it's slow this morning. The weather is so nice outside."

"I'm on file," Silas said. "So is she."

Peri turned to him as Kelly's entire demeanor shifted three tax brackets up. "I am?"

Silas took the palm-size keypad Kelly had enthusiastically handed him. "We are two blocks from your old apartment," he said as he typed in first his, then her name. "You're on file."

Kelly beamed at the cheerful ding, turning to see the two holograms that shimmered into existence at one of the stages. "You're on file," she said happily as the two mules in their silk boxers and black panties and chemise began to interact with each other on basic programming.

"Welcome back, Ms. Reed. Dr. Denier," Kelly said as she took the keypad and read the screen. "Have a seat and feel free to look through the catalog. I've put you at table three. I'll be right back with some refreshments. Coffee mocha for you, ma'am?" she said, glancing at her readout. "Straight black for you, Doctor?"

Peri didn't remember setting up her profile, but the simulation "talking" to Silas's double looked up-to-date. "Sure," she said, not realizing until just that moment how wide Silas's shoulders were. And was she really that short beside him?

She stifled a shiver as Silas set a light hand on the small of her back, escorting her to the small table overlooking the commons, bright with light and busy with people living their lives. She could see everything, and for the first time in ages, she felt safe. But then her butt gave a twinge and her tension swung back around as she tried to find a comfortable position.

"Can't try on coats half dressed," Silas said as he swiped through one of the two glass catalogs and quickly chose a classic pair of black pants, striped shirt, and matching tie. Peri's mule clapped her hands and jumped, showing her belly button, and Peri hid a smile. Marketing at its finest. But even she had to admit it looked good. She glanced sidelong at Silas. Really good.

"I'm going to change your drink," he said, eyes furtive as he suddenly stood. "Trust me?"

"With my drink order, sure," she said. "What are you really doing?"

He chuckled sheepishly. "Calling Howard. He's going to want to run his bug detector over you before I bring you in."

Peri leaned back in the cushions, arms over her chest. "Yeah, I wouldn't trust me either."

"Oh, stop looking for shoes to throw," he said sourly. "I'm going to be right over there. Pick yourself out something. That blouse is awful."

"I think Allen bought it," she said, mollified as she pulled the second tablet to herself and brought up the women's section.

"It looks like something he'd like," he said, already walking away, and Peri smiled.

But it faded fast, and her gaze fell to her palm where her message to herself stood out in harsh letters. Opti would never let her out, unless it was in a body bag.

Mood tarnished, she quickly dressed her mule in a tight, thigh-high evening dress, a wash of color at the collar to show off her slim neck and a pair of six-inch heels to bring her closer to Silas's mule's height. They looked good enough for a night on the town—a really expensive night—and she started, sighing when Jack's presence was suddenly standing beside her. "I hope you like what he brings back," he said as he sat down, his

514

arms spread across the back of the wide chair to own the space. His suit rivaled the one Silas's mule wore on the stage, now sharing a glass of not-there wine with her double.

"Me too." Fidgeting, she turned to Silas at the center counter, talking on his own phone. "It's probably some foo-foo drink with too much sugar."

"I meant," Jack said, pulling her attention back, "I hope you like the memories he brings back. He wants to, you know. Damn psychologist anchor."

Peri frowned. She was here to buy her way out of Opti, not defragment memories. Besides, how would she know what was real and what was false?

"Here he comes," Jack said as Silas approached, two ceramic mugs in his hands.

"Try this," Silas said as he put the one with the cinnamon stick before her with a satisfied firmness. "I guarantee you'll like it."

Silas began to sit, and she watched in amazement when Jack all but fell out of the chair, scrambling to get out of the way and swearing as he strove to maintain the illusion that he was real. Oblivious, Silas took his place, clearly eager for her to try the frothy, steamy drink.

It looked like it had too much milk, but she took a taste, turning it into a long draft when she found it creamy but not too rich, spicy without hiding the nutty flavor. Eyes closing, she held a swallow on her tongue, savoring it. "That's good," she said, and Silas beamed, sipping his own straight-up black coffee. "You're an anchor, aren't you," she said, and he hesitated. The all-too-familiar feeling of having said something stupid came over her. She should know that already.

"Sort of." Silas drew his tablet back to himself. "How did you guess?"

Peri stared out at the commons, trying to let it go. "Trained anchors have a feel about them that's easy enough to pick up on. You've never worked in the field before, though."

"You're not nearly smart enough," Jack said snidely as he fingered a display of silk ties.

"You're not nearly careful enough," she said, wishing Jack would shut up. Silas had said he was tied to her intuition. Apparently something about Silas bugged her. Smiling, Peri hoisted the coffee. "Thank you. This is good."

"I saw your diary. When I was an unwilling guest at Opti," Silas added at her sudden disquiet. "I'm sure half of it was invented to scare me, but they left enough of you in there to convince me it wasn't fake. It's something you said you liked last year, so . . ."

Not knowing if she should be flattered or creeped out, Peri watched their mules interact. "You figured I wouldn't remember it. No, I don't. Thank you. I appreciate you giving this back to me."

"Blah, blah, blah." Scraping his blond hair out of his eyes, Jack tried on a black tie. "You have an expiration date, babe. Cut to the chase."

Silas was clearly pleased. "I thought it might make you feel more like yourself."

"It does." Peri leaned back, ankles crossed as she tried to relax, not liking that he knew more about her than she did. "How long until Howard gets here? I left Allen doped up, and if I'm not there when he wakes, they'll know I pulled the tracker."

Head down, Silas looked through the coats, trying several on to make Peri's mule clap her hands. "He's on his way. How are you doing?"

Jack snorted, and, surprised, her head rose. "How am I doing? Seriously?"

Silas looked up. "Yes. How are you doing? I can't ask that?"

Peri darted a look at Jack, now on the stage with the other beautiful pretend people. "I'm pretty confused right now," she said sarcastically. "Forgive me, but I've got this memory of you shoving Allen through a window—"

"That's fake," he interrupted.

"We know that, dumbass," Jack said loudly, and Peri set her mug down hard.

"I know that." She hadn't meant it to sound nasty, but that's how it came out, and she touched his hand to convince him she wasn't mad. "It would take more than the weight of one man to break the window. It's supposed to be bullet-proof." She furrowed her brow, angry at herself for having trusted so blindly.

"Do you want me to fragment these fake memories?" Silas said, and she shook her head. It was all she had, false or not. "You don't trust me yet," Silas said. "That's okay."

Annoyed, she shifted her mug around. "It's not about trust. It's about me needing to make the right responses, and if you take them away, I won't. You were an Opti psychologist, weren't you? Until Opti fired you?"

He stiffened. "I *quit* Opti. They didn't fire me."

Peri took a deep breath, ready to broach what had been on her mind since last night. "Silas, that picture you gave me triggered a memory knot of Jack and me."

Silas's expression blanked. "Are you okay? Have any more snarled up?"

"No. And I don't know why except that the knot was of a real memory, not twin timelines," she said, wanting him to say it would be okay. *How could something that beautiful be bad?* "Even if Jack was lying to me, even if he was a bastard and used me, I felt centered that night. Beautiful. Safe." Silas followed her gaze to the simulations, not seeing Jack standing beside her and Silas's mules like a jealous boyfriend.

"Mmmm." Silas's sudden worry was obvious. "He's here now, right?"

She nodded and Jack blew a sarcastic kiss at them. "Here comes the psychobabble BS," Jack said. "Ignore it, babe. He doesn't have a clue what's going on."

"I wouldn't worry about the memory knot," Silas said. "As long as they aren't centered around twin timelines, they're just your way to remember artificially destroyed memories."

Artificially destroyed . . . They can do that?

"But what about Jack?" she asked, setting her outrage aside for the moment. Opti had lied to her about everything else, why not the missing time associated with a draft, too?

Silas shrugged. "Frankly, I'm surprised he hasn't broken up. But if he's still there, then the twin timelines I left in you are still there, too."

"You left twin timelines in me?" she whispered hotly, lowering her voice when the man cleaning Silas's coat intruded to hang it up on the purchase rack near her chair. Warm, Peri leaned over the table. "What kind of an anchor are you?"

"A damn good one. You're still sane, aren't you?" he said tightly, eyes on the man as he went into the back room. That was debatable, and he shifted under her accusing stare. "The proof that Opti is corrupt is in your mind. I couldn't fragment either line without destroying the truth," he finally admitted. "I tied three years of latent memories of Jack to your intuition so the inevitable hallucinations would distract you from tearing your mind apart. Peri, I'd take you in to the alliance myself and defrag them, but without something to prove your loyalty to them, they'll scrub you themselves."

Scrub as in artificially destroy. Peri slumped in the seat and stared at him, her trust in Opti falling utterly apart. "I'm just a big Etch A Sketch, huh? Don't like what you see? Give me a good shake, and write what you want." It was getting easier to say, but the bitterness was chiseled deeper with every new realization.

"That's not true. Peri, you're in control of your own destiny."

"Bull," she said calmly, angry as she turned off her mule so she wouldn't have to look at it up there with Silas and Jack. "My actions stem from what I remember, and my memories are a made-up mix of lies and falsehoods. And now you tell me the years I've lost are *artificial?*" she said, voice rising. "I trusted my anchor to tell me what decision to make until I remembered everything—and he betrayed me. *Don't* tell me I'm in control of my destiny until you've lived without knowing what's real and what's not."

Her soul hurt, and she didn't want to talk about it anymore. On the stage, Silas's mule became sad, straightening his tie and tugging his coat as if finding his courage to start again.

"I want asylum, Silas. Can you give it to me or not?"

Silas rubbed the back of his neck and turned his simulation off as well. With a snort, Jack wandered away, heading for the half-dressed mules in the front window. Peri hoped he'd leave. "If that's the chip we want? Probably," Silas said. "Let me see it."

She pulled her purse up and onto her lap. "God help me," she said as she took out her keys and wedged the bell off the key ring. Damn it, she was going to trust him, and she watched herself, unbelieving when she just gave it to him.

The bell looked tiny in his hand, and he squinted at the chip. "Huh," he said softly. "How lucky is it that he put it on the one thing that made it out of your apartment."

She nodded. The collar had dagazes all over it, but only she or Jack would know that made it important. "That cat is the only thing that feels real to me. Apart from my car and a bag of yarn," she said.

Silas tucked the bell away. "If Howard says it's the list, I'll call you."

Her head snapped up. "Call! I want to go now," she complained, and Kelly, coming to check on them, turned and went back into the back room.

Mistrust flared when he shook his head. "Opti doesn't know you broke the memory implants, do they?" Silas said. "You should be okay for a day or two. Once we get it uncoded, the alliance will grant you asylum."

"This sucks," she said bitterly. Maybe she wasn't as nice as she thought. She had killed her own anchor, after all—and she'd *loved* him. "Please don't betray me. If you do, I'll have to kill you." Angry at herself for having trusted him, she stood. "I'll probably have to kill you anyway, but I'd rather do it because I was told to, not because you lied to me."

"Peri . . ." In a rush, Silas stood. Breath held, she waited, making a fist around her note to herself, hiding it. "Peri, about Jack." He hesitated until she looked up. "If you have an issue with Jack not suppressing the twin lines, any at all, forget Opti and find me. Try not to draft in the meantime. Even in the best case, Jack will be able to repress the twin timelines only so long, and then you will—"

"Yes, I know, MEP," she finished, the threat so constant it had lost a lot of its bite. "Don't call me. I'll call you. Tomorrow. If I run, don't follow me. Got it?"

She turned and walked out. Hunched into her coat, she hustled back to the elevated, feeling Silas's eyes on her every step of the way. Her heart pounded as she took the stairs, her world seeming to shift and realign to something new and far more dangerous.

"Jack?" she whispered, and he was suddenly beside her on the stair.

"Yes, Peri?"

She halted on the platform, the wind in her hair fresher as she looked straight up into the camera, not caring if it recognized her. All she had was this instant. To try to remember her past would drive her insane. But for the first time, she found strength in it, not fear.

"Don't leave me yet," she said. She'd seen what happened when drafters fell into memory-eclipsed paranoia. Unable to trust anyone, they usually killed themselves to make the confusion stop.

"Never," he said, and somehow, she thought that even more dangerous.

CHAPTER
THIRTY-FOUR

Peri halted outside Allen's apartment door, her hand falling when she saw that the fortune cookie slip she'd left between the door and frame was gone. *Great.* "I'm going to go nucking futs," she breathed, glancing up and down the empty hallway.

She could walk away, find Silas, and hope to God that chip was Jack's list.

She could pretend she'd drafted and lost her memory of the entire morning, which would result in Opti rehab and ultimately another scrub.

She could admit that she'd taken out the tracker and be the pissed, angry drafter. She could let her temper go. She could demand some answers. Make a reckoning.

The choice was obvious, and squaring her shoulders, she tried the knob to find the door was unlocked. Tucking Allen's key in her purse, she walked into an empty, silent room. There was a small strip of medical tape on the kitchen counter, the tracking bug still stuck to it.

So it's going to be like that, then. "A-A-A-Allen!" she exclaimed, eyes narrowing at the small noise from the bedroom. "Get your ass out here. I've got some questions for you." She faced away from the bedroom door as she took off her coat, watching her back through the dim reflection of the closed fireplace doors. But she turned in surprise when it was not Allen but Bill who walked out, dressed in his usual suit and tie, his office shoes gleaming and his hair combed to perfection—a soothing, utterly convincing smile on him.

Peri, you work with actors, she thought as she finished folding her coat and let it fall on the couch. *And not lame ones, either,* she added as Allen shuffled out behind Bill in his pajama bottoms and a white shirt, still rumpled and stubbly from sleep but very much awake.

"Peri," he said darkly, rubbing his arm where she'd injected him. "What the hell are you doing?"

"My question exactly," she said with a bold confidence she wasn't sure she could back up.

Maybe the medical office had called Bill, since he was the one who had set up the original appointment. "Should I be pissed at Allen or you about the butt bug?"

Bill's smile widened as if it was a big joke. "Me. It was for your safety."

"Bullshit." Arms crossed, she sucked on her teeth, eyes flicking from one to the other as the men exchanged a silent look that screamed volumes. They were both in on it. She hadn't been sure until just now. "Bill, can I have a private word?"

"Ah, hey . . ." Allen lurched forward only to be jerked to a halt by Bill's raised hand.

"I think that is an excellent idea. Allen, make some coffee."

"And keep the drugs out of it," Peri added as she crossed the living room to the den, standing outside it as she pushed the door open with one arm and waited for Bill.

Clearing his throat, Bill rocked into motion. Peri's eye twitched as he passed within inches of her, smelling of cologne and his breakfast. Pulse fast, she followed him, shutting the door and leaning back against it. Bill was standing with his rump resting on the edge of the desk. Reaching a foot out, Peri closed the lid to the laptop to prevent any easy eavesdropping.

Bill watched until her foot was back on the floor. Then he sighed, playing the part of the concerned boss. "You want to explain why you drugged Allen and took a walk?"

Peri pushed off the door and sat in the swivel chair across from the desk. Best to keep as much to the truth as she could. "Shopping. I want a new anchor. Today. I've tried working with that man and it's not happening. He's slow on locks. I've never *seen* him drive. He won't spar with me, so I only have his word he's good at unarmed combat. All he's done is make waffles and plane reservations! His lousy recon put my memory in jeopardy last night. Forgive me if I didn't want him with me when I picked out some new clothes, because what's in my closet sucks. I don't trust him, Bill. Something is wrong. I can feel it in my gut."

Bold, demanding, and ticked off. It might work. It might not. A lot depended on how secure they thought their fake memories were.

Bill's almost hidden worry began to dissolve and a knot in her began to relax. "Your unease is simply an artifact of your recent memory loss," he said, pulling a tissue from the nearby box and coming closer.

"The one that *Allen* can't bring back," she muttered, forcing herself not to move when he leaned over her, his thick thumb wiping off her excessive eye makeup.

"You've always been slow on defragging your memory," Bill said soothingly, doing first one eye, then the other. "Don't put this black shit on yourself anymore. You have such a beautiful face. Such a long slender neck."

"I can't work with him, Bill," she said, taking the tissue and finishing the job herself. "I drugged him with his own pharmaceuticals, for crying out loud. I don't want him watching my back. He's dangerous, and not in a good way. Who else do you have coming up in the ranks? Anyone who can make a decent cup of coffee? That's a good start."

Bill settled back into the second chair, the leather creaking. She could practically see him thinking *What a bitch,* but since that's what she was going for, she didn't care. Smiling fondly, he shook his head, his heavy hands laced over his middle. "You were able to bring him down because he trusted you," he said, and she rolled her eyes. "I think you owe him an apology. But first, I want to know why you took the tracking device out."

"Because I'm not a dog?" she said loudly. "If I find one again, I'm done. I've managed this long without a proper anchor." Playing the wounded drafter, she put a hand to her mouth and stared at nothing. "Maybe I don't need one," she muttered.

She froze when Bill leaned forward and took her hand. Her pulse hammered, but she stayed carefully passive as he turned her hand palm up and rolled her fingers back. Her scrawl to return to Allen's apartment hid Silas's number. "Mmmm," he questioned.

"I wanted to be sure I got home," she said, sniffing as if embarrassed.

"Working without an anchor isn't an option."

Her head tilted, and she didn't need to fake her anger. "Then give me an anchor who knows his *job!*" she shouted, hoping Allen heard her.

Bill arched his eyebrows. He was seemingly convinced, but about what she wasn't sure. "I'll talk to him."

Exhaling, she tried to appear confident. "And no more butt bugs."

"No more butt bugs," he echoed, and her lips parted at his quick compliance.

"Really?"

Nodding at her disbelief, he reached behind his jacket to the inner pocket. "The alliance knows to look for them now," he said as he extended a small baggie holding a capsule. "Welcome to the latest and greatest."

Peri looked without reaching. "You want me to drop my pants and bend over?"

"I want you to swallow it," he said stiffly. "It's a low-dose radiation marker. It won't harm you, but it will stay in your system for a year. We will know where you are and where you've been. Even those you've been in contact with, to a limited degree. It's experimental, and only a team's handler knows the signature." He smiled.

"You're a ghost, Peri, the first Opti agent to get this. My best deserves the best."

Radiation marker? Mistrusting it, she hesitated as Bill encouraged her to take it. It could be anything: drugs to knock her out, poison to kill her. She could wake up in Allen's bed tomorrow having forgotten everything and she'd never know.

"You just happened to have one in your pocket?" she questioned.

He shrugged, not a wisp of guilt. "After your little walkabout this morning, I deemed it was time to take it out of research. You really cut that tracker out yourself?" he asked, laughing, and she hunched in embarrassment.

"It's not funny," she said, and after a last chuckle, his mirth ended.

"Take it."

His tone was flat, demanding. She hesitated, not sure how much he knew or suspected. But realizing it was going to end up in her one way or another, Peri slipped the capsule into her mouth and swallowed.

Immediately Bill's mood lightened. Smiling, he got to his feet, hand extended to help her rise. Her slim fingers looked tiny as they fitted into his, reminding her of him in the gym breaking boards and bringing down men. *My God, his hands are huge.*

"You're my best drafter, kiddo," Bill said, and

she jumped when his arm landed heavily across her shoulders and turned her to the door. "That comes with responsibility. We're not letting you out of our theoretical sight for even an instant."

Great, she thought, stomach rolling. If she threw up, would he make her take another? "So do I get a new anchor?"

"No," he said, and she drew him to a halt before they could leave. "I'll talk to Allen," he said in a fatherly tone. "Tell him to step it up. You worked well together before. I know you will again. He needs to find closure, too. He trusts you. Let go and trust him."

Like that was going to happen. "Bill . . . ," she warned, and he put his hands in the air as if in surrender.

"Okay, okay," he finally relented. "I'll talk to Sandy and see what we can do. I've got someone in mind, so don't mention this to Allen—just in case we can swing it. Deal?"

Eyeing him, she backed up from the door. "Deal," she echoed him as her heart pounded in her ears.

"I'm proud of you," he said softly as he opened the door. "You've come a long way."

As in a long way in becoming his tool. "I only want to be my best."

"You are already that," Bill said as he ushered her into the living room.

───── CHAPTER ─────
THIRTY-FIVE

Silas's friend's seats at Comerica Park were in the sun, and whereas it was usually too hot, today Silas felt good, the early-spring air still holding the morning's chill. Two hot dogs and bottled waters sat waiting beside him. He'd asked Peri to meet him here, and the thrum of anticipation running through his background thoughts ebbed and flowed with the noise of the crowd as the Tigers tried to bring the inning to a close.

The memory of sitting in these exact seats with Peri was an ache, but that wasn't why he had wanted to meet her here. The crowd itself gave them a measure of protection. The multitude of doors couldn't be locked. Even the park's security that Opti itself would have to contend with helped. But if he was honest, he had wanted to meet her here because Peri loved the game, and he was hoping memories she couldn't recall might help cushion his bad news.

Silas pulled his cap lower, hunching deeper into the hard seat. The chip she'd brought him wasn't the list. He was out of options, mistrusted by the alliance and an enemy of Opti. He was here to tell her to run and never stop.

Brow furrowed, Silas ran a hand over his freshly

shaven chin before resettling his sunglasses in a nervous twitch. His eyes roved over the stands thick with orange and blue, the noisy throng excited at the fresh beginning April always brought. Pulled by a familiar silhouette, Silas's gaze darted to one of the entrances.

God almighty, she looks good. It was a relief not to see her in those gaudy clothes that Allen must have picked out, more herself in her usual black slacks and a white blouse cut to show off her long neck. The sophistication was a little much for the stands, but the Detroit Tigers hat and sunglasses toned it down, and no one gave her more than a second glance.

His brow eased at a feeling of pride. No longer was she the deadly but anchor-dependent doll that Opti had made of her. Her fiery independence was reasserting itself through the cracks of Opti conditioning and lies—as long as he could keep them from scrubbing her again.

The crowd's noise swelled as she met his eyes. Unmoving on the stairs, she hesitated as if listening to something only she could hear, then scanned the stands for something only she could see. *Please don't run,* he thought as he stood, trying to convince her he only wanted to help. He took his glasses off, pleading with his eyes. Breath held, he waited . . . and finally she decided, head down and expression unreadable as she made her way up the final stairs.

Peri stopped at the head of the row. "Nice seats,"

she said, and an anxious need to do something filled Silas.

"They belong to a friend," he said as he picked up the box of hot dogs and edged down to give her his chair so she wouldn't have to slide past him. Behind them, a man complained about not being able to see, his tirade cutting off when Peri took her glasses off to stare at him.

"You look great," Silas said, and her expression shifted to one of surprise.

"I went shopping again. This time on Bill's tab and with a vengeance." Peri sat down, and Silas felt a knot ease. "I'm going to give everything in my closet to Goodwill. You look . . ."

"What?" Silas said, knowing his jacket and jeans were coarse next to her polished sophistication, but where Peri could get away with silk and linen at a ballpark, he couldn't.

A faint smile quirked her lips to erase a worry line. "Content."

Content? She thinks I look content? Flustered, he watched as her eyes lifted to the stands, and another level of tension was rubbed out by the announcer's patter and a stanza of music from the organ. It was the sound of summer, and it eased over him like the sun.

"Hot dog with mustard, no ketchup?" he said as he eagerly proffered the box.

"How . . . ," she started, eyes lighting up as she reached for it. "My diary?" she asked drily.

"Lucky guess this time," he lied.

"Sure it is," she said as she took it, startling Silas when her fingers brushed his.

It was how she liked them, and he couldn't help but watch her unwrap it, her eyes closing as she took a bite. Her *mmmm* of pleasure sent a shiver through him, and he warmed when she noticed, eyeing him askance as she chewed and swallowed.

"Me eating a hot dog makes you happy?" she questioned as she wiped the corner of her mouth with a pinky, and he felt himself flush deeper. "You're an easy date."

"Beautiful woman, beautiful day. What's not to like?" he fumbled, turning his attention to his own dog and trying not to look like a dork.

Peri sighed, but it wasn't a bad sound. "Silas, I'm not stupid."

He took a bite, glancing sideways at her. "I said you were beautiful, not stupid. Despite what popular media would have you believe, they are not mutually inclusive."

"I mean, we've done this before."

Shocked, he turned to face her. "You remember?"

"No, but you do. I've never seen you this relaxed."

"Funny how not having a gun pointed at you does that," he said.

"So . . ." She eyed him mischievously. "Were we like boyfriend-girlfriend?"

He choked on his hot dog. "Ask me tomorrow," he managed, feeling his neck go red.

"I might not remember you tomorrow." She crossed her knees. "Yesterday you followed me from Allen's apartment," she said as she put her dog down and reached for a water. "Knew exactly where to take me so I'd relax and maybe give you something you wanted."

His mouth went dry; he felt as if everything was unraveling. "It's not like that. I'm not manipulating you."

"Yes you are." She tried to open her water, but it wouldn't budge. "You're doing it now. Meeting me at the ballpark. Taking me to Mules. I love Mules. Reminding me of my *favorite* coffee. I'd be angry except I have the feeling that you're doing it for you as much as me."

"I am not!" he protested, but it sounded lame even to him.

"I'm willing to overlook it," she said as she gave up on the water and handed it to him. "But I want to know if you're doing it because you want to or because you have to?"

Discomfited, Silas cracked it for her. "What does your gut say?"

She took the bottle back, looking out over the field in silence. "Ask me tomorrow," she finally said. Sighing, she took a sip of water and set it down. "Howard has good news, yes?"

Silas cringed. He couldn't look at her, angry at himself, at Fran. Peri couldn't have known what that chip was. But even he had to admit the likelihood that Opti was using her even now.

"Not good news," Peri amended, her eyes empty of recrimination.

"Can't you let me enjoy even half an inning?" he grumbled.

Peri picked her dog back up. "You have until I'm done with this bodacious hot dog. Mmmm, you don't mess with the dog."

Silas settled back but the mood was broken. For a moment, they were both silent as the art of the game stole over them, of science and muscle, of physics and psychology.

"I remember coming here with my dad," Peri said, eyes on the field. "He taught me the game from the stands. The original park at the corner. My mom thought the park was filthy, and she didn't like the new boxes either, so that was kind of the end of it after he died."

Silas hunched, straightening when his jacket pulled. "Sorry to hear that."

Lips twisted into a smile, she looked at him and adjusted his hat. "But I'm here now, with you, Mr. Tomorrow."

Silas's jaw clenched. Her smile was perfect, the sun making her skin glow and her eyes vivid. He wanted to bring it all back, every little thing. But there was nothing left. Allen had wiped it all away. And he had helped.

I should have told her that I loved her, he thought, breath shallow. Maybe then she would have had a choice. But he'd hidden his love, giving her no choice but the one that Allen offered. And who wouldn't have chosen glory over an empty apartment? He was a fool, and all he could do now was try to give her the knowledge to save herself.

"You okay?" Peri asked, the sun glinting on the tips of her thick black hair.

"Fine," he said tightly, eyeing the park's drones. They were low-Q and harmless, but he didn't like how easy it would be to slip a high-Q, facial-recognition one among them. "How is Jack doing? Is he here?"

Peri cast about as she wiped her fingers on a napkin. "No," she said, sounding surprised. "And that makes you happy because . . . ," she prompted.

Silas shrugged, not liking that he was telegraphing his mood so loudly. "It just means you're comfortable," he said, hiding behind a sip of his drink. "And if you're comfortable, it's a good bet that no one is sitting in the stands watching us."

Peri scanned the nearby stairs, but there were only fans to look at. "Seriously?"

He nodded. "Jack manifests when you think something is wrong. He's not infallible, since he only knows what you suspect, but I trust your intuition more than, say, . . . Allen's word."

She chuckled at that. "Yeah, I don't trust him either," she said. "He knew my ass was LoJacked."

Silas smirked, and she turned to him, head

shaking. "Good God," she said, not angry at all. "You're happy I don't trust Allen?"

He couldn't help his laugh, and her smile turned real. "I can't keep anything from you, can I? But you're not done yet with your hot dog."

"Yes. I am." She shoved the last bit in her mouth. Chewing fast, she swallowed, washing it down with a gulp of water before turning to face him. Silas's pulse quickened, but just then the inning ended and he looked past her to the suddenly moving people. The announcer's voice was almost lost amid the thousand conversations starting all at once.

"Getting under the alliance blanket is going to be a little tricky," Peri said in the new noise, glancing darkly at the man knocking into her on his way to the food court. "Opti found out I removed the tracker and made me ingest a new radiation marker."

Silas's head snapped around. "What!"

"It's not that big a deal," she said, almost amused as she leaned closer to be heard. "Don't freak out, okay? I can muddle it when I want with a little barium syrup."

"They knew you were gone and didn't scrub you?" he asked, trying to wrap his head around this.

Peri's expression twisted wryly. "No."

Silas's hands clenched so hard on his water bottle the cap cracked. She was chemically tagged? What the hell was he supposed to do now? They were using her, blatantly using her to get to the alliance. Cold flowed through him, and he ran a hand under his cap, scanning the moving people for black suits and sunglasses. "This is really bad," he said softly.

"So I take a low-dose of barium syrup to mask it," Peri said, her eyes narrowing as her confidence wavered. "Or wear a tin hat. It isn't anything we can't work around. Opti doesn't know I've broken their memory implants."

Which was exactly what she would say if she really was working for Opti to bring the alliance heads in on a platter. Silas's chest began to hurt. Fran had told him Peri couldn't be trusted and to bring her in for "retirement." He didn't want to believe it. He wouldn't.

But then Peri jerked to look behind her at that recently vacated chair. "Ahhh, shit on a shingle," she whispered.

It had to be Jack, and a slithery feeling crept through his spine as she watched something that wasn't really there. "What is he saying?" he whispered.

Peri's eyes scanned. "That something is wrong and I have to go. I'm tending to believe him. Thanks for the hot dog. It was nice. Which way to the car?"

She stood, and he rose as well. "Uh . . . ," he said unintelligently. But he had no plan, no thought other than to take her and go. And with the chemical tag, the alliance was doubly out.

Peri looked him up and down, his fear feeding her own. "I *gave* you Jack's list. You've got what you want."

Silas's brow furrowed, and he took her elbow. "What you brought us wasn't Jack's list."

Her face went white. "Yes, it was. It had to be," she insisted as the music blared. "It was on my cat. His collar is the only thing that survived my apartment."

Silas shook his head. "It was a listening device."

Her lips parted, and he saw her world fall apart in the sheen of her eyes. "Oh my God," she whispered. "They heard everything." Her eyes shot to his, panicked. "They know everything we said! That I'm lying to them!"

A part of Silas was relieved. She was afraid. She was telling the truth. "No they don't," he tried to soothe her, but her arms were stiff under his hands. "The unit was damaged. You said you got it off your cat. Well, those things can't take being outside for long. Opti hadn't had a chance to change it out. They didn't hear us, but Peri, it wasn't the list, and the alliance won't trust you."

Peri's wandering attention came back to his. "They'll never believe me," she said, and his fear swelled when he saw her new determination. She was going to run. She was going to try to do this on her own.

"I have to go," she said, pulling away from him.

"Where?"

"I don't know," she said. And then she simply walked away.

"Peri!" he called, but someone had cut in behind her, and he had to wait. In three seconds, she was gone, out the way she'd come in.

"Move!" Silas pushed past the man on the stair, ignoring the angry protests as he shoved through the tight inflow of people. Peri's slim form slipped gracefully past the throng like water while he was more like the rock everyone else was crashing against, but finally he was through the crush and in the cool underbelly of the stadium.

"There you are," he said, spotting her weaving through the crowd to an exit. He saw her note the two men at the exit gate. They were in suits and lacked the park's lanyard identification, and she smoothly turned and went the other way.

Shit. She was in flight mode, and he lurched after her, calling her name when he caught up to her so she wouldn't overreact.

"What do you want?" she rasped as he touched her elbow and she spun, shocking him with her wet eyes. "I don't need an anchor. I don't need anyone."

"You're right," he said as he brushed a finger under her eye, and she moaned and turned away. "You don't *need* anyone," he said, pulling her to a stop again. "But that doesn't mean you need to be alone."

Lips parting, she let that spill over her, her shoulders losing their tension and her eyes showing her heartache. "I don't want to be alone. I want to sit in the sun and eat another damn hot dog. I want it to be done, Silas. I want it to be done!"

"We can figure this out." Still holding her arm, Silas looked over the moving throng as the announcer began his between-inning patter. "Together. Trust me, Peri. One more time."

She took a breath to answer, but he already saw it in her eyes. And then she jerked, her attention going over his shoulder. "Gun!" she shrilled, shoving him back.

Silas's arms pinwheeled as he caught his balance. His head snapped up. Peri was poised for flight, and a red-fletched dart skittered on the floor between them.

"Run!" he said, grabbing her elbow and yanking her into motion.

Peri sprang ahead, slipping from him as Silas pounded behind her. The two attendants followed, one yelling into a two-way. "I didn't know they were here," Peri got out between breaths, when she'd slowed enough that Silas could catch up. "Opti wasn't supposed to be here."

"It's not Opti. It's the alliance," he said. "No, keep going!" he shouted, pushing her to an employees-only door, when she almost stopped.

"Why are we running?" she asked as they spilled through it and into a quiet hallway.

Grimacing, Silas dead-bolted the door, starting at the sudden pounding on it. "Come on. This has to lead somewhere."

"You told me you were alliance," Peri said as she jogged beside him. "Are you or not?"

"I am," he ground out. "It's Fran, Taf's mother. She'd rather believe that you bewitched her daughter into believing your lies than that her daughter might be a better judge of character than she is."

"Taf?" Peri bit her lip as she recalled the young woman. "I don't get it."

They turned a corner and Silas eased their pace, looking for an exit. "Fran is the head of the alliance. Taf ran off with you instead of backing up her mother. There was a gun involved, and Fran's pretty pissed off about it."

"Swell. I ran off with the daughter of the head of the alliance? They're never going to believe me," Peri said bitterly. "Why are you just telling me this now?"

"Oh, I don't know," Silas smart-mouthed. "I couldn't wedge it between you cracking my rib and the hot dog."

The sudden crash of the distant door slamming behind them jolted them into motion.

"Go!" Silas shouted, pushing her.

Peri sprinted ahead for the fire door, hitting it

full-force since fire codes would have it unlocked from this side. The heavy door thumped into the wall, and Silas ran after her, skidding to a stop when three men straightened from a car waiting in the sun.

"Get her!" one cried as weapons were pulled.

Silas's heart seemed to stop as Peri continued to head for the wide square of light and her freedom, going full-tilt off the raised platform to roll upright and running upon landing. Her hat was gone, and her black hair gleamed when she reached the sun and the men at the car.

"You in the black! Stop!" one shouted, and Peri hesitated to look back for him.

"Don't shoot her!" Silas shouted, knowing the pause was fatal. "For God's sake, Peri, don't draft! You might go into a full MEP!"

Two men crashed into him from behind, knocking him down and wrestling his arms behind his back. But his eyes were fixed on Peri, his eyes closing in heartache when she slowly rose from her crouch and yanked a dart from her arm.

"No!" Silas shouted as she staggered . . . and then . . . drafted before it could take hold.

Silas gasped, shocked at the breadth of her reach as she yanked everyone in a half-mile radius into a blue haze of hindsight. His mind seemed to expand as time became malleable, and with a sudden pop he could almost feel the world reset with a crystalline clarity of lost chances.

CHAPTER
THIRTY-SIX

"**P**eri! Wait!" Silas shouted as he ran onto the loading dock, and Peri spun, putting her back to the Dumpster and edging deeper into the shadows instead of into the sun and her freedom. She was drafting, and for the first time, a new fear slid between her thought and her reason. Silas thought she was going to go into MEP? If Silas's tinkering didn't hold, she wasn't only going to lose her past, but her mind.

"Stop!" Silas exclaimed as two men fell on him, and Peri backed farther into the alley. "I can talk her in. You're making this worse."

"You shut up," the man holding him said, kicking his knees out from under him, and Peri crouched, reaching for her pen pendant and jerking it open.

TRUST NO ONE, she wrote, eyes fixed on the two men creeping closer with the caution of Bushmen circling a lion. She shifted the pen's position to gouge.

"No!" Silas protested as she silently rushed them.

"Watch it!" someone cried, and Peri crashed into the nearest man. He shouted, dropping out of her way when the pen buried itself deep between his shoulder and his neck. Teeth clenched, she shoved him at the other man the jolt of her breakaway lanyard snapping through her. She darted left at the pop of a weapon. She was going to make it. She was going to make it!

And then the world hiccupped. She was running. Men were shouting behind her, and she didn't know why. But she didn't slow down, confused as she zigged when a red-fletched dart pinged on the window of the car she was passing. Heart pounding, she looked at her palm.

Trust no one.

It made perfect sense and none at all. She'd come here to buy her way into the alliance, but she didn't remember talking to anyone. She'd lost at least ten minutes, maybe more. But it was that she might have damaged Silas's patch job that struck fear into her. She'd be fine if she could just . . . get away!

"Jack?" she shouted, and she saw him thirty feet up the street, gesturing for her.

"Don't stop!" he exclaimed, and she gasped when a man came out from behind a car and she plowed right into him, crashing them both to the pavement.

"No!" she howled as a dart hit her and her arms were pulled behind her. She fought until there were two, then three men sitting on her. Someone held her face to the ground, and her eyes screwed tight when a foam insert was wedged into her ear. A hum of sound stifled her ability to draft. She couldn't breathe, and finally she gave up, her heart thudding and adrenaline making her head hurt. She clenched her fist to hide the writing on her palm—her fear—even as a plastic strip ratcheted tight about her wrists behind her back.

"Peri!"

Still on the ground, she spit the dirt from her mouth and turned her head. *Silas?* He was in the grip of two men as they moved to get him in a van. He was cuffed and there was a new welt on his cheek. Was it Opti who had her, then? Oh God, how had they known she was lying?

She kicked fruitlessly at them as they hauled her up. Her teeth clenched when they tossed her into the van as well, and she landed on Silas. His elbow jammed into her gut and she lost her breath even as she struggled to find her knees. The door slammed shut, and she fell when the van accelerated fast.

"Peri, stop fighting. You're making it worse. I'm not going to let you go into MEP."

Peri wiggled until she was off him. There were no windows, and she pressed into a dark corner, trying not to fall as the van rocked. The hum in her ears and the drugs in her system made her nauseated. She knew that she'd set out to talk to Silas and buy her freedom, but she couldn't remember how she'd gotten here or what had gone wrong.

At the other side of the van, Silas slowly got himself upright. "You drafted," Silas said breathlessly. "Just relax and breathe. It's going to be okay. Opti doesn't have us. It's the alliance. Turn around. Let me get that audio blocker out."

His voice was soothing, but she mistrusted it. "Alliance?" she whispered as the van leaned into a long curve that said entrance ramp. "Then why are you cuffed? You said *you* were alliance." She couldn't remember how she'd gotten to the ballpark. The unreasonable fear wound tighter about her heart and squeezed. She couldn't breathe, and she pulled her knees to her chin and dropped her head, trying to relax.

But the harder she tried, the more the panic grew, the unknown hammering at her, eating her alive. It was that patch job. It was falling apart, and when it did, she'd go crazy. She *was* going crazy.

"Look at me." Silas knelt before her, but she stared at the ceiling, terrified. The van was running full-out on a straightaway. She had no idea where she was going. She wanted to draft and keep drafting, but the drugs in her wouldn't let her, and she hung in a hell of her own making of doubt and panic.

He inched forward, and her eyes shot to his. "Peri, I'm an anchor," he said calmly, and she recoiled as far into the corner as she could. "You know I am. I was there when you drafted. I can bring it back, and with that, the rest will return. Trust me. At least let me get that earplug out."

Her mouth was dry, and she couldn't swallow. *Trust no one.* "I can't," she whispered, confusion swirling through her, muddling her thinking.

"You have to," he said, inching closer, his eyes showing his pain from his bound wrists. "Listen to your gut. It was a tiny draft, but you're teetering on collapse. Look at yourself. This isn't you. Undo my hands. Let me help."

"I can't," she said, almost pleading for him to help her, but he had turned to show her his back. His fingers looked swollen, the binding too tight.

"Please," he said, and she saw the bent nail in his grip. "I know you're confused, but I can fix this. You have to trust me."

Her heart was thudding and she felt sick with the motion both outside and inside her head. "Okay," she whispered. "But if you make one move I don't like, I'll kill you for real."

"Fair enough," he said, and she carefully moved to put her back to his. His fingers felt cold when she touched them, and he hissed when the nail slipped, gouging him. But his sigh was real when she finally got the tab wedged and he pulled out of the zip cuff.

"Your turn," he said, and she jumped when he plucked the earplug out and the hum ceased. She was freed even faster, and she rubbed her wrists as she backed to her corner, that same unreasonable fear cramping her chest.

Scared, she shook her head, warning him off. "You stay back. Hear me?"

"Do you remember how you got to the ballpark?" he asked as he took her hand, not letting go when she tried to pull away.

"Let go. Let go!" she demanded, her fear hesitating when he turned her hand over and put that nail in it as a talisman. Her breath caught, and she stared at it as half a lifetime of protocol and effect beat on her. She *wanted* to remember. He was an anchor, and she was out of her mind. "I don't remember how I got to the ballpark," she finally groaned, desperate. She needed to trust him to survive.

"That's okay," he soothed as he took her other hand, a spot of calm in her chaos. "It was only ten minutes ago. That's within normal tolerance. It's just shock. When you calm down, it will come back on its own. Do you remember shopping?"

"Yes," she said, the relief enormous as she looked at her clothes, remembering. That had been this morning. She hadn't lost everything. It was going to be okay. And she began to calm—to think.

"Peri, let me in," he said softly, his urgency a thin thread.

Not knowing why, she closed her eyes and nodded. Exhaling, she felt his presence slip in behind hers, gasping when his masculine shade of thought colored her memory of her trip to the mall. He was there, with her, and her shoulders slumped in relief so deep it hurt.

"It's okay," Silas was saying, but she hardly heard him as a thick exhaustion covered her, swimming up from nowhere. "You've only lost fifteen minutes or so. Let me bring it back."

"Make it stop," she mumbled, hardly aware of him in her thoughts as he turned her memories that way. "Please make it stop."

"You were running with me," he said, and she saw it through his mind. "It was the alliance, and I told you why they were after us."

A flash of his angry emotion pulled her memory of it into existence, and her feelings of betrayal crowded out his anger until his emotions reasserted themselves and they found understanding. For a moment, they both looked at the memory together, seeing it from the other side, finding common ground, something they could both accept. Perhaps she'd jumped too quickly to a conclusion that was wrong. *Perhaps,* he thought, his emotion mixing with hers, *I should have been honest with you about being on the outs with the alliance.*

"I was cuffed at the loading dock," he said. "They shot you and triggered a draft."

Her eyes were shut and her body went slack as the first memory of being darted rose into existence and Silas dissolved it. She saw herself through his eyes: furious, determined, obstinate as she looked for a way to survive. She didn't remember it that way, and she felt him take in her emotions of fear, betrayal, and desperation—and they were as real as his vision of her strength.

"I didn't betray you," he whispered as he pulled her to him, and she believed him with a certainty as real as the nail in her grip. "I didn't know they were there."

And as that reality became firm in her mind, her world stopped spinning. Her chest eased and her breaths came and went more easily. She drowsed, the warmth of Silas's arms around her as their memories meshed and hers became real. There was only one draft left in her, the tiny space of double time reduced to one.

She was at peace for what felt like the first time in months, and like an addict, she hung in a haze, not wanting it to end. "You're good at this," she slurred, and his hand gentled her head against his shoulder as the van swerved and jostled.

"I used to be," he said, his breath shifting her hair. "Go to sleep. Let it firm up. When you wake, you'll have your entire morning back. It's going to be okay."

She doubted that, but she fell asleep right there in the van, confident she would remember everything she'd lost today, holding that nail as if it were a diamond.

CHAPTER
THIRTY-SEVEN

Stomach clenched, Peri did a final pull-up, straining as she hung from the decorative ironwork that had been installed for the sole purpose of making the underground wine cellar look old. It couldn't have been in place more than ten years by the look of the resort-size log house they'd hustled her through yesterday, filthy and cold from her ride in the back of the van.

Tucked away in the Kentucky mountains, the high-tech, expansive getaway mansion only looked rustic, with its highly landscaped indoor-outdoor pool, restaurant-size kitchen, and multiple entertainment areas all connected by an engineered waterfall and subtle, state-of-the-art security system. She hadn't seen anyone when they'd brought her through the first floor, down the elevator, and to the wine cellar, but the three stories of windows overlooking the valley had given her a view of acres of isolation that she could get lost in, figuratively and literally, if she could escape. *But not without Silas.*

She dropped to the floor, Silas's talisman nail stuffed into her boot for safe keeping pinching between her toes. There was a heating duct, but nothing had come out of it in the hours that she'd been stuck down here with the dusty reds and whites, all good but nothing exceptional. She'd checked.

Slowly Peri collapsed to sit cross-legged on the artfully stained flagstones. *Imported or manufactured?* she wondered as her sweat went cold and she closed her eyes. Silas had given her a top-notch, professional defrag. She'd been lost, but she didn't feel that way now. Even imprisoned, she was still riding the high of that one exquisite return of memory.

Her psyche had been tampered with so badly that what should have been an easily handled draft had pushed her over the edge. She'd been in the first stages of catastrophic memory-eclipsed paranoia, totally losing it, and Silas had not only stopped it dead in its tracks, but returned her memory. He was good. Really good. And she couldn't stop thinking about him and those few moments they'd shared at the ballpark.

Eyes opening, Peri scanned the dimly lit, luxurious wine-tasting den past her iron-barred door. She hadn't seen Jack since Silas's defrag. Maybe she didn't need him anymore. She'd never felt so much at peace, even if her life was falling apart. Again.

The distant sound of the elevator pulled her straight. Dampening the flash of adrenaline, she steadied herself. It would've been helpful to have known that Silas was currently on the outs with the alliance, but even so, she doubted his accommodations were as severe as hers. As it stood, her next move hinged on whether he had told the alliance that she had a radioactive tag, shining like a lighthouse to draw Opti in. That she could hear the muted sounds of people gathering above her made her tend to believe he hadn't.

She had no doubt that Opti was going to track her down through her new radioactive beacon, and she was still trying to decide if she was going to warn the alliance about it or not. Much depended on whether they trusted her. She wanted out, but if they weren't going to give her asylum, she'd be better off with Opti, where she'd have a chance to run.

Another metallic thump, and Peri twitched, cracking an eye as she sat in a lotus position. But her eyes opened wide when she recognized the feminine voice raised in demand as Taf's, the young woman who had been with Silas at Eastown. *The daughter of the head of the alliance.*

"You've checked me twice. Will you back off. It's not like you can bake a file into a batch of muffins. I didn't even make them. Gawd!"

The clatter of heels on flagstone vanished as Taf and two security suits strode into the carpeted wine-tasting den. Taf had a bundle of clothes in one hand, a covered basket in the other. "Lights up!" she demanded, and the dim lighting brightened against the rich décor, silent black flat screen, and informal seating around a central gas fireplace. "Make yourselves at home, gentlemen," she said, pointing at the white couches. "Munchies are at the bar."

"Ma'am," the one with glasses protested, and Taf jerked to a stop.

"Look, Brian," she intoned, glaring at them both until they fidgeted in their black suits. "I don't care if you sit or stand, but you will *back off*. I have ten minutes, and I don't want you hanging like vultures."

Peri could smell muffins, and her stomach growled.

"Yes, ma'am. Five minutes."

"*Ten* minutes," the blond woman protested even as she came forward. "She can't eat in five minutes. You tell my mom they can wait. These things never start on time anyway. Someone always forgets about the time zones and they have to be tracked down."

Still sitting behind the barred door, Peri watched the woman drop the clothes on a nearby table so she could push one of the chairs around to face her. Only now did Taf's bluster falter as she stood before her with the basket of muffins, and Peri cringed inside at her look of hopeful expectation, hope that Peri might remember something they'd once shared, something that was important but that she'd forgotten. "Ah, hi. Are you hungry?" the woman asked hesitantly.

Peri got up, her muscles chilled from the cold floor. "I'm sorry. I don't remember you. It's Taf, right?"

"Don't worry about it. Most of my friends don't remember our nights out, either." Pinky in the air, she pantomimed sipping wine from a nonexistent glass. "Here. Fresh this morning."

Taf paused at the bars, then tilted the basket so it would fit between. Peri took it, the warmth through the wicker and linen liner pleasant on her fingers. "Thanks. If it helps, I know that I like you, even if I don't know why." Her lips quirked at the muffins. "And it has nothing to do with you bringing me breakfast. Emotions linger when events don't." Chuckling, she took a bite, adding, "Why am I feeling as if it has something to do with my mom?"

Beaming now, Taf sat forward on the plush white chair, the picture of wealth and privilege as her perfectly styled hair bumped about her shoulders. "I can answer that. Both our moms are control freaks. We met at a horse event. You were asking for help to rescue Silas from Opti so he could defrag some information, and my mother tried to exchange you for him instead. Howard and I rammed the van you were in to get you free. I thought that was going to be the end of it, but when you went off to rescue Silas, we came along to help."

The cranberries were almost burning hot, and

Peri swallowed fast, enjoying their tangy sweetness. "Silas said there was a gun involved?"

Taf nodded enthusiastically. "Oh yes. I got to shoot someone in the foot and drive the getaway car. I, ah, brought you a change of clothes," she said as she glanced at the guards. "They should fit."

Peri set the basket down, wiping her fingers on her pants before reaching for the bundle. "Thank you!"

"There's an athletic body wipe in there, too," Taf said, looking eager to help. "I've used them before in a pinch. They're almost as good as a shower." She turned to the guards playing with the fireplace, turning it off and on with their voice commands. "Big strong men afraid to let you shower!"

Peri found the packet, her mood brightening. "Thank you very much!" she said, dropping back deeper into the wine cellar and out of the guards' sight.

"This place has twelve bathrooms, and they won't let you into one. Barbarians." Taf's attention went to the guards again to make sure they kept their distance as Peri stripped to her skivvies. "I can't bust you out this time, but I can at least help you look good for your lynching."

The body wipe was a spot of clean, and Peri relaxed at the chill menthol scent. "It won't be that bad," she said as the dampness air-dried with the heat of her body. "I've got something they want, they've got something I want. Win, win."

Slumped over her knees, Taf shrugged. "Silas said that chip wasn't the list."

She's been talking to Silas? The feeling of an impending something grew, but she felt almost normal as she slipped into the tailored navy blouse and slacks and buckled the tiny belt. Taf had good taste. "I've got more than that," she said, coming forward as she tapped her head. "There's no reason we can't work together."

Taf's eyes brightened, and she handed Peri a brush. "You remember?"

"No, but it's in there. Silas can get it out." Peri ran the brush through her hair, then checked out her distant reflection in the bar mirror. Not her best effort, but a hundred times better. "Thank you."

Taf stood up, and the suits came forward. "I hope you're right."

"Me too," she said, then jumped, outraged, when a dart buried itself in her thigh.

"What the hell is *wrong* with you!" Peri exclaimed as the guard with the glasses lowered a dart gun and Taf protested hotly. She immediately jerked it out, but the smooth metal against her fingertips felt fuzzy. It was too late, and the chalky taste of a jump blocker coated her tongue.

"Maybe you shouldn't keep busting the audio blockers," the guard said, and she threw the dart down to look at the tear in her new slacks.

"Those pants are Chanel," Taf complained. "Brian, this is coming out of your paycheck. Open the door."

But the other agent had his stopwatch app going on his phone, and Peri knew they wouldn't let her out until they reached some arbitrary number that made them feel safe.

"Put them on," Brian said, tossing in a pair of cuffs.

Peri's jaw clenched at the metallic ping as they slid across the flagstones.

"No one said *anything* about cuffs." Taf was furious, face red and lips in a tight line, but Peri put them on, glad they let her do it so her hands were in front instead of behind.

"Don't worry about it," Peri said as the guard with the phone nodded and tucked it away. It was irritating, and they'd slow her down, but if she wanted out, she'd get out. In fact, seeing her cuffed would make them careless.

Brian unlocked the door. Immediately Taf grabbed her arm, yanking her onto the carpet. "This way," the young woman said, glancing back at the two men as she stalked to the elevator. The weapons of the men behind her were holstered but unsnapped. She could probably take them out with minimal risk even cuffed, but why bother when they were clearly headed upstairs?

"If you move too fast, you'll be shot," Brian said, then gave her a shove. "Go."

He got a dark look instead of the foot in his face that she wanted, and eyeing him appraisingly, Peri stepped into the elevator.

One of them hit the button for the fourth floor, and the panels slid shut. She only remembered seeing three floors, but then the doors opened with a cheerful *ding* to the window-lined, octagonal aerie she'd noticed from outside when she'd arrived. She'd thought it was only decoration, but the enormous room was at least fifty feet in diameter and was set up for high-class entertaining, with a neon-strewn bar against one side and a circular comfort pit of white couches taking up the majority of the space.

The vista out onto the cloudy mountains was almost overwhelming, with an astounding 315-degree view, even in the light fog. It was hazy and overcast, and a line of storms threatened. A biting whiff of electronics came from the small camera on a tripod set in the middle of the circular room. Lines snaked from it to a card table, where an awkward tech guy in an off-the-rack suit fussed over two glass-technology tablets. It was clearly a teleconference, and Peri watched an aide come up a staircase, furtively crossing the camera's line of sight to whisper in a security guard's ear.

Howard sat glumly at the bar under the restraint of an agent, and a confident older woman, draped in jewelry and attitude, stood beside the camera in the middle of the room, her white business dress tight and her heels making her tall. Her hair was done up in a French chignon, and before her on the couch and in front of the camera was Silas.

Peri's breath caught, and she stumbled to a halt on the thick rug as something struck through her. He didn't know she was here, clearly angry, his neck red and his muscular shoulders pulling his shirt tight as he sat on the edge of the indulgent couch with his back to her and argued with that woman. Peri's thoughts went to the note she'd written to herself not to trust anyone, and she wished she could take it back.

"Mother, why is Peri in cuffs?" Taf said loudly, and the tech guy had a fit, waving his hands for her to be quiet.

Silas jumped, emotion crossing his face as he turned to her. Peri moved to join him only to be pulled back. *This domineering woman is Fran? The head of the alliance?* Peri looked between Taf and Fran as Taf continued to argue, seeing not the resemblance, but the resentment when Fran's cheeks reddened and she told her daughter to be quiet.

"Shut up!" Brian barked, and she started when he poked her.

"I haven't said anything," Peri protested. "Why don't you go poke Taf? She's the one who won't shut up."

"You still maintain your actions were for the

benefit of the alliance?" Fran said as Taf was pulled to the bar where Howard tried to mollify her. Fran's attitude was so familiar that Peri felt as if she should know her, but nothing was clicking.

"I do." Silas shifted on the couch so he could see Peri. It put him at odds with the camera, and the tech guy made an exasperated sigh and went to adjust it.

"From our first encounter in February, Peri Reed has been looking for asylum from the same corrupt Opti faction that we're trying to eradicate. My actions and those of the people with me were to prevent her from being returned to Opti—where she would be scrubbed and remade into what they wanted. Our actions were never intended to betray the alliance but to prevent a mistake that would set us back another three years. It's time to end this, Fran."

"I agree," the woman said with so much bile and frustration, a sudden doubt erased Peri's confidence. Something was going wrong. "But let's finish with you first. You ran with her, Denier. After you were instructed to bring her back in. You refused to disclose where she was until we could do nothing. How do you explain that?"

Silas's expression was peeved. "You were hell-bent on giving her back to Opti. I never agreed to that."

Fran took a step closer, almost in front of the camera. "That's where she belongs. She doesn't have what we need to bring Opti down, and I don't think she ever will."

Peri's lips pressed. Clearing her throat, she said loudly, "I do. I simply need Dr. Denier's help to dig it out."

"On the couch . . . ," the tech guy bitched. "Say it in front of the camera on the couch. The mic doesn't pick up the back of the room."

"Then tell grabby fingers here to let go of me," Peri said, yanking out of the agent's grip again. *I'm going to take those glasses of yours and shove them up your nose.*

Fran waved the tech guy back to his station. "You'll have a chance to state your case shortly, Ms. Reed. Please refrain from comment until then."

"I should be allowed the opportunity to regain my memory before an inquiry," Peri said loudly, and the woman narrowed her eyes. "That's what this is, isn't it?"

"If there are enough credible witnesses, your recalling your actions won't factor in," she said, then turned to Silas. "Nothing has been changed by what you have said. You'll join Howard in protective custody until such time as we can be certain of your loyalties."

"My loyalty is to the alliance," Silas exclaimed, but an agent had come forward at Fran's directive and pulled him to his feet. The screen on the tech's temporary desk showed only an empty couch, but the chat room associated with it was busy.

Peri's gut clenched as they forced Silas to sit at the bar beside Howard and Taf. Her past made her appear both guilty and untrustworthy, and her association with Silas wasn't helping.

"Your actions show that your loyalty is to yourself," Fran said, gesturing for security to bring Peri forward to take Silas's place.

"Thinking for oneself does not imply disloyalty," Silas said, but it was likely no one outside the room heard him. "She thought she was giving us the information we needed," he added as Brian manhandled her forward. "She shouldn't be standing before you justifying her actions. She should be in conference with you to bring Opti down!"

Pulse fast, Peri scrambled for a way to make this work for her. Clearly Silas hadn't told them about the chemical tracker. Opti was likely on their way, to find out where she'd gone if nothing else. And Opti was coming. She could feel it—brewing just over the horizon like a summer storm.

"Enough," Fran hissed. "Get her on camera."

That man shoved her again. Peri had had enough, and she spun, arms jabbing out with a palm thrust to break his nose. Brian fell back, screaming and clutching his face. Peri froze, cuffed hands in the air as safeties clicked off, but Howard only laughed.

"Someone get Brian a towel," Fran directed tiredly. "Can we move forward, please?"

"Peri, this isn't how I wanted to do this."

It was Silas, and Peri's expression blanked. Someone else had said nearly the exact same thing to her—right before her world fell apart the first time. First chance she got, she was going to run and keep running. But she wouldn't leave without Silas. He'd brought her back, given her something to build herself on. His own people were turning against him. She didn't know which side was right, but she knew how that felt. The alliance and Opti could tear themselves apart for all she cared.

Finally they got Brian behind the bar with a pack of ice. The new agent at her side was more polite, and Peri smiled at his gesture for her to continue, putting a sway in her hips as she made her way to sit in front of the camera.

"Please state your name," Fran said, though it was obvious everyone knew who she was.

"Peri Reed," she said as she settled herself into the white cushions and the technician adjusted the camera.

"You're here to account for your crimes done under the auspices of Opti," Fran began, careful not to get her face on camera, "your actions against humanity, and your efforts to reduce the inherent rights of every citizen. If found guilty, you'll be taken from here and permanently stripped of your ability to draft."

Peri's head snapped up. "I thought this was to

discuss what I had to offer you in exchange for asylum."

Fran's thin lips pressed as she scrolled through a tablet. "You thought wrong. We're going to make you normal, Peri Reed."

"I am normal." Peri glanced at Silas, whose expression mirrored the surprise and horror she knew were evident on her own features. "The only way to eliminate my ability to draft will leave me unable to make any long-term memories, and that's if you do it right. Pardon my concern, but you can't possibly possess the equipment or the finesse. You'll make a vegetable out of me."

Fran put on a pair of diamond-encrusted bifocals and brought her gaze back from the hazy mountains, thick with the coming rain. "Your actions carry their own sins. You're accused of the murders of Hans Marston, James Thomas, Daniel H. Parsole, Kevin Arnold, Thomas Franklin, Nicole Amsterdam, and, most recently, Samuel Smity."

Seven deaths, most of them probably people who'd been in the wrong place at the wrong time. It bothered Peri that she didn't remember most of them. Taf had gone pale, and even Silas looked uncomfortable. "Hans beat his children and mutilated other men's wives to convince their husbands to do what he wanted them to. I did the world a favor. Kevin Arnold was an accident. He didn't move when I told him to, and someone shot him as he went over a fence. I don't remember the rest," Peri said, ignoring the rising murmur of outrage behind her. "You can't try me for something you might have made up."

"You've been linked to a multitude of corporate espionage events that resulted in massive illegal gains in the private sector," Fran continued, peering down through her glasses. "I have them listed here, if you feel the need to refute them. Numerous accounts of theft or arson to eliminate records detrimental to Opti personnel . . . several mentions of technological terrorism. Most of them involving biological warfare." She peered accusingly at Peri over the glass tablet. "We're not sure what you were doing in old Russia, but I'm not liking that the Korean ambassador developed Legionnaires' disease the same week you were there and died of complications. Here's my favorite, though. Under the cover of installing a U.S.-friendly government, you set in power an extremist group who went on to commit a nationwide genocide, more commonly known as the White Plague."

"That wasn't me," she whispered, going cold. "That was Nina and Trey." She looked at Silas, seeing his empty expression. "I didn't do that!" But a faint memory ticked in the back of her skull, a wisp of unfragmented memory of trying to sneak frightened people past a blockade as the night lit up in a fiery hell behind them. Maybe she'd been there, but it had been to stop it, right?

But even as Peri thought it, doubt paralyzed her. Had she ever been anything other than Bill's tool? Had she believed everything Jack had said because he'd rubbed her feet and made her dinner? Sick to her stomach, she looked up when Fran said, "How plead you?"

Silas stood, shoving the sudden hands off him. "How can you stand there as if you've never bought a drafter's skills before, Fran?"

Fran covered her mic, and the tech guy jumped. "I am not on trial," she hissed, furious.

"Maybe you should be." Silas fell back into his chair, pushed by security.

"Everything I've done is for the benefit of mankind," Fran said earnestly, but her face was red from more than anger.

"End justifies the means, eh?" Silas said bitterly, and from outside, thunder rolled between the hills. "You are a hypocritical elitist," Silas accused, straining against the guards' hands. "How dare you, Fran. She's been used. By you most of all, turned into something she might not come back from. How dare you accuse her of this? *You owe her!*"

"Mother, this is not fair!" Taf exclaimed, pushed back to the windows with Howard.

"Fair doesn't enter into it," Fran said coldly as the three men kept him unmoving. "You're correct in your diagnosis, though, Silas. There's no way she can come back from this. She is a tool. And she needs to be destroyed before she brings us all down. You either perform the incision, or you will remain in alliance custody for the rest of your life."

Peri was numb as the thunder grew and beat on her. Had she been blind to Jack's lies for three years, or had she known and gone along with it?

"Uh, guys?" the tech geek said, eyes on the mountains as he stood over his tablets.

"I won't do it," Silas promised. "I'm *not* going to mutilate her so you can hide your guilt. She volunteered for this. Everything she's done has been for the alliance. You have a responsibility to *fix her!*"

Volunteered? Volunteered for what?

"Guys! That's not mine," the tech guy said, pointing, and someone gasped at the massive high-Q drone hovering just outside the window. Three seconds later, a military helicopter thumped overhead. Behind it, half a dozen more rolled over the mountains. It hadn't been thunder. It was a flight of Black Hawks, no insignia marring their sleek black shadows against the low clouds as they roared overhead and swung back around. Fast and light.

Fran paled. Spinning, she turned to Taf. A house alarm began to sound, filtering up through the stairway.

Opti was here.

CHAPTER
THIRTY-EIGHT

"**G**et them to the cars!" Fran shouted, hustling to the bar and physically pulling Taf to the elevator. "You"—Fran pushed an agent toward Taf—"escort my daughter to a secure location. I want Reed out of here. Now! Move!"

"Fran, it's not Peri's fault!" Silas shouted as he was shoved to the elevator.

A security man yanked Peri to her feet and all but dragged her to the carpeted stairs. A frustrated anger was spilling through her, but she wasn't ready to act. She'd been ready to put herself at the alliance's mercy—and they had condemned her. Going back to Opti wasn't an option, but neither was the alliance.

"It is over, Silas," Fran said as the elevator filled with Howard, Taf, Silas, and the bulk of the security. "Either she just gave us to Opti, or they're using her without her knowledge and will continue to do so within the alliance's shadow. Either way, she needs to be ended."

"I won't mutilate her," Silas argued with Fran as the doors slid shut to leave the tech guy panicking over his equipment.

"Downstairs!" Brian demanded, his nice white shirt bloodied by his nose, his Glock pulled and pointing at her. Peri turned, catching herself against the railing when he shoved her.

The thumping of the helicopters was a heavy pulse she could feel through the walls. Tension pulled like a ribbon through her, shredding her mental fog and bringing on a new clarity with each step. She was not going to an Opti cell, and she was not going to stay and be lobotomized by the alliance. There were two guards and one of her. Doable—even if she was cuffed.

"Keep going!" Brian said. "All the way to the garage," he added, shoving her a third time as they reached the first landing. Peri caught herself with a little hop. Pissed, she put her back to the wall, staring at the two men with their weapons pulled. She could hear gunfire coming up from the great room. Someone was screaming. Opti had the house. She had to get out of here. *Not without Silas.*

"Brian, push me again, and I'm going to jam your balls into your esophagus," she said, inviting him to try.

"Yeah?" He reached for her. Leaning back into the wall, Peri kicked up and out. Brian screamed, doubling over to put his head conveniently within her reach. Cuffed hands clenched around themselves, she slammed them down on the back of his head.

"Hands up!" the first man screamed, and she head-butted him, sending him cascading down the stairs in a pinwheel of arms and legs. His handgun went off, and plaster flaked down.

Jaw clenched, Peri dropped to Brian, her cuffed hands searching for the key. "Thank you," she sang out merrily when she found it, unlocking her cuffs and taking his weapon before leaving him in a puddle of misery.

She found the second man groaning on the second-floor landing. "Now, aren't you glad you weren't shoving me?" she said as she locked him to the railing and took his weapon, too.

"Don't leave me here," he said, eyes desperate and holding pain as another flurry of gunfire rang out. It sounded like a war down there, and Peri watched through a narrow window as another of those big helicopters landed, its blades assaulting the air to make it beat like a heart about to explode. Twelve people in assault gear got out and ran to the nearby barn.

From below, more gunfire sounded. "Come back with my daughter, you sons of bitches!" Fran screamed, and Peri went cold.

Silas.

He'd been with Fran in the elevator. Numb, Peri ran down the stairs to the great room. The biting scent of gunpowder grew thick, and she jerked to a halt as she reached the end of the stairs and looked beyond.

The elevator stood open, riddled with bullets and splattered blood. An alliance guard was facedown before it in a pool of blood. The front door was shot to hell and missing, fire-suppressive smoke drifting lazily through the landscaped grounds beyond it. Five men in Opti-issued gear were crouched behind an upended couch, changing out their clips as they prepared to reopen fire on a small cluster of people pinned in the kitchen. It had to be Silas and Taf. There hadn't been time for anyone else.

"Now!" one of the Opti men yelled, and four agents stood together, peppering the kitchen with fire as they slowly advanced.

"Will someone give me a friggin' gun!" Fran screamed from behind the stove, and Peri strode forward. If Silas was hurt, she was going to lay down some serious pain.

The man who had remained behind the couch looked up at her. Mouth open in surprise, he raised his weapon. He was too slow, and Peri's foot connected with him, knocking him back. His weapon arched into the air and she caught it, using its own momentum to smash it into the man's windpipe. Gagging, he dropped, his hands clutching his throat as he choked.

The butt of the rifle smacked her free palm, and she checked the clip and the safety in one smooth motion. *Good to go,* she thought, wiping the man's spittle off it before bringing it to her shoulder and shooting out the drone hovering in the middle of the room. Spinning wildly, it crashed into the fireplace.

"It's her!" someone shouted, and all hell broke loose as Silas bellowed in fury and came out from behind the counter, big gun blasting.

Peri shot once, twice, and actually hit someone on the third try. Shrapnel peppered her, and she ducked behind an overturned desk. "Mmmm, nice," Peri whispered as she stretched a foot out and dragged two discarded handguns into her reach.

"Get off!" Fran screamed in outrage, wrestling with a man. Teeth clenched, she dropped out from his grip, pulling him off balance and knocking him to the floor. "Will someone give me a goddamned gun!"

"Here!" Peri shouted, checking the clip and throwing one to her.

Fran caught it, and Peri gasped when someone grabbed her from behind. It was Brian, and a jab to his kidney and then his throat, and he was out again—this time for good.

Peri's leg hurt, and she ran her hand down the side of her calf. *Sticky?* Her fingers were red.

Crap. When did I get shot?

"Fall back! Fall back now!" came faintly through the gaping doorway, and Peri's head snapped up. It was Bill, and if he was leaving, he had something he wanted, because he sure as hell didn't have her. Ears ringing and the stink of gunpowder thick in her nose, Peri sank back down behind the desk, her hand clamped on her throbbing leg as she watched a man crawl to the door. If Bill was here, Allen probably was too. *This has potential.*

"Where's my daughter!" Fran screamed as she fired on everyone running for the door. Peri ducked, and when she looked up through the sifting dust, the crawling man was unmoving, his neck contorted at an unnatural-looking angle.

"I said fall back!" Peri heard Bill cry out again from outside amid more firing.

"You okay?" Silas called as he found her, looking fantastic with that semiautomatic rifle propped on his hip. It was pointed at the ceiling, but smoke was coming from it, and he put his hand up when Fran screamed at him, gun shaking as she pointed it in their direction.

"Shit, Fran! It's me!" he shouted at her. "Get control. They're leaving."

"They have Taf!" she raged, face red and coiffed hair flying. Fran was looking at Peri, and she felt herself blanch, sitting half behind a desk and holding her leg as it slowly leaked. "They have my daughter," Fran said, her voice breaking as she fell against a shot-up couch and let her weapon slip from her. "Peri, please. Get her back for me. They're going to use her, hurt her until I give them whatever they want. She's my *daughter!*"

Peri's hands were red as she ripped the silk couch throw to bind up her leg. The bullet was still in there, but it hadn't cut though anything but muscle. Fran might be domineering, obnoxious, and simply wrong, but she loved her daughter. Maybe they could find something together that Peri had no hope of finding with her own mother. "Okay," she said, and Fran almost sobbed.

"You're shot," Silas said, pale, and Peri pushed him back with a bloody hand before he could touch it. Why did they always try to touch it?

"I'll be fine." But her stomach lurched when she tightened the knot. "I'll get Taf," she said as she stood, reaching for the desk when vertigo threatened. She could pass out later. *It doesn't matter that I don't remember why I care about her. I feel. I know.*

"Thank you," Fran whispered, and Peri glanced at the ceiling when a loud, ominous thump came from above. Dust sifted down.

"You can't do this," Silas protested. Peri edged around him, weaving through the broken glass and chipped stone for the door, but her pace slowed at a stabbing pain. *It's not that bad,* she told herself, her grip on her weapon slick with sweat. "I'll find her."

"Damn-fool woman." Silas kicked a fallen chair out of the way as he strode after her. His eyes were pinched with stress, and he glanced at Fran before taking Peri's arm and slowing her down. "Peri, don't shoot Allen," Silas said, and she squinted at him. She could smell the house burning, and smoke was rolling down the stairs

577

like fog. Fran was losing more than her daughter today. The house was a wash.

"Why not?" she asked him, and he stared blankly at her. "Why can't I shoot Allen?" she asked again as they paused on the porch. Thunder, real thunder this time, rolled back and forth between the hills. Two men and a woman were running to the helicopter waiting to the left of the pool. Well, the men were running. Taf was kicking and screaming.

"Help me get that bird in the air," she said, bringing her rifle up.

"Peri!" Silas shouted, and then her ears went numb as she fired half the magazine at it.

The helicopter took off at the first clink of a bullet, long before Bill reached it. He slid to a stop, pushing Taf at Allen when he turned to the house and saw her standing on the threshold of the burning house. Clearly angry, he shoved them both toward the nearby detached show garage.

"Where's Howard?" she asked as she lowered the weapon. She'd try to take them both out from here, but she wouldn't risk hitting Taf.

"Doing his doctor thing," Silas said, and then he sighed and started down the log steps. "Well, let's get them before they steal one of Fran's cars."

Shaking her head to get her ear to work, Peri limped after Silas, following the sounds of Taf screaming insults as she was dragged through the manicured gardens. There was a thump of a door closing, and Taf's protests were gone.

"I'm serious. Don't kill Allen," Silas said again as they approached the building, where a shiny red Ferrari gleamed just past the glass garage doors.

"Look, my ear isn't working really well right now, but I could have sworn you just said don't kill Allen." Peri tried the heavy door, finding it locked.

"That's exactly what I said," Silas said as she limped to the front of the garage, eyeing the midlife-crisis mobile through the first glass garage door. "No!" he shouted, hand raised as she lifted the Glock this time.

Teeth clenched, she did a controlled burst to take out the entire door. It crashed to the ground and shattered, missing the car. "And the rolling icon of testosterone is fine," she said as Silas came up from his instinctive crouch. "Let's go."

Taf's screams for help drew them on, and Peri limped fast, passing sleek cars on raised rugs and under spotlights. Someone was a car hog. "Let me go!" Taf howled, and Peri pushed into a controlled jog. *If we don't get her in the next thirty seconds . . .*

As one, Silas and Peri swung around a decked-out Porsche to see Bill and Allen dragging Taf to a mundane service van. *I truly hate vans.* Peri raised her rifle.

"You might hit her," Silas said, and she lowered it, agreeing, as she abandoned the car to inch closer.

"Shut her up," Bill snarled as they reached the van and he shoved Taf at Allen as he went to open another garage door.

Peri lurched to fall against the next car, leg throbbing as she quietly used the hood to steady her aim. Silas scuffed to a halt beside her.

"My mother is going to be so pissed!" Taf shouted, and Allen knocked her up against the van, making her gasp in affront. "Hey!"

Peri shifted her aim to Allen. She hated him. Bill might be corrupt, but Allen had lied to her, tricked her, lulled her into complacency, stolen three years of her life. She exhaled, finger tightening.

"Shut up," Allen threatened. "Or I'm going to hit you. Understand?"

"Yes," Taf said, and then her jaw clenched and she punched him right in the gut.

Allen's face twisted in anger. Taf fought wildly, and Bill slammed her into the side of the van with an utter disregard for human frailty. Taf slumped, out cold.

Exhaling, Peri shifted her aim to Bill and pulled the trigger. Bill's eyes widened as the single slug buried itself in the van's side. "Go!" he shouted, manhandling the limp woman into the van and vaulting in after her. Peri turned her aim to Allen.

"No!" Silas knocked her arm so that it was only chipped cement that hit Allen as he crawled into the front seat of the van.

Frustrated, Peri stood as the engine roared to life. "What the hell are you doing?"

"Their wheels," Silas said, white-faced. "Take out the wheels!"

"You going to let me shoot this time?" she said, using the Glock to take out the tires. She fired until it clicked to nothing; peeved, she tucked it in the back of her waistband. Swerving, the van ran into a pillar.

They weren't going anywhere, and having a moment, she rounded on Silas. "Why can't I kill Allen?"

Silas looked her straight in the eyes. "Allen is alliance."

Jaw clenched, Peri pushed her rifle into Silas's chest. "Like hell he is!"

Silas looked at it, probably estimating his chances of getting it off him before she could pull the trigger as slim. Thick smoke drifted past the opening to the garage. She could hear the fire trucks called by the house's automatic security. "Allen is alliance," Silas said again, voice uncharacteristically soft. "Think about it. He's a lousy anchor, isn't he? What has he actually brought back for you? Anything?"

Taf cried out for help, struggling as Bill ousted her from the busted van and began dragging her to another car. Allen limped behind them, casting furtive glances at her and Silas.

Bullshit. Peri took aim at Allen since Bill was

hiding behind Taf. Silas shoved her arm, and the shot went wild.

"Will you stop doing that!" Peri shouted. She could hear men outside, but didn't know whose side they were on. "Why didn't you tell me before?"

Silas tried to take the rifle from her, but she wouldn't let go. A car door slammed shut, and an engine started. "Because the alliance thought you might turn him in if you knew," he finally said. "They didn't trust you."

Her grip on the weapon eased. *Allen is alliance?* But she wasn't buying it, and she struggled for control of the rifle.

"It was your idea," Silas said in exasperation as he let go and she fell back with her weapon. "Damn it, they're getting away!" he exclaimed as the car's engine roared.

My idea? Leg throbbing, she staggered after Silas as a black car bounced out into the sun. "I'll get Allen, you get Bill," Peri said, halting in the open garage door and bringing the rifle up to her shoulder. Exhaling, she shot out those tires.

"Peri . . . ," Silas warned, and she grinned at him as the car careened to a stop. From inside, she could hear Bill bellowing.

"Fine, I won't kill him. Just mess him up a little," Peri said as she jogged painfully forward. "You coming or not?" she called over her shoulder.

Her heart thudded. Reaching the car, she yanked the passenger-side front door open. "Get out!" she demanded. Bill was behind the wheel. Allen held Taf before him like a shield. He looked pissed. Taf looked pissed and disoriented. *Allen is alliance?*

"She said get out!" Silas exclaimed as he yanked the driver's-side door open.

Allen shoved Taf at Peri, using the sudden movement to escape. From the other side, Bill launched himself at Silas. Taf landed on Peri and they went down. Peri rolled her off, getting to a crouch with her weapon, searching out Allen. Bill was shouting into his phone, his voice going distant as he ran. What sounded like a dozen men began yelling amid more gunfire. A Black Hawk was back, thumping in the near distance. Peri didn't know who else was surrounding the vehicle, and she didn't care.

And then she saw Allen running after Bill's retreating backside.

Rolling to her stomach, Peri took aim—and pulled the trigger.

"No!" Silas shouted, and Allen jerked to a halt when the dirt sprayed up in front of him. Allen pulled his attention from Bill, the bigger man never slowing down as he ran behind the building toward the helicopter and was gone. Allen's eyes met hers, and she smiled at his white face. Screaming in anger, she scrambled up and lunged at him, bowling him over and straddling him.

"I should just kill you right now!" she shouted, the butt of the rifle pulled back to crush his throat, and he stared up at her, his face smudged and his glasses knocked askew.

"Allen, she knows!" Silas shouted. "She just doesn't believe it yet!"

Under her, Allen seemed to steady. His gaze fastened on her, and his fear seemed to vanish. "You won't kill me because I haven't killed you first," he said, smiling though he was clearly in pain. "It's okay, Peri. It's over. All of it. You did good. Stand down."

Peri's lips parted, and, shocked, she did nothing as they were suddenly surrounded by the alliance, all of them screaming at her to put the gun down and get off Allen. Allen waited, her weapon ready to end his life.

"Peri," Silas called out. "Listen to your intuition. It's over."

But her intuition was gone. All she had left was a need to trust someone. Anyone.

Her eyes met Silas's, and in a swift motion, she pulled the weapon away from Allen and clicked the safety on. She tried to toss it aside, but as soon as he was clear, someone plowed into her, knocking her down. She didn't struggle, letting them pull her arms behind her. Her shot leg was in agony, and she blinked the dirt out of her eye as Taf and Silas protested that she was okay and to let her go. She didn't feel okay. *Allen is alliance? It was all my idea?* "I don't know my own life," she whispered to herself in disbelief.

Fran appeared and said, "Let her up." The weight on Peri was shoved away so she could breathe. "I said, let her up!"

"She doesn't remember anything," a man said, his pistol pointed at her. "You can't let her go. She's been brainwashed!"

"She's not brainwashed, she's just forgotten," Fran said bitingly. "The woman just brought in half the corrupt Opti agents for us and saved my daughter. How much more proof do you need that she's not gone native? She's one of us. Let Reed up!" Fran shouted, and Peri cautiously sat up, her leg throbbing as she looked at the weapons ringing her.

"Where's Bill?" she asked as Fran crouched beside her, looking odd in her tight dress, now torn and smeared with grease and dirt. Peri slapped the woman's hand away when she tried to look under the makeshift bandage, and weapons were brought to bear again.

"Will you all just relax?" Fran barked, and then to Peri, just as annoyed, "Out of your reach. One of his birds came back. He's gone." Her expression shifted. "He didn't get Taf. Thank you." Blinking fast, she beckoned for a med officer. "Get Agent Reed an ambulance. Today, maybe?"

Two men in fatigues with slung rifles ran to

get a stretcher from an arriving ambulance. She would have protested, but her leg was throbbing and she felt sick. Her head hurt, too, and she looked at the weapons pointed at the ground, and then at the second ring around them pointing outward. The house was on fire, but several people were coming out of it. She recognized Howard, his shoulder under another man's as he helped him walk, and the horrid tightness in her face eased.

She hadn't found Jack's list, but it felt as if she'd found something vastly more important. She'd landed safely, and not just her, but the people she cared about. That she didn't remember why she cared didn't matter. She was here, they were here, and no one was pointing a gun at her—mostly.

Maybe it would all be okay.

"Did we win?" Peri asked as she squinted up at them.

From beside a chuckling Taf, Silas laughed. "Hell if I know."

CHAPTER
THIRTY-NINE

Peri pulled her coat tight across her shoulders, her spirit low and her shot leg throbbing as she sat at Overdraft's bar. The place was empty but for Allen banging around in the back room and Silas at the fireplace. He was trying to get a fire going to warm the place up, but Peri could tell he wasn't laying it right. All the heat from his matches and half-burned paper was not being trapped—wasted up the flue. A part of her wanted to slide from the stool and fix it. Another part, the indifferent, complacent part of her, didn't care. Her focus blurred when he swore under his breath, his words tickling something in her brain. She'd heard him swear at a fire before. Her memories had more holes than Swiss cheese. It could be anything.

"You'll never be rid of me," Jack said as he tucked behind the bar and helped himself to a mug of beer. She knew he wasn't here. She knew he wasn't filling up a glass. She knew he wasn't downing it with his Adam's apple bobbing and a thin ribbon of beer escaping to run down his chin—but it sure looked as if he was.

Jack was a constant reminder of everything she hated about herself: her insecurity, her dependence on others, a show of strength that was just that—a show, nothing more. And she wanted him gone, even if that meant she'd never have a memory of what had happened that night. She'd killed the man she loved. Why would she want to remember that?

"You think *Allen* wiping that night will do any good?" Jack mocked as he leaned over the counter. The beer spilled onto the bar surface, and Peri wondered if she'd feel anything if she wiped her hand across it. "Opti is in you, babe.

You liked it. You were powerful and that turned you on. Now you're nothing but a dangerous liability who can't remember shit. That's why you didn't tell the alliance they were coming. You *want* to go back."

Peri's eyes flicked past him to Silas swearing over his fire. The government, embarrassed at the unfolding story, had granted the alliance control of Opti's shutdown, and at Fran's urging, Silas was taking up management of Overdraft, maintaining a way for Opti's anchors and drafters to come in without reprisal. "I can't get this stupid thing to light," Silas grumped. "The instant this place starts making money, I'm ripping it out and putting in a gas burner." He straightened, sighing when the gray smoke turned black and vanished.

Restless, Peri spun the stool, her disjointed attention landing on the oddest of things: one of the bulbs in the lotto kiosk was out, three of the tables had claw feet while the rest did not, and the wall-size gaming screen in the lounge was making an almost unheard squeal of faulty electronics. Her attention went to the clock on the microwave behind the bar, and at exactly noon, the at-table menus all reset—just as she knew they would. *Why do I know this stuff?*

A thump from the back room made her jump, but it was just Allen, and he shouted he'd found a footstool. Silas stood dejectedly before his defunct fire, his hands on his narrow hips as he waited for something to happen. "Peri, you're better at this than me," he complained as he wiped his ash-coated fingers on his jeans. "You want to take a go at it?"

"Sure." Peri slid from the stool. Leaving her coat at the bar, she halted when she realized she'd not only drifted from her intended path, but that she couldn't bring her eyes to the dance floor.

Frowning, she forced herself to look at her feet, heart pounding as she inched them out farther. But her attention wandered. . . . A dark presence at her shoulder became Jack, insufferably confident as he looked at the same chunk of yellow floor, whispering, "You're never going to be rid of me. You *like* who Opti made you into, and I'm going to haunt you until you accept that. You're bad, just like me, and without me, you're nothing."

"Liar," she breathed. Wavering, she stared at the floor. Her head throbbed, and Jack chuckled. Something had happened here. She knew this. She would remember it.

"Peri?"

She looked up, the world cycling outward in shock. Allen and Silas both looked at her in concern. Her hands were in fists, and she shook her fingers free. "Did I draft?" she asked, not remembering Allen coming back in, and Silas shook his head, clearly worried. Allen's weak smile was uneasy, and Jack, still holding his beer, snickered, brushing by her with arrogant confidence.

"You'll never lose me, Peri. But go ahead and try. You're more fun when you're fighting." Smirking, he sat on the raised hearth, patting the stone beside him.

"You were trying to break the loop," Silas said as he put a log on the fire—which promptly collapsed. "The sooner we get this done, the better."

"You think?" Anxious, Peri took the brown plastic footstool from Allen and set it clunking down before a straight-back chair pulled before the fireplace. Jack snickered when she sat on the low stool, her knees almost up to her elbows.

The silver threads in Jack's black shirt glinted as he crouched beside her, whispering in her ear. "So many bad things we did, you and me. I'm going to be here, babe," he said, tapping his temple. "Reminding you of every single one of them, because you *enjoyed* it. And you think you're going to let it go? Never. Not my girl. Bill is right. You're the best, and you don't let your best go. Ever."

Allen sat down behind her and tucked close. Shifting awkwardly, Silas edged toward the bar. "Ah, I'll just be over here."

"No one needs you, piano man," Jack said loudly, and Peri flushed. He was getting aggressive. He'd vanish for good if they did this right, and the illusion seemed to know it, her subconscious fighting her, lying about who she was. *It's a lie. It has to be*.

Peri bowed her head as Allen's fingers landed on her shoulders, pushing deep into exactly the right places. It was hard to relax with Jack staring at her. *I don't need you anymore,* she thought as she closed her eyes, and finally she began to relax.

"Little whore," Jack muttered.

Tension slammed into her. Sensing it, Allen sent his fingers to scrub at her scalp. "I'm sorry, Peri," he said softly. "The last thing you need is more holes in your memories, but the only way to be rid of him is to destroy both timelines. I promise you'll get the straight story, but any direct memories will be gone, along with Jack."

"Never . . . ," Jack whispered, and she shivered.

"You're fighting," Allen complained. "Let me do this, or Silas will never let me hear the end of it."

That brought a smile to her. True, Silas was more talented, but Allen had firsthand knowledge of what to remove, and she leaned back into him, even as she pondered the wisdom of letting him into her head. She'd shot at him, beaten him, left him for dead, berated him. Why should he help her?

"You're blocking again," Allen said wearily. "I don't hold you to actions done in the name of closing Opti down. It was your job. We all volunteered for it."

Crouched with his breath tickling her ear, Jack whispered, "But you hold yourself to them, don't you, babe. Because you enjoyed it. Even Africa. Admit it," he whispered. "You liked who you were—or it wouldn't have taken three years to figure out. Don't let them steal that from you. You're alive when you're bad. Don't let them kill your soul."

Peri's pulse quickened. She hadn't enjoyed the ugly things she'd done while at Opti. The people she'd hurt or killed were real. The wrongs she'd done were real. To have enjoyed it would make her foul. She hadn't.

"You did," Jack whispered, and her eye twitched.

"I'm trying," she whispered, and as Allen's fingers eased her into a light trance, a flash of Jack lying on a yellow floor, a blood-soaked scarf pressed to his middle, rose up.

Oh, God, he'd been dying, shot in the gut. Jack had lied to protect her. Bill was corrupt. Sandy and Frank. . . . They'd fought. She had thrown a knife at Sandy and missed.

"That's the one, Peri," Allen said, his presence in her mind becoming clearer. "Remember everything. I'll take it away."

Jack's breath seemed to brush her cheek. "It never goes away. You're a bad person. You like who you were, and you miss it already."

He was giving voice to her deepest fear. Flashes of that night came fast and without order. Blood on her hands. Her scarf pressed against Jack's middle. The sound of breaking glass. Sandy's long hair flying before her as she fell back to break the bar's mirror. Peri couldn't make sense of the disjointed images. Allen scrambled to catch them, but they were too fast and she wasn't letting him in deep enough to destroy any of them.

"Peri," he pleaded. "Please. I need to do this."

Maybe I deserve to be left in the chaos of my own creating, she thought.

"You do," Jack whispered, his breath sending her hair to tickle her neck. "I'm going to take you there. Right now."

With a sudden twist, the entire night came back in a flash. Both timelines sparkled in irreconcilable clarity. She gasped, jumping to a stand. Her pulse thundered as she spun to Allen, his mouth gaping as he stared at her from his chair. He wasn't supposed to be in a chair. He'd been by the bar, throwing Frank's rifle to her.

"I shot him!" she cried out, staring at the stage where Jack had fallen, his belly punctured. Slick blood covered the floor, smeared where he'd gotten up. Terrified, she looked at her blood-covered hands. But her chest had a hole in it, and she staggered. The mirror was broken, and Sandy's soft sobs rose from behind the bar.

Scared, Jack ran for the door. In her mind, she lifted the rifle to her unblemished shoulder and blew a hole in his back.

"He's dead!" she groaned as the memory of Jack

slid to the floor, unhelped and uncared for. No one was moving to save him. Not even her.

"Allen! What the hell are you doing! You *want* her in MEP?" Silas shouted.

"She used the framework you left to twist control from me! What did you do to her?"

Peri turned to the bar. Panic joined her confusion when the mirror was unbroken and Silas stood there instead of Frank. She backed up, eyes darting for a way out.

"Easy now," Allen called, and she spun. Silas moved, and her eyes flicked to him. Both men were between her and the door. She was trapped.

"Stay back," she warned, fixated on the space on the floor where Jack had died. "Where's my rifle? I had a rifle!" Spinning, Peri looked at the door, shocked to see it clean and unblemished. Her heart thudded as she whirled to the stage. There was no blood. But she had shot Jack. "Someone tell me where Jack is!" she screamed.

Silas came forward, hands raised in placation. She kept moving, looking for a way out.

A tiny, rational part of her knew she needed to stop, but instinct kept her backing up almost into the fireplace. She could go no farther, and she grabbed a fire poker.

"Peri, relax," Silas said calmly, and she jabbed the poker at him to keep him away.

"He's dead, isn't he," she said, iron held tight. "Is Jack dead?"

Angry, she took a step forward, and Silas shifted. "I'm sorry about this," he said, and then she swung at him. Swearing, he blocked it, twisting the iron from her grip. She screamed, furious when he grabbed her wrist and spun her into a submission hold as they went down and hit the floor together.

"Call Fran," Silas said to Allen as he wrapped his legs around Peri in a wrestler hold, and she howled, flinging her head back. He leaned out of the way and she hit nothing.

"Hold still," he grunted, binding her with his own arms and legs. "Just. Hold. Still," he panted, gripping her tight. "It's okay. Allen fucked up your defragment, but it's my fault. I never should have done what I did. Remember me. Remember me, Peri, and let me in! I'm your anchor! Trust me, damn it!" he shouted, angry. "Be still and let me *fix this!*"

"Let go . . . ," she wheezed, gasping when he reached into her mind as if it were his own and pulled up an image of Jack standing before the door, his gun smoking. It was aimed at her, and her chest felt as if it was being squeezed to a singularity. "Jack!" she screamed, and froze as she felt the memory burn to ash, the edges of it folding in on itself until it was gone. Under it was the memory of Jack running for the door, leaving her as if the last three years together had meant nothing. Then her, blowing a hole in his back.

"Oh, God, no," she moaned, knowing it was true. She had gone to Opti to find the corruption, but she hadn't been able to break from it and had become the tool she'd gone in to expose. He'd never loved her, not really, and she sobbed as Silas crumbled the memory in the fist of his mind and it was gone. But the pain remained, staining the folds of her brain.

Silas has done this before, and then a flash of insight poured through her, flooding the very gaps that Silas had just made. Allen had been in Opti to protect her, playing the part of the corrupt Opti agent to keep her safe. He'd been there to allay Bill's concerns at her lapses as she balanced on a knife's edge. Only now did she realize why he'd never tried to defragment anything. She *knew* him, and he'd been afraid he'd missed something when she'd agreed to let him erase all memories of him . . . and Silas.

Silas? she thought, feeling his stark determination as he manhandled her memory of the night back to the forefront of their joined thoughts, but she refused, seeing within him a faint image of a wind-calmed boat stuck in the middle of a lake, of laughter and music—and a toast to a future success. In a sudden wash, she realized it was Silas's memories she was seeing, a shadow of their joined past during the year they'd spent together preparing to take Opti down. They'd both been there, Allen and Silas, countless nights spent over take-out and schematics and personnel files, of flirting banter at the rifle range, and the keen bite of testing each other's dexterity skills in the gym. Allen had been there too, but she'd agreed to the year-long preparation because of Silas. She'd loved him, but he hadn't loved her back, and she had no reason to say no when the year of preparation was over and the game was ready to be played. She had loved Silas, and she'd agreed to let that die. Wanted it to, maybe, when he hadn't noticed that she'd fallen in love.

You loved me? Silas thought desperately, and she groaned when he wrenched her thoughts back to Overdraft, flipping through them with a frighteningly cold intensity, burning everything to ash. Memories of the night at Overdraft flared into short-lived, doomed existence, ugly emotions feeding them as oxygen fuels a flame. And though the memories were destroyed, the emotions lingered to coat her mind like smoke on the ceiling. It should have been cleansing, but all that grew from the fading memory of the night was a heavy depression. She'd done this to herself. She had forgotten love. And for what? Glory?

Jack was right. She was a bad person.

Her fight to be free collapsed into a soft trembling.

"Is she okay?" Allen whispered, and Silas's hold on her eased, both the arms he had wrapped around her and the mind he had entwined with hers. Her heart ached as he let go. She was alone. She'd done it to herself.

"That depends," Silas said, and the cool air of a deserted bar touched her skin where there'd once been warmth. His arms slipped away, and she huddled on the floor where he left her. The scrape of his shoes on the yellow floor serrated through her as he went to get her coat and draped it over her. "Give her a minute to catch up."

Catch up. That was a good idea. She felt as if she'd been away for a long time and had come home to find everything changed. She was the one who was different, the truth making her feel ugly and ashamed. Forehead on her knees, she wondered what she was going to do now.

Tilting her face, she saw Allen and Silas sitting on the hearth. Silas's back was bowed in fatigue or sorrow, or maybe both, she couldn't quite tell. Allen looked guilty. Did he know she remembered him? Did he know she knew about the year they'd been together, the three of them planning and agreeing to this? That she'd asked him to destroy all memory of it?

"Thank you," Allen said raggedly. "That construct you put in her felt self-aware."

"It was." Silas didn't look at her. "There were enough latent memories of Jack for it to be fully realized. It had to be for it to be flexible enough to keep her sane until the memory could be defragmented. It's gone now."

What kind of monster am I that I could have given up on love so easily? For glory? They remembered her, and all she had was disjointed images. But if not for them, she'd still be Opti. She would have continued to accept the lies she'd molded about herself, be what Opti said she was. She was the sum of what she'd done, and she'd done so much that was ugly and wrong.

Exhaling, she pulled her head up, knowing she must look hideous with her hair mussed and her eyes red. "Jack is gone," she said, edging up to sit on the low hearth, feeling his absence to her core, shivering as she recalled his breath on her neck, the way he made her feel powerful, dangerous—alluring.

Peri was at a loss, not knowing what to do next—not today, tomorrow, next week, or even five minutes from now. When she'd known nothing, she'd had goals and ideas. Now that she knew the truth, she was detached, distant, drifting aimlessly. Numb. Not remembering love.

Silas poked at the fire, and she flushed as she remembered hitting him with the iron. *Peri, you're better at this than me. You want to take a go at it?* Had there been firelit nights between them? She didn't remember any.

"You never would have done any of those things if you'd known the truth," he said, and a lump filled her throat. It was hollow psychobabble bull. She didn't believe a word, and anger began to edge out the numb feeling. She had blinded herself. Jack had been right. She'd enjoyed it.

Allen handed her a drink, his phone pressed against his ear. She took it by rote, uncaring. "Yes, she's fine. A little depressed, but what did you expect?" he was saying, talking to Fran maybe? She'd been the one to okay this long-running, deep-undercover op. Peri still didn't believe she'd ever been alliance. She must have been someone else five years ago. Naive. Stupid, certainly.

She stiffened at the clank of the fire tools, pulling her coat tighter about herself when Silas sat beside her. "You're a good person," he said.

"Am I?" she said bitterly. Her past suggested otherwise, as did the growing ache inside her. She missed it, God help her, she missed it.

He ran a hand over his stubble, his eyes on Allen hunched over his phone and walking away as he talked in a terse, hushed voice. Nudging the door to the back room open, Allen slipped out. The silence grew. Peri's thoughts went to Silas holding her on the floor. She felt no shame for having fought him. She'd been out of her mind, and he'd known it. "Thank you for fragmenting the timeline."

Silent, Silas reached into his coat pocket and held out a squat, tattered book. She didn't reach for it, and after a moment, he set it between them. "I saved this for you," he said, his voice hiding something. "Along with a box of things you set by for when this was over. It's all from the year we prepped for this. We have some of your early talismans, too. Your life is not lost. Everything is there. You can remember who you were."

Her jaw clenched, and she forced it to relax. She picked the book up, feeling the worn leather against her fingertips, knowing how supple it would be if she opened it. But this book wasn't her. She was so far from it now it would be like looking at someone else. "Thank you, but no," she said, handing it back.

From the back, Allen's voice rose in anger, saying, "Screw you, Fran. You know shit."

Silas folded his hands around hers, sealing the book in her grip. "Keep it for a while," he said. "Stick it on a shelf. You may want it later."

She was too tired to argue, so she wedged it in an inner coat pocket, vowing to throw it out as soon as she had the chance. "Is this my psychologist talking?" she said, trying to at least pretend that everything was okay, and he leaned across the distance between them, cupping a hand on her cheek and smiling. The hint of pain she'd always seen there was gone.

"Your friend," he said.

Her gaze fell and he pulled away when the door to the back room swung open and Allen strode in, ticked. She could guess how the conversation had gone. Fran still didn't trust her. Hell, she wasn't sure she could trust herself. Peri's emotions grew more and more erratic. Silas had said he'd been her anchor, but it made her feel utterly alone. He wasn't her anchor now, and after this long without one, she wasn't sure she wanted one. She wasn't sure she wanted anything anymore.

"Fran can eat shit and die," Allen said, clearly angry. "Peri, you did good. Better than good. Opti is on the run and we're picking them up as we go. You're going to come work with Silas and me here at Overdraft to bring in the stragglers, and everything will go back to normal."

It was getting harder to breathe. She didn't feel like she'd done anything at all. "Can I go?" she said suddenly, and both men stiffened in surprise. "I mean, there's no reason I can't go back to my apartment, right?" she amended, and Allen got a lost look on his face. "I need to think for a while," she lied, just wanting to leave.

"Um, we were going to meet up with Fran in about half an hour," he said slowly. "Lunch, that's it. Are you hungry?"

"She just realized what this whole mission cost her," Silas said. "You really think she wants to eat? God, Allen, use your brain."

"Hey! I'm just making sure she's not hungry," Allen said belligerently, and Peri stood, cutting short his retort.

"Can I borrow your car?" she said, and Allen fished his keys out of his pocket. "Thanks," she said, taking them from his slack fingers. Jaw clenched, she headed for the door, the weight across her shoulders growing heavier with every step.

"Are you coming back?" Silas questioned, and she hesitated.

"I, ah, sure. I just gotta get a few hours of sleep," she lied, rubbing her forehead. It hurt. "Tell Fran thank you for the job offer."

Allen scowled at Silas, his expression shifting as he turned to her. "I can drive you."

"No, I want to be alone." Head down, she went for the door. "See you tomorrow."

Fat chance of that, she thought, but it was something to say.

"She shouldn't be alone," she heard Allen say. "What if she drafts?"

"Then she forgets," Silas said. "Give her some time. She'll be okay."

The Opti logo in the stained-glass window mocked her, and it was all she could do not to punch it. Angry and depressed, she stiff-armed the door open. The bright light was a shock. She'd forgotten the sun was up.

"But she's a drafter. Drafters are never alone."

"She is," Silas said, and Peri's heart lurched at the truth of it. "She can handle herself. You want to make her mad? You just keep following her."

The door finally shut behind her, cutting off their heated conversation. Peri hesitated in the cement-

and-pillar silence as she scanned the parking lot. The bordering trees were finally starting to leaf out—except for the one in the corner. It was as dead as she felt, reminding her of her favorite tree at her grandparents', the one sheltering a long-forgotten grave. Depressed, she took her phone from her back pocket and left it on the planter where they'd find it. Her chest hurt. She felt so alone, and being with other people made it worse.

There was a huge space in her where Jack had been, a space that had once been warm but now held only bitter ash. Behind it was a gap of about a year that she'd probably never have back. She hadn't even missed it until now, hidden by Silas, obliterated at her request by Allen. A year to fall in love, maybe. And she'd destroyed it.

Chin rising, she strode to Allen's car, feeling the wind cut under her coat as she fastened it shut. The leather upholstery was cold as she got in behind the wheel. Putting the car in drive, she spun it around and cut across the fading lines for the exit.

The sudden tears caught her off-guard and she blinked fast as she pulled into traffic, making a right because it was easy. She didn't know where she was going, but she knew she didn't want to go to that ground-floor apartment. Her gut was so tight she felt sick. Everything she remembered was Opti, and Opti was corrupt. She didn't remember the past that everyone kept telling her about. The past she remembered was one of hurting people and ending lives—and of feeling powerful doing it.

Sniffling, she wiped a hand under her nose. It was post-fragment blues. She'd get over it.

But her heart jumped when a dark shadow sat up in the backseat.

"Hi, babe," Jack said, and she touched the brakes, head jerking forward and back.

"Damn it!" Peri shouted, checking her mirrors to see if anyone had noticed. "I want you to leave. Leave me alone!" It hadn't worked. He was still there in her head!

"Alone?" Jack snickered. "That's the last thing you will ever be. Just keep driving."

He leaned over the back of the seat, arms draped along it, and her shock turned to anger.

"Where am I going, Jack?" she said bitterly. "I have a past that I don't remember. Not just one, but two. I have people telling me they're my friends, but the only friends I remember are corrupt Opti agents. I *am* a corrupt Opti agent, but I'm also an alliance officer with a military retirement plan I don't *remember setting up!* Where am I going, Jack? Where?"

He tightened his tie and fixed his hair in the rearview mirror, almost laughing at her. "Wherever you want, babe. You're the one calling the shots. On one side you have a well-funded, poorly organized do-gooder organization destined for failure. On the other, you have massive political pull, an almost godlike authority, the ability to make real change . . . and me." He smiled in a way she'd once found charming, and her stomach churned. "I'd take the latter if I were you. It's more fun."

Jaw clenched, she looked at him through the rearview mirror. Silas's efforts hadn't worked. This . . . *thing* was still with her. Allen, she remembered suddenly, had always been better at destroying memories. *Good God. I can even smell him,* she thought, his aftershave pinging on a hundred lost memories.

"I talked to Bill," Jack said, his breath coming and going on her neck. "Agents are coming in, finding him, looking for answers. Opti isn't dead, not by a long shot. I told him you might still come home. You know Opti is where you belong. It's why you're out here driving with no destination. If you were alliance, you wouldn't have walked away. You would have told the alliance that you have a chemical tag in you. We can go back to the way it was, only I won't have to lie to you anymore. We were good together, weren't we?"

Peri's lips parted when he touched the back of her neck to move a strand of her hair. His lips met her neck, wet and warm, and tingles spread in a wave when he pulled on her skin, sucking, promising more.

Holy shit, he's real!

CHAPTER
FORTY

Shocked, Peri yanked the car to the left, careening into an empty parking lot where the ferry docked. Jack cried out in surprise as he was flung against the door. Heart pounding, she stomped on the brakes and he hit the back of her seat, swearing. Keys still in the ignition, Peri lurched out of the car, heart pounding.

Feeling unreal, she paced back and forth between the car and the dock. Jack was in Allen's car. *He's in Allen's car!*

She froze when the back door opened and Jack got out. Her injured leg hurt, and she felt her empty pockets. She had no phone, no knife, nothing.

"I shot you . . . ," she said, then went colder yet when he stretched, rubbing the back of his neck as if embarrassed. He was alive. "What are you doing in Allen's car?"

"I was going to kill him. A little payback between him and me. This is better."

She began pacing again, trying to figure this out. "Damn it, Jack. How long have you been watching me?" she asked. She hadn't killed him. He was there. Alive.

Shoulders rising and falling, he leaned against

the car. His fair hair fluttered in the wind off the river when he turned to look up the road the way they'd come. "Not long. It's amazing what you can come back from. Sandy kept me alive until the ambulance got there. Three weeks in intensive care, and then Bill had me in the hole after that, hoping I'd tell him where the chip was with the list." He touched his chest, smiling. "I never told him, Peri, because I love you, even if you shot me. I did shoot you first, after all. It's still in your damn knitting needle."

Her eyes flicked to his, reading the lie about love, but the truth in where the chip was. *My needles?* she thought, seeing how the Opti-approved stress relief might have survived to stick with her. Her project bag was with her cat at Allen's.

"Bill let me out after you pulled that tracker out of your ass and started complaining about Allen. It wasn't until yesterday that he needed me, though. Needed us." He chuckled, head shaking in mock dismay. "What an epic failure, losing most of his force and all his credibility. Not to mention his free movement." He smiled, confident and full of himself. "It's good to be needed. Bill says you talked to me when you were alone. That's sweet. I knew you loved me."

"Damn it all to hell," she whispered, cold. She had loved him, loved the way he made her feel, but everything was tied to a past that was *wrong*.

"I missed you, babe, but I knew you'd come back. The alliance is a joke, and you're better than them. Opti is power."

He flicked the top of Allen's car—nice, but nothing like the sleek icons of power she'd always had—the best of everything, and when it wasn't, they got on a plane and found it. Bill might have lost a lot yesterday, but his house was now spotlessly clean and he was already setting up shop again, this time unburdened by government guidelines and the illusion of legitimacy. *And he wants me to come back.*

"Get out of here," she whispered. "If I ever see you again, I will kill you. Then draft so I can do it again."

But his smile grew wider. "Not without you. Come on. You want this."

Oh God. He was right. Jack would fill her up, infuse her with feelings of warmth and strength. She couldn't move when he pushed himself off from the car. Her heart thudded as he got closer, and she backed up a step, but only a step. Eyes closed, she felt the wind off the bay shift her hair when he tucked it behind her ear. He was real. She hadn't killed him. And . . . she knew him. He knew her past.

"That's right," he whispered as he leaned in, kissing her so softly it sent a shiver through her. "You remember us. Maybe not everything, but enough. Remember the hotel? The last time we made love?"

Her shoulders eased as his arms went around her, familiar and right. He smelled of his after-shave, and she knew exactly how his stubble would feel. Her rising hand shook, and her chest clenched when she touched his jaw. He was home. It made everything else, the guilt, the shame, and her longing, pale under its force. She had nothing, and he held it all, a return to when she was strong.

"I gave you everything, treated you like the deadly princess you are," he whispered, his fingers easing her tension away as they ran under her ear to the base of her neck, reminding her body of the feel of him. "You'll never find that from anyone else. Come with me. I can bring everything back. Everything. You won't need talismans—I'll be your talisman."

She ached for the feeling of being cared for, loved. It would be so easy.

Stop! a tiny part of her screamed, flickering under the wave of contentment Jack breathed into her. It had been so long. So long. *So tired . . .*

"Peri!" a distant voice called, and Jack stiffened.

"Son of a bitch," he muttered, pushing back from Peri and turning to look.

Peri's heart pounded as guilt and self-loathing poured over her, making her knees go weak. *What am I doing?* Silas. He was running, but so far away.

"Babe?"

Peri's resolve to leave him returned in a cold wash of reality. "I can't do this."

His hand ran across her cheekbone, slipping down to hold her shoulder. "I know," he whispered, and then she gasped when the gun in his hand went off, the slug thumping into her with the force of a kick.

She gasped, her fall arrested by Jack as he held her to him. Her chest exploded into pain, and she couldn't breathe as he eased her down. She blinked, looking at the gun in his hand and seeing the smoke drift idly from the muzzle. Faint on the wind, she heard Silas screaming her name, but she couldn't look away from Jack. "You shot me," she choked out.

"Sorry, babe," he said, gentling her to the cold pavement like a lover. His eyes were trained on her, and she saw not the cold calculation of a murderer she had expected to see, but something resembling heartache. "It will be our secret, okay? I'll just tell Bill you said yes and that you got shot by accident afterward."

"Why?" she said, staring at the sky. "Why!"

He stood, handgun ready as he watched Silas, not her. "It doesn't look like it, but I just saved your life. You need me. You need the way Opti makes you feel. Draft. I'll take you home."

She couldn't believe this, and her hand felt her chest as she choked on the pain. *Son of a bitch . . .*

He'd shot her, shot her so that she'd draft and save herself, and forget everything that had been made clear to her today so she could be a pawn of Opti once more. He was counting on it. "I can't believe you shot me." The pain redoubled, but she blinked, her searching fingers coming away in the startling realization that though she felt as if she'd been kicked by a mule . . . there was . . . no blood. Instead, a page from her diary peeked from between her fingers—her past had saved her after all. *You have got to be kidding me.*

Oblivious, Jack stood above her, the wind shifting the hair into his eyes as he frowned at Silas. She felt something within her war with itself as he swiftly brought the gun up, sighting it at Silas. She could do nothing and Jack would take her home. No one would blame her, and she would be everything she wanted to be. Her soul cried out for it.

But that wasn't who she wanted to be.

Groaning, she rolled, knocking into Jack as the gun went off.

"Peri!" Jack shouted in anger as his shot went wild.

A low, guttural snarl rumbled through her. Grit pinching her palms, she rose. Jack turned at the sound of her boots scraping on the pavement, but it was too late as she launched herself at him.

They crashed into the car and went down; Jack's

face was awash with surprise. "You didn't draft! How!"

"I didn't have to," she snarled, then head-butted him to get him to let go of her.

He cried out and her hands were free.

Grabbing her head, he slammed it into the concrete dock.

Stars blotted her sight. Gasping for breath, she hit his face with her elbow, and he shoved her away as his nose gushed bright red blood.

She rolled, cursing herself. She'd lost the advantage of surprise, and with it, her chance at the handgun. Pages from her diary were slipping from her, and Jack's expression became ugly as he realized why his shot hadn't done anything. "That is so clichéd," he said as he staggered to his feet and brought up his handgun.

"It goes with the joke you made of my life," she said, then dove to the pavement when he pulled the trigger.

The bullet winged away and Peri came up into a fighting stance, staggering when her wounded leg gave out. Jack followed her down, pinning her to the pavement, and she stopped, feeling the hard blunt end of a pistol against her kidney. He was inches away, feeling both familiar and threatening atop her.

How many times have we played this out? she wondered, then gasped when chunks of concrete peppered them, cutting her face and making Jack look up.

"Why do you care!" Jack shouted, and the pistol lifted from her to point at Silas.

Peri jerked her arm free and smashed her palm into his already broken nose.

Jack screamed. His fist lashed out. She couldn't move to escape it, and it hit her full-on.

Pain exploded in her face. She couldn't see. She struggled to keep from vomiting as vertigo swamped her.

And then she could breathe as Jack was ripped off her.

Bleary, she rolled to her stomach. Silas and Jack fought hand-to-hand on the concrete. Gasping, she sat up and looked for the gun, spotting it flung off to the side. Holding her stomach, she pushed herself up and staggered toward it. He'd hit her so hard she couldn't walk straight.

"Silas, get clear!" she shouted, and he howled, getting in one last punch before he rolled to his feet and away.

Jack lurched upright. Expression wild, he didn't see her as he screamed and went for Silas. Her hand trembled, and she shot at the ground at his feet. Shrapnel sprayed up, and Jack halted, his head snapping around. Arms held out before her, Peri pointed the gun and shook. She had him!

"Peri?" Silas shouted, hunched and afraid to

move. "Oh God. Don't kill him. He's your past. You need him to tell you your past!"

"I don't need him!" she raged. She wasn't scared. She was angry with herself for being tempted, knowing that it would always be there. The cracks would never mend. She wanted what only Jack could give her, and she hated that part of herself, even as it kept her alive.

Slowly Jack pulled himself to his full height, his eyes going from her to Silas. "You're not going to shoot me, babe."

Her arms shook, but her gaze never left him. "Stop calling me that!" she shouted, her throat going raw. "And why not? You killed me first." The words were hard as they fell from her. Hands quivering, she said, "Silas? Will you take this for me?"

Silas eased up beside her, and the muzzle of the weapon steadied as he took it. Jack's expression went grim. Being careful to stay out of Silas's line of sight, Peri eased up to Jack. She was almost light-headed from spent adrenaline. It would pass. Grunting, she kicked the back of his legs to make him kneel, and he hit the pavement hard. "I want very much to shoot you," she said from behind him, her words hardly above a whisper. "But Silas is right. You're useful." Reaching behind her coat, she brought out the damaged diary and tapped it against his bloody face. "One way or the other."

Jack clenched his teeth, and she backed up, not trusting that his desire to remain unshot was stronger than his desire to throttle her. "If he moves, shoot him," she said, retreating to stand with Silas. "Can I use your phone?"

"Back pocket."

Her eyebrows rose, and she gave Jack a smile as she fished it out. "You knew Jack was alive, didn't you?" she asked Silas.

"I didn't know he was in Allen's car," he said, and Peri made a sad laugh. "Fran wouldn't trust you until you settled it with Jack. Peri. It's truly over. Are you mad at me?"

Over? It wasn't over. She'd almost said yes to Jack. She'd wanted to say yes, and even though she had said no, it sickened her. She couldn't go back to the alliance now. She didn't trust herself—and they would never trust her.

"You can't stop this," Jack said softly, the blood flowing from his nose. "They will come for me. And when I get free, I will find you. I will—"

Peri took three steps forward. Hands in fists, she snapped a sharp front kick at him, flicking his head back and knocking him down. Grunting, he levered himself up, hand on his chin as he sat on the pavement and stared silently at her.

Shaking, she backed up to lean against the car. She shouldn't have done that. Her leg was in agony. Swiping the phone app on, she called

Fran. The line clicked open, and Fran's intent voice barked, "Silas? Talk to me."

Peri's eyes went to Silas, his aim unwavering from Jack. The wind gusted, drawing her attention to the loose pages of her diary, shifting in the wind.

"Silas, are you there?"

Peri jerked herself back to the present. "It's me. Silas and I are at the ferry dock. Can you send someone to pick up Jack? Silas has him at gunpoint. I'd appreciate you locking him up. And thanks for the offer to work for you, but I'm going to have to pass."

Silas's face became ashen, and Jack chuckled, his eyes on the muzzle fixed on him.

"I'm leaving now," Peri said into the phone but talking to both of them. "Don't follow me. Tell Allen I need his car for a few days but I'll leave it parked illegally somewhere next week so he can pick it up at impound. Oh, and, Fran? You suck."

"Agent Reed—"

Peri ended the call, setting the phone down on the pavement where she wouldn't run it over when she left. Almost immediately it began to hum.

"What are you doing?" Silas asked, but she said nothing as she dropped her diary next to it, not caring if more pages blew into the water. Head high, she limped to the car. The keys were still in it.

"Peri!"

Silas fidgeted, unable to move for worry that Jack might get away. Jack was laughing, bitter and vindictive as she opened the car and got in, lip curling that it smelled like Jack. There was guilt for leaving Silas, but it was outweighed by the horror at the temptation that she knew Jack presented. She hated him for laughing. He knew why she was leaving—running away. She wanted what he offered, and she didn't dare tempt herself again.

"Don't let him move until they get here, okay?"

Frantic, Silas divided his attention between her and Jack. "Where are you going? Peri, talk to me!"

"Somewhere else," she said, then slammed the door shut.

"We can fix this," Silas called out. "I promise."

She started the car and rolled the window down. "I'm sorry. I have to. And thank you."

"Don't do this. God bless it, woman!"

She thought she heard shots as she drove away, but there was no change when she looked in the rearview mirror. Silas was standing there horrified, unable to stop her as he held Jack unmoving. The son of a bitch was laughing, and helpless tears slipped from her. She angrily wiped them away. She didn't deserve to cry.

She was close enough to the bridge to Canada that she would be across it before Fran's call could stop her. She didn't need a passport to go over the bridge, not with her enhanced driver's license. They'd think she was just a woman on the way home. She probably had time to stop and get her cat and knitting. The clothes she'd leave, though. Allen's taste in women's fashion still sucked.

Her helpless bark of laughter sounded fanatical, and she turned the radio on to distract herself from her thoughts. Her heart was breaking, but she couldn't stay. Jack was alive, a temptation she didn't know if she could resist. She couldn't be that person anymore, someone so dependent upon others that she was a danger to herself. So she would leave, and go somewhere far away, pick up the pieces of her shattered facsimile of a life and start anew.

She was done with it. Done with it all.

EPILOGUE

I should have worn white sneakers, Peri thought as she strode purposefully through the wide corridors with their uniform handrails and hidden, indistinct lighting. Her borrowed scrubs were a pale blue to match the stripe on the wall, and a forgotten machine lit up in alarm as she passed it, reacting to her mild radiation level.

She just kept going, taking a dust cap in passing from a nurse's station and tucking her short hair under it. Behind her, two nurses and an aide went to fuss over the machine.

Pulse fast, she read the names on the doors, trying not to glance in and ruin what little privacy the residents had. She found the one she was looking for across from the communal living room. Someone was at the baby grand, playing music from the forties as three patients and a nurse sang.

MRS. CAROLINE REED.

Head down, Peri took the clipboard hanging on the door, hiding her face from a passing orderly. There was a current picture of her mother, and Peri's heart clenched at the fading hint of the strong woman Peri had once railed against, the strength and determination hidden under the wrinkles and indistinct focus. Beneath it was a brief description of her life, the highlights and accomplishments: marriages, siblings, divorces. Peri wasn't on it.

The orderly turned the corner. Steeling herself, she knocked. The door was hard against her hand, and it made hardly any noise.

"Yes. Come in!" a strong but quavering voice called.

Peri unclenched her jaw, forcing a smile on her face as she pushed the door open. "Hello," she said, shutting the door carefully behind her.

"Finally!" her mother said, sitting in a chair all alone in her robe, looking out the window to an empty bird feeder. "Just how long were you going to let me sit here? I've got things to do today other than wait for my stylist. New girl, eh?"

She swallowed, blinking fast. *She doesn't know me.* "I'm sorry I'm running late," she said, glancing at her clipboard like it meant something. "What can we do for you today?"

"The usual."

How many times, Peri wondered, *have I said the same thing to hide the embarrassment of not knowing what's going on?*

Heart aching, Peri helped her mother sit up straight, trying not to notice how light she was as she turned her to the huge mirror that was there to try to make the small room look larger. Her mother's chin was high, her anger that she didn't know what her usual was was obvious.

"A style it is," Peri said, reaching for the soft brush beside the bed. "We can skip the wash if you like. Your hair is in wonderful condition. You take very good care of it. Is it getting too long? Would you like me to schedule a cut next week?"

"If you would," her mother said, her thin, age-spotted fingers coming up to play with the ends. Peri remembered it as jet-black as hers was, but now it was pale, a hint of the original, a whisper, like her mother herself. She was looking vacantly at their reflection, seeing something other than what was there.

Peri slowly brushed her mother's hair, taking

what she had today and not letting regret color it. "Has it been a busy week?" she asked, focusing on how the hair felt slipping through her hands as she cared for her mother.

"About the same," she answered, voice distant. *She doesn't know, doesn't remember.*

"Family?" Peri prompted, hoping for something. A story. A recollection. Anything.

"Oh, yes," her mother said, brightening. "Did you know my daughter is studying to be a dancer at the Met?"

"Is that so?" Peri's chin trembled, but she smiled as she ran a lock of hair around her finger, trying to get it to stay. "That's wonderful. I always wanted to be a dancer."

"She's very good. Very graceful." Her mother smiled, pride lighting her face. "So much more graceful than I am. And she'll do it. That girl has more grit than anyone I know. I don't know where she gets it."

I got it from you, Peri thought, blinking fast.

"I'm so proud of her," her mother said wistfully. "I wish I could have told her."

"I'm sure she knows," Peri said, finding peace in the moment because that was all she had, all any of them had. "I'm sure she knows."

Center Point Large Print
600 Brooks Road / PO Box 1
Thorndike, ME 04986-0001 USA

(207) 568-3717

US & Canada:
1 800 929-9108
www.centerpointlargeprint.com